Myron MacHutchens

No Justice
No Peace

A Cautionary Tale

Mythical Legends Publishing

A Mythical Legends Publishing, First Edition

Copyright © 2017 by Myron MacHutchens
First published by Mythical Legends Publishing, 2017
Publisher@mythicallegends.com
http://mythicallegends.com

ISBN **978-1-943958-16-0**
Library of Congress Control Number: **2017905843**

Printed in the United States of America

9 8 7 6 5 4 3 2 1

Introduction

This book is not for you. Because too few readers will be able to read this story without descending into anger rather than understanding the reasons why it had to be both written and published.

When my white contemporaries asked me why I felt compelled to write this novel, my answer was that no matter where I traveled across this country, the subject has never been discussed in terms of a cure for the inequities African Americans suffered on a daily basis just short of four hundred years from their ancestors being shipped here as slaves.

Even our first African American President of the United States was unable to promote any substantive discussion for fear of further alienating and frightening America's conservative whites, far too many of whom are demonstrably racist. The question that always sat in the back of my mind was how long are America's blacks going to have to wait for equal justice under the law; how long will it be until they are treated the same as whites by the police, the courts, and the penal system?

I also questioned why the United States Department of Justice did nothing at all to bring equality to America's criminal justice system. But after several years of research, I discovered that the idea of justice for all was one of the greatest fictions perpetuated in American culture.

As of this date, the current Attorney General is Jeff Sessions, who is an avowed racist who has already overturned recent advances in holding police departments accountable for promoting and maintaining racist practices against the very people they serve. We also have a President of the United States sued in the 1970s for his company's racist practices in property management. Collectively, the president and his appointees are determined to erase decades of progress in ensuring everyone in the United States is treated equally.

What's been done in this novel is to present the only means of finally achieving the promise of equal protection under the law for African Americans. The proof of this thesis is that after three hundred ninety-seven years of whites killing blacks with relative impunity on this continent, virtually nothing has changed. Oh some may argue that this _____(fill in the blank) or that_____(also fill in the blank) is better for African Americans, but the fact is that white conservative men from the American Legislative Exchange Council wrote legislation for Red States that extended the privilege of killing blacks without consequence to civilians with Stand Your Ground laws shows that the more things change, the more they are exactly the same.

I expect anger from both blacks and whites who read this story. But white America—we whites—have to own it. Prove me wrong, make America treat Blacks like white men before this cautionary tale comes true. Prove me wrong before preemptive self defense becomes a necessity for any black man, woman or child who is forced to deal with any white police officer. Prove me wrong before whites become a statistical minority in this country and begin to suffer the tyranny of the majority.

Myron MacHutchens
April 20, 2017

No Justice
No Peace

Chapter 1

Jackson looked past the yellow police tape at the body lying in the street; another black man's body devoid of life in broad daylight, getting soaked in the persistent drizzle. Off to the side was the white officer, who had shot the man lying in the street, being debriefed by the ranking lieutenant with fellow officers keeping the growing crowd away from the shooter.

Voices were getting louder from the crowd, but no apparent family member related to the victim was present nor anyone who was with the man before he was shot.

Jackson pulled a monocular from his pocket and focused on the name tag of the shooter, seeing it said "Benson."

He jotted the name down and the number of the squad car he had driven along with the current date and time and tucked the notebook back into his pocket to keep it dry. He looked around to see if he could spot anyone who witnessed the incident.

Off to the side were a teenage couple under an umbrella surrounded by a small knot of people; several bigger men keeping officers at bay.

Jackson edged over to the group and eased up next to one of the men, black of course, standing between a Tampa police officer and the couple. He nodded at the man not bothering looking at the white cop as he made his way toward the couple.

". . . no, he wasn't doing anything at all. He was walking carrying two bags of groceries, not bothering anyone," the young woman said pointing to the twin bags spilled on the ground.

"Then what happened?" Jackson quietly prompted drawing glances from several of the assembled.

Jackson Richards was a freelance reporter and Internet blogger standing six feet tall with a slight build with medium brown skin. His features were thin but pleasant, and his voice was smooth and soothing.

The young man picked up the story tipping the umbrella toward the man lying in the street. "He was walking along when the cop car drove up, and the cop rolled down the window. We couldn't really hear what was said, but the brother raised his hands, still holding his bags when the cop got out of the car."

"He wasn't doin' nothing, just holding the bags when the cop put his hand on his gun and shouted that he wanted to see some ID," the woman said.

"The brother lowered his left hand . . ." the young man began.

"Was he still holding the bag?" Jackson interrupted.

"Sure was," the woman replied.

"He reached down to put the bag on the ground,; and when he reached for his back pocket, the cop shot him four times!" said the man.

"He didn't have anything in his hand?" asked Jackson.

"Hell, naw. And the first thing the cop did when the brother hit the ground was to look around to see who was watching. When he saw us, and that old man over there, he shouted for us to keep back," the young man said, nodding toward an elderly man talking to two police officers on the other side of the street.

"Did the officer touch the body?" Jackson asked.

"He checked the brother's neck, but he didn't do anything else. That cop in the white shirt took the man's wallet when he arrived, but there's no sign of a weapon, and they couldn't plant one on him with all of us watching," explained the young man.

"I do some online reporting for some Black news sites,; would it be all right if I contact you later about the entire incident?" Jackson asked. He then saw the young woman pull on the man's shirt as she whispered in his ear.

Jackson waited patiently while they made up their minds.

"Do you have a card? We can get back to you—maybe," the man said, holding out his hand.

Jackson gave the man his card and watched as the couple read his name and the Web site.

"Yeah, maybe we'll give you a call," the man said.

"Thank you. I would appreciate hearing from you. It's always best getting an observant, uninvolved party to help tell the real story, not the one the cops want to tell," Jackson said, watching the two nod in agreement.

"This is your cell phone number?" the woman asked.

"It is. Call me anytime."

Jackson slowly edged away from the couple, nodding to the same brother keeping the cop at bay, meandering through the crowd, eavesdropping.

The crowd had grown larger in the short amount of time Jackson had been on the scene. The humidity was cloying,; the air almost liquid. The temperature, in the nineties, jacked up the discomfort, and crowd, overwhelmingly black, was getting louder and angrier as the minutes ticked by.

Once he'd seen and heard enough, Jackson headed back to his rental car parked several blocks away. When he got into the car he turned his custom police scanner on in time to hear the call for the coroner's office dispatch to the site to pick up the body.

Jackson fired up his tablet and waited for it to log onto the Web. He made a quick stop at the Tampa Police Department page and did a search for officer Benson, finding out his first name, Earl, and that he was a six-year veteran of the force. He then logged into a secret, highly encrypted site that his tablet could only access because of a special app that managed the highly encrypted traffic.

He logged in, then created an incident report with the date, time and officer's name, planning to get the victim's name and background information once it was released. He added some brief notes on the locale and then logged off.

In the fifty years since Ronald Reagan was elected President of the United States, a radical change in law enforcement occurred. Police departments in major cities and small towns alike, became virtual paramilitary forces. Their arms, uniforms and tactics became those of anti-insurgency units trained in war,; no longer simply civilian forces to uphold the law. And along with these changes came a corresponding change in the legal system where prosecutors, lawyers and judges became a direct conduit for nonwhites to be immediately incarcerated in a profit-driven prison system regardless of the evidence, that is when the nonwhite "offender" wasn't simply killed outright.

Despite national outrage, far too many in positions of power turned a blind eye to the activities of increasingly belligerent local police forces. And here America stood, a land of infinitely greater peril for any man of color, with young black men thirty-five times more likely to be shot and killed by a police officer than any white man.

The wealthiest four hundred families in America had been running the country using their lap dogs, the Republican Party, for decades. For nearly two generations they had propelled over half of the nation's wealth into those families' hands. And though Republicans hadn't seen the inside of the White House since the disastrous eight years under George W. Bush, they were doing their best to keep the country moving toward an oligarchy-run police state.

Conservative organizations like The American Legislative Exchange had been crafting laws for "Red States," extending the privilege of the non-consequential murder of black men and teens to white civilians. Laws like those grouped under the title "Stand Your Ground" were frequently used by whites in Red States like Texas and Florida where the killing of blacks was excused because white shooters felt threatened by the mere presence of a black male, and the juries all went along with the notion. White police officers and civilians had their automatic get out of jail free card for the murders merely stating, "I feared for my life."

The ubiquity of the dumbing down of America, which began with Richard Nixon having declared war on the intelligentsia, continued unabated. Elementary schools had been scoured of any classes that provoked analysis of the issues of the day, the same with high schools across America. Students were deprived of any classroom exercises that taught cause and effect, now with testing standards designed to graduate students just smart enough to make change at McDonalds.

College was only for the monied elite, or athletes who made the colleges and universities that great sports revenue and were often cut loose dumber than when they enrolled.

Republicans also made sure that middle and underclass Americans scrambled for the few remaining jobs across the country having presided over changes to the trade laws and tax codes that eliminated 46,000 manufacturing companies in a single decade. The number of jobs sent offshore were legion, leaving the United States absent the manufacturing capacity that once ruled the world. The world's economy was laid low by the criminal greed of the white elite bankers.

Whatever the machinations of those driving American culture forward, Jackson was invoking serious respect in online and broadcast media for his sober, factual coverage of the nation's police shootings. And though some local departments tried to refute some of the rather obvious conclusions in Jackson's reporting, even the FBI largely agreed with the statistics published in Jackson's blog, "Jackson's Real Deal."

In the fifteen years since the events in Ferguson, Missouri, little had changed despite a worldwide condemnation of the killing of unarmed, innocent boys and men of color with the now-familiar "Hands Up, Don't Shoot" and "I Can't Breath" refrains when history tragically repeated themselves. Jackson's Real Deal Web site contained thousands of comprehensive reports of police-involved incidents of violence against the very people they were supposed to protect.

-=#=-

Jackson Richards grew up in the northern suburbs of Chicago. He came from a family of culturally invisible African Americans. He was raised by his mother and father, both of whom had respectable, upper middle class jobs. His mother was the accounting department head for a medium-sized hospital while his father supervised a crew of engineers for the regional transit authority.

He attended public schools, and along with very respectable SAT and ACT scores, he easily scored an academic scholarship at the University of Illinois Urbana-Champaign campus in journalism specializing in digital media. He had no police record,; he had never been arrested. He didn't own a hoodie, nor did he sound like actor J.J. Walker when he spoke, except when it suited him. He favored jazz over rap and was an accomplished sketch artist by the time he graduated.

In his Sophomore year of college, Jackson created a Web site that aggregated over fifty college and university basketball and football scores, including game statistics, only stealing a half hour of his time each morning to aggregate. It became the go-to destination on his campus until word-of-mouth spread. Soon, he had two other students populating the content who he was able to pay out of local and national advertising as the site's popularity grew.

By his second year of online operation, he had to move the Web site off the campus network because it was drawing too much traffic. By then he was pulling in about $5,000 in advertising revenue each month, mostly from beer and sporting goods companies. However, he struck gold in his senior year when ESPN Sports advertised televised college games on his site. By the time he graduated he had $700,000 in the bank and a half dozen offers to buy the site, which he eventually sold to the ESPN Sports Network for more than enough money to retire on.

Jackson was smart, savvy. He approached everything he did looking at every angle he could think of before he chose the path to be taken,; this included his romantic life as well. It was no secret on campus he was well off while he was in school, attracting his share of co-eds interested in his attentions, and his money. But Jackson was no fool. He knew he was too young to be saddle with a wife or children while he was in school. Nor was he interested in forming a relationship with someone in school with the expectation that they would marry upon graduation.

When he did graduate, Jackson decided to take a rail tour around the United States. He first returned home to spend some time with his parents. Since it was summer vacation, his younger sister (by two years) was also home. The entire family took some time off together. They went to several concerts, the local amusement park where Jackson coaxed the entire family to ride the park's fastest roller coaster together; all-in-all, a good time was had by all.

MYRON MacHUTCHENS

Jackson discussed his plans to see the country by rail. His mother helped him plan out his route, sharing the task of researching the various long-haul Amtrak passenger lines, schedules and destinations. Over dinner they would all discuss various historical sites, national attractions and notable cities, planning the best routes to take and when the best times for layovers would be in the cities along the way. As it was approaching the beginning of July, they decided that arriving at the nation's capital for the Independence Day celebrations would be a great kickoff for Jackson's tour.

Armed with what his mother insisted was the necessary count of socks and underwear, a snazzy backpack equipped with solar cells to keep his mobile phone and tablet charged by sunlight alone, and a year's Amtrak Ameripass,; Jackson departed from Chicago's Union Station on the Capitol Limited with Washington, D.C. his destination.

Chapter 2

"Good morning everyone, it is 6:00 A.M., and the temperature has already reached 81° in Manhattan. Time for the news," the radio announced before a hand slapped the button on the top of the clock to turn it off.

Andrew Simmons cracked an eye toward the clock knowing full well what it was going to show him. Simmons was one of the top urban planners working for one of the largest consulting firms in New York. In the eight years since he had left military service and joined the firm, Simmons had been all across the United States and in a dozen countries, first contributing to, then leading engineering and design projects in urban planning. His expertise was public transportation infrastructure which didn't much surprise his old friends from the army. His advancement through and deployment after US Army Sniper School was characterized by methodical planning and execution, often literally, of his missions. His missions inevitably paired him with white spotters, but his accuracy and attention to detail gave him a reputation of unbroken success without mishap, injury or a team member's death.

Now, he lived on Long Island and commuted to and from the firm's tony office suite in Soho reading the morning's news on his tablet during the commute.

Although he was staying home to get some work done in peace without everyone constantly asking him questions on this or that project, his attention was caught by the news of the shooting of another innocent, unarmed black man in Tampa by a white cop. He breezed through the story, did a search for more information about the incident and inevitably landed on the Jackson's Real Deal Web site. He read the reporting of the facts posted, including the shooter's name, noting that an internal investigation by the Tampa Police Department was underway.

Simmons shook his head after he finished reading, finding that the majority of the news coverage was just rehashed information from the initial Tampa newspaper report. His anger over the continued injustices fellow black males faced in the U.S. never showed. Neither did his feelings about the racist nonsense he faced in the military. His response to the racists crap he faced in the army was to be better than any other man he competed against and to do so without comment, letting his actions do all his speaking for him.

Once he left the service, he parlayed his Bachelors in Engineering into a nice gig with the company he still worked for, and with his same methodical way of doing things, worked his way up through the ranks. He was now one of the top three consulting engineers for the firm. In addition to making a very respectable seven figure salary, he brought in over one hundred million dollars in revenue per annum. This fact alone gave Simmons a great amount of freedom, specifically the freedom to manage his own time without interference.

Just as he was getting out of the shower he heard his mobile phone ring.

Dripping water across the bedroom, he grabbed the phone off the night table and answered.

"Hello?" he said, wiping water from his body with the towel he grabbed along the way.

"One Shot! What's up, killer?"

"Get the fuck out! Is that really you?" he replied.

"In the flesh, so to speak."

The caller was a voice from the past, Anthony Dawson, former USMC sniper who later went to work for the CIA. The two initially met in the African Congo where their individual assignments chanced to bring them together in a bar in Tanzania before Dawson was dispatched to Uganda and Simmons was off to Rwanda, both tasked to eliminate particularly vicious warlords with a penchant for killing hundreds of their own people at the drop of a hat to keep "order."

"Brother, you are a hard man to find, or at least you were, at first. Found out where you worked, called up and told them I was a buddy from way back and sweet-talked your number out of the nice chick who answered," said Dawson, chuckling.

"I forget; did I leave you holding the bag on that bar tab?" Simmons replied, also laughing.

"Not at all. Just was thinking about you the other day and decided to see what you're up to."

"Cool beans. And you, still in the family business?"

"Now that's a good question. But if I had to tell the truth, no. I left all that spookiness behind. Hey, I'm in New York for the next couple of days, how 'bout I buy you dinner and we can catch up? You have time in the next day or so?"

"My time's basically my own this week. How about tonight?" Simmons asked, mentally checking his calendar.

"Good enough. How well do you know the city?" asked Simmons.

"Name a place, I'll find it."

The two set up the time and restaurant, then concluded their call. Simmons was more happy than curious about Dawson's call. The two belonged to a select fraternity of men who had precision killing in common. He breezed through the day, checking out the requests for quotes on an engineering project for the city of Detroit and one in Dubia.

The day passed quickly, and when Simmons looked up from his work, he saw that he had to get a move on if he wanted to be on time.

When he arrived at the Italian restaurant not far from the UN Plaza Hotel, he saw Dawson hanging out just off the entrance.

The two hugged then quickly went inside out of the heat. Simmons gave his name to the hostess who crossed off his name in the reservation book and took them to a table. A waitress was there as they sat who quickly took their drink orders after she set a basket of warm bread on the table.

Once she was gone, Simmons said, "Damn, Dawson. You're the last person I expected to hear from these days. How the hell are you?"

Dawson sat back and took a sip of water before answering.

"Pissed off and ain't gonna be talked out of it. You see that shit in the news today about that kid murdered by a cop?" he asked.

"Yeah, first thing this morning."

"You know how many that makes this year? And the year ain't even half over."

Simmons shook his head. "No, how many?"

"Thirty-four."

"No shit?"

"No shit. You ever check out Jackson's Real Deal online? He's got a running count for every year since the site went up. Today's was the thirty-fourth killing of an unarmed black person this year."

Simmons was silent for a moment, then said, "That's the one page I generally don't click on. But I have checked it out."

"It piss you off, One Shot?"

"Hey, call me Andy. No one needs to know," Simmons said in a low voice.

"I get you, no offense, man."

"None taken," Andrew said bumping fists with Dawson.

"Yeah, it took a little while before I started answering to 'Tony' when I got out."

"How long have you been out?" Simmons asked.

"Six years in September."

"What have you been doing since?"

"Logistics for OpFor International. It pays better than the old family did, and I don't have to wear the Ghillie anymore. I wear what I want, and most of the time I get to sleep in my own bed at night," Dawson said then paused while the waitress dropped off their drinks.

They clinked glasses and sipped in silence.

"So tell me, what is it you do today?" Dawson inquired.

"Mostly civil engineering. I have a team that solves problems for municipalities around the world. I guess I'm out of the country about two to three months a year. We do traffic, water infrastructure, green tech, most anything you need in a town or city to support the population," he explained.

"You like it?"

"Yeah. It's like problem solving on a macro level. Plus, it's never boring."

"You miss the life at all?"

Simmons looked into Dawson's eyes and slowly shook his head. "I'm through doing Uncle Sam's dirty work."

"I hear ya' brother. You still keeping sharp?"

"About once a month. Why?"

"Just wondering."

Simmons burst out laughing startling Dawson.

"Man, you are still some piece of work. You call me completely out of the blue, suggest we get together, and then don't have a damn thing to say? Brother, just spit it out; you in some kind of trouble? You need money? All you have to do is ask; we've eaten the same mud and bled the same blood. What's mine, is yours."

"Hey, you know that goes both ways. But it ain't nothing like that. I have something I want to talk to you about, but I'm not sure how to lay it out. There's risk involved for me and maybe for you," Dawson said quietly.

"What the fuck are you talking about? Risk to me? How?"

"Hey, I said maybe." Dawson paused and took a good swallow of his drink then lowered his voice even more and said, "I hear there's a movement growing that's focused on ending these murders in this country," then paused to see Simmons' reaction.

Also lowering his voice, Simmons said, "That would be some trick. They've been killing us ever since the first black foot landed on the shore. That ain't going to be easy. You know there's been a handful of vigilantes who've popped cops. But they all got caught or killed. Plus, most of the cop killings just got whole neighborhoods rousted and more than a few folks shot in revenge."

NO JUSTICE, NO PEACE

The conversation paused when the food arrived, and they dug in.

A few minutes later, Simmons asked, "So how's that going to be done? How do you change a half-millennium tradition?"

"Good question. When you ask fifteen different people you get fifteen very different answers. Academics intellectualize the problem and talk about changing societal paradigms. But the shit hasn't changed, so where's the intellectual imperative been? You talk to the militant crowd, and they want revolution and killing whitey. That shit ain't gonna do anything but get a whole lot of black folks killed. I read The Spook Who By The Door and Siege way back when. This country has too many guns and crazy white folks to pull the triggers for that to be a winning strategy." Dawson paused.

"So, your people have an idea how to change America's pastime of killing us?" asked Simmons.

"Not sure yet. What's that line from Macbeth? If it were done tis done then twere well. And yes, I've read a book or two."

"Whatever the—the cure, for lack of a better term—there's got to be a shock and awe component to it," Simmons observed.

"No doubt. That's the reason I looked you up. You were hands down the best mission planner I ever met. One hundred percent mission success rate; no one has ever hit that number since."

Simmons shook his head, "That's because I was determined that Momma Simmons' favorite boy always came home. Are you looking for shooters?"

"No, at least not yet. These folks are trying to see what can actually change in the US because everything that's been tried in the past hasn't done a damn thing. But it's past time for a change. What I'd like you to do is toss some ideas around to see if you can come up with something, anything, that would make white cops stop killing us."

Simmons barked out a laugh. "Yeah, wouldn't that be the shit! Hell, man, I wouldn't know where to start."

"Just think about it. We'll get together in a few weeks and see what you might come up with."

"Yeah, sure, whatever," Simmons said already trying to figure out where to start.

Their conversation swung around to the more mundane, lives, loves, dreams, etc. Simmons found out that Dawson lived in Texas, not far from the OpFor training compound, just west of San Antonio. Neither was married, although Simmons had a close friend with benefits who was his usual companion when he had a business event to attend, or when he needed a night out; the arrangement suited them both.

Dawson worked hard and played hard. He hadn't settled down, at least not so far.

When they finished eating and were standing outside the restaurant, they exchanged email addresses. Dawson pulled Simmons into a hug saying, "You are definitely a sight for sore eyes, One Shot. Stay frosty, I'll catch up with you the next time I swing through town."

As he walked to the garage, Simmons went over the conversation, spoken and unspoken. If one was stupid, the whole visit appeared to be recruitment for a paramilitary vigilante team. But Dawson wasn't stupid, neither was Simmons. They would more than likely be bounced out of any mission like that, that is if they didn't desert first.

But it was a good intellectual exercise, how to stop a practice that had been going on as far back as when whites themselves arrived on the continent. A practice so imbedded into the fabric of the country that it persisted essentially unchanged for over four centuries. How could you stop white cops from murdering innocent, unarmed blacks? There was little consequence the police faced, maybe sitting behind a desk for thirty days and some additional paperwork. But since the law, the prosecutors, the fraternal orders and far too many judges were enablers in the murder of innocent blacks, the legal route was a useless path to justice. For the last generation, those Stand Your Ground laws had extended cover to ordinary citizens who shot blacks with shooter merely having to tell juries (if charged at all) that "they feared for their lives" and they were almost all automatically found not guilty of any wrongdoing.

What would stop a rogue white cop from pulling the trigger? Could anything stop him from pulling the trigger?

A good number of people had debated the idea, probably ever since blacks were first brought to the continent. Surely freed slaves who were automatically assumed to be runaways dealt with the topic daily.

More recently in the previous several generations the arguments swung away from more laws, increased accountability, which proved useless, to revenge killings of rogue cops. Sneaking up on unsuspecting officers and opening fire had a precarious success rate at best. And even if the officers were killed, the blowback to the black community was just more innocent people killed by twitchy cops bent on revenge.

It was something Simmons had been thinking about off and on for quite some time, often triggered when time he read about another innocent black man, child, or woman killed by a white cop. When it got down to it, he was willing to do most anything to make it stop.

Chapter 3

Jackson carefully observed the news coverage of the Tampa shooting investigation over the following two weeks, publishing updates in his online database of police-involved shootings, and noticing that the record of the Tampa shooting had been accessed over three-hundred-thousand times since it had been posted.

The Tampa Police Department, the mayor, and the district attorney were under enormous pressure to indict Officer Benson as soon as possible. Demonstrations at City Hall were staged daily with protestors arriving at sun up and lasting well into the night. The growing frustration of both blacks and whites concerned with social justice was so evident; the district attorney was under pressure to indict regardless of the grand jury's findings.

The Tampa Bay Times reported that while under suspension, Officer Benson was in an undisclosed location in the city while the investigation moved forward. A fluff piece on his family reported that they had been relocated to another location, presumably out of town.

Jackson noted both facts in the online record, dated for today. When he was done, he perused the national news looking for any new cases of officer-involved shootings. He knew statistically that there were three or more such shootings every day in the United States. His online database had collected more than seven thousand shootings since he put the site up on the Web. And even though several departments in the federal law enforcement community readily admitted the fact that Jackson's records were better organized and better researched than most of theirs, still, many police-involved killings simply never made it into the national news.

Just as he was about to log off his site, Jackson received an alert notifying him that the Tampa Grand Jury was due to release their findings on the officer-involved shooting after the close of business the coming Friday. Jackson chuckled as he read the bulletin. They always do that, he thought, trying to bury bad or controversial news when everyone was on their way to their weekend.

He clicked on his travel agency link and looked into flights to Tampa over the next few days, scheduling a Friday morning flight. That would give him a little time to nose around before the district attorney's press conference.

=#=

Officer Benson was tense, having spent the previous week essentially a prisoner in a hotel on the outskirts of Tampa. He had been sequestered by the Chief of Police as the grand jury got closer to releasing their findings.

Police Chief Daniels immediately sent a dozen officers to Benson's home to maintain order, making sure that everyone in the house stayed safe. He then suggested that Officer Benson send his family away for the time being, and that Benson, himself, hide out away from the press and anyone else.

Just after Benson had eaten lunch, the phone rang.

"Yeah, hello," he said, remembering not to use his name.

"Daniels. How are you holding up, son?"

"I'm fine if I don't turn on the damn TV. It ain't too friendly out there, Chief," he said nervously.

"Well I'm calling to set you at ease, Earl. The District Attorney is not going to indict. He called to give me the heads up and to post up some officers around City Hall. I'm sending two extra cars to guard your home to keep anyone from throwing rocks at the windows or whatever."

"So how long do I have to hole up over here? It's driving me nuts. If the DA isn't going to indict, I should get back to work, right?" Benson said hopefully.

"Let's see how the local news coverage goes once the DA makes the announcement. It's not like you're there on your dime. Be patient,; it'll all blow over soon. It always does. How's the wife and kids?" the chief inquired.

"They're fine. Susan and my mom have been taking them around to all the parks around Orlando,; they're supposed to go to Disney World in the morning. I really miss 'em," he said morosely.

"Why don't you join them for the weekend? And we'll see what Monday or Tuesday looks like," offered the chief.

"Hell no! I want to go back to work. You can't let these civilians pressure you, the DA's going to say that I did nothing wrong! This isn't right!"

"I suggest you calm down, son. Or did you forget who's running this department? Maybe you're thinking that you'd be happier working somewhere else?" Daniels said letting the threat hang out there.

After a few moments, Benson said, dejectedly, "I hear you, chief. But I ain't leaving town just in case everything calms down over the weekend. I want to be ready to come in as soon as you tell me the coast is clear."

"All right, Earl. I'm not going to make you leave town, but you keep your head down. I'll keep you posted and have someone keep an eye on your house. Stay cool,; it'll all be over soon," Daniels said then hung up. Seconds later, he ordered additional coverage on Benson's home and dispatched another patrol car to circulate around the hotel where Benson was staying.

The call had gone out earlier for additional off-duty officers to gather at Police Headquarters for a special afternoon briefing. The plan was to deploy the additional officers around City Hall to direct traffic and keep any demonstrations orderly.

Chief Daniels started the briefing promptly at three o'clock with the room filled to overflowing.

"Okay, let's get started. Everyone have their deployment chart?" Daniels asked looking around the room.

Seeing hands raised, he continued. "We're closing surface streets to vehicular traffic for a two-block radius. Any authorized traffic will be directed in and out on Kennedy Boulevard, but no vehicles any closer than a block away from the building. There will be no demonstrators or the press any closer than across the street.

"I want all press credentials scrutinized and for each member of the media to provide at least two pieces of picture identification before they are allowed through security screening. CNN will be allowed to broadcast the video feed to everyone else who wants it. I don't want a shit load of cameras blocking up the place."

One of the officers near the back of the room raised his hand.

"Yes, what is it?" asked Daniels visibly annoyed at the interruption.

"Sir, do you know what the grand jury is going to recommend? Is that why this show of force?"

Daniels shook his head, a wry grin on his face. "Even if I did know, there's no way I could tell anyone before the announcement by the DA. Regardless of which way the grand jury goes, a whole lot of people are going to be pissed off; it's our job to maintain order. That's your job and responsibility, keep peace on the streets."

A captain raised his hand. "Will we be issuing riot gear? I don't want my troops to be caught with their pants down if it gets out of hand—"

"Things aren't going to get out of hand!" Daniels snarled. "Everyone hear me? I don't want anything to happen that causes a shit storm in the press. You all get me?" he spat out. "You all know the plan. The van will be circulating with helmets, shields, and the usual riot gear. If you need it, it'll be there. Are there any other questions? No? Then let's get to it."

Even as the Tampa officers were deploying, a crowd had already gathered at City Hall. Jackson Richards was queued up with the rest of the media representatives, waiting for access to the building. He chitchatted with several of the talking heads from the local television stations, getting a sense of their perspectives, and the likely way the coverage would go depending on the grand jury's recommendations. Several of the media people were aware of whom Jackson was, but had never met him. Jackson was bemused when two of them asked for his autograph. Fortunately, where they were queuing was on the shady side of the building in the day's heat, with the temperature hovering in the low nineties with humidity to match.

At half past six, the members of the media were let into the building in a single file, and had to pass through metal detectors and serious scrutiny of their credentials. Jackson watched as more than a few were turned away, very upset at being denied admittance.

Jackson and the rest were conducted to the room where the DA would make his statement. There were eighty or so people all talking to each other, speculating on the grand jury's findings. The consensus was that given the witnesses who had been all over television in the days after the shooting, and their description of the officer's actions the odds were running five to one on the DA handing down an indictment.

The media representatives were confined to the room without anyone from the DA's office showing up until an hour later; at least the air conditioning had the room comfortable. And when the mood of the assembled was threatening to explode in frustration, District Attorney Nelson Parker entered with a phalanx of suits trailing behind him.

As he took his place at the podium, the others flanked him from behind,; Parker organized his notes and cleared his throat.

"Good evening, everyone, I'm District Attorney Nelson Parker,; thank you all for coming. In the grand jury's examination of the facts presented, the testimony of twenty-one witnesses, including that of Officer Earl Benson, transcripts of the police radio traffic and three calls to 911, with more than one hundred exhibits, the grand jury has recommended that no charges be filed against Officer Benson—"

The room erupted with shouted questions, rising to an almost painful din. Seconds later, the crowd outside was dimly heard as someone in the room must have texted the finding by phone. The shouting continued several minutes after Parker raised his hands indicating his desire for order. When the room began to quiet down, members of the media waited for Parker to resume.

Once the room went silent, Parker continued. "As I was about to say, the full grand jury report will be posted on the city's Web site next week. Until then, I have very little to add at this time other than to state that as far as this office is concerned, the investigation into whether or not to charge Officer Benson is concluded; there will be no charges filed."

Jackson listened as questions were thrown at the DA, who either said that the information sought would be available online next week interspersed with more than a few "no comments."

After fifteen minutes of DA Parker's stonewalling, Jackson made his way out of the building only to be met with a wall of sound that was almost a physical assault on his person. Even though the crowd was on the other side of the street, their shouting was deafening. The officers around the building looked nervous, questioning the prudence of not being issued their riot gear. Even with the S.W.A.T. van parked in the loading dock, the officers knew just how quickly things could get out of hand.

Jackson walked into the street and into the crowd. Several people asked him what was said, and he told them, raising his voice to a shout to be heard over the din. He kept moving, quickly leaving the crowd behind and walked back to his hotel.

Once in his room, Jackson grabbed a bottle of water from the room's fridge, turned on the television, and tuned to one of the local stations. He figured he was too late for any special bulletin but was content to wait for the 11:00 P.M. news. He pulled his tablet out of his bag and connected to the hotel's public Wi-Fi. Once connected, he logged into his server and began to update the information on the grand jury finding, thin as it was. He then saw several interviews of the victim's family and friends. The victim, Robert Wilson, was described by everyone interviewed as a good churchgoing man with no criminal record whatsoever. Community leaders from the black church in Tampa pleaded for calm knowing that were there to be massive demonstrations, any kind of civil disobedience or violence would visit more misery on nonwhites in unhealthy measure.

Deciding to grab a bite while he waited for the local news to come on, Jackson took his tablet down to the hotel restaurant, and while he ate, caught up on the news and sports around the country. The news about the Tampa grand jury recommending not to indict Officer Benson was already all over the news sites on the Web though none had anything new to report. Jackson was convinced that he was in for breathless speculation from talking heads with absolutely nothing factual to report.

After a fairly good meal and a couple of beers, Jackson returned to his room to watch the coverage of the DA's announcement and to see whether or not someone from the police department went on record. He chuckled when every local channel announced that the mayor was unavailable for comment then got upset when the head of the local chapter of the Fraternal Order of Police spouted off the usual bullshit about the police departments around the nation were the "thin blue line" that kept law-abiding citizens safe on the streets and in their homes. When he had exhausted the local coverage, he switched over to CNN wanting to see what the national coverage looked like.

He was about ten minutes into the show when there was a special bulletin banner splashed along the bottom of the screen. His interest perked up when he saw that the bulletin was about an explosion in Orlando.

When CNN broke for the local reporter, Jackson saw that the epicenter of the explosion was a house destroyed due to a suspected gas leak. The local video showed the remains of a two-story frame house whose ruins were completely engulfed in flames. There didn't appear to be any damage to the homes on either side of the one on fire, but the burning rubble of the exploded house was only about three feet high above ground.

He was only listening with half of his attention until the newswoman making the on-scene report disclosed the owner's name and identified her as the mother of Officer Earl Benson, the officer just cleared of any wrongdoing in the Tampa shooting investigation.

-=#=

Office Benson was in his underwear, laying down watching a movie when the phone in his hotel room rang. Picking it up, he heard the chief saying his name before he could speak.

"Earl, Earl, are you there?"

Sitting up, fearing someone had done something to his home, Earl answered in panic, "What's up, chief?"

"Have you been watching the news, son?"

"No, I was catching a movie. Why? What's wrong?" Earl said, now completely freaked out.

"Was your family visiting your mother in Orlando, son?" Daniels said soberly.

"You know they were. Why, what happened?!"

"I'm sorry to be the one to tell you, but it appears there's been an accident. There's been an explosion at the house, the fire department says it was gas-related."

Benson nearly dropped the phone as all strength drained from his body, his mind just couldn't process what the chief had told him.

"Earl! Are you there, son?"

After a moment he said, "I'm . . . here."

"Is there any chance they were out to a late dinner, somewhere out of the house?"

In shock, Benson was able to reply, "No, Susan always had the kids in bed by nine o'clock." He paused, trying to get himself together. "Did they find anyone yet?"

"No, the Orlando PD said that until they get the fire completely out, there's no way to be able to tell. Son, do you want me to send someone over there? Whatever you need, just ask. I could stop by—"

"No, no—I'm going to go home and get a few things and go there. I have to know—"

"That's not a very good idea, Earl. There's nothing to know until at least tomorrow. Let the locals do their job. Your being there isn't going to help them, or you. I know telling you to get some rest is a waste of time, but I don't want you going off half-cocked. I want you to stay put the Orlando PD will be calling me with any updates; I'll keep you posted, son. You hear what I'm saying, stay put. Do I have to put someone in the room with you, Earl?"

Earl was just shaking his head, trying to get his mind wrapped around the possibility that his entire family was dead. "Yeah—I hear you." Benson paused, then asked, "You gonna be in tomorrow?"

"Of course, son. I want to make sure I know exactly what's going on."

"I'll see you in the morning. I want to know what they find. Otherwise, I'm going to see for myself."

"I understand. I'll be in by seven."

Earl just hung up the phone, grabbing the television's remote flipping around until he landed on CNN, showing the home on fire in a window onscreen while the talking head in the studio was rehashing the Tampa DA's announcement, mentioning that the home on fire was that of Tampa PD. Officer Benson's mother, April Benson. He then tried calling his wife's mobile phone and listened as it rang then went to voice mail. He left word telling her to call him as soon as she got the message, and then almost threw the phone across the room before getting hold of himself.

When Daniels got off the phone he called the front desk of the hotel and inquired whether the room across Benson's was available. When informed that it was, Daniels booked it and informed them that a couple of officers would be by shortly for the room.

MYRON MacHUTCHENS

When he concluded that call, Daniels then called on his two best protective detail officers and dispatched them to the hotel to keep an eye on Benson's room, to make sure no one tried to get at the officer, and to make sure Benson stayed put.

Chapter 4

When Officer Benson arrived at the station the next day he had to run the gauntlet of protestors already camped out outside the police department but still being held across the street. When people saw him, recognizing him from his ID photo online and shown in the press they shouted all manner of insults, demands and a few, their joy over his mother's home being blown up in the previous night's explosion.

As he walked to the chief's office everyone he passed offered their condolences, some even wanting to know if there was anything they could do for him. Benson was stoic, but thankful for the outpouring of support. By the time he reached the chief's office, he at least felt that his fellow officers had his back.

"Come in," came the reply to his knock.

When Chief Daniels saw who it was he quickly got to his feet and came around the desk to shake Benson's hand and clap him on the back.

"I'm so sorry, Earl. We're all praying that no one was home. Have you had any success contacting your wife?"

Benson shook his head. "All my calls go straight to voice mail."

"I dare say you probably didn't get much sleep. . ."

"None. All I could do was switch from channel to channel, hoping. . ." Benson rubbed his eyes in fatigue. When he started to speak, his voice broke. "I know that it would be a miracle."

Daniels came around the desk and laid a hand on Benson's shoulder as he watched the man weep silently.

"Orlando PD hasn't called yet, last I heard, at 4 A.M., was that the fire department would be able to start sifting in a couple more hours. Could you get some rest if you were at home? Or would you like to put off going home for a bit, son?"

Shaking his head, Benson said, "I'd prefer to either be here or go to my mom's home."

"That's pretty much out of the question. No one wants you hanging about over there. The fire department has to determine the cause of the accident. I know that's scant comfort to you at this point, but we have the same policy here.

"I appreciate you're wanting to be here, but you're beat. You haven't had any sleep, and I dare say you're also in shock. My advice is for you to go back to the hotel and let me coordinate everything from here. I was told I'd be called if any information becomes available. I promise I'll call you first thing."

"It's my family, I deserve to be here—or there," Benson morosely said.

"You're not even fit for duty, not like this. I'm here for the duration, and if I have to leave, the Orland PD has my mobile number. Nothing's going to happen that I won't know about immediately. I'm strongly suggesting that you go back to the hotel. Stay there. The doc is here. She came in just in case you needed anything. Do you need something to help you get some sleep?"

"Hell no! That's all I need is to sleep through a call from Susan. Barring that, I want to hear anything you find out. I am tired, but my mind's running around like some bat-shit crazy rat in a cage! I need to know, chief."

Daniels got up from his perch on the corner of his desk and went to his phone. "I want you to see the doc before you head back to the hotel. You straight?"

"Yeah, whatever."

"And leave your car in the lot, I'll have Simpson and Clark run you to the hotel."

Chief Daniels called the department doctor, who often doubled as the in-house psychologist, and let her know Officer Benson was on his way down. Once Benson left the office, he arranged for officers Simpson and Clark to provide transport to the hotel. Daniels figured that have a pair of female officers escorting Benson back to the hotel would lessen the chance of him deciding to go off on his own.

He also called the protection detail stationed across the hall from Benson's room to let them know that they should remain there for the duration.

Chief Daniels was a twenty-eight-year veteran of the force, first in Phoenix, then in Tampa for the last fourteen years. His first thought when the explosion was reported was that there might very well be a nefarious cause. The timing was suspicious, especially in light of the district attorney's refusal to file charges against Officer Benson. The liaison officer in Orlando had also voiced the same concern. So far, publically, the explosion was being investigate as a simple accident, but Orlando's arson investigators were on the job examining the wreckage of the home.

Daniels was frustrated that there was nothing that he, or anyone else, could do until the arson investigators completed their examination of the wreckage. If the explosion was deliberately set, then Daniels had one hell of a mess on his hands. The chief was actually glad for the opportunity to catch up on some of his paperwork, somewhat distracting him from the anxiety of waiting for a call from Orlando. As far as he was concerned, he had covered all his bases, hopefully not overlooking anything of note.

-=#=

Jackson had arrived in Orlando early in the morning. His first stop was to visit the Public Information Officer for the Orlando Fire Department, and he was not received particularly well. At first the PIO just handed Jackson a release stating no more than had been reported in the news the previous night, stating, "That's all we have so far. The investigators are pouring through the wreckage as we speak. When anything new comes up, we'll probably have a news conference to let you all know what might, or might not, be found."

Jackson thanked the man, then made his way out of the building. He then got in the car and using his mobile phone's GPS app, drove to the site of the explosion.

The street had been cordoned off at both corners so Jackson parked the car a block away, got out and walked down the opposite side of the street to join the group of onlookers filling the sidewalk.

After a few moments, Jackson sidled up to an older black woman watching.

"Did they find anyone in there yet?" he asked in a friendly manner.

She shook her head and said, "Not so far. I got here about an hour ago but nothing yet."

The crowd watched as seven firemen were carefully going through the debris. After a little over thirty minutes, one of the firemen gestured excitedly to the others who gathered to see what the fuss was.

All of a sudden, they all stopped moving, standing motionless and silent. A hush came over the watching crowd, guessing that a body had been found.

Two police officers moved to block the crowd from surging forward as two other patrol cars quickly arrived, bringing crowd control reinforcements.

Moments later a van from the coroner's department arrived and the firemen helped set up a tent adjacent to the burned out rubble as the watching crowd was silent.

Once the tent was up and a stretcher was brought into the rubble, two of the firemen started clearing the area while two others stood by with the stretcher. When the area had been sufficiently cleared, all four lifted an unrecognizable, charred form onto the stretcher and immediately covered it with a thin, rubber sheet. As they lifted the stretcher, several men in the crowd removed their hats as the firemen carried the stretcher into the tent.

Jackson knew it would be useless trying to get any information from the police officers or firemen even with his media credentials, but he was determined to remain to see what the body count would finally be. He was also entertaining the notion that the explosion was in response to the Tampa DA's grand jury recommendation not to indict Officer Benson.

He watched as the firemen left the tent while the man and woman who had arrived in the Coroner's van carried their gear into the tent. The fire department crew returned to the rubble, carefully shifting the larger burned bits of the former structure, seemingly sobered by the discovery of their first body.

Ten minutes later another body was discovered. When they lifted it on to the stretcher the crowd could see it was very small, most likely a child. And as two of the crew were taking the stretcher into the tent, one of the others signaled that he had found another body in the debris.

When the forth body was recovered, Jackson left. He knew the identities of the four bodies and was certain that there would be no further macabre discoveries. But what he was becoming interested in was monitoring the investigation into the cause of the explosion, whether or not the gas leak was accidental or deliberate. If it was deliberate, Jackson wondered if Officer Benson was going to be brought down by mishap as well.

-=#=

Someone was knocking on the door, pulling Benson out of a troubled sleep. He got up and staggered to the door, surprised that he had fallen asleep at all. "Who's there?" he asked, trying to shake the tendrils of grogginess away.

"Earl, it's Sam Daniels. You awake, son?"

"Yeah, yeah—I'm awake," Benson said, opening the door.

Chief Daniels walked into the room, pushing the door shut behind him, and began without preamble, "I'm really sorry, son. They've found four bodies, two of them small enough to be children. I arranged to send dental records to ID them; the bodies are in a pretty bad way. I'm very sorry, Earl. It doesn't look good."

Benson fell back on the bed, tears welling up in his eyes. Daniels crossed over to the bed and squeezed Benson's shoulder while handing him a flask. "Have a drink, son."

Benson waved away the flask, got up and went into the bathroom, closing the door behind him.

When the door shut, Daniels automatically looked around for Benson's service weapon and located it hanging from the chair at the room's desk. Listening carefully, Daniels could hear the water running in the sink, deducing that Benson was probably getting himself cleaned up.

Moments later the door opened and Benson came out, his hair combed and face obviously washed. He went over to the chair and started pulling his clothes on.

"Thank you for coming by to tell me personally, chief. I'm going home to get some clean clothes on and then head to Orlando to make the arrangements."

Daniels just stared, seeing that Benson wasn't going to be talked out of going this time.

"Fine, Earl. But I'm going to have someone escort you, you're in no condition to drive. Hell, maybe you'll get some sleep on the way," Daniels said, pulling his mobile out and dialing.

"Smitty? Yeah, it's me. Call Simpson and Clark and have them pack a bag, they're running Benson to Orlando, probably staying overnight. No, I'll be bringing him to the station, have them meet us there and have an unmarked gassed up and ready to go. Yeah, thanks." he ended the call and turned to Benson.

"So, here's what you're going to do. You'll be escorted to Orlando, I'll call ahead and let the chief there know you're coming. He told me earlier that if you were to come, he'd extend you every courtesy. Let Clark or Simpson do the driving, I doubt you'll be able to come back tonight. Stay over and take your time tomorrow. I'll expect to see you on Monday, at the earliest. If you need more time, take it. Pack up your things, I'll run you over to your house and then take you to the station to meet the ladies; you'll be taking an unmarked squad."

It only took a few minutes for Benson to get packed up and out of the hotel. When they arrived at his home, there were a dozen protestors being held across the street by several patrolmen. Fortunately, they didn't shout anything at Officer Benson as he walked from the car to the front door. The stop at his house was bittersweet and opened up an almost overwhelming sadness. Daniels tried to keep Benson's mind on the mundane details of packing his bag to keep him focused.

When they were finally at the station, Chief Daniels gave some brief instructions for Simpson and Clark, letting the women know the Orlando chief's contact numbers as well as the address of the city's morgue.

Once the three were on their way east, Chief Daniels allowed himself to relax. He knew that the report from the Orlando's fire investigators wouldn't be completed for at least a day or so, he could get back to his regular routine after hopefully getting to take Sunday off.

-=#=-

During the drive back to Tampa, Jackson's mind was furiously working through the implications of Benson's mother's home exploding being a deliberate act in retaliation for the killing of unarmed Robert Wilson. No, not just the murder, but getting away with what any right-minded person would call a heinous crime. Furthermore, what if this wasn't just a single act of retaliation and only the beginning of some kind of trend?

Shaking his head, Jackson decided to table any further consideration until he dug up something of substance. He turned on the radio, set it for the AM band, and scanned up the dial for a local talk radio station, steeling himself for the inevitable low-brow assault of conservative on-air, so-called talent. Having settled on a Tampa station, Jackson was waiting for the local news to see if any new details from the district attorney's office had been released.

He drove along, only half paying attention to the radio when his attention was drawn to a special bulletin.

"Justine Parker, wife of District Attorney Nelson Parker, along with their son Edward, were killed in an accidental explosion at the American Sun service station on Rogers avenue while she was refueling the family minivan. The owner of the station, Peter Johnson, stated that Ms. Parker was using one of the self-service pumps when the explosion occurred. Four other customers at the filling station were injured by the explosion and have been transported to St. Luke's Hospital. One is listed in serious condition. There has been no statement from the Office of the District Attorney at this time. Stay tuned to this station for breaking details as they occur."

How does that saying go? Once is an accident, twice is coincidence, and three times is enemy action, thought Jackson. He knew that he wasn't going to be the only one thinking this was no random accident, someone was sending a message. Looking at the markers along the road, he saw he was only forty miles from Tampa and couldn't wait to get back. But wanting to get back as quickly as humanly possible didn't spur him to increase his speed, he was entirely too smart to give any white cop in the south the opportunity to turn him into another tragic statistic.

When he arrived in Tampa, Jackson first stopped at his hotel to drop off the car. He turned on the room's television to check out the news and was stunned by the national reports of no fewer than eighty-six deadly accidents, all involving the families of white officers involved in the deaths of unarmed, innocent blacks who had managed to avoid prosecution.

U.S. Attorney General Simon Thatcher was giving a statement being carried by nearly every channel.

". . . no doubt that these accidents are the acts of a deadly, organized group of vigilantes and will not be tolerated. No one is allowed to take the law into their own hands, no matter what issue they have. We are coordinated with local authorities to merge investigations focused on determining exactly who is behind these heinous acts. Now, I have a few minutes to take some questions."

The room erupted in a cacophony of shouted voices, quieting when Thatcher pointed to one of the reporters.

"Mr. Attorney General, has anyone privately claimed credit for these acts that you're not able to reveal to us at this time?"

"No, Allen. And even if that were the case, I couldn't say so. Next," he said pointing to the other side of the room.

"Obviously someone is killing family members of cops who killed blacks. Where is the starting point of your investigation going to focus, and has your office notified local departments of officers, local district attorneys and judges involved in similar police-involved killings?"

Thatcher waited a moment before answering, then said, "Sadly, the FBI, the agency responsible for keeping national crime statistics, doesn't have a ready-made listing of the white cop on black citizen incidents across the entire country. However, they are working closely with the DOJ and the various local police departments to identify families at risk."

"Excuse me, sir. There is a resource that has a list of all officer-involved killings for the past decade; what about Jackson's Real Deal Web site?" someone asked, with Jackson pumping his fist in excited triumph at being mentioned. That mention alone was sure to jack his site visits up into the millions.

Thatcher nervously cleared his throat before answering.

"All departments of the federal government are using every possible resource to try to uncover the people behind these crimes, I would imagine that Mr. Richards' online database is just one of many resources we're looking at."

Jackson sat down, realizing that going to the police department was a waste of time,; this was so much bigger than Tampa's lack of indictment of Officer Benson. He pulled out his tablet, logged on to the hotel's Wi-Fi, then logged into his site. It took several minutes to log in indicating the traffic was already astronomically high. He made a note to call his service provider to increase the number of servers handling the traffic for his site. Jackson was infinitely glad he had never added a public comment section to the site, he had foreseen exactly what a mess that would have been, especially now.

For the time being, he was going to have to put together a private database of the white families killed in this latest wave of violence and checking the correlation between his listing of cop shootings and the families who were killed.

Chapter 5

Andrew Simmons was in San Francisco consulting on the design of a new water reclamation system needed to combat over two decade's worth of drought. He and two other engineers from the firm were working with the public works department studying the feasibility of building and operating desalinization plants along the coast. They were in the middle of planning the right-of-ways for the massive water pipes that would bring the desalinated water to the interior pipes of the city for distribution to the businesses and homes along the northern edge of San Francisco. They had been working on the least costly routes, the ones that impacted the fewest residents and businesses needing to be relocated.

Being Friday, they were trying to get as much done before the weekend began because the city's planning department staff were not able to work overtime due to city policy. Andrew's crew were all staying through the weekend, both engineers were single and looked forward to a couple of days free in town. Andrew had thought about flying back to New York and catching a flight back early in the morning Monday, but he didn't really have any reason to make the round trip.

When six o'clock came, they decided to bag it. Knowing that his people wanted to hit the town, Andrew said his goodbyes when they exited the building and stepped into the street to hail a cab. Seconds later, a sedan pulled up with the window rolling down and Tony Dawson's voice shouting for him to get in.

Andrew got in and buckled up as Tony smoothly took off into traffic.

"Somehow I get the feeling that this isn't just a coincidence," Andrew said, slapping five with his buddy.

"Obviously. Although I was on the west coast, in San Diego, on business," Tony said, laughing.

"And you knew I was here. . . how?"

"Easy, called your office and told them we were buddies in the service; got the same woman who gave me your mobile number."

Andrew cut a glance at Tony that said, bullshit, but let it go.

"Yeah, whatever. Where are we going? I'm starved," Andrew asked.

"There's a great seafood place on Fisherman's Wharf that I've always liked. How's that sound?"

"Just so long as we get there quick."

"We're less than ten minutes away."

The two traveled in silence with Andrew watching the city go by outside the window. Once they arrived, Tony parked, and the two walked down to the end of the wharf to the restaurant.

When they'd been seated and their drink orders taken, Andrew just said, "Well?" making Tony burst out in laughter.

Tony twirled his glass, took a sip, then said, "Give any thought to what we talked about?"

"You know I did."

"Come up with anything?"

Andrew's breath hissed out between his teeth, then he said, "Given the circumstances I can't see anything happening without a wholesale sea change of the top policy-makers in the country. Even then, there's still the cultural inertia. Shit, breaking a half millennium habit in this country isn't going to go easy. Frankly, I don't think it's possible." He paused, to take a sip of his drink. "I don't see how it can be done without a hell of a lot bloodshed. A whole lot of white folks and black folks are gonna have to die to make it happen."

Chuckling, Tony said, "You're probably right. But does that mean it shouldn't happen?"

"Yeah, that's the sixty-four-thousand-dollar question. If it won't happen otherwise, then the saying 'you can't make an omelette without breaking some eggs' would never be truer. So let's just get down to it. What do you want of me?" Andrew asked pointedly.

"Nothing."

"Bullshit. You show up into my life without notice, and you roll up on me all the way across the country to talk about armed insurrection," Andrew said holding up his hand to forestall any comment. "I'm not done. I've given the idea a lot of thought, and I can't say that I wouldn't want to do something, anything, to set things right. But I can't see how you and I could get together enough trained black folks to pull it off," said Andrew, shaking his head.

"May I speak?" Tony asked, a bemused smile on his face.

Andrew just waved his hand, go ahead.

"I'm not here to recruit you for anything. All I wanted was to see what your perspective is and to give you a heads-up. Things are getting worse, not better. And if something were to jump off, people like you and me are going to be put under a microscope, folks with skills, skills in warfare with proven track records in the killing of men."

Andrew lowered his voice even further. "What the fuck, Tony? What do you know? What's going to jump off?"

"I don't know anything specific, just some rumblings. Someone I know mentioned that if that cop in Tampa gets off, that this could just be the last straw."

"Wasn't there something in the news about the Tampa grand jury's findings being released today?" asked Andrew. "Level with me, is the shit going to hit the fan tonight?"

"I can't really say," answered Tony.

"Can't, or won't?"

"I really don't know, but watch your six. If you get the notion to take a little vacation, take this," Tony said, handing him what looked like a business card. "Memorize the information on that card. You never know."

Andrew tucked the card in his pocket without looking at it.

"I swear to you that I've done nothing to put you at risk. I'm just looking out for you—watching your back," Tony assured him.

"You hanging around for a while?"

"Nah, I have to get back to OpFor in the morning. Just wanted to swing by and say hello and give you the card," Tony said, gesturing toward Andrew's pocket.

"One day, you're going to fuckin' tell me what's going on. Until then, I've still got your six. Stay frosty, man," Andrew said, paused a beat, then continued. "Anyway, I'm hanging around Frisco until Thursday or Friday. I have a team here working on water management; probably too mundane for the likes of you," Andrew said, chuckling.

"No doubt. If the water doesn't come out when I turn on the tap, I call a plumber," Tony said, both of them laughing.

The conversation went on for just over two hours before they paid the bill, left the restaurant, and wandered around the wharf. They chatted about missions past, with Andrew fighting the urge to constantly scan the surroundings looking for threats. He knew something was up but believed that Tony did have his back. That didn't allay his fear that he was somehow a target, but for what he had no idea.

They spent another hour wandering around reminiscing, maintaining light conversation. And later, Tony took Andrew to his hotel. When the car pulled up to the hotel's awning, Tony got out and came around to give his nearly life-long friend a hug, whispering in his ear, "Stay frosty. I'll be in touch." They then shook hands, and Andrew watched as Tony drove off.

Andrew knew that Tony wouldn't jack him around which is why he took his friend's warnings seriously. His frustration over not knowing where a threat could come from wasn't something he could do anything about so he did his best to put it from his mind. The problem was that the events of Orlando and Tampa blasted across every cable and satellite channel over the weekend only served to force him into a mode of behavior that hadn't been present since he left the service.

-=#=

By Monday morning, the pontificating about the weekend's coordinated killings across the nation was deafening. The fact that no one was holding back wild speculation that some heretofore unknown black power group was responsible for the murder of one hundred eighteen whites, all family members of white police officers, district attorneys and judges, only served to make targets of blacks across the nation. The nation was literally in the grips of terror, a terror that was all the more frightening for its justification of visiting revenge on whites who even other whites honestly believed committed murders for which there were no consequences.

The FBI was coordinating communication between local police departments. The White House had the Justice Department begin to draw together a task force designed to discover and respond to those responsible for the wave of violence.

In every death, there was nothing to indicate that there was any foul play whatsoever. Each and every death of an officer's, district attorney's or judge's family members, other than all of them occurring within hours of each other, showed no sign of having been the result of deliberate design. All manner of special investigators were looking for any evidence of something other than divine providence.

The cause of deaths included explosion, single-vehicle accidents, carbon monoxide poisoning, accidental drowning, accidental electrocution, heart attack, stroke, and on and on. However, not a single death was caused by a firearm of any kind, one-on-one violence or personal attack, but dead they all were. No one was spared, not children, nor spouses of any gender; no one.

It was the children killed in the myriad accidents that provoked both the harshest criticism of the yet unnamed organization behind the killing spree, as well as the most fear. It was less than seventy-two hours since the first explosion in Orlando, but the United States of America was in a full panic.

As the hours passed Monday, the death toll kept rising with several families caught in hiding, although death failed to touch any of the police officers who had killed innocent or unarmed blacks across the country.

In a few cases, the officers' direct presence appeared to have protected their loved ones, but in two cases once the families were sequestered in what the officers believed were safe circumstances, and the officers left, both families died under highly suspicious circumstances.

This was an uprising perpetrated by a completely unknown entity. By the time Monday passed into Tuesday, another forty-four whites had died in inexplicable accidents. The country came to a standstill Tuesday morning, Andrew and his two white engineers returned to New York while flights were still moving about the country. After being glued to the news reports, Andrew was astounded by the scope of what the country was experiencing. He was tempted to call Tony but refrained. He couldn't know for sure if Tony was involved in what was going on and given the massive resources needed to pull off this kind of operation, he was content to wait and see what shook out.

What Andrew knew was that whomever was behind all those accidents was someone well-funded, someone with a virtual army of specialists in covert operations, specialists that rivaled or exceeded the expertise of those employed by the Central Intelligence Agency. This was unprecedented, an unspoken declaration of war with nearly five hundred years of history coming home to roost.

On the flight back to New York, Andrew began to examine exactly how he would have put together the assets needed to pull off this operation.

The first thing he realized was that the operation had to be years in the making, that someone had begun planning the overall operation years in advance. First the gathering of intelligence on every white police officer's lives, their family's schedules, relatives, nearly every facet had to be monitored and recorded. Just the surveillance alone would require a legion of undercover operatives. The information necessary to have created all those accidents wasn't something that one could just look up on the Internet, it called for actual human assets to obtain and implement. People needed to be shadowed: homes places of work, schools and a host of other facilities and locations had to be cased.

And in those places that had to be prepared for their inevitable accidents, untraceable prep work had to be done. Just thinking about the prep work alone made Andrew revise the time line backwards to more than five years.

This operation also took money-massive amounts of money to set up. What would be the source of that amount of money? In most cases it would take a government, or perhaps organized crime, to fund an operation that extensive. Since whites were being targeted, the source of the funding couldn't very well be another government, and using one as a source represented risk if word leaked out. Long-term planning, a nearly unlimited money source, and the skill sets of top counter insurgent operatives numbering in the hundreds. And let's not forget Information Technologies support; hardware, software, perhaps even access to those resources through the Internet. Surveillance, physical and digital, would be a large part of their operations Andrew figured.

By the time the flight arrived in New York, Andrew was awed by just how enormous the resources people behind the mass killing had to have. He calculated that somewhere between one hundred and four hundred people were needed to run the operation and at least tens, even hundreds of millions of dollars could easily have been spent over the previous decade through the present to make it all happen. And the organization would have to be all black. That was the most impressive facet of the operation, and not because of the perception that African Americans lacked the skills needed to pull off the operation, but that no one had leaked the coming events for their own personal gain. That was always the risk in large-scale, secret operations.

Once he got home, Andrew immediately turned on the national news finding out that the death toll, as near as the media could figure it, had reached in the neighborhood of eighteen hundred people-almost entirely women and children. . . and a few pets. The most terrifying part to law enforcement was that there was no communique, no declaration of war, no manifesto published explaining exactly what the people who were killing the families of police officers and those in the legal profession who had provided cover for the murder of unarmed, innocent blacks wanted. An update carried by CNN reported that families of white men acquitted of murder using the south's stand your ground legal shield were also dying under suspicious circumstances as well.

While he was unpacking, Andrew noticed that there hadn't been a single instance of a cop-involved shooting of any black adult, teen or child reported since the previous Friday night, and it was already Tuesday evening. Although he deplored the loss of life, he thought the strategy was brilliant. And entire country brought to its knees in the name of social justice, and no one had a clue who was behind it.

-=#=-

Federal Court of Appeals Judge Alvin Bridges had never been so busy in his life. He had published a book entitled The Entire System Is Broken: Throw It Away and Start Over, which, up until now, was mostly read by law students and legal scholars. But one of the conservative-leaning cable channels had discovered the black judge's completely factual recounting of the systemic injustice blacks faced in America's legal system and convinced him to sit down for an interview.

When Judge Bridges was completely unapologetic for the conclusions in his book, conservatives later tried to paint him as the cause of what was happening across America. Bridges laughed at the notion, stating that what the country was experiencing was four hundred years of American injustice coming home to roost. And furthermore, that whites were seeing what the systematic insults, injuries and murder of blacks had wrought. What completely frustrated conservative pundits was the fact that Judge Bridges remained completely unapologetic no matter what provocations they threw his way. And the sound bite that was picked up and replayed on every other news channel, social media and video Web site was the judge asking, "How's that white privilege thing working out for the country now?"

Chapter 6

President Marcus Temple was seething with rage when he convened his National Security Team. It had been a week since Tampa Officer Benson's family had died in the explosion, and the FBI, the US Marshals, and every other arm of law enforcement had nothing, no leads, not even a hint of where to begin.

"This is completely unacceptable. We're sitting here with our thumbs up our asses, and the country is experiencing the worst insurgency in its history. And none of you have uncovered any hint of who is behind it! This is bullshit. I'd love to fire the lot of you if it wouldn't just add to the monumental panic out there. What do you have to say for yourself," he said gesturing to the director of the FBI.

"My people are tracing leads—"

"What God damned leads? You have leads? What have you found since your notes from yesterday?" Temple demanded.

"Uh, nothing concrete yet, sir. But we're beginning to compile a list of past combat vets who have the kind of skills this operation calls for," the director replied.

"And just what kind of profile are you looking at?" Temple snarled.

"Well, combat skills, counter insurgency training, infiltration—"

"And black! Right?" the president interrupted.

"Well yes, and no. Not exclusively black. Some of our analysts believe that there's not enough black talent out there to field this large and effective an operation," the director explained.

The rest of the people in the room were silent realizing the racist implications the director of the FBI had voiced.

"Really, now? Is everyone else of the same mind as Ryan? That blacks are incapable of pulling off something this big, this coordinated?" Temple said looking around the table. "Don't you realize it's that kind of thinking that got us into this damn mess in the first place?"

Temple looked at the director of the NSA and asked, "I can't believe that this was pulled off without your people never having twigged it. This has to have been in the works for years, and you still have nothing? Hell, you've recorded every phone call in this country for the last thirty years, copied every email since the 1990s, and you have nothing?"

"Mr. President, my people are creating new filters right now to go back through our captures," NSA replied.

"How long is that going to take, and how soon will you have results?" Temple demanded.

"I'm uncertain, sir."

Temple banged his fist on the table startling everyone. "This is unacceptable. I want results, and I want them yesterday."

"Sir?" said Attorney General Thatcher.

"What, Simon? You have something, anything?"

"Not at this moment, but I do have a concern," Thatcher began.

"Well, what is it. Speak up man."

"Given the nature of this operation, shouldn't we be thinking about isolating African Americans in sensitive positions, reducing their access to information about the investigation, just in case?"

"How stupid are you?" Temple asked in genuine anger. "And it's not just you. I'm sure there's a number of you sitting around this table who don't realize that's the kind of thinking that got us here. No, we don't start treating people in our own departments as insurgents or enemy combatants no matter their race.

"Unless you have direct knowledge of someone who is a member of the organization that planned and executed these killings, you leave everyone the hell alone; just find these people. What's the death toll up to now?" Temple asked the FBI.

"As near as we can tell it's now over four thousand people, sir."

"What? That many?" the president said in shock.

"Yes, sir. They come in spurts, and there may be some that we've missed since they all look like accidents. There's no sign yet of direct action against any of them. It's damn frustrating, sir. Based on all the local police departments and the investigations we're running, for all practical purposes these killings could be the biggest coincidence in history, but we know better. It's just spooky how none of the killings can be attributed to anything but accidental death. Frankly, sir, and I know you're going to be pissed to hear it, so far we're chasing ghosts," the director said waiting for an outburst from the president.

The room was silent, everyone waiting for the president to speak. When he did it was in quiet desperation. "Look, I know that everyone here is doing the best that's humanly possible. I share all your frustrations. But I'm the guy who has to go before the nation Monday and explain to the American people, to the world even, how this country has failed its people. And that includes all the innocent blacks killed since the boats first started bringing them here.

MYRON MacHUTCHENS

"The latest estimates suggest that north of twenty million blacks have been killed in this country. And anyone honest knows that a scant minority of those killings were justified. And if you want to know what I mean by justified, or how I would judge the killing of a black male in this country justified, I imagine that they were white and see if the justification for their death still holds true. Too many times it does not. We have a serious problem in this country about race. The fact that there's not a single person of color, not to mention any women in this room, is proof enough of that.

"It appears that in around a decade whites are going to be a numerical minority in this country, we are all aware of that. The lengths whites are going through to maintain their privilege in this country are tearing us apart. Fear is the leading killer in this country. And now we have someone who has decided to level the playing field,; someone we have no idea how to fight, let alone find. Find me something, anything, gentlemen."

-=#=

Washington, D.C. police officer, Jerry Stackhouse, was in a panic. He had spirited his family away from the city and was on the run in Arizona. He had changed vehicles twice, shaved his mustache and stubble of a beard, and had his wife dye her blond hair black explaining to his two children that they were on a "special" vacation.

Every black face he came across caused a chill of fear in Stackhouse. He had no idea who he should be afraid of. His killing of eighteen-year-old Leonard Pitts had sealed his family's fate.

Pitts had been walking down the street with his girlfriend when Officer Stackhouse received an alert over the radio about a convenience store robbery nearby. Stackhouse was cruising the neighborhood trying to locate the robbery suspect when he came upon the pair.

Calling for backup, Stackhouse cut the couple off with his squad car and exited, gun out, shouting for the two to lay down on the ground. Pitts moved to shield his girlfriend and raised his hands.

Stackhouse continued to order the two to the ground at the top of his lungs. When Pitts turned to move away from his girlfriend, Stackhouse fired eight rounds, stopping only as Pitts fell to the ground. The girlfriend dropped to her knees, trying to help Pitts, ignoring Stackhouse's shouted orders, crying as two additional squad cars arrived.

Three more officers exited, guns drawn, all shouting for the woman to lie down on the ground. She continued to lean over Pitts, crying, with his blood all over her hands.

NO JUSTICE, NO PEACE

One of the newly arrived officers ran up and jerked her away from Pitts' body and slammed her to the ground, kneeling on her back as he jerked her arm back to snap the handcuff to her wrist, repeating the maneuver for her other arm. He then stood up, his foot on her back to keep her on the ground.

At that moment, officers several blocks away had located the robbery suspect and took him into custody. Meanwhile, Pitts was dead, and the woman with him now had a dislocated shoulder, contusions and a broad scrape along the side of her face.

Officer Stackhouse was exonerated from any wrongdoing. His defense was that he feared Pitts had a concealed weapon. The department called the discharge of his weapon appropriate, barely mentioning that Pitts was innocent of any crime and didn't even match the description of the robbery suspect. As for the woman with Pitts, she eventually sued the department in civil court and was awarded four million dollars in damages for her injury and the fully inappropriate treatment she received at the hands of the police.

On the run, Stackhouse was acutely aware of the news from around the country. He also saw that officers involved in shootings of African Americans were not the targets in the deaths-just family members or close friends. His calculation was that as long as he kept his family close and out of sight they would be safe.

He had no real plan, his flight across the country was born of fear and desperation. His wife Clare knew why they were on the run, but her only concern was keeping their children safe. Neither parent fully expected to be successful. The media was all too happy to document the details of the other deaths, making spectacle of most tragic death.

Even though it was midday, Stackhouse was exhausted, having driven straight through the night. The kids, six- and eight-years-old, were restless having spent the last twenty hours in the minivan. Wanting a cup of coffee and a bite to eat, he pulled off the road into a chain hamburger restaurant.

"I'm exhausted, let's get a bite and let the kids play for a little while," he said to Clare.

"Good idea. Has anyone been following us?" she asked looking back along the road.

"Not that I could tell, and I kept my eye out. Relax, I'm pretty sure we're fine."

Stackhouse parked the minivan well away from all the other vehicles in the lot and then sat them at a table inside where he could keep an eye on the vehicle while Clare and the children ordered their food. When they returned, Stackhouse immediately gulped down half of his coffee scalding his mouth.

The kids were happy to be out of the car and ate quickly so they could play in the attached playground area once Daddy had checked it out.

When he returned to the table, he said to his wife, "I'd like to stop some place to rest up for a day or so. I think it should be safe. We've left no tracks, we're using cash and we don't look like we did before we left," he explained.

"I can read just as well as you can. These people, whoever they are, are superhuman. Not one clue? No death attributable to anything but accident? And did you see about that officer's family in Chicago that was in protective custody? The meal they brought in gave them all food poisoning. That's not supposed to be so immediately fatal, yet they died almost immediately. Jerry, I'm terrified," she said.

"I know, baby. So am I, but what else can we do? I'd like to head north once we reach California and keep going until we get into Canada. I can get us some good IDs once we get there, but it's still a long way. If we take our time, and are careful, I think we can make it," he promised. "Tell you what, get on that tablet and see what's nearby. Maybe something with a kitchen so we don't have to go out but once."

Stackhouse had picked up the tablet at a closeout sale paying cash and also paying the store to set up his account using his, then, current fake identity and prepaying for network access for three months.

While Clare looked up lodging, Stackhouse checked out the minivan and then strolled over to the indoor playground to check on the children. Seeing everything was okay, he returned to the table.

"How's this look?" she asked, spinning the tablet around so he could take a look. The place she had found had individual cabins, a rustic wild west kind of motif. "You can see if anyone drives up to the cabin, we can also see if we can get the one farthest away from everyone else."

"Good call. Let's give the kids ten more minutes, grab some burgers to take with us, and check the place out." Looking at the directions to get to the motel, he said, "Looks like it's less than an hour away. Take the girls to the restroom before we take off, hopefully they'll fall asleep in the van."

Once they were all in the van, Stackhouse pulled into the filling station next door and filled the tank, picked up a crate of bottled water and some snacks. They then started off toward the motel.

The drive was easy, and like Stackhouse had hoped, the girls almost immediately fell asleep. When they arrived at the motel, Stackhouse arranged for a cabin well away from the pool, the entrance and slightly away from the other cabins. He parked along the far side of the cabin, and when Clare and girls were inside, Stackhouse changed the license plate on the back of the minivan, watching to see if anyone spotted him. When he went inside, he was happy to see that the girls were ecstatic that they had bunk beds to sleep on.

Clare had put away the snacks and was filling ice trays with water. "We're going to have to get some groceries for tonight and tomorrow."

"What do you think? Shouldn't we all go together? Truth be told I'm dead set against splitting up for any reason. The only chance I have of keeping you safe is with you all by my side. At least if someone comes for you I have a chance." Stackhouse said.

"No you don't, Jerry. Don't fool yourself. I agree always being together is the best choice possible. But the girls need some time out of the van,; let's give them some time to unwind before we go out shopping. We also need to find a Laundromat in the next couple of days, maybe even get the girls some new outfits," Clare suggested.

"Can we hold out for another week? Maybe until we get to Canada?" Stackhouse asked.

"I'm sure we can," she said, lowering her voice. "Do you think we can get them some new books to read?"

"Sure, find a bookstore, and we'll stop on the way out of here," he promised.

The family settled in for the afternoon, playing several games of Chutes and Ladders with the girls winning all the games. Then they got cleaned up to go grocery shopping.

Nothing untoward occurred on their trip around the area, stopping at a produce stand and a family-owned grocery getting staples for a couple days. And when they returned to the cabin, Stackhouse preceded the girls and Clare inside, ensuring that everything looked untouched.

Clare had the girls help her prepare dinner while Stackhouse checked out the heater, knowing that the nights in the desert could be rather cool.

Dinner was a complete success, and a relief to Clare who preferred the girls ate healthily. The cleanup went quickly, and then they all played several board games until it was time for the girls to go to bed.

Once they were on their way to sleep, Clare called her husband to the table to talk.

"I've been looking at the news coverage and there's two reports of families who tried to get away into Mexico, and both ended up dead. Is Canada going to be any different?" she said, worriedly.

"Honey, I honestly don't know. If we did give them the slip, if I managed to break our trail, we just might make it," he said reaching over to squeeze her hand reassuringly.

They eventually moved to the couch and quietly watched a movie on the tablet with Clare curled up against him. When the movie was over, Clare decided to take a shower while Stackhouse debated whether or not to take a tour around the motel grounds.

Thinking that nothing could happen in the time he took to walk around scouting the lay of the land checking for any threats, probably no more than half an hour to forty-five minutes.

He stuck his head into the bathroom and let Clare know he was going out and leaving his spare handgun on the counter under a hand towel. He then left the cabin locking the door behind him.

He first checked the minivan even looking underneath trying to spot any sign of tampering. Once he was reassured, he continued his stroll trying to look like he was just taking a casual walk around getting some air before he turned in for the night.

Stackhouse went into the motel office and got the free shopper paper to peruse when he got back to the cabin. He went and checked out the pool seeing it closed at 10:00 P.M. By then, he'd been out of the cabin for just over fifty minutes so he headed back. When he unlocked the door, he saw that Clare was already in bed so he quietly started to undress.

Minutes later, his head began to hurt, and he was having trouble concentrating. He fell to his knees dizzy, confused. Before he could pass out, Stackhouse pulled himself to the door and with incredible effort, managed to pull it open. The inflow of air began to clear his head. As he began to regain his faculties, he quickly ran back inside and opened all the windows. He then went to get his wife and kids out of the cabin. Shaking Clare, he shouted her name getting no response. He then grabbed both girls out of the bunk beds and carried them outside, laying them on the ground. He then returned inside and picked up Clare from the bed and carried her outside laying her on the ground.

When he couldn't get any response he noticed that her lips were dark blue. He quickly checked both girls and found their lips were also blue. He felt everyone's necks, looking for a pulse, and he could feel no movement at all. He jumped up and went to bang on the door of the nearest cabin. A man answered, ready to give who was banging the what for when Stackhouse pleaded with the man to call for an ambulance.

Returning to his family laid out on the ground, he was completely nonplussed, not knowing where to start. He blew air into Clare's lungs, then quickly did the same to both girls as the man whose door he banged on quickly arrived with two teenaged boys in tow.

The man began to perform CPR on one of the girls as the older of the teens did the same for the younger girl. The three continued CPR on the woman and girls until the ambulance showed up, and the paramedics jumped out to examine them. The first one put stethoscope to Clare's chest, looking for a heartbeat. He then asked Stackhouse, "How long has she been like this?"

"At most no more than forty-five minutes," Stackhouse replied desperately. He saw the paramedic checking his wife look to the second paramedic and shook his head. As his heart dropped, the people from the other cabin stood back giving Stackhouse some room.

Seconds later two Arizona state police cars pulled up, their headlights illuminating the three bodies on the ground with Stackhouse kneeling next to his wife, his head in his hands. The more senior Arizona State Police officer went to get the situation from the paramedic, finding that all three of the deceased appeared to have died from carbon monoxide poisoning, and that the man on the ground was assumed to be the woman's husband and father to the two young girls.

Stackhouse didn't move as the paramedics covered the bodies. The senior police officer approached him and crouched down to try to get his attention.

"Sir? Sir?" he said, gently touching Stackhouse on the shoulder prepared for any kind of reaction.

Stackhouse lifted his head from his hands to look at the officer obviously in shock. The officer gently lifted Stackhouse by his arm and got him to his feet, then led him to a picnic table several yards away while the other officer circulated and ordered everyone back to their cabins. He then began to unroll the familiar yellow police tape, cordoning off the scene. He then retrieved a camera from his squad car's trunk and shot the scene from several angles. When he was through outside, he cautiously entered the cabin, turned on the overhead lights and took pictures all around. He concentrated on the probable causes of the monoxide poisoning, shooting close-ups of the thermostat and the gas-fired, wall-mounted heater then exited quickly.

He returned the camera to the trunk then radioed headquarters and called for an evidence technician. When he finished the call, he turned off the headlights, throwing cover to the bodies on the ground.

Meanwhile, the senior officer with Stackhouse waited a few moments, letting the man get over his immediate shock. When he saw some emerging awareness in Stackhouse's eyes he gently asked, "Can you tell me your name? Or maybe just let me take a look at your ID if you don't feel up to talking yet."

Stackhouse fumbled for his wallet and gave the officer his real identification.

"Jerry, may I call you Jerry?" he asked getting a nod. "I'm sorry to have to ask, but can you tell me what happened here?"

"I'm Sergeant Jerry Stackhouse, and I was involved in an accidental civilian shooting a year ago," he tiredly replied.

The officer at first didn't get what Stackhouse said for a few moments, then his eyebrows shot up and he muttered, "Holy shit!" Raising his voice, he called to the other officer, "Eddie! Get over here!"

The two stepped a few feet away from Stackhouse as the senior officer told Eddie what was up. Eddie then hurried away to use his mobile phone to call the Phoenix, Arizona office of the FBI to pass the information along. He also wanted to see if they had any special instructions about what was now a crime scene. When he gave them the GPS coordinates of the motel, the FBI agent informed him that someone would be there in less than an hour. Eddie then radioed the local office again, informing them that the FBI had commandeered the site and would they dispatch a couple more officers to help secure the site until the FBI arrived.

The manager of the motel was called on to pull some picnic tables across the drive, isolating the cabin until the FBI arrived, and the younger officer repositioned the patrol cars to obstruct the view of the bodies from the rest of the motel grounds.

When the second officer rejoined Stackhouse and the officer, he heard Stackhouse explaining, "...and the second I pulled the trigger I knew it was a mistake. He was only eighteen-years-old, and when we searched him he had no weapon at all. By the time the ambulance arrived, he had already bled out. There were two investigations, one by the department and one by the Justice Department since it was in D.C. The department exonerated me of any wrongdoing, and the Justice Department declined to charge me."

"And when all this craziness started, you were hoping to get away," the officer said, making a notation in his little book.

"Exactly. Clare, my wife, thought it was a waste of time, but she agreed to try to run," Stackhouse said, sighing. "What's the latest body count," he asked.

"I'm not sure. I quit watching when it got over a thousand. It's pretty fuckin' vicious out there."

"Anyone in your department?" asked Stackhouse.

The two officers passed a look between them before the elder said, "We had six."

"And?"

"All dead, all their immediate families, and the one who was single had his girlfriend, mother and brother killed; all under accidental circumstances," he replied making air quotes as he said accidental.

"This is fucked up. No one has any clue about who is behind this; everyone's running scared. The FBI guys who investigated our guys found exactly zip about who was behind the killings," the officer said.

Stackhouse slowly shook his head. "We're fucked."

"Maybe yes, maybe no. When these people are caught, there's going to be hell to pay. These motherfuckers will pay the ultimate price," he promised.

"From your mouth to God's ear," Stackhouse intoned sardonically.

Chapter 7

The Federal Bureau of Investigation was the lead agency coordinating the collection of data on the rash of officer-involved shootings family's deaths. They set up the task force, formally called Operation Family Matters.

The special agent in charge, Sheldon Willis, had been with the bureau for seven years, but had already distinguished himself coordinating a multinational task force effectively fighting the counterfeiting of American currency around the world.

Willis had a free hand to call in whatever resources he needed to chase down any lead to those responsible for the unprecedented killing spree. He also didn't fall into the trap of excluding African American resources from the task force. His number two was Special Agent Sharon Jefferson, a black agent with twelve years of experience fighting organized crime and top-level banking fraud. Willis wanted the best, the kinds of assets most likely to find those responsible. He also wasn't afraid to publically express both his fear and respect for those behind the killings.

Willis and Jefferson were closeted together in their customary morning meeting going over the reports received through the night.

"Still nothing from the NSA?" Willis asked.

"They just reconfigured the new filters early yesterday. I've gotten nothing from them so far," she replied.

"Who did you get over there for the task force?"

"Sam Dobson. He said he'd worked with you on the counterfeit operation intercepts. Any problem with him?" asked Sharon.

"No, he's perfect. We have anything for the White House before the president does his speech that you could find?" Sheldon asked, hoping.

"Just the current body count. All told, since last night's count we're looking at forty-seven hundred and eighteen," she replied.

"That's insane! How the hell do they do it? There's never been anything like this in history. Forty-seven hundred killings without a single clue— hell, without even an indication that these deaths were deliberate. What's the latest one?"

Paging through a pile of papers on the conference room table, Sharon pulled out a sheet and read. "We've got a family outside of Phoenix, two little girls and their mother. It was carbon monoxide poisoning. They were on the run, started out here in D.C. Says here he shot a kid in cold blood, claimed he thought the kid had a gun.

"What was he doing in Phoenix? Vacation?" asked Sheldon, looking at the sheet Sharon had passed him.

"He told the Arizona State Patrol officer who filed the report that the he was trying to run, hoping to get to Canada," she explained.

"Yeah, look how good that worked for those two who sneaked into Mexico," Sheldon said soberly.

"Does the Phoenix office need any additional manpower there? If we're going to get any leads at all, we're going to find them in the newest cases," he suggested.

"We're tapped out. We can pull people from other cases, but we have no reserves," she said picking up a folder. "We're short on about one-hundred-sixty cases where the locals requested us to assist."

Sheldon sat back and groaned in frustration. Sharon waited to see where he was going to go next.

Leaning forward, he said, "These people scare the shit out of me."

"Like fearing for your life, or your family scared?" Sharon asked beginning to worry.

"No, not at all. But I can't see where we get any traction with the investigation without a clue to go on. And I know that we're the best in tracking down clues, but look at all this, "he said picking up a handful of reports, "There's not a single clue, a single mistake, something, anything we can move on."

"This is what we do. It's obviously going to take time," Sharon reassured.

"And if we don't find anything? Then what? Nearly five thousand killings go unsolved?"

"If that's the hand that's dealt."

"Is that Sharon the FBI agent talking or a black woman," Sheldon asked raising an eyebrow.

Sharon looked at Sheldon in disbelief waiting for some kind of punch line. When one didn't come, she stood up and said, "I'm going to get reassigned, asshole."

Sheldon quickly stood, apologizing. "You know I didn't mean it like that. I'm just completely stressed. I have the utmost confidence working with you on this task force. Don't go, I didn't mean anything, I fucked up and miss spoke."

"Too bad, Sheldon. But you're right about one thing, you seriously fucked up," she said as she left the room.

Word spread quickly with most of the agency split over who was at fault. Some said that Sharon didn't want to help find those responsible for the accidents, and slightly more expressing that what Sharon went through was exactly why African Americans couldn't get a fair shake in the United States. When word inevitably leaked out to the Washington, D.C. media, the story went international in less than a day.

Understandably, the President of the United States was not pleased. He ordered a complete review of the Bureau and its racial hiring, firing and promotion policy, causing no end to the scrutiny and controversy. In the weeks since the first explosion in Orlando, the entire law enforcement of apparatus of the country was chasing its tail. In the rare circumstance where some over overzealous cop or prosecutor arrested someone who they stated they had absolute proof that the person in custody was either a person of interest or even the perpetrator of a killing, they were forced to release them with an apology. They were all going nowhere fast.

-=#=

Jackson Richards was in high demand with hundreds of media outlets across the globe trying to get him on camera. He was forced to post a blanket "thanks, but no thanks" message on his site. He was deleting hundreds of inquiries a day from his inbox.

He instead filled his time with updating his database with the few cases he had overlooked as well as information about some of the others where additional details had come out in the press.

Ironically, a good amount of the Internet traffic to Jackson's site was now coming from overseas. His hosting company had tripled the number of servers managing Jackson's Web site to accommodate the huge increase in traffic.

There was no real reason for him to leave his home in Chicago because the events unfolding were happening so quickly all across the country. He spent some time catching up with his family even helping do some home improvement projects with his father. He could easily have hired the best tradespeople to do the work, but his father refused any such notion, happy for something to do in his retirement.

One afternoon, Jackson's mother pulled him aside and asked, almost in a whisper whether or not Jackson knew who was behind the killings happening across the nation.

Jackson laughed and assured her he had no idea who was behind the accidents. When they sat down to dinner that night, the discussion turned to speculation on what it would take to pull off the various "accidents" across the nation. His father said that though he abhorred violence and killing of any sort, he thought it high time that the killing of innocent blacks got the serious discussion it needed.

His mother, on the other hand, couldn't say enough about the kind of people who were visiting the killings on those who had murdered in the first place. When Jackson asked her whether she had any sympathy for the officers and the rest of their family members left behind, she said, "Maybe once I'm done mourning the millions of black folks murdered in this country without so much as a howdy-do, perhaps I might have a tear left over for the dead ones and their families."

Jackson and his father looked at each other, and both shrugged their shoulders at the same time. His mother, watching, began to laugh sending the other two into laughter along with her.

America was coming to a realization that there was an organization, a clandestine group operating in the country with no one having a clue who they were. African American leaders being interviewed when asked to speculate on who might be behind the rash of killings, were carefully noncommittal. When asked how they felt about the many deaths, most at first hid behind statements abhorring any loss of life. But when pressed, they begin to turn the question around and asked those interviewing them if their people, their race had suffered almost half a millennium of murders without consequence, how would they feel if their son, daughter, husband or wife was killed in the street with no consequences befalling the shooter? To date, no answers were forthcoming.

It would be fair to say that the feelings of most African Americans were mixed. Many lauded the fact that a brand of street justice was being handed out against those who murdered blacks in recent times. However, there were also many who feared that retribution by frightened and angry whites would not bode well for the black community. Most hoped that the events of the day would make vigilante-minded whites think twice about taking matters into their own hands.

A serendipitous effect of all the simultaneous accidents was that not a single unarmed African American had been shot or killed by a police officer since the explosion in Orlando. And since whites who chose to murder African Americans using stand your ground defenses were also suffering the same fate as the police officers, white America was finally paying attention to what blacks had been saying for decades. For once, whites were completely on the defensive. Even the usual strident voices who repudiated African American claims of bias, slights, and systematic prejudice were nearly silent in light of the massive number of police killings as evidenced by the number of families who had perished in the previous weeks.

The Whites House, in the name of the President, sent out a statement calling for calm, promising that everything possible was being done to halt the accidents and bring everyone responsible to justice. Even to President Temple, the statement read by his press secretary sounded weak, tentative even.

When word reached President Temple of Agent Jefferson's demand to be reassigned from the number two position on the Operation Family Matters Task Force, he immediately summoned her and SAIC Willis to the White House. Arriving in separate cars, neither agent said a word to the other as they were checked in and their side arms stored in the Secret Service's office.

When they arrived in the Oval Office, President Temple greeted them both warmly, shaking hands and posing with each for the White House photographer.

Once they were seated and his offer of drinks declined, he dove right in.

"What in the hell is this thing between the two of you all about, and why do I read about it in a dozen news outlets before I hear it from you?"

Jefferson and Willis both began to talk in rapid-fire fashion making Temple raise his hands silencing them both. Once they were quiet, the president gestured to Agent Jefferson to go ahead.

"Sorry, Mr. President. What I was saying was that since SAIC Willis did not have full confidence in my loyalty, he would be best served if someone white replaced me."

Hearing the word "white" made President Temple sit up straight and raise a questioning eyebrow at SAIC Willis.

"Mr. President, that's not entirely accurate at all," he began.

"Then why on earth would she get that impression in the first place?" Temple asked.

Willis was silent for a moment, then said, "Because I said something monumentally stupid. As soon as it was out of my mouth I knew I was wrong, and I tried to apologize."

"Was his apology genuine, Agent Jefferson?" asked the president.

"As much as it could be."

"Then why did you demand a transfer off the task force?" Temple asked.

"Because he, like most whites, has no idea just how much his prejudices and racism is built into his makeup. And no offense, Mr. President, you probably have no idea either," she said.

President Temple threw his head back and laughed. He continued laughing for a few seconds before he regained control. He wiped tears from his eyes and said, "Ain't that the truth. The only good thing to come out of this crises is the realization of the fact that the majority of whites really have no idea how deeply ingrained that crap is. Although to call it crap is to diminish the evil done in its name, knowingly or not.

"SAIC Willis, I'm going to hazard that if you've given any thought to Agent Jefferson's demand for transfer, you're seeing exactly how much of what's made all these people have their accidents, to be factual, lives in us all."

Turning to Agent Jefferson, he asked, "And how much of that kind of bullshit have you had to put up with at the Bureau, Agent Jefferson?"

"I'm sorry, Mr. President, what do you want me to say? To be honest, my being a woman has been more of an issue than being black. That's not to say that I didn't experience prejudice from above and below. I have to work twice as hard to get half the credit in the Bureau; in life even. All black people do, Mr. President. As for what's been happening with the task force, I'll say this: if whites hadn't been murdering blacks in this country ever since blacks landed on the continent, none of this would be happening."

"No one's saying that life's been a paradise for your people, far from it. But whatever the complaint, there's no excuse for killing nearly five thousand innocents. Make no mistake, we will catch whomever is behind this. Yes, they're effective, and yes, they've been very careful. But the bureau is expert in working all the angles and clues until they find the people responsible. The question we're here to answer is, can you two make up and work together?" President Temple asked the two.

Willis looked at Agent Jefferson waiting to see if their relationship could be salvaged.

"I'm sorry, Mr. President, Sheldon. If I return to the task force, it will be just another in a long string of swallowed insults for no better reason than my skin color. I'm a better investigator than SAIC Willis, better than most at my pay grade at the Bureau. But do you know what would happen if I was made head of the task force? All hell would break loose, starting with questions about my loyalty based on the color of my skin. And, Mr. President, I'm two grades below where I should be given my experience, my achievements and my time in the Bureau. Unless someone decides to seriously address this issue, I just don't see anything changing," Agent Jefferson said her gaze at the president unflinching.

"Then that's that. I understand and sympathize, Agent Jefferson. You're going to have to find yourself another Number Two, Agent Willis. I daresay this has been a teachable moment for everyone. Agent Jefferson, I would like to offer you the liaison job on my national security team. I can virtually guarantee you will see none of what you've been experiencing working here in the White House," President Temple promised as he stood with the agents scrambling to their feet.

He led them to the office door pausing to shake hands with SAIC Willis and bid him good day. Temple then turned to Agent Jefferson and said, "I'm going to have my Chief of Staff show you around, and I'd like you to stick around for this afternoon's meeting. Is that okay with you?"

"Of course, Mr. President. I should call my supervisor and let them know about—"

"Already done, Agent Jefferson," President Temple said, grinning broadly.

"How did you know?" Sharon asked.

"Just a good guess on my part," he said escorting her out of the office and handing her off to the Chief of Staff.

Chapter 8

Andrew took a chance and texted Tony when he arrived home, just saying for Tony to give him a call when he was free. He had checked in at the office and found nothing that would require his presence, leaving him plenty of time to check out the news from around the country.

As he watched, Andrew revised upward the number of people it would take to pull off such a massively effective operation. The part that intrigued him was the fact that every death documented was completely absent of any overt sign of foul play other than the fact that someone was dead. With nearly five thousand people now dead, Andrew figured those who were responsible had to number over a thousand.

As he was watching the news coverage which by then had gotten pretty repetitious, Andrew's phone beeped signaling an incoming message. When he grabbed the phone and took a look, the message from Tony simply said, "tomorrow."

Since he had nothing better to do, Andrew packed up his favorite rifle's traveling case and decided to put in some practice at his usual shooting range in White Plains. As he exited the building's garage, he noticed that traffic was sparse on the expressway going out to the range. He wondered how big a financial hit the deaths were costing the country.

When he arrived, he was greeted warmly by owner Matt Rails, also a graduate of the US Army Sniper School. Matt was half Navaho, half Black and one of the few snipers who had earned Andrews respect in the fine art of killing.

"Man, are you a sight for sore eyes," Matt said slapping five with Andrew. "Is it just coincidence you're stopping in with all this madness going on, Drew?"

Andrew grinned and said, "What do you think?"

"Hey, I have no idea what to think. The whole thing's crazy. Is it true that every one of those deaths were all accidents? I don't mean that they were random or anything, but they were set up in a way that there's been no clues, no sign of foul play?"

"If what they've been saying in the news is true, that's right. And you and I both know that ain't possible. My guess is that the best of the best have been working on this for years," Andrew speculated. "And other than the fact that not a single victim was shot, I have to think that some of the kinds of people you and I know and have worked with are involved."

"Brother, ain't that the truth. Trouble is, people of our caliber don't come by regular-like, so it's been impossible for me to see any patterns here. Honestly, I was surprised to see you. I figured that if anyone was working with the people responsible, it would be you. Although now that I think about it, you being the best of us, maybe you were too high profile. I will say this," Matt began, lowering his voice, "whoever is behind this scares the shit out of me."

"I spent the last few days trying to figure how I would plan this kind of operation, and nears as I can tell, this has been in the works for years. And a goodly amount of cash has to have financed it too," said Andrew, shaking his head. "Anyway, how's business?"

"Quiet since this all started, but before there was a bump in Wall Street types with new handguns—about a third of them purchased new from me. I'm sure I'll be seeing another bump when all this calms down. Lot of scared white folks out there, cops especially. If it weren't for all those dead bodies littering up the place, this would be great entertainment. When this is all over, I'd love to meet the person or persons who put it all together. You shootin' today?" Matt asked.

"Yeah, can you set me up?"

"Outside, right?"

"Yeah, I want a long lane," Andrew informed him.

"Take the last lane. I have a silhouette set at five hundred meters. That okay? Or were you looking for something else?" Matt asked.

"That's fine. I'm going to fire maybe fifty rounds to tighten up my game."

"Let me know when you need to change the targets. Just hit the intercom, and I'll send Pete out through the trench."

"Thanks, Matt," Andrew said, grabbing his case and heading out to the range.

Andrew went outside and walked to the far end of the firing line. He set up at the last lane, assembling his Windrunner M96. It was a very effective weapon, firing a .50 caliber round, accurate to over two thousand meters. Although unofficially, Andrew's skill added at least another five hundred meters on to that.

Andrew loaded four, five-round magazines, then loaded the first one into the rifle. He took note of the two flags downrange to calculate the speed of the wind. Adjusting the scope to compensate for the expected deflection of the round in flight, he began the routine that calmed his heart and focused his entire attention on sending the round exactly where he wanted it.

His breath quieted becoming smooth and deep. His trigger finger started loose, then imperceptibly began to tighten against the smooth metal. And when everything in focus came together, the Windrunner fired, sending the bullet downrange. Less than a moment later the bullet tore through the head of the silhouette, off center to the right, about an inch from where the right ear would be on a man. After inspecting the target, Andrew adjusted his aim and repeated the routine sending the next round into the center of the target's head.

Andrew quickly fired, then again, and once more. When he inspected the target through his spotter scope, he was happy to see that the holes his rounds had made could be covered by the saucer for a coffee cup.

He loaded a full magazine and chambered a round and repeated firing as the familiar rhythm quickly came back. He fired twenty rounds, and then called Matt over the intercom to have the target changed and then fired another twenty. Satisfied, he took the time to disassemble and clean the rifle before heading inside to briefly chat.

"All set, Drew?" Matt asked

"Indeed. It all comes back easily. While I'm thinking about it, why don't you come into town, and I'll treat you to one fine dinner?" Andrew suggested.

"You crazy, One Shot? All that traffic, all those crazy-ass people? You have got to be kidding. Tell you what, call ahead next time, and I'll cook us up something on the grill. Be better than anything you get in those fancy restaurants," promised Matt.

"You're on, till next time."

The two slapped five, then Andrew left to head back into the city. During the drive, he tuned to the local talk station and listened as a steady parade of whites called in demanding that something be done about vigilante African Americans making all the accidents happen. When the host persisted in explaining that there was no evidence to connect the deaths with anyone in particular, Andrew laughed almost continuously at the completely unhinged conspiracies issuing forth. One thing that always seemed to pan out in America was that there were entirely too many idiots, willful idiots, who saw no need for deeper exploration into the world around them.

The state of American culture was testament to the general sloth of the American psyche. These killings were a shock to the system, proof of the neglect that a privileged, white majority had woven into the fabric of life's existence in the United States from its inception. And it was patently obvious that those white men calling in somehow felt that the legitimate complaints that African Americans had been voicing, at least for the last hundred years, had no basis in fact at all. In their monumental guilt they became whining apologists for wrongs continuously perpetrated even when everyone knew better. That was where the proverbial moral rubber met the road.

Fed up with the stupidity of low-information white people, Andrew tuned in one of the university jazz stations and listened to it all the way home. When he arrived, the first thing he did was clean and oil the Windrunner. Just before he put it away the lobby intercom rang. When he answered a male voice announced that he was an agent from the FBI and would like to have a word with Mr. Simmons. Andrew identified himself and inquired about the purpose for the interview. The agent insisted in coming upstairs, not wanting to conduct business over the building intercom; he sounded vaguely annoyed. Andrew chuckled to himself and invited the agent upstairs.

Five minutes later there was a polite knock on the door. When he opened it, Andrew was greeted by two agents, a man and a woman, showing him their identification and with the man introducing himself as Agent Greer, the woman as Agent Carson. Gesturing them inside, Andrew conducted them to the living room and invited them to sit. When they were all seated, Greer launched right in with the questions.

"Mr. Simmons, you're of course aware of the series of unprecedented deaths over the past two weeks, are you not?"

"I am," Andrew replied determined to make them work for anything they would get from him.

"And would you have any idea who is behind these deaths taking place across the country?" asked Greer.

"I do not."

Greer and Carson exchanged glances.

"Do you know where Anthony Dawson might be at this time?"

"I do not," Andrew said a slight smile showing on his face.

"Do you find what's going on amusing, Mr. Simmons?" Greer asked, hostility clearly in his voice.

"No, I don't."

"Then what the hell are you smiling about?"

"At how stupidly transparent your line of questioning is, and how misdirected the investigation appears to be," replied Andrew.

Greer looked like he was about to explode when Carson laid her hand on his arm as she broke in and asked, "Excuse me, Mr. Simmons. Why do you think the investigation into almost five thousand deaths is misguided—"

"I said misdirected, Agent Carson."

"Okay then, misdirected. Please explain why you believe this?" she asked.

"Because you've mentioned Tony, and you're here. And I wouldn't be a bit surprised if you also knew I went out to White Plains to shoot at Rails' range," he said nodding to the disassembled rifle on the dining room table. "Also, you both saw the Windrunner sitting over there and didn't even raise an eyebrow. All of this says to me that you're investigating former black military specialists looking for a connection between us and those responsible for these deaths."

"And the misdirected part, Mr. Simmons?" prodded Agent Carson.

"Not a single one of those who died was shot, or the victim of direct violence, unless the media is withholding that information. But I'd hazard that no one has found anyone who could be pointed to with evidence they were directly murdered.

"So some idiot gets the notion that snipers, specialists in insurgency and the like, probably the one or two black CIA spooks out there," he said busting out in a grin, "could be doing the wet work for this operation. Pretty stupid if you give it a single moment's thought," Andrew concluded.

"And you would know that how?" Greer asked, almost casually.

"Because I used to plan ops like these, but not with the psychotic need to make sure the death looked like an accident. On a handful of missions, yes, but they were the exception, not the rule. I admit I'm both impressed and scared shitless of the capabilities I've seen already," admitted Andrew. "I guess that this has to be more than a few years in the planning, maybe a decade. And the cost in the hundreds of millions, billions even."

"What about the manpower?" asked Agent Carson.

"Easily over a thousand, maybe closer to a couple of thousand operatives to collect data and arrange the deaths to look like accidents. If any one of those people had died in isolation, no one would have seriously suspected foul play. This has to be driving the Bureau and all the rest of the agencies absolutely bonkers. You all definitely have your work cut out for you," Andrew said.

Both agents were silent for a few moments then Carson asked, "And you have no idea where Mr. Dawson is at this time?"

"No I don't. Last I heard was he was heading back to OpFor's headquarters."

"And when and where was that, Mr. Simmons," Greer said, pulling a notebook from his jacket pocket.

"Last Thursday, at a seafood restaurant on Fisherman's Wharf in San Francisco," said Andrew, declining to mention the text message unless either of the agent's did.

"Was this a planned meeting?" asked Greer.

"No, we just happened to be in town at the same time."

"Do you and Mr. Dawson keep in close touch?" Greer asked, making a notation in his notebook.

"As a matter of fact, no. I hadn't seen Tony since he left the service and went to work for the CIA. I assume you know his history as well as I presume you know mine. As for telling you where he is right now? I don't know. Why not call OpFor?" Andrew suggested.

"You mentioned that you have given some thought on what it would take to carry out an operation that would kill so many in such a short time window. That the resources would be considerable in time, manpower and financial backing," said Greer.

"Is there a question in there, Agent Greer?" Andrew asked.

"If you were going to look for those behind these deaths, where would you start?" Greer asked.

Andrew didn't answer. He weighed telling them the truth, or telling them why he wasn't going to answer. A few moments later he simply said, "I have no idea."

"Really, Mr. Simmons? A smart guy like you should have some idea, especially since you were in the same line of work," Greer said, that sneering tone back in his voice.

Fuck it, thought Andrew. "You want to know something?"

"Very much so, Mr. Simmons," said Agent Carson.

"I don't have any idea who's behind all of this, and I doubt I'd tell you if I did. I don't agree with the loss of life, but nothing short of something like these deaths was ever going to stop the killing of innocent blacks in this country." He paused thinking about saying more then figured, what the hell.

"Look, you're here wasting everyone's time. I'm guessing that the Bureau, along with the rest of the other law enforcement apparatus in the government, is taxed to the gills trying to find those responsible," he said seeing an almost imperceptible nod from Agent Carson. "I'm good, and I have no idea where to start an investigation like this. Maybe hope some surveillance camera somewhere in America saw something that these people overlooked, but that's a long shot; hell everything's a long shot. So, I gotta ask: how the hell do you run an investigation like this when your superiors do things so stupid like sending you here to interview me? And furthermore, do you really expect to find the people behind these deaths?"

"Damn right we do!" exclaimed Greer.

"It's what we do best, Mr. Simmons. We look for that single thread and we follow it until it connects with other threads until we get who we're looking for. And even though I didn't think you would be helpful in this investigation, I understood why we had to speak to you," Agent Carson explained.

"Well, I'm betting that you're never going to catch the people behind this. And I'll be glad if they do get away with these killings, because you know what?" Andrew asked, getting to his feet.

"What's that, smarty?" Greer sneered.

"Ever since that first explosion in Florida, not a single black man has died from a cop killing him. And if this what it takes to stop hundreds of years of tradition, then more power to those behind this," Andrew said then pausing for a moment. "Thank you for stopping by. This interview is over."

Seeing that any further questioning would be a waste of time, Agent Carson nodded toward Greer, stood and made her way to the door. Before she walked out she turned to Andrew offering her business card saying, "I understand how you feel, Mr. Simmons. But if you come across anything that might help prevent any more people dying, please consider giving me a call. That's all I ask, think about it. Thank you for your time, good day."

After he closed the door, he looked at Agent Carson's card, considering just throwing it away. But after a moment, he tossed it on the hall table and returned to cleaning the Windrunner.

-=#=-

Jackson had just finished having lunch with his mother when he received an email message from the White House informing him that he was invited to attend the president's press conference. Jackson had put in the request along with hundreds of other electronic media representatives the previous week not believing he had any chance of winning the media lottery when he filled out the online form.

After glancing over the notification and the list of requirements the White House and Secret Service expected of him, Jackson immediately replied that he would gladly attend.

Only after he gave the invitation some additional thought, he began to question exactly how he made the cut. When he showed his mother the message, she squealed in excitement and hugged him around the neck in joy.

"My baby's going to the White House!" she kept repeating.

When she started to wind down, Jackson extricated himself from her grip, explaining with a laugh that he had to breathe.

"I'm going to call your father and tell him the good news. Don't you go running off anywhere," she admonished.

Jackson endure the excitement and pomp his parents heaped upon him and made his way out of the house as soon as he could explaining that he had to prepare for the trip to Washington.

Once he returned home, he quickly booked a flight and went over the electronic packet of instructions the White House sent in response to his R.S.V.P. Since his mobile phone camera was better than broadcast quality when shooting video, he wouldn't be bringing any additional gear the Secret Service would have to take apart for their security sweep of those attending the press conference. There was no possibility of Jackson, or anyone else, to take an old-style "selfie" with POTUS.

Jackson was also looking forward to the trip to Washington for an additional reason. His best friend from college lived there. She was an international law attorney with her own practice. The two were often companions when one or the other had an event to go to on and off campus in the good old days.

Her firm had a dozen attorneys, twenty support staff, and was well regarded in the Georgetown legal community. Her success, and the driven way she ran her practice, was something in common she shared with Jackson. They saw the same attitude in each other in school, and though they had much in common, they never got to the point of serious dating. But they had kept in touch.

When Jackson sent her a message letting her know he would be in town. She immediately replied that she would leave her evening open so they could get together for dinner.

Chapter 9

Jackson arrived at Washington National Airport the night before the press conference. Since he had no checked baggage, only his carry-on, he went directly to the cab stand to get a ride to the hotel. When he walked outside the baggage claim area of the terminal, all of a sudden, a cab quickly cut in front of the line of cabs waiting for passengers.

He chuckled to himself as he watched the cab cut in the line of cabs waiting to get to him and the angry faces of the other cab drivers. He thought things must be very tight if the cabbies were so determined to grab an inbound fare.

When he got in, he directed the driver to his hotel and sat back to try to enjoy his drive.

"You that Internet blogger guy, Jackson?" the cabbie asked out of the blue.

"Why do you ask?" Jackson replied. "I'm somewhat surprised you would recognize me given that my picture isn't really posted anywhere. Who are you?"

"Just a guy tryin' to make a livin', if you know what I mean."

Jackson took a close look at the cabbie's license, noting the name, Reginald Parker, and that the driver was a fairly nondescript black man in his mid-thirties. He had a short-cropped beard and under his cap, appeared to still have most of his hair. What was striking about the man was the intensity of his eyes as they watched the traffic around them and would periodically glance at him in the rear-view mirror.

After a brief pause, Jackson answered. "To answer your question, yes, I am Jackson Richards. I'm still curious why you would recognize me. What's up, brotha?"

The cabbie didn't immediately answer as he merged into the traffic heading into the city.

"I was asked to keep an eye out for you. My name's Reggie."

"Why were you keeping an eye out for me?" Jackson asked wondering what was up.

Reggie reached down and picked up a package off the passenger seat next to him and handed it to Jackson through the open security window separating them. "Here, this is for you. Open it when you have some time to follow the instructions. And don't do it out in public. Wait until you're in your room or something."

Jackson took the proffered package and inspected it. It was slightly larger than a piece of notebook paper and about an inch thick. The paper was standard shipping paper with no markings on it.

"Okay, I'll bite. What is all this all about?"

"I'm just following directions."

"Whose instructions?" Jackson immediately asked.

"I got nothing else for you. Just follow the directions."

After trying to get more information and being met with silence, Jackson quit trying. There would be enough time to sort out what was going on when he checked into his room.

The rest of the ride was entirely normal. Jackson paid the cabbie then went inside and checked into the hotel. Once in his room he dumped his bag on the bed and unwrapped the package. When he opened the box within, he saw a tablet computer, a charger and nothing else.

He turned the tablet on and watched as it logged onto the local cellular network. Once connected, he tapped on a simple icon labeled "Start Here."

The tablet's Web browser opened up and automatically navigated to a blank page with his name on it and a space for him to enter his mobile phone number. Intrigued, Jackson did just that.

As soon as he tapped the "Enter" button the screen cleared. Five seconds later his mobile phone rang.

He looked at the incoming number and grunted when he saw the display showed an unbroken string of question marks.

"Hello?"

"Please excuse the song and dance, Mr. Richards," a deep voice answered. The person on the line was clearly a mature black man by accent and diction.

"So what's this all about?"

"I have a story to tell you. Do you have the time?"

"I do. I have the entire evening free. Your method of contacting me definitely has me intrigued. Can we meet?"

The voice on the other end of the line laughed. "That would be something now, wouldn't it? Unfortunately, that is impossible, Mr. Richards. But I guarantee that the story I tell you will be worth your time. You game?"

Jackson thought about the possibilities. The chances were that with all the cloak and dagger getting in touch with him gave a fifty-fifty chance this would be a waste of his time. "Go on."

"Allow me to begin a couple of generations ago at the height of the American Civil Rights Movement, Mr. Richards. No matter what was advertised as a change in the way blacks were being treated in this country, one thing never changed; the killing of black men, first by the police and then ordinary white citizens with relative impunity."

"Yes, I know this very well. I report on this issue often—" Jackson began.

"I know this very well, Mr. Richards. This is why I employed the extraordinary means possible to not only contact you, but to give you plausible deniability. Allow me to continue."

"Please do, I'm definitely intrigued."

"A little more recently you had a sitting president, Ronald Reagan, demonizing blacks with his thinly-disguised fictitious welfare recipients, read blacks, who were supposedly gaming the system unfairly.

"You combine this lying in the media, all day, every day, beating the drum of the lawless, criminal, thug black male, and it became an essential part of the nation's consciousness."

"Then came the conservative organizations like the American Legislative Exchange Council who continue to write legislation for Red states like the Stand Your Ground laws that gave white men the perfect excuse for killing blacks. You combine that with prosecutors, judges and juries perfectly content to allow whites to kill blacks because they claimed they 'feared for their lives,' and this country's culture gave us the perfect storm. But I know I'm not telling you anything that you don't know, am I, Mr. Richards?"

Jackson gave a wry chuckle, "As you well know, all of this is quite apparent to me. . . And with the destruction of the country's economy under that junior mope at the turn of the century, things got steadily worse."

"And then what, Mr. Richards?"

"And then the country elected a black POTUS—twice—and that scared the living shit out of whites when they believed their built-in privilege was about to disappear. With the racial shift in the population scheduled to put them in the minority in less than a decade, they're doing everything possible to stave off the changing of the guard," Jackson replied.

"You're entirely right. Blacks are being denied the right to vote, schools are being destroyed educationally and economically, and Nixon's plan of fostering the ubiquity of the dumbing down of America rolls on.

"Red states are raising white students who are dumb as dog shit by not teaching science, civics, math or social studies. You have a sizable white population out there who think the Flintstones cartoon is a documentary, and the Earth is only six thousand years old.

"However, in the service of cutting to the chase, we believe that it's time to make a change in this country. It's time to stop the senseless and consequence-free killing of blacks in the United States as you've seen."

"Indeed," Jackson said ironically.

The voice on the other end of the phone laughed heartily. "Let me ask you a question. Can you think of any other way to truly level the playing field and prevent whites from killing unarmed, innocent blacks?"

Jackson was silent as his mind ran through scenario after scenario all leading to dead ends. After several minutes of silence, he finally answered.

"I can't come up with any other path to make them stop," Jackson replied soberly. "Any change in the law is definitely not in the cards. With the courts, prosecutors, judges and juries perfectly willing to facilitate police shootings of innocents, legislative change is useless. Demonstrations, civil disorder and the like are also useless. You have a complicit media owned by the wealthiest whites in America only concerned with amassing more wealth. Sidestepping them with channels like social media wouldn't be effective either."

"Okay then. What was the bottom line of the killings of black men before all these accidents occurred?" the man asked Jackson.

"I guess the fact that when white cops have the opportunity to pull the trigger on any black man, there was nothing to stop them. Obviously there's no real moral or ethical reason stopping them. And they are terrified or resentful of blacks in general; pulling the trigger is the easiest thing in the world for them. And knowing that there's no consequences for their actions, what's to stop them?"

"Exactly. What had to happen was to change the paradigm, to present cops with a situation where they will experience the worst punishment possible should they murder an unarmed black. We have done that."

"May I ask, who is we?" Jackson asked, not really expecting an answer.

"Who are we, indeed. I dare say you didn't really expect me to answer that question, did you, Mr. Richards?" the man asked, chuckling.

"Not really. And given the circumstances, it's probably for the best. What do you want of me, mystery man?"

"To warn you."

"About what?" Jackson asked.

"That you're under very heavy surveillance. And for you to take care going about your daily routine. The government is trying to determine whether or not you're associated with the people who arranged for these thousands of accidents," the man explained.

"What about this call? Surely the NSA is monitoring every call in the country," said Jackson concern in his voice.

"This call is not subject to their monitoring, do not be alarmed. If you have any understanding about what it's taken to do what we have done, you know that we must have secure communications," he explained. "It was incumbent on us to warn you about the doings around you. This is likely the only time we'll be in direct contact, Mr. Richards. You have done invaluable work for the country which I dare say very few will appreciate."

"Uh, thanks, I guess. If, and I stress if, I wanted to try to get in touch with you, is that going to be possible?"

"I think not for your safety and for mine. But hang on to the tablet, you just never know. Good bye, Mr. Richards," the man concluded, and the call disconnected.

The screen of the tablet cleared, then the normal screen populated with app icons appeared.

Chuckling to himself, Jackson examined the tablet, digging into the operating system, looking for any sign of modification. It only took a few moments until he realized that if the person who arranged for thousands of deaths across the country leaving no clues behind, custom programming a tablet, and getting it into his hands then concealing that special programming wouldn't be much of a problem. He powered off the tablet and stuck it in his bag, laughing out loud when the thought of carrying it into the White House flashed through his mind.

He pulled his own tablet out and fired it up. Once connected to the network he logged into the Real Deal site and checked the admin console he saw that there was still increased traffic originating both inside and outside of the country. Once again, he was extremely grateful that he hadn't included a reader's forum on the site. He could only imagine the kinds of comments that would have been posted.

He turned on the television and tuned to national news for some background noise while he checked out his usual online information sites. He made a few electronic notes for later research, reviewed the schedule for the next day and then decided to get a bite in the hotel's restaurant.

Through the meal, Jackson went over the conversation he'd had with the nameless man on the phone. He knew that there had to be an organization behind the deaths, and the sheer number of them indicated that the people behind the so-called accidents had to be a pretty significant number, well-funded and professional. He'd seen various talking heads trying to spin the notion that African Americans couldn't have pulled off all those deaths on their own, that they had to have help, many saying from another country. But for an entire race conditioned to doing twice the work to get half the credit, finding several thousand with the needed skills and the ability to keep their mouths shut would have been child's play.

The part of the conversation that was worrying, but not unexpected, was the fact that the government had him under surveillance because of his Web site. It would be easy to conclude that his site was the signpost pointing to those who were killed. Which brought him around to the media invitation to the president's press conference. Why him, especially now?

Jackson wasn't in the habit of worrying about things over which he had no control. But to be contacted by the most sought after people, probably in American history, merely to let him know something that he had figured out on his own was troubling.

The only question he had at the moment was did the White House include him in the media representatives to lure him into questioning or custody. And since he wasn't going to find out until the next day, Jackson did his best to put it from his mind.

The next day, Jackson prepared for the White House, leaving everything behind except for his key to the room, wallet, his lanyard of press credentials and his smartphone. Once he arrived he was led, along with the other media representatives through security screening, then into the briefing room. Interestingly enough, he hadn't met a single person in the room previously.

All the media representatives had been screened and let into the room forty-five minutes before the press conference was about to start. The veteran reporters from cable and broadcast television were all chatting with one another, a number of print journalists were also catching up with each other.

A couple of media reps sitting near Jackson politely said hello, but none of them seemed to know who he was and, frankly, he preferred it that way.

When it was ten minutes until they were to begin, everyone was told to take their assigned seat as the two camera crews adjusted their color balances. When it was time for the president to arrive the room grew silent. Right on time, President Temple entered the room.

"Good afternoon, everybody. Thank you for coming. I have a statement to make and then time for a brief number of questions.

"This country is facing an unprecedented set of circumstances that have led to the death of four thousand, eighty-four people at last count. And although each and every one of those deaths appears to have been accidental, no one in law enforcement at the federal or local level believe that those killed were the victims of divine providence. They were killed by persons unknown. Most likely a group that believes that they have a right to take the law into their own hands.

"The Department of Justice has convened the largest, most comprehensive criminal task force in the history of this country. We are examining every single death to the most rigorous degree and leaving no stone unturned."

"We know we are looking for an organization that is methodical, and has demonstrated a disregard for life that will not be tolerated.

"Currently the Justice Department is running the investigation. The FBI is supplying the majority of the agents investigating the killings, and the other agencies, like the United States. Marshals and the NSA are providing logistical support where needed," the president said, pausing.

"I will not be answering any questions pertaining to the specifics of the investigation at this time, nor will the Attorney General or the Director of the FBI be answering any questions at this time either. So I'll entertain several questions—Stan, I believe you're first."

Jackson saw one of those in the front row stand.

"Thank you, Mr. President. Has anyone in law enforcement identified anyone behind these deaths? Any single individual at all?"

"I cannot answer any question about the specifics about the investigation at this time," Temple answered, a trace of annoyance in his voice. "Margaret?"

"What does the fact that victims in all these deaths are directly related to cops involved in black civilian shootings say about the state of law enforcement in this country, Mr. President?"

President Temple was silent for a moment, obviously working out how to answer.

He let out a heavy sigh, then said, "Only an imbecile would think that the playing field in the criminal justice system hasn't been level for as long as it has been in existence. And there are those who believe that African Americans are punished disproportionately in a number of areas including traffic offences, drug-related arrests and a whole laundry list of crimes numerous studies have proven over the last hundred years.

"There are those Americans who believe that so many police-involved shootings of African American men, women, teens and children are indicative of a lack of value placed on black lives. To ignore this belief in this investigation would be foolish. Marty, I believe you're next."

"Thank you Mr. President. Playing devil's advocate, I would like to ask you to speculate on what it would mean for this country if we don't find those responsible for these deaths?"

"I can't answer that, Marty. I believe that those responsible for this wave of killings will absolutely be caught and made to pay for their crimes. I will not rest until justice is done," Temple said shaking his finger at those in the room. "Regardless of the state of crime and race in this country, no one gets to kill almost over four thousand people just because they think life is unfair. Okay, Judith?"

A black woman in the second row stood. "According to our research department, Mr. President, not a single officer-involved shooting of an African American has occurred since the explosion in Orlando, Florida. Could we take that circumstance continuing forward for several months, for example, as a game changer in the four hundred year tradition this country has enjoyed in the killing of blacks? And if so, wouldn't that be a Mission Accomplished in actually eliminating the murder of blacks by police officers in this country because of this group's tactics?"

Jackson chuckled at the immediate uproar in the room as people shouted in indignation over the presumptions in the reporter's question. And it took more than a minute to get the room quieted again.

Giving the president a bemused look, Judith said, "I withdraw my question, Mr. President," and sat down. The room was silent, people looking from the president to the woman who asked the question, waiting to see what was going to happen.

President Temple's face betrayed nothing, but his eyes didn't leave that reporter.

"Don't think I don't know what African Americans think about justice in America, I do. And though I have no experience in the kinds of lives they have at the hands of a bigoted white majority, only an ignorant fool would discount their complaints. So, if you're asking me if I think the ends justify the means in this case, I do not. There's no excuse for killing, no matter the circumstance."

The woman immediately stood up demanding a follow-up. "If that is your answer, Mr. President. Then what about Thomas Jefferson's quote, 'The tree of liberty must be refreshed from time to time with the blood of patriots and tyrants?' Surely, the tyranny of the murder of a population that unarguably built this country from the ground up only to be denied equal access to the American dream, to be shot with impunity by white police officers and now to have that privilege extended to every white man in the country terrified of anyone with black skin is worthy of some bloodshed, Mr. President. After all, no one in this room has ever asked you how you felt about the hundreds of the innocent, unarmed black men shot and killed since you took office. I would like to know how the leader of the free world feels about the slow motion attempted genocide of the black-skinned people in this country?"

The room erupted in chaos, once again. With the same reporter shouting, "What about the tyranny of the majority, Mr. President? What about blacks suffering the tyranny of the majority for over four hundred years, Mr. President?"

President Temple looked out over the room, looking like he had lost control of the press conference. He decided that if he didn't get control, all hell was going to break loose across the country.

Holding up his hands to signal for quiet, he waited a few moments in silence then said, "Okay, you want a discussion on race in this country, let's at least start one.

"Have innocent African Americas been murdered in this country for far too long? Absolutely. And should African Americans continue to, as a race, have a lower standard of living in America because of systemic prejudice and racism? Absolutely not.

"So what do we do to change that? We tried to address systematic deprivations beginning with Affirmative Action programs. But when ignorant conservatives, white conservatives mind you, got into office around the country they characterized programs that were designed to try to level a playing field tilted for hundreds of years as reverse discrimination.

"Whites in this country, and that includes most of you," he said, pointing around the room, "are guilty of ignoring the fact that in this country, whites refuse to relinquish their built-in white privilege.

"So now we have a lawless organization that has decided to take matters into their own hands. They have murdered thousands, admittedly a drop in the bucket compared to the number of blacks killed since being brought here as slaves as Judith pointed out. But murder is wrong, it is a crime, and those responsible will be caught and punished. Thank you," he concluded, picked up his notes, and lead the way out of the room, his two aides scrambling to catch up.

Well that was special, Jackson thought as he got to his feet. As he reached the end of the row of chairs, he was stopped by a White House aide who leaned close and said, "Mr. Jackson, if you have a few minutes the president would be honored to have a few words with you."

Stunned, Jackson didn't understand what had just been said.

"I'm sorry?"

"The president would be honored if you would consent to having a few words with him," the amused woman repeated.

"Um, sure. When?" he answered.

"Just step out and let everyone else leave, and then I'll escort you to his office."

Jackson waited with the aide until the room cleared of everyone except for a couple of technicians, and then they set off with a Secret Service agent as escort. When they arrived at the President's Study, Jackson saw that President Temple was sitting behind his desk watching the video of the press conference on his computer screen.

The aide and agent let Jackson into the room and closed the door behind him. President Temple got up from behind the desk and came over to Jackson, his hand out.

"Mr. Richards, thank you for stopping by," he said as the White House photographer moved in to take several pictures of the two shaking hands.

Jackson was glad he had worn a suit, and asked how he could get copies for his mother.

"They'll be brought in as soon as they are printed, I'll sign them and then they'll be framed. They will be ready before you leave," Temple promised.

"Thank you very much, Mr. President. I really appreciate the consideration."

"Don't mention it. Would you like to sit down?" Temple asked leading Jackson to one of the couches.

Once they were seated, the president gestured to the computer on his desk and said, "Not my finest hour, was it?"

"Mr. President, that was a no-win situation. I think you handled it as best you could," Jackson said easily.

"You are too kind, Mr. Richards. In any case, I'm sure you're wondering why the invitation. Am I correct?" Temple asked, his eyes twinkling.

"Would this be about my being investigated by the task force, Mr. President," Jackson replied, not pulling any punches.

"Partly, but I highly doubt you've had anything to do with what's been happening around the country. Although whomever is behind these killings wouldn't go wrong using your database as a roadmap. Let's just get this out of the way, do you have any idea who is behind these murders, Mr. Richards?" Temple asked.

"No, I do not," Jackson said, as the office door opened and the woman with the questions was ushered into the room.

Both men rose to their feet as she entered the room. President Temple crossed over to the door and led her to Jackson introduced her as

Judith Spencer, independent correspondent at large.

"I haven't been knocked out like that since my boxing days at Annapolis, Judith. I see that you haven't changed not one little bit since we worked on the president's campaign in Boston way back when!" he said, sounding delighted.

"Mr. President, it was you who told me to never pull my punches. I was just following an executive order," she said, her laugh setting off Temple's.

Jackson was confused. In the briefing room the two acted like arch rivals, or combatants, but obviously they appeared to be the best of friends.

"Mr. Richards, we've been close friends for over twenty-five years. This country has to address the problem of race. Now I abhor the killings, but they have put race front and center, and I fully intend to take advantage of that fact. Judith suggested that you just might be able to advise me on how to go about planning out the way forward," said the president.

"Me? But what about the investigation?" Jackson asked.

"Would you expect me to make an offer to you about working with the White House without doing a background check on you?"

"And what did you find out about me?"

"Nothing, absolutely nothing other than the fact that your accomplishments speak for themselves," Temple answered.

"And who do you think turned the president on to you? Someone who used to check up on her son's football scores on a Web site called CollegeBox a few years ago," Judith said, surprising Jackson for the second time that afternoon.

"Nothing that's said in here is recorded, so feel free to say what's on your mind," Temple informed them. "Whomever is behind these killings is smart. They came up with the only means of stopping cops killing innocent blacks in the street. We weren't going to see any legislation that was going to move race to the front burner like this has any other way, changing the status quo. Killing the cops wouldn't matter to those predisposed to pull the trigger on anyone black,; there's no downside for the cops except for riding a desk for a few weeks. And there's a segment of the population drawn to law enforcement because they're bullies, racists, wife beaters and the like."

Jackson pointed at President Temple and asked, "So if I'm hearing right, even though the people behind these killings have to be brought to justice, you're not above using what they've done to try to improve the lives of blacks behind it, right?"

"In a nutshell."

"Could this just be a way of keeping close tabs on me?" Jackson asked, looking at Judith to see her reaction; there was none.

"Partly, but you have demonstrated the kind of skills, and the intelligence we need helping to make policy in this country behind the scenes. But unrelenting scrutiny, political polarization and an overly intrusive press keeps too many of the best minds from serving in government. Judith has been a trusted advisor to me for several decades. Imagine what the press would say if they knew the truth about our little performance today?"

"I get you. But you'll have to excuse me if I don't quite believe you, at least not from the start," Jackson said cautiously.

"That, and the fact that you won't be showing those pictures to too many of your friends, if I'm not mistaken," Temple said with a laugh.

"Can't stop mom and dad from showing off. But you're right, I'm not about to mention this conversation to anyone and mind you, I haven't agreed to anything yet. Clearly, I want to know more about what expectations you have for me," Jackson said.

"Well, if you have the time, let's just talk about that," President Temple invited. "Lunch anyone?"

Chapter 10

After a six-day moratorium on the accidental death of police officer families, sixteen more died. Sixteen in one day restarted the panic and the media rhetoric with a vengeance. Given the performance by President Temple at the press conference, conservative media was ratcheting up the call for someone else to lead the task force. For President Temple to have admitted that African Americans had legitimate complaints was anathema to those conservatives whose primary goal for several generations now was the redistribution of wealth into the hands of a very small minority of the country's white über wealthy.

Jackson returned to Chicago, the president's offer still on the table. He and Judith Spencer had traded contact information before leaving the White House, intending to get in touch in a day or so.

When he showed his parents the two pictures of him with the president, he had to endure two hours of their fawning over him; it didn't even matter that he didn't get to ask the president a question during the press conference.

Once he had arrived home, Jackson turned on the tablet the cabbie had given him and just left it on. He was hoping that the no-name man would want to get in touch with him. He played around with it for a few hours now that he had some free time. Unfortunately, he didn't find any sign of hidden apps or deeply buried malware code, but he wasn't really a programmer. So, as was his custom, Jackson put it out of his mind.

One of the evening news magazine shows Jackson was watching did a full hour's segment on several of the accidents. They covered the explosion in Orlando for the first segment, including interviews with the chief of police and the lead arson investigator. The conclusion of the investigators was that based on the evidence, the incident was the result of an accidental gas explosion. There was no evidence to conclude otherwise, even though it was the lead off incident for thousands of narrowly specific deaths to follow.

The second deaths reported on were those of a family under round-the-clock police protection in a secret location. They had died of botulism borne of food brought in from a local restaurant. Several other patrons of the restaurant had symptoms of the toxin though none had died.

MYRON MacHUTCHENS

The police officer's girlfriend and his twin boys had died even before an ambulance arrived on the scene. Investigators had found questionable cleanliness in the food prep area of the restaurant and traces of the bacterium that produced the deadly nerve toxin. The interview with the Miami Police Department's Public Information Officer speculated on the likely source of the toxin and discussed how someone could have found the secret location where the family had been sequestered.

The conclusion was that those bent on locating and killing the relatives or loved ones of those officers likely had nearly unlimited resources and very possibly inside access to law enforcement data. Speculation about the unknown force behind the killings traveled down several different crazy lines of thought.

The third case covered was that of Officer Jerry Stackhouse's family's death by carbon monoxide poisoning while they were on the run in Arizona. This time the local FBI PIO was interviewed about the circumstances behind the deaths.

She began with the facts about the cabin they had rented, that the family wasn't using their real names, and that the deaths of the officer's wife and two daughters occurred during a forty-five minute window when Officer Stackhouse was inspecting the motel grounds.

All three cases only served to further elevate the level of fear across the country. The ominous conclusion was that the people behind the thousands of deaths across the country were African Americans of superhuman powers. The network's talking head stopped short of calling for prophylactic action against African Americans by law enforcement, especially in the Department of Justice, but only just.

Singling out blacks for exclusion or special treatment played right into the hands of those presumed behind the killings in the first place. And the last thing anyone wanted, except for the really hard core racists who wanted to capture, incarcerate or kill every nonwhite in the country, was to be the cause of any further murders of innocent blacks.

There was no one to point to, no one to blame except an America that fostered the murder of its black citizens for hundreds of years. It was as if whites in the United States had some form of collective amnesia about the millions of blacks murdered; the overwhelming majority innocent of any crime but the misfortune to have been born with black skin.

It was amazing to Jackson that so many whites still refused to admit that the root cause of the thousands of deaths was institutional racism borne of white privilege permeating every segment of American society.

Flipping through the cable news channels, Jackson found the rebroadcast of a congressional hearing on race covered by C-SPAN held earlier that day with Judge Alvin Bridges testifying about many of the assertions in his book, The Entire System Is Broken: Throw It Away and Start Over.

Judge Bridges was in the middle of his opening statement when Jackson tuned in.

". . . for whites to believe that the problem is as systemic as it is, and that somehow the complaints of African Americans over the last one hundred years are exaggerations. Or, that claims on a widely tilted playing field in law enforcement, employment and access to the American dream are overblown forms the basis for the resentments we see today.

"The election of a half-black President of the United States only served to inflame the fear and hatred of African Americans by small-minded whites convinced that they were going to be subjected to the same treatment visited on blacks by whites down through the ages.

"And given the egregious nature of the treatment endured by African-origin blacks in this country, it is fair to characterize the events of the last several weeks as a rebellion against unlawful oppressors," Judge said to the growing sound of audience comment and unrest.

"Come to order," Senator Wilson said banging his gavel on the table before him. "Quiet please, everyone settle down, or I will be forced to clear the room of spectators. Please continue, Judge Bridges."

"That concludes my opening remarks, Senator."

"Those are very provocative words, Your Honor." Senator Wilson offered.

"Indeed they are, Senator. Though they are no less true," Judge Bridges said calmly unsettling Senator Wilson and the rest of the panel. "And let me comment for the record that I find it curious and inappropriate that not a single person of color is seated on the panel. This reminds me of countless congressional panels on women composed exclusively of men," the judge said to gales of laughter from the gallery.

Senator Wilson was silent for a moment as the rest of the panel had the nerve to look insulted.

"Are you trying to be provocative, your honor?" asked Wilson.

"Not at all. I merely pointed out a fact. I leave the implications of the composition of the panel for others to decide."

Senator Wilson frowned briefly, then continued, "Moving along, Judge Bridges. Would you summarize the conclusion in your book concerning America's legal system for the panel? As briefly as possible, please."

"I'd be happy to. Given the inescapable statistics, going back over four hundred years, the U.S. legal system has continuously passed laws designed to disproportionately punish blacks leading to disenfranchisement in voting, in employment, in banking and even the communities where blacks can live. Furthermore, there are whole communities where there are virtually no older black men to be found because of racially biased arrests, incarceration, and killings.

"It should be noted that the United States legal code is not only racist, but over ninety-five percent of the legislation passed since nineteen eighty has been corporate-friendly at the expense of the average American citizen.

"The criminal code is just as unequally enforced in terms of class. How many people on Wall Street went to prison for stealing middle class wealth in the initial decade of the 21st Century? Four, that's how many. And those four went to prison for having cheated rich white Americans, not for nearly crashing the world's monetary system and destroying trillions in investments—"

"The reason you're here, Judge Bridges, is to discuss racial inequality and the judicial system— " Senator Wilson interrupted.

"Oh but I am, Senator," Judge Bridges interrupted right back. "I know you're a Republican, and that your entire political philosophy is the redistribution of wealth to the very top earners in the United States, but can't you be honest enough to admit that much of the judicial inequity is based on your party's political platform?"

Several members of the panel were clamoring for a chance to speak, but they immediately quieted when Senator Wilson banged his gavel.

"Your Honor, I would like to remind you that you are an invited guest to these chambers, and partisan political bickering has no place here. And that goes for everyone else in the room as well."

"Beg your pardon, Senator. I believed that there would be a measure of honesty in these proceedings. Had I known better I wouldn't have wasted the Senator's nor the rest of the panel's time. Allow me to state what I believe we're here to discuss, and then you can correct me if I'm wrong,"

"Proceed," was the senator's sour reply.

"We have witnessed the deaths of over four thousand people in this country whose only commonality is the fact that they were family members, friends and pets of police officers involved in unpunished killings of innocent and unarmed African Americans. We are here to try to address the circumstances surrounding a group of people deciding to change a nearly half-millennium tradition in the United States of America by creating unthinkable consequence for state-sanctioned murder of the descendants of former slaves.

"I believed you invited me here for a discussion about striving to make the law fair, to grant equal justice under the law to nonwhites and to offer some public platitudes to give the people at home some glimmer of hope that things could change. But I submit that they have already changed."

"Do tell," the senator urged, intrigued by where the judge was taking them.

"In the several weeks since the first death of a police officer's family in Orlando, Florida, not a single innocent African American has been killed by a police officer. Since statistics kept for the last one hundred years have shown that every four days, on average, an innocent black person has been shot by a white police officer. It appears that whomever is behind the deaths of all those officers' families has done what apparently couldn't be done by law enforcement agencies themselves, couldn't be done by legislative fiat, nor by presidential executive order.

"The deed is done. And if those behind the deaths are not identified and/or caught, the change in this country is likely permanent," Judge Bridges concluded.

Muttering ran through the gallery, angering Senator Wilson. He looked at each member of the panel, inquiring by eye if anyone wanted to speak. Finally, the junior senator from South Carolina, indicated he wanted to speak.

"Judge Bridges, am I to understand that you approve of the tactics of this unknown group?"

Bridges laughed, his reaction to the question completely unexpected. "Is that what I said?" he responded.

"You sounded like—"

"Excuse me young man. I'm a little too old to play childish word games. I'm sure you can review my remarks and see the answer to your question," the judge admonished.

Senator Wilson took the brief pause to speak. "Need I remind you—"

"No, you do not, Senator. But even you, with all your years of experience chopping words, have to admit that the question was argumentative and a waste of this body's time. However, to answer the question, no I do not approve of the actions of this group or organization. But there is something to be said for their results.

"Let's be perfectly honest here, there was absolutely no reason for the United States Government to change the status quo regarding the killing of blacks until several weeks ago. Now, whites are reaping the consequences for their actions throughout history in a way that's never occurred in this country. Consequences and repercussions that have never been levied on white men before have completely changed this country forever."

"You do sound like you admire these people," Senator Wilson accused.

"I admire the brilliance of their tactics. To kill the police officers who have killed innocent African Americans would be pointless. Far too many drawn to join police forces across the country are bullies who just want to crack some heads. And they get away with that kind of mentality and behavior because the rank and file officers, the departments and the fraternal orders protect the dirty and the clean with equal fervor.

"I dare say that no one in this room has ever heard of any Fraternal Order of Police castigating one of their own even when the evidence of malfeasance is without doubt. There's never an excuse for a police officer killing a child yet that happens in this country as much as once every other month. And it defies credulity that only black children get shot by police in this country, white children shoot each other or themselves. Up until now co-equal justice for blacks and whites has been a fantasy in this country. And though I have detailed a number of areas where reform would have made a difference in my book, the people behind these deaths have rendered my academic suggestions moot."

"How do you mean, judge?" Senator Wilson asked.

"Because leveling the playing field, of sorts, has begun in spectacular style. Begging the senator's pardon, but this hearing is premature. We need to see what long term changes happen as a result of these numerous deaths. The Department of Justice has to locate those responsible, because if they don't everything is going to change permanently."

"Just what do you mean by that, judge?"

"I would like to suggest this to this panel, your committees on race and all the people who are watching these proceedings, if the people behind these revenge killings, and make no mistake that's what they are, are never caught, or even assuming only a few of them do, this country will never be able to go back to the indiscriminate killing of African Americans by cops or anyone else for that matter," Judge Bridges promised.

Senator Wilson looked at the rest of the panel members, then he scanned the spectators, all silent, waiting for his next question, or at least his response to Judge Bridges' testimony. He said nothing for a few moments, then he finally announced, "We are in recess until one o'clock this afternoon." He banged his gavel, stood and immediately hurried from the room.

Judge Bridges smiled watching the senator and the rest of the senators file out. He just sat there until some of the notables who were sitting directly behind him came forward to shake his hand wanting to discuss the things he said. While he was talking to several people from the gallery, an aide approached and handed him a note excusing him from the afternoon's session.

The coverage of the panel concluded with the usual C-SPAN camera panning over the crowd until the clock reached the top of the hour. Jackson wondered exactly what Senator Wilson gleaned from the judge's testimony given that the direction of the country's response was being dictated by persons unknown.

Jackson wondered if the man who contacted him was at all connected with the government, or law enforcement even. He had to come from somewhere, thought Jackson. Figuring out the why of the deaths was easy even for white folks. What wasn't easy to figure was how the group was organized and how they recruited. And the most important mystery, how they kept their existence a secret.

Jackson flipped up and down the cable channels looking for more news and stopped on CNN reporting on an incident where a police officer's dashboard camera showing him beating an elderly black man that even his department commander couldn't explain. The film had been around for under a week, the victim beaten and hospitalized days ago. What caught Jackson's ear was the reporting that the officer's son was involved in a rollover accident in his pickup truck and was hospitalized in critical condition. Preliminary investigation suggested that the pickup truck blew a front tire, causing the truck to career out of control, hitting several parked cars before rolling over.

Jackson wonder whether this signaled a new phase in revenge being visited on cops who merely beat or otherwise injured innocent blacks; he hoped so.

Chapter 11

One of the inevitable results of the thousands of deaths of officer family members was a hardening of police department attitudes toward America's blacks especially those protesting their treatment at the hands of police officers.

At least the various local police departments were scrupulously careful to avoid anyone using deadly force against demonstrators. And those demonstrating, knowing of the departments' caution, pushed the limits of their actions as far as they could seemingly provoking the kind of response neither side wanted.

In Los Angeles, demonstrators were marching over the beating of a seventeen-year-old, black student arrested for being in the wrong place at the wrong time. The teen suffered a broken wrist and the loss of three teeth at the hands of the L.A.P.D.

Protestors were marching around the L.A.P.D. headquarters building chanting, "No justice, no peace," over the fact that the two officers who made the arrest and beat the teen were immediately cleared of any wrongdoing. The young man was merely returning home from a late night run to the store for his grandmother and clearly didn't fit the description of the person who had robbed a nearby liquor store an hour before.

The police department erected barriers around their headquarters and redirected traffic a block away from the building on all sides, keeping demonstrators across the street from the building.

Though loud, and covered by a scattering of local media, the demonstration was fairly peaceful. As evening fell, the ranks of the demonstrators grew and the chanting was replaced by belligerent shouting at the ranks of police surrounding the building.

The department deployed weapons loaded with rubber bullets and beanbags in response to the rising hostility, but the officers on the street refused to be drawn into an armed confrontation. That is until rocks and bottles were launched toward them from the interior of the crowd of demonstrators.

When one of the bottles hit an officer in the leg and exploded into shards, the office next to him fired a rubber bullet blindly into the crowd across the street. Seconds later his head exploded, completely shorn from his body. The crowd went silent then people started running away from the police line in panic. Another officer raised his weapon and fired into the crowd, and his head also exploded in a mist of blood and bone. Several other officers prepared to fire in retaliation when the order was broadcast to "stand down." Unfortunately, two additional officers fired into the crowd and immediately died in a bloody mess. The line of officers was ordered back toward the building, getting them into a position where they could quickly get inside for protection.

Emergency services personnel arrived on the scene and saw that there was nothing to be done for those who had fired into the crowd. Officers on the street were not able to tell where the kill shots originated, but reinforcements were arriving from all over the city to try to contain all the demonstrators, preventing them from leaving the area until they could be searched.

A block away, on West 3rd Street, two squad cars rolled up on about fifty people fleeing the area, and the four officers leaped out to try to contain the crowd. Two of the officers emerged from their cars, guns drawn, and one of the others was carrying a shotgun. The remaining officer, who was black, didn't have any weapon drawn.

The four approached the fleeing crowd and tried to stop their running away from the perimeter around headquarters where the shots were fired. None had brought a bullhorn, and they were trying to shout above the crowd to for them to halt. The crowd was unable to hear the shouted commands and kept running down the street away from police headquarters.

The officer with the shotgun pointed it in the air and fired two times. Before the sound of the second shot had a chance to dissipate, his head disappeared in an explosion of red mist. Several of those in the running crowd screamed and their speed away from the area increased even more. The other three officers overloaded the radio frequency calling for medical assistance, announcing "officer down."

The police tactical command channel was a mess. Cops were calling in various sources of the kill shots at the same time tactical command was ordering everyone to stand down and holster their weapons. Someone in the street was targeting police officers, and in every case, the officer had drawn and fired their weapon; this did not go unnoticed.

Given the events of the previous few weeks, this was something new, something frightening. This was the first example of direct action against an officer.

The L.A.P.D. quickly cordoned off the streets for four blocks around headquarters and was searching every person within before letting them proceed out of the area, searching cars moving through the area as well. They were looking for anyone suspicious, hopefully carrying the specialized weaponry a sniper needed to have made the kill shots. The officers were more scared than angry, and for once, they were treating the people in the area with unaccustomed respect; no weapons drawn or unnecessary manhandling.

The people being detained picked up on the fear of the cops containing them and were cooperating. No one wanted any escalation of violence, either more cops being killed or the police firing on the crowd.

The local media was not able to immediately get the information about the officers struck down, only that several had been shot. The only coverage was from one local crew on hand shooting background video footage of the protestors. No one from the department was willing to go on camera in the confusion until they were ready so the media was ordered out of the area along with everyone else.

The Los Angeles Police Department had never suffered this kind of attack. Officers were dead with no suspects to be found. Investigators were convinced that no one in the nearby crowds of demonstrators had been responsible because the damage to the corpses of the downed cops could only have been done by large-bore bullets, easily heard within several blocks of being fired.

This was fear on a whole new level. Apparently someone had a problem with cops firing on the predominately black demonstrators and prosecuted the transgression in spectacular fashion.

The police department maintained a perimeter around the headquarters three blocks deep with no one allowed into the area by any means but on foot. By morning, the area was on full lock down while investigators tried to locate the source of the shots. And even though the L.A.P.D. was not commenting on the killings, numerous people who were in the crowd were interviewed all over the news describing their version of the night's events. By noon, a snippet of a mobile phone-shot video briefly showing what looked like an officer stricken and falling to the ground was uploaded to the Internet and ran almost continuously on every cable and broadcast news show.

Several law enforcement officials across the country appeared on local and national news shows announcing that if the officers had been assassinated then a state of war existed against those who committed the killings.

The problem was no one had a clue who was behind the officers' killings nor the thousands that had come before. With the killing of the officers who had discharged their weapons at the demonstration, the FBI Task Force was immediately stretched even thinner. The higher-ups at the L.A.P.D. didn't even have to make new policy for the rank and file cops on the street, none of them were anxious to take a chance at getting their heads blown off.

Los Angeles Mayor Julie Rodriguez called a meeting with the Chief of Police and the head of the local office of the FBI. She demanded a quick investigation, and that the person or persons responsible be immediately caught.

"Madam Mayor, according to our ballistics experts, the shooters could have been anywhere up to a kilometer away from the officers. They were probably outside of the area that was immediately quarantined, and as we know this morning, were not apprehended," reported the Chief of Police.

"And just who would have the skill to make those shots, chief?" Mayor Rodriguez inquired.

"Six of the officers on our S.W.A.T. team to start with. At least that number of former military living in the area I would imagine," the chief replied.

"We've already asked the military to run the names of former snipers who live in the state to begin with in our parallel investigation," added Special Agent Jacobs. "Although it would be short-sighted to assume that the shooters only came from former military living in California. There are hundreds of discharged specialists across the country—"

"And how many are black?" the mayor interrupted angrily.

Jacobs, African American himself, paused, surprised that the mayor would ask the question with such undisguised anger. "Somewhere in the neighborhood of four hundred twenty just from the last twenty years, all originating from U.S. Army Sniper School. We haven't received the numbers from Special Forces, the Marines, et cetera. We have no idea how many more may have been trained by independent security companies, mercenaries and the like. Chief, have you recovered the munitions fired?"

"We have all but one, I'll have them delivered to your people this afternoon. So far they are all .50 BMG rounds. It appears they may have been fired from the same weapon."

"Sad to say, but that's damned impressive shooting—" started Agent Jacobs.

"Don't you fucking tell me that you actually admire whoever killed my officers—" Mayor Rodriguez began only to be interrupted by Jacobs.

"Madam Mayor, I would suggest you get hold of yourself. Just because I'm black doesn't make me your God damned enemy. And just because you're mayor doesn't mean I have to put up with any childish, racist bullshit from you."

Chief Loeber started to object, but Jacobs cut him off before he got out a word.

"I will be spoken to with respect. I'm exactly like the two of you wanting to see those who killed your officers brought to justice. But I will not tolerate any race-based nonsense from either of you or any of your people. I'm lead here in L.A. for the Bureau whether you like it or not. You're welcome to try to get me replaced, but I highly doubt you will get your way."

The chief and mayor were both silent, neither willing to say what was really on their mind so Jacobs continued. "A lot of things are changing in this country as a result of the events of the last few weeks. We all know it. But if we fall victim to the ugliness of race politics, we're simply not going to find and prosecute the people behind these thousands of deaths. Now, are we going to be able to work together?"

"I apologize for my rudeness, Agent Jacobs," began the mayor. "The deaths of my officers has us all on edge, and no, your local lead on these killings will not be a problem; I can assure you of that," she said, getting a nod of agreement from the chief.

"For your information, these killings don't make my job easier. Too many small-minded whites are willing to believe that I have sympathies for the killers just because I'm black. For the record, I do not. I want all those responsible brought to justice because of how it marginalizes African Americans in positions like mine. Make no mistake, I not only know my job, but I have even stronger motivation to catch the killer or killers responsible because of my color. Now are we straight?" Jacobs asked.

"Absolutely," Chief Loeber replied immediately, moving to shake Jacob's hand. "Let me know if you need any of my peoples' help."

"You have my office's full cooperation, Agent Jacobs. I only ask that you keep us apprised of your investigation. What the chief said goes for my people as well," Rodriguez added.

Agent Jacobs stood, as did the others, said goodbye and left the room.

Once he was gone, Rodriguez gestured for the chief to sit.

"That was special," she said sarcastically. "He definitely has a chip on his shoulder."

"He's entitled. He's one of the best in the office, we've worked with him a bunch of times. I never gave a thought to how this might affect his own official relationships. What worries me is that from here on out, we're going to have to evaluate our trust of our black officers on an ongoing basis. I can't afford to take their loyalty for granted nor can I treat them at all like hostiles. All anyone knows is the people we're hunting are very good at both killing and not getting caught. My forensics people inspected the .50 cal bullets recovered and other than rifling marks, they're unremarkable and off the shelf as opposed to hand turned. Unless the FBI already has a match for the barrels they were fired through, the bullets are a dead end unless we find the weapon. By the way, I've ordered my people to make damn sure their lives are in danger before they even thinking about unholstering their weapons. This means the next high-speed chase through the streets is going to be damned interesting. From here on out everything has changed for my people."

"And the dead officers are all white, are they not?" asked Rodriguez.

"They are."

"What does that suggest to you?"

"Nothing specific. The force is mostly white and Latino now. Bad luck or statistical happen chance, no one can tell. But I can say this with certainty, we're in an entirely new phase in an undeclared war. Someone out there has sent the clear message that police brutality against blacks will not be tolerated."

"And how does that effect your peoples' behavior?" the mayor asked.

"Hard to say long term. Don't quote me on this, but I'll bet that in the near future we're going to see a lot of white officers leave the force—and maybe that's a good thing. Hopefully, it will be the bullies, the cops who pull the most citizen complaints. It would help in the long run. But for fuck's sake, I'll be damned if some rogue vigilante group out there dictates how I police this city," the chief said, clearly angry.

"What I'm afraid of is that you may not have a choice," she said quietly. "It's not a race riot this time. Now, we're looking at someone who can essentially kill with impunity. Someone at least as skilled as your own S.W.A.T. personnel, and capable of killing without leaving a trace of their actions. This country is definitely in uncharted territory," she concluded.

-=#=-

"Hey buddy, sorry it took so long to get back to you. I was out of the country makin' that cash," Tony said when Andrew answered the phone. "And before you ask, no I haven't been anywhere near L.A."

"Did I ask?" Andrew said, laughing. "But since you mentioned it, what do you think about that thing?"

"From the diagram in the L.A. Times, that was some damn fine shooting. But nothing above average for the folks we know. There were so many sight lines outside of half a mile, the paper's right; the shooter could have been anywhere over a klick away. Anyone call to question you yet?"

"Hey, you know my life's an open book, Tony. But I will say this, the shit's getting deep. From thousands killed in untraceable accidents, to killing cops who fire on demonstrators, this is escalating with no real end in sight," Andrew observed.

"Yeah, no shit. And they can't start killing us just because that's what got this whole thing started in the first place. Hey, you got any time off coming up? I'd love for you to come on down and take a look at OpFor."

"I told you, I'm done with that."

"I know. It's not a recruitment thing. I'd just like for you to take a look around and give me your opinion. And hell yes, I would love to spend some quality time on the range with you; usual stakes, a hundred bucks a shot," Tony said, then paused. "Just give it some thought, One Shot. And don't give them an excuse to roust you, you hear?"

"I hear you. Let me check on work stuff. I'll call you in the next few days and let you know. Now that you mention it, I could use some time away even if it's only for a few days," said Andrew.

"Good. Let me know. I should be here at home for the next few weeks. Call me. Catch you later."

Andrew seriously thought about making the trip to Texas. He was very curious about what Tony had been hinting about ever since he'd gotten back in touch. It may not be about the group or organization behind the cop family killings, but there was something. He really wanted to know what it was. Just as he was about to get on with his day, he received a text from Tony inquiring about what kind of rifle he was using these days. Andrew laughed and sent the information on his Windrunner along with a smiley face, deciding that he would head south as soon as he could shake loose.

Tony, once he received Andrew's texted reply, called OpFor's armorer to make sure there was a Windrunner and ammo in stock. Then he considered how and where he was going to talk to Andrew about the thing that had been on his mind for the last year. The next time the two were together, the conversation was going to be very interesting and very direct.

Chapter 12

Special Agent Sharon Jefferson had never been "ma'amed" or addressed by her title so much in her life. Working directly with the White House and the other departments of the federal law enforcement apparatus was a completely enlightening experience for her. And sitting in on the afternoon security briefing nearly every day was an eye opener.

Today, she was returning to the FBI Task Force Group and meeting with SAIC Sheldon Willis, who by now knew what an ass he'd been with her at the onset of the task force.

The impromptu meeting was about the sniper killings in Los Angeles. When she arrived the full-wall display in the conference room had a satellite image of the streets surrounding the L.A.P.D. Headquarters out to about ten blocks. Small, bright dots were placed at the location of each downed officer. Leading away from each location was a cone indicating the probable location of the shooter.

Jefferson took a seat in the middle of the table so she would be able to see everyone clearly as well as the wall display. She knew everyone in the room by sight except for one agent looking closely at the overhead view on the display, making notes.

There was a quiet buzz in the room as several agents were talking, when SAIC Willis came into the room, everyone got quiet waiting for him to lead the meeting.

"I see we're all here so let's dive right in. Everyone got the update on what happened last night in L.A., right?" he asked, checking around the table. "Good. On the display are the locations of each cop shot and killed last night. We have Gordon Banks here today to brief us. Gordon's the Armorer for the Bureau, Gordon?"

"Good morning, everyone. Let's take a look at the display here," he began, zooming the display to show the block L.A.P.D. Headquarters sat on in the middle. "What we have here are the locations of the L.A.P.D. officers killed. These cones coming off their locations indicate the extent, left and right of the probable location of the shooter. The L.A. office has received five expended bullets, all .50 caliber, and the preliminary analysis indicates they were all shot from the same weapon so we're concentrating on this area here where all these cones overlap. We have no acoustical record of the shots, no video, just these three dead officers."

He panned the display to show two more cones. "And here, we have two additional officers killed a block and a half away, also killed by the same weapon. Based on the local analysis the shooter had to be located on this arc," he said, drawing in a larger cone encompassing all five downed officers leading outward for several blocks. "As you see, there are thirteen structures identified as locations with the blue dots from which the shooter could have operated. Local PD have isolated each location for our people to inspect the buildings. Any questions, so far?"

Willis raised his hand and asked, "I understand that SAIC Jacobs has asked for a download from the military of all discharged personnel with sniper training, is that available to us yet?"

"It came in about 6:00 A.M. I scanned it and then posted it to the task force database. We have someone on it in my department, but I doubt we're going to find anything just from the list. The bullets were off the shelf, not custom-turned—virtually untraceable.

"Again, what this set of killings demonstrates is that the people we're hunting are extremely well trained and, so far, virtually untraceable. The bullets are being brought here, but it's highly unlikely that we'll find anything more than the L.A. office did. What's very concerning is that we have to assume that the people behind all the killings are as good as they come. And even though I have every confidence that we will find them, it's going to be a long slog."

"Thanks, Gordon. Anyone else have something to add? Questions?" Willis asked.

"What about the NSA filters?" Sharon inquired.

"Nada. Neither telephone calls, nor email messages. They informed me that they are now screening trillions of SMS messages, maybe someone was careless and texted something we can call a lead," Willis reported. "But I'm not really hopeful."

"What about the packet-sniffing of the old TOR network? Are these people avoiding the normal lanes of the information superhighway, to use an old school term?" one of the other agents asked.

"Same thing. Nada," Willis replied.

"If it weren't for the fact that we're looking at a black revenge thing, several people on the president's National Security team would like to believe that a foreign government might be behind it," Sharon offered. "But why African Americans? What's the play, internationally speaking?"

"National disruption? Hell, the stock market has lost twenty-five percent of its value since this whole thing started," Willis replied.

"I doubt it. All the exchanges around the world are taking a beating.

No one's getting rich off of this, not even the nay-sayers who short everything," a women agent at the end of the table observed.

"This is the work of Americans, probably black, who are setting out to change the racial paradigm in this country," said Sharon, seeing the other three nonwhite agents all nodding in agreement.

"So, what we have today is direct action against police shooters, in addition to family members getting offed," said one of the black agents, his name slipped Sharon's mind.

"If you take a look at this," he continued as he brought up a display of the entire nation, "the distribution of the family deaths is all across the nation. And running didn't help the cop from here in D.C., his family was suffocated just outside Phoenix."

"Logistics have estimated no fewer than a thousand people have to be working with this group; probably closer to two thousand. They also insist that this operation has to have been on the drawing table for at least a decade, and we had no clue they even existed. We also have to think about the money needed to pull off an operation like this; billions the analysts say," said Willis.

"The number two over at ATF is convinced that it's white supremacists trying to finally start a race war to the death. But those guys are too stupid to pull off something like this. Most of them can barely read. So far, these people have been way smarter than we are. What we're going to have to do to catch them is an unprecedented amount of leg work especially if the NSA can't come up with any hints as to who these people are. Strap in, everyone. This is going to be a long ride. Anyone have anything else? Okay, give your latest to Agent Jefferson to take back to the White House before you head out," he said, handing her a data solid containing everything from the big board.

"How are they treating you over there?" Willis asked.

"I've never been ma'amed more in my life." Sharon replied.

"Yeah, they're big on formality over there. It's just respect, though. You hearing anything I should know about?"

"Not really, except for the president's pissed off that this has escalated into direct confrontation with the killing of cops. If they don't find anything out in L.A., the president thinks we're hosed; the whole task force, that is," Sharon reported. "The public's demanding action, at least loud mouthed whites are. I'm hearing mixed signals from African Americans. Some are quite happy with the status quo, others are worried what the eventual fallout is going to be after the killers are caught."

"And you? What do you think, Sharon?"

"I want the best of both worlds: no more innocent blacks killed by cops, and the people responsible caught and punished."

Willis laughed.

"What's so funny?" asked Sharon, about to get pissed.

"Nothing about what you said, it's just that I can't remember the last time the country had a win/win situation like that in a major crime spree. That would be the shit!" Willis said, smiling.

"From your mouth to someone's ear. Well, times a wasting, I'm going to head back," she said, getting to her feet.

"Good enough. Wanna catch lunch later in the week?" Willis asked still trying to make up for being such an ass when the task force began.

"That'd be nice. See what you have up for Thursday. Call me," she said as she left the room.

When Sharon returned to the White House, the first thing she did was to upload to the secure network the data SAIC Willis had given her. She then sent out a message to everyone on the internal task force distribution list with links to the uploaded data.

A few minutes later, the Chief of Staff called to get Sharon's evaluation of the meeting, and whether or not anything had been discussed that wasn't covered in the upload. He also inquired into how SAIC Willis was treating her, knowing why she was appointed to the White House in the first place.

"He's fine. He invited me to lunch. I think he's still trying to make up for being an idiot in front of everyone," she explained.

The Chief of Staff laughed and said, "I wouldn't let him off the hook just yet, keep that leverage as long as you can. Gotta run. See you this afternoon."

When she hung up the phone, Sharon turned to managing the virtual mountain of email she had received since the day before. However, the bloom wasn't yet off the rose of her assignment at the White House. She was receiving the update stream from the task force and as well as the national security team. She was tapped into an information stream that was up-to-the-minute to a degree she hadn't known existed. She had a glimpse of the Presidential Daily Briefing once and was astounded at the level of detail there was, not to mention the scope of the elements of risk and danger across the globe that could come to roost in the United States or negatively affect the country's assets worldwide.

The intelligence gathering capability of America's investigative services was unbelievably enormous, and yet none of the vast information gathering assets had uncovered even a hint of the vast operation that had killed thousands of Americans. The attacks at the turn of the century on September 11th numbered less than three thousand deaths. There were more blacks killed by white cops since the 21st Century began than everyone killed on 9/11.

Sharon spent the rest of the morning going through the latest dispatches from the task force, making her own notes on ideas and leads she wanted to follow up on later. She was especially interested in looking over the databases of the discharged military snipers to see if there were any likely candidates who jumped out at her. But after spending a couple of hours pouring through the data, there were absolutely no clues to be found.

She wrote up her summary and added it to the general analysis folder on the network. She then logged into the FBI's secured servers and looked over the information posted by the Los Angeles office, preferring to see it for herself.

For the rest of the day, Sharon continued her research until it was time for the afternoon national security meeting. The meeting was brief, most of the discussion centered around the killing of the cops. It wasn't lost on anyone that firing into the crowd was the provocation for the killings, but the killing of police officers elevated the seriousness of the adversary they were facing. The FBI's assessment of the skill of the shooter, once the analysis of the shots had been completed, was grudgingly high. The probable site from which the shots were fired was a hair over two thousand yards from the officers stationed around the building; a difficult shot for even the best of snipers. But to hit a total of five officers with only five shots from that distance put the task force on notice that the people they were chasing were the highest of trained professionals.

The focus now was on unearthing any clue as to who was behind the killings and reshaping American culture. There was no debate that it was long past the time for the tradition of murdering blacks to stop in the United States. But what was fueling a good deal of resentment and anger in white Americans was the fact that it was being forced on the country shoved down their collective throats as it were.

African American militants, all being monitored by various branches of law enforcement, were beginning to voice their opinions on the change in police behavior but were careful to not state that they in any way approved of the loss of lives. Their refrains all cynically started out, "Now I don't approve of anyone killing another human being, but . . ." making for an uncomfortable silence in response from white America.

The current leader of The Nation of Islam in Chicago was asked, after giving a sermon on "The evils of white men through history coming home to roost," that with his claims of cherishing life, did he not mourn the deaths of the families of the nation's police officers. His response was,

"After mourning the murder of millions of African-related peoples' lives at the hands of whites in this country, I have no more remorse in my soul left over for a handful of whites killed in the service of making this country live up to its ideals in equality and liberty." He continued, asking, "Why has no one begun the conversation on how many people with colored skin are languishing in prison because of the corrupt nature of the police in this country? It's been the state's cottage industry of the last fifty years. No, until that egregious wrong is also corrected, this country will continue to reap what it sowed."

Public calls for investigating and/or arresting all such voices were heard throughout the conservative community. But the U.S. Attorney General was not going to be pushed into such precipitous action, and even the local police departments were wary of even the appearance of such persecution.

Sharon's research into the local investigations found eighteen African American community leaders under direct surveillance for signs of collusion with those who could be connected with those behind the killings.

Just before she was going to bag it for the day, a note from the C.I.A was added to the task force database indicating that all eleven black clandestine agents on the payroll had been cleared of any outside involvement. Sharon laughed to herself figuring that someone over there must have remembered the 1969 novel, The Spook Who Sat by The Door by Sam Greenlee, or the movie adaptation of the book that appeared several years later. At least someone's on the ball over there, Sharon thought as she made her way out of the building and out to her car. She wouldn't be surprised if the CIA wasn't deconstructing every passage in the book for clues to those killing cop families and now, cops. Simply put, black rage terrified white America and always had. Black superiority in strength, endurance, sports, and sexuality, whether real or perceived, only served to enhance white inferiority, producing an abiding fear and hatred for them.

As she left the White House grounds, Sharon wondered again if she was also under close surveillance as well. Ever since she left the task force, she assumed she was. All her computer work in the White House was recorded, as was everyone's working in the building. Well, they're not going to find anything on me, she thought as she drove toward Georgetown where she shared a townhouse with her partner, Felicia Davenport, a labor law attorney originally from the Bay Area in California.

The two had met at a professional mixer sponsored by Felicia's law firm. They spent the majority of the time that evening in a lively discussion on the politics of gender, finding they had a number of things in common. And in less than six months, they decided on a trial period of living together, settling on Sharon's place because it had more space though Felicia kept her place in the event it didn't work out. They'd been exclusive now for six years with the Bureau unconcerned about previous generation's superstitions and prejudices about same gender couples.

When she parked in the building's garage, she saw that she had beat Felicia home. Once inside, she quickly changed into some gym wear and plopped down on the sofa with a glass of wine, turning on the national news.

As she figured, this day's hysteria, as she commonly referred to it, was on the spectacular killings of the L.A.P.D. officers. The talking head was breathless with speculation about a coming race war. So much for fair and balanced she thought, finishing off half of her glass.

Moments later, she heard keys in the door. Seconds later, Felicia rounded the corner and saw Sharon on the couch. She gave Sharon a kiss then asked, "Anymore wine left?"

"I just opened the bottle. How was your day?" she asked as Felicia poured a generous glass for herself.

Joining Sharon on the couch, she said, "Nothing that a glass of this and a hot shower won't fix. You?"

Nodding toward the television coverage of the shootings, she replied, "Everything's escalating now that direct killings have occurred. That they were cops is a gut-buster. Now, we know that a badge doesn't mean a thing to those people."

"Aren't they more than likely our people," Felicia said, eyes twinkling over the rim of her glass.

Sharon laughed with the day's tension beginning to drain out of her. "More than likely. But so far there's no hint of a clue to follow."

"Hey, how'd it go back at the FBI today? Is Willis still sucking up to you?"

"He invited me to lunch. That's some kind of progress, I guess," she replied unenthusiastically.

"I know it's a pain in the ass, the politics of gender, of race, sucking up for a promotion or whatever. But you're handling it well," Felicia said. "You're in the White House for shit's sake!"

"You're right," Sharon admitted, finishing off her wine. "I'm going to work out. What do you want to do for dinner?"

"I'm bushed. If you don't feel like cooking either, let's go out; nothing fancy."

MYRON MacHUTCHENS

"How about Chinese," Sharon suggested.

"Done! Call me when you're going to hit the shower, I'll join you."

"No problem."

Chapter 13

Jackson was quite happy that his part in the work he was doing with Judith Spencer largely consisted of deep data mining into some of the cases of cop-involved shootings, and the ancillary personnel involved in the officer's getting off in a civilian shooting. The two tried to get grand jury testimony, accessed local newspaper archives, and gathered televised statements in the service of gathering the most comprehensive overview of the targeted cases possible.

Their theory was that by amassing all the data of the target cases, they might be able to trace the same investigatory path of those who killed the officer's family. Understand the tactics of those they sought would be a very good first step in divining the methods behind the killings.

This kind of research was bread and butter for both Jackson and Judith, and he had set up a protected online database where the two of them could add information gleaned from the cases they researched.

Jackson kept the tablet from the mysterious man powered up all the time hoping that contact would be made again. He knew it was a long shot, especially given his new relationship with the White House. That relationship couldn't have been overlooked by someone with the ability to kill thousands of people without a trace.

Just out of curiosity, Jackson looked through his Real Deal database to see when the last time it had been this long between cop shootings of an innocent black and was astounded when he found it had been over forty years. He was ambivalent about the fact; happy that no one had been shot since the Orlando explosion but still angry that such shootings were a constant in the fabric of American tradition for as long as whites arrived on the continent.

Jackson was also ambivalent about the idea of the people they were seeking getting caught. His opinion was somewhat harsher than that of his parents who were afraid of the repercussions African Americans would suffer should the people doing the killings be caught. Jackson thought if they never got caught, blacks would receive a measure of "justice" they had never experienced since their ancestors were originally kidnaped and brought to America.

When he had opportunity to discuss the broader matters of their investigation, he found that Judith too had mixed feelings about the people they were seeking. Her job as a journalist had put her in situations that exposed her to man's inhumanity to man far too many times.

Judith had dealt with scores of police departments across the U.S., and they were universally hostile to the media, especially to a black journalist investigating the possibility of wrongdoing by one of their own. But she was good, very good, at her profession. More often than not, her disarming manner in interviewing managed to get those with whom she spoke to reveal things that others didn't get. But she was seldom allowed access to the cops involved in the shootings so she made do with interviewing everyone else involved to put together a picture of what most likely happened.

Because of their different personalities, Judith was spending almost all of the time on the road leaving Jackson with an unaccustomed long period of time at home in Chicago. What started out as a little side research with an old friend drifted into something else.

Jackson had a high school friend who had ended up going through the Chicago Police Department's academy when she graduated college in down state Illinois. Angela Williams was now a Sergeant in the Nineteenth District on Chicago's north side.

He called her wanting to hear what the department's response to sixteen of their officers' families being in the mix of those dying. She had described the scramble to try to protect the families of the officers they knew were immediately at risk, and the hasty in-house research to identify any others back down the line. When Jackson asked if there were successful in saving any of the families, Angela sadly told him no.

Over the last few weeks, they had gotten together half a dozen times. The last time together they had ended up on Angela's sofa necking, but hadn't gotten very far before Jackson's native caution pulled him out of the mood. Angela wasn't at all surprised and didn't take it personally. So when his phone rang, Jackson was surprised it was her.

"What's up, lover boy?" she said when he answered.

"Hey, come on you know I didn't mean—"

"Jackson! Cool out, I didn't mean anything by it. But check this, I got some news for you," she said, excitedly.

"Like what?"

"You know that cops were shot in L.A., right? Well the Bureau is actively investigation military snipers all across the country."

"Black ones, I'll bet," Jackson said sardonically.

"Of course."

"How many are out there?" he asked.

"The preliminary list is about four hundred. But from the shots taken, they're really only interested in the cream of the crop. That means only the top thirty or so," she replied.

"Any of them live around here?"

"Only two, a guy in Hanover Park and one of our own S.W.A.T. guys. That went over like a lead balloon when word got out. The local FBI is taking care of interviewing the other guy. But the department isn't taking this new development lightly. If cops are being targeted, then the situation has just gotten a whole lot more dangerous—for everybody."

"Yeah, I can see that. But the L.A. cops shot into the crowd first," Jackson clarified.

"True. But anyone willing to so brazenly kill cops can't be allowed to be free."

"So where is everyone on catching these guys?"

Angela was silent.

"I see," Jackson said. "So the sniper thing hopefully might identify someone in their ranks, right? By the way, what did your S.W.A.T. guy say when his name came up?"

Angela laughed and said, "I heard he started cussing up a storm, calling everyone in the locker room all kinds of motherfuckers when he was told. The lieutenant hauled him into his office to get him calmed down. It was epic!"

"I'll bet. Hey, I heard of a new sushi place in Evanston. Want to check it out?" Jackson asked.

"Sure, when?"

"What's good for you?" he asked.

"Tomorrow? I have that continuing ed. class tonight."

"Sounds good."

"Okay, I'll run home and change. You can pick me up there about 6:30. That cool with you?"

"See you then."

After he hung up, Jackson tuned to KTLA's cable TV channel and half-listened for the next update on the cops who were shot. Online, he saw that the names of the cops had been released, noting that one of them had lost his girlfriend because he had killed a black teen during what he called a routine traffic stop gone bad. The L.A.P.D.'s investigation cleared him of any wrongdoing (Jackson was getting damn tired of hearing that word).

What was readily apparent was that the direct killing of cops had just added a deadly dimension to the hunt.

-=#=-

When he saw Andrew exit the San Antoine airport terminal, Tony honked twice to get his attention. He popped the trunk, got out to shake hands, and pull Andrew into a hug.

"Glad you made it, my man. How was the trip?" he asked as they got in the car.

"Hang on," he said, angling the rear view mirror. "Yep, just what I thought."

"How's that?" Tony said, looking back through the side view mirror.

"Dark blue sedan, one lane over. Cat that was on the plane with me just jumped in that unmarked car. "

"Spook?"

"No doubt. Let's go straight to OpFor and see what they do," suggested Andrew.

Looking around, Andrew smirked and said, "Nice car. The missus let you use it today?"

"Actually, this is my grocery car, all clean electric. If I don't use the air conditioning I get around three hundred miles on a charge. I have a rice-burner for my daily commute," Tony explained. "If you want to go riding, I got a buddy who'll lend me his bike."

"We'll see. First things first, let's see what this asshole is all about."

Tony took the direct route out to OpFor's compound, neither rushing or intentionally holding up traffic. Halfway there, just outside of town, Tony asked if the car was still back there.

"Yeah, three cars behind us."

"Well, they ain't getting into the gate, no matter what kind of badges they've got. We'll be there in five minutes," Tony said, giving Andrew the heads up.

The final couple of miles were spent in silence while Andrew kept an eye on the government sedan.

Minutes later Tony turn on to the long gravel driveway to the main entrance of the OpFor training compound. Andrew watched as the government car slowed as it went by the driveway, traveled about a hundred yards down the highway then pulled a u-turn and drove past in the opposite direction.

"You saw that?" Andrew asked.

"It'll be interesting if they send someone by to knock on the door."

"Yeah, but you have to figure that they've got the entire compound photographed from space," Andrew reasoned.

"They did that years ago when they hired us to do protection and anti-insurgency when the company began getting government contracts. I wouldn't be at all surprised if they didn't send someone through for training to see if we're on the up-n-up. You got some shootin' duds in your bag, otherwise I can get you some fatigues," Tony offered.

"That would be great."

Tony led them to the locker room so Andrew could change then went to fetch their weapons and ammo from the armorer. When Andrew was ready, Tony took him out to the firing range.

They made their way to the far end of the line with the farthest targets and began to prepare their weapons on the table behind the line.

Andrew inspected the Windrunner, disassembling the rifle laying the parts out on the table before him. He ran a cleaning pad through the barrel and lightly oiled the parts, pleasantly surprised that the parts and trigger mechanism were so clean.

He reassembled the rifle and loaded the magazine. He then looked up at Tony and asked, "Ready?"

"Absolutely. One hundred-fifty yards, standard stakes, right?"

"Just like you said over the phone," Andrew replied, laying down at the lane next to Tony's. he inserted a pair of compression ear-buds before pulling on the ear protectors. Then he pulled his shooting glasses out of their case, set the case aside, and put them on.

"Take a few shots to see how she fires," Tony suggested.

Andrew began his routine, calming himself, focusing on nothing but the target downrange. Tony was using the spotter's scope, watching Andrew's target.

"Bam!" the first shot echoed.

"Three centimeters, eleven o'clock," Tony announced as Andrew adjusted the scope on the Windrunner. Seconds later, the second shot rang out.

"One centimeter, nine o'clock."

"Okay, I'm good. You ready?" Andrew asked.

Before Tony could answer, a group of five people, four men and a woman, exited the building and were quickly approaching down the line towards them.

"Sorry about that. I may have mentioned you were inbound to do some shooting to a couple of the folks here," Tony said apologetically.

They both got to their feet then Tony introduced Andrew to the others, one of whom Andrew recognized from being a class behind him at sniper school.

"I'm sorry, I don't remember your name, but we came up together, right?" asked Andrew.

"Yes, sir. Lance Baldwin. I was about nine months behind you. Nowhere near your record, sir," he said.

"As long as we're all on the same team. That's all that matters, Lance," Andrew said, shaking his hand.

"By the way, Tony. I was told to inform you that some local fed wants to interview you, and as he said, your guest," said the woman introduced as Michelle Young.

"Thanks for the heads up, Michelle. Did they say when they were coming by?" Tony asked.

"Around three."

"Plenty of time. You all here to watch?" Tony asked.

"Damn right. We weren't going to miss out on the famous One Shot here on our range. We wanted to see if the legend was real," Michelle said to the chuckles of the others. "That's a lot of rifle you have there, One Shot."

"Michelle here thinks she's the best shot at OpFor," Lance explained.

"That's only if you go by kills and scores here in the range," she replied.

"And what do you shot with?" Andrew asked.

"Same as Tony," she replied, nodding toward Tony's Barret M98. Both Tony and Andrew preferred older weapons to the newer, lighter composites.

"Want to take him on, Michelle?" Tony offered.

"You mind, One Shot?" she asked Andrew.

"Not at all," he replied with a predatory grin.

"Same stakes. A hundred a shot. Who goes first?" she asked.

"Ladies first, of course," Andrew replied.

Tony gave Michelle his ear protectors, seeing that she already had her glasses out and was putting them on.

The two shooters took their positions on the ground as Lance turned on the monitors telescopically showing the targets down range.

Michelle started her breathing routine, took note of the wind flags down range and began to squeeze the trigger. When the shot was away, the five clustered behind the monitor, peering closely to see where the bullet hit.

"Center ring, half outside the line," Tony announced. "Not bad."

The spectators turned to the monitor on Andrew's target and waited.

Andrew's shot came about ten seconds later.

"In the bullseye, eight o'clock," Tony announced.

Michelle's second shot was completely in the bullseye at the three o'clock mark.

Andrew's next shot was as close to dead center as they could tell. One of the others whistled in admiration.

Michelle's next shot was close to dead center, slightly high.

Andrew powered the next shot almost exactly through the previous hole. The gallery was silent as Tony said, "Same hole."

Michelle looked over at Andrew in both slight disbelief and respect.

She then looked down range, completely blocking out the distraction of the guys behind her, and the knowledge that Andrew was watching as well, and slowly squeezed the trigger.

"Dead center," Tony announced, to the whistles from the others.

"Dead center," Tony announced after Andrew's shot.

"Bullseye, seven o'clock," Tony said on Michelle's last shot.

"Fucking same hole!" Tony said incredulously on Andrew's final shot.

One of the others took off to run the trench and get the targets. When he brought them back they could easily tell whose was whose by the size of the holes through the paper.

The center of Andrew's target was a hole you could cover with a half dollar except for the hole in the lower left of the bullseye.

Michelle pulled her wallet out of her back pocket and handed Andrew three one hundred dollar bills. "Damn, you sleep with one of those?" she said in admiration.

"Used to. That's some mighty fancy shootin', ma'am. Where did you learn?" Andrew

 inquired.

"At home. My mother taught me. She's a marine!" Michelle said proudly. "Tightened up on some of the math, and got to try out some of the latest, greatest weapons here at OpFor and really liked kickin' it old school," she said, slapping five with Andrew and the others. "So what's that fed want with the two of you?"

"To see if we were in L.A. shooting cops," Andrew replied. "At least me, some spook was on the plane with me coming here. They followed us to the gate to see where Tony was taking me then they took off."

Lance shook his head then said with aa chuckle, "Man, you dark folks just can't catch a break, can you?"

"Andrew's a civil engineer now. But obviously that doesn't stop them when they're running this scared," Tony explained.

"I guess they have to check him out. Did you see how far out those cops were capped? It had to be two clicks. That's easily within One Shot's wheelhouse; it's on record," Michelle said with respect.

"Maybe so. But these assholes knew where I was when the cops were shot; Tony too. I'm thinking they want us to do their work for them and rat out anyone we think could have made those shots—anyone black that is," Andrew said bitterly.

"You want us to run interference for you all? They'd never find you in the compound if we don't want them to," Lance suggested.

"That's a great offer, but I can't lay low here forever. Besides, I have nothing to hide. Let 'em come. Let's go inside so I can clean the weapon," Andrew suggested.

"No way. I got this," Lance said, reaching for the Windrunner.

Andrew blocked him from retrieving the weapon saying. "Thanks, Lance. But this is my deal. I shoot, I clean. But I have no problem with shooting the shit with you all while I work. This OpFor looks like a pretty slick operation. Why don't you all bring me up to speed?"

When they returned to the range lounge, Michelle and Andrew disassembled and did the light cleaning while the others, Eric, Matt and Luther (Andrew didn't remember their names until reminded) gave him an overview of the security and logistics company. They all hung around until two FBI agents stopped by to speak with Andrew and Tony. All of them wanted to listen in on the conversation, but when the agents realized that they were facing a hostile audience, they insisted on the four of them adjourning to the privacy of one of OpFor's conference rooms.

Chapter 14

"I'm Agent Barnes,; this is Agent Santos. Thank you for seeing us."

"Why didn't you just sit next to me on the flight down here? We could have had a great chat," Andrew said, recognizing Barnes. "I know, you were trying to see if I was going to meet a cadre of super niggas bent on taking over America, right?"

"Mr. Simmons, there's no reason to make this a hostile meeting," Santos said. "We're not here to accuse or harass. You know why we're here. We want to locate the person who killed five police officers in Los Angeles. That man apparently had the same set of skills as you in your previous job. It's a very special skill set, and we would have to be fools to discount your possible assistance in finding a sniper who can fire five kill shots from two kilometers away."

"Don't you mean a black sniper who could have fired those shots, Agent Santos?" Andrew said casually.

"We're not afraid to admit it, Mr. Simmons. Wouldn't you be doing the same thing were you in our shoes?" asked Barnes with a smile that didn't reach his eyes.

Andrew chuckled. "Fair enough. But why were you shadowing me? I was interviewed in New York just a short time ago."

"No cops had been shot from two clicks away back then," Barnes reminded.

"And the first person you all thought of was One—Andrew here?" Tony said.

"We know his nickname, Mr. Dawson. That's why we're here. And we really would like to find out if either of you have any idea who we might be looking for? We're looking at a pool of several hundred possibilities, and any assistance you could give us would be more than welcome and could save lives," Barnes replied.

"Yeah, yeah. Save lives, and all that bullshit," Tony said.

"It sounds like you have some sympathies with the killers—" Santos began.

"Don't, just don't," Tony said. "I'm CIA trained so let's not try to insult my intelligence,; you're really not that smart."

Santos was visibly pissed and started to say something when a gesture from Barnes cut him off.

"If you'll stop and think about it, gentlemen, it's a new world out there. I wonder if FBI agents who kill innocent black men will start to see their families have accidents too?" Tony said belligerently.

"You know, that's pretty fucked up for you to say," Santos said, getting a head of steam up.

"Whoa, whoa, there gents," Andrew said, holding his hands up. "Let's all take a moment and cool down. I really want to talk about this. Everyone cool?"

The others nodded and waited for Andrew to say his piece.

"Here's what's happening in this country today. Someone, who we all presume is black, is changing American culture. The killing of blacks by cops, for the time being, is over. What was supposed to be your job was coopted by someone else. You were supposed to rein in rogue cops, but you and the Justice Department just didn't give a shit enough to do your job protecting African Americans.

"Someone stole your march in spectacular fashion. No one black has overlooked the fact that there hasn't been anyone advocating for our protection and that whites are completely satisfied with their built-in privilege. You all like your privilege so much you never cared about anyone else until you started having to pay for murdering blacks.

"So here we sit. You looking for us to help you find the instrument of our liberation so you can most likely kill them," Andrew lectured calmly. Before anyone could interrupt, he continued. "Since you're here, you obviously have no idea where to look. You have no clue who you're looking for. And based on my own experience, the people you're looking for have been working together probably for a decade or so; and that's right under your noses. You're so sucking hind teat that a month's-long investigation hasn't gotten you anywhere. Now, tell me I'm wrong."

Neither agent spoke up. Neither did Tony.

"So, what we have here is a situation where no one can help you. You can't find anyone who's behind the killings. I dare say that there's an organization operating in America with better capabilities than the FBI, the NSA, and every other investigative arm of the government. You have the NSA, filtering their petabytes of recorded phone calls, emails and text messages looking for a clue, and nothing is there.

"This should demonstrate beyond a shadow of a doubt that all the stomping on this country's civil liberties in the name of security were worthless. All those doomsayers in the government who preached unlimited data collection, unfettered listening in on domestic telephone calls, and vacuuming up every single email that crossed the globe got you exactly NOTHING!" Andrew nearly shouted startling Tony.

Everyone remained silent, mulling over what Andrew had said.

"So, neither Tony or I have any information about the people you seek. We probably wouldn't have been considered in the first place given how easy it was for you to approach us. And yes, I could have made those shots, but I didn't. And no, I'm not going to help you find them because frankly, the ends has justified the means. Your organization's collective failures have brought us here; the Department of Justice's failures have brought us here, but note that whomever is behind this killing spree has done what you all failed to do. And frankly, I'm not too broken up about the status quo at this time. The FBI, et al, are completely outclassed in intelligence and operations. I suggest you cease wasting your time here and get on to where you actually have a chance of finding your betters."

Agent Barnes looked over at Santos, neither having anything to say. Then he stood and offered his hand to Andrew and then to Tony. He then said, "Gentlemen, thank you for your time. You have given us, me especially, some serious things to think about." He then offered his card to Andrew and said, "I completely understand how you feel, and frankly I've never thought about this investigation in the manner in which you described it. But if you do run across something you think I should know, I hope you call."

As they exited the conference room, Agent Santos just said, "Gentlemen," nodding his head toward each of them.

"Whew! Brother, you are something else," Tony exclaimed once the agents were gone.

"But was I wrong?"

"Absolutely not. I never could have laid it out like that. Hell, I never even thought about it like that. And for them to just walk off like that— you're something, you know that, Drew?"

"I don't know about all that. But I am hungry, and I need a drink. How about you?" Andrew asked.

"Good idea. I have something I want to talk to you about, anyway," Tony explained. "The gang wanted to take you out to dinner, so that's where we'll be tomorrow night."

"I'm going to grab a shower and get back into my duds."

"Just have someone show you to my office when you're ready."

Andrew showered, washing away the dust from the range and the flight down, then grabbed a fresh shirt out of his bag. Dressing quickly, he stopped someone outside the locker room and asked where he could find Tony. When he arrived at Tony's office, he and Michelle were chatting. When she saw Andrew, she immediately perked up and said, "We were going to treat you to dinner tonight, but Tony said he's got stuff to talk to you about. So we're going to reschedule for tomorrow and maybe you can tells us what was up with the FBI."

"That sounds great! I'm looking forward to it," he replied, smiling, and then was surprised to get an impulsive hug from her.

"See you tomorrow," she said, almost skipping out of the room.

Andrew looked at Tony, clearly wondering what was up.

"She's been looking forward to meeting you ever since I mention that I knew you. You have one hell of a reputation in the ranks, and my stock has actually increased around here because of my knowing you! Anyway, she worships you. She knows everything about you, your stats, everything. Whatever you do, just don't break her heart."

"Hey, I'm not going to bang her, for fuck sake," Andrew said, lowering his voice.

The relief on Tony's face was clear.

"You have a thing for her?" Andrew asked, wondering what was up.

"No, it's not that. She's like everyone's little sister here, and most times she's just as good as you on the range and on missions. . . well almost."

"Don't sweat it, man, it's cool."

"You know she's already bragging about how she lost to you on the range. She's going to ask you to sign your target, by the way. I'm sure she's going to frame it."

"I'd be happy to do it. I'll let her know tomorrow. NSo,o where are we going to eat?" asked Andrew.

"How about some good old Texas barbeque?"

"Sounds like a plan."

They took off in Tony's electric, heading into downtown San Antoine with the temperature still in the mid eighties. Andrew kept his eyes peeled, looking for any tails, but saw nothing. When they arrived at the restaurant, they dropped the car off with the valet and went inside, thankful for the air conditioning even though the smoke from the open pit grill filled the building.

Once they were seated, Andrew said, "Okay, you've been wanting to talk to me ever since you showed up in New York. This place is loud as hell, so give: what the hell is up?"

Tony's eyes slid around the room, checking for anyone displaying any interest in them, then bent his head toward Andrew to be heard easily.

"Two years ago, I think, I was contacted by those people. I was asked if I wanted to work on a confidential project that would last several years. I swear,; I think it's them."

"What else did they say?"

"Not much. As you can see, they play their cards pretty close to the vest. Hell, every cop, FBI agent, whatever is looking for those people and there's not a hide nor hair of them to be found," Tony said.

"They leave you any way to get in touch?" Andrew inquired.

"No."

"And no word since then?"

"Nothing. I was half hoping they might have contacted you, too."

"I haven't been approached by anyone like that. Maybe they thought I was too high profile for them. Judging by Michelle's reaction to me, I'm still pretty well known in certain circles. Plus, doing the engineering thing puts me in touch with too many folks on a monthly basis for me to just disappear.

"I have to imagine that no matter how many people are working on this, they have to have regular lives. So who are they? Are they people we know,; people we pass by on the sidewalk? Or are they some kind of underground organization, literally, that sends out their agents to set these families up for deadly accidents and monitor cops at demonstrations? Their capabilities scare the crap out of me, and yet they have my utmost respect for their planning and execution. I'd have a hard time telling anyone I was better than they are," Andrew said, shaking his head.

"That's what I'm talkin' about! When you were saying that shit about super niggas, I just about shit because that's exactly what they are," Tony said, almost whispering. "Sorry to say, I don't have a single problem with what they're doing, and that worries me."

"I get you. It kind of worries me too. What's the fallout going to be if they're caught? All the racist assholes in the entire country are going to be loaded for bear and gunning for any face darker than white," Andrew said, then sat up straight as their food was brought to the table.

The two began to eat. Andrew had ordered a slab of spareribs and the obligatory plastic bib, and Tony settled for a ribeye steak.

"Man, I haven't had anything like this in way too long."

"Been eatin' all that foo-foo New York food. A man needs some real meat, cooked over an open flame to remind him of his ancestral roots!" Tony said, laughing.

Andrew wiped sauce off his hand, grabbed his glass, and then drank down the rest of his beer. He then looked around for their waitress and held up his empty glass, getting a nod from her.

"So what if they do find the people behind all of this, and white folks go completely nuts, then what? I've made some arrangements,; maybe you should be thinking along the same lines too, One Shot," Tony said earnestly.

"Way ahead of you, son. I have two Windrunners with five hundred rounds. I have three different handguns,- all 9MM. I have two thousand rounds of ammo for those. And I have some special party favors squirreled away, too. So when the shit hits the fan, where do we meet?" Andrew asked, chuckling.

"The food's much better down here," suggested Tony.

"Yeah, but it's easier to get lost in the crowd in New York," Andrew countered.

"Brother, dark skin is dark skin. They'll find you no matter where you are in the Big Apple."

"But this is red neck central! Too many untrained white assholes with guns down here."

Tony laughed, "Okay, I have to give you that!"

"Seriously, though," Andrew said, lowering his voice, "you thinking that we're really in for it?"

"If whitey catches them? Hell yeah! Maybe not us specifically, but consider this: the man's never going to let the country get in this position again. You know what that means for guys with our training; we're most likely dead. And it's in our best interests to make sure, if we can at all, that they never get caught," Tony said soberly. "So, we're in it no matter what. That's what I wanted to tell you. And judging by our guest's conversation this afternoon, not a moment too soon."

"What about your people here? Would you trust them if you had to bug out?" Andrew asked.

Tony thought about it for a few moments. "Yeah, I think so—most of them at least."

"Better find out, just in case. Hey, are we really talking about this?" Andrew asked, almost in a whisper.

Tony looked around the room and just shrugged. "Better safe than sorry."

Their mood for the rest of the night was sober, with their conversation populated with the sickest jokes they both knew; gallows humor. When they'd finished dinner, Tony took them to the bar where many of the OpFor specialists hung out. And Andrew wasn't surprised to see Lance and Michelle sitting with a couple of guys he hadn't met yet.

When they arrived, and the OpFor folks saw them coming through the door, Tony and Andrew's mood climbed right out of the basement. Michelle, and the others, were quite happy to see Andrew, and their mood was infectious.

Andrew and Tony entertained, telling stories about operations they had been in. Tony explained that Andrew was not only a shooter, but a master of planning and logistics.

"And you're wasting your time in civil engineering? What's up with that?" Michelle asked.

Andrew paused a moment, trying to figure the best way to explain.

"You see, it's like this: it wasn't the targets that bothered me so much, it was the pointless machinations that our superiors were putting the entire military through. I started feeling like Sisyphus," said Andrew.

"Who?" Lance asked.

"The guy who kept rolling the boulder up a hill, right?" Michelle guessed.

"Exactly," Andrew said, pointing at her. "The body count kept getting higher, but we weren't making any real progress. I was a little too young for Afghanistan, but it was essentially the same thing in Yemen. You know how many times those cocksuckers tried to send me to Africa? Just because I'm black? Too God damn many!"

"Why didn't you go Tony's route? No offense, Andrew," Lance asked.

"None taken. It just wasn't the right fit for me. In the military, I was almost always in on the planning."

"He's right. More often than not, some analyst who's never been in the field did the mission profile, which we had to change once we were on the ground," Tony explained. "I once finished a mission, barely getting me and my spotter out safely, and when I got back, the analyst started to cuss me out for going off-mission. My spotter got in his face and threatened to tear his head off if he ever put either of us at risk while his ass was safe at home watching a ball game on his couch."

"Tony's a pure pro, otherwise the CIA never would have hired his black ass," Andrew said. "You guys are lucky to have him on board at OpFor."

"Stop, stop! You're making me blush. Go on, tell me more about how fabulous I am," Tony said to the laughs of the others.

"Say, are you guys allowed to discuss what the feds were looking for this afternoon?" Lance asked.

Andrew looked over to Tony, and saw from his slight nod it was all right. "They wanted to know if either of us had any idea who might have shot those cops in L.A."

"No shit? Why you—oh for fuck's sake, I know why," Lance miming a face-plant with his hand. "Just because you all were both trained, they just assumed you would know? That's fucked up!"

"One of those guys was on my flight out here, tailing me," Andrew explained.

"Is there something we should know, Tony?" Michelle asked quietly, as they all leaned in a little closer. "You two need some help?"

Tony took a pull from his beer and replied, "Not that we know of. But me and Drew did talk about it. Kind of thinking through the where-fors and what-nots. Trouble is, I can't drag One Shot here away from that fancy eatin' in New York."

The entire table laughed at Tony's sardonic tone. Soon the conversation turned back to the kinds of missions Andrew had planned and executed, with Andrew wanting to know what kind of support and training OpFor had them doing. It was easy to see that the snipers didn't have much respect for the assignments that were little more than them acting as mercenaries, guns for hire. But they all got excited when they talked about the new technologies they got to play with; artificial intelligence-based drones, the newer stealth helicopters that were nearly silent, and the cutting-edge reconnaissance satellite technologies.

Lance pulled out his smart phone, and did some fancy tapping on the screen, and then turned to it show the screen to Andrew. On the screen was what must have been the bar they were in, showing the traffic on the road and in the parking lot in real-time.

"Holy shit? They let you do that from your phone?" Andrew exclaimed.

"Not officially. But we use the tech for so many of our government contracts that they don't waste time anymore making and deleting our accounts every time. There's two parts to the app, one tracks the satellites in orbit, the other accesses the satellite's cameras. We can access the network nearly anywhere in the world," explained Lance.

The merry band closed the bar, and discretion being the better part of safety, Tony made sure he could leave the car in the parking lot until morning. They took Andrew's bags from the trunk and then grabbed a cab back to Tony's place.

Chapter 15

After a momentary respite from officers' family's dying, a new rash of accidents began, most nonfatal. It took nearly a day for the task force to figure out what they all had in common. It turned out that all the family members were of officers who had lied in court testimony resulting in innocent black men being imprisoned.

The first thing that crossed SAIC Willis' mind was that the people behind these accidents had the research abilities of the KGB. Even though the pattern was known, it was still very difficult to find all the families at risk across the country. Too many white police officers had lied in the last generation for the FBI to have compiled any substantive database of who might be at risk.

But once Agent Willis assigned the data collection task to the Justice Department, it blew his mind how many known cases of lying testimony by police were on record. What was troubling was that the cops whose families were suffering mishap were hard to ferret out until mishap occurred. What was readily apparent was that there was an epidemic of police officers everywhere who had not given truthful testimony.

At first, everyone on the task force wanted to discount the accuracy of the nefarious group behind what was being called street justice by conservative media. But as the cases were examined by the task force, in each instance, once the impartial eyes of the Justice Department dug into the investigation, the evidence and the testimony, is wasn't difficult at all to determine that the cases stunk. To compound the indelicate fact that there were a whole lot of dirty white cops across the country, municipalities were being sued by wrongfully imprisoned inmates, family members and local chapters of the American Civil Liberties Union. And still the Fraternal Orders were doing their level best protecting all those dirty cops, even when incontrovertible proof was exposed.

The backlash police departments across the country had focused on them was getting harder and harder to discount by law and order hardliners. The need for imposing accountability on cops who, through the years, counted on white privilege to shield them from their illegal, corrupt, and negligent behavior that the rest of America, white America, turned a blind eye toward was now impossible to ignore.

MYRON MacHUTCHENS

People were beginning to discount the notion the FBI Task Force continued to champion, that of bringing the perpetrators to justice. There were enough leaks from the task force so that everyone generally knew they still had no leads. And now those killed, maimed, or injured because of the actions of their police officer spouses were beginning to be considered by more than a few as necessary collateral damage in the service of bring justice to an entire race after four centuries.

The very action of taking revenge for past transgressions against African Americans by law enforcement and America's legal and penal systems was graphically illustrating exactly how black men didn't stand a chance of receiving justice in America. Jurisdictions, both large and small, were guilty of the wholesale denial of civil rights to blacks. The majority of whites in the United States still felt the centuries-old tradition of white privilege was simply fiction. But that was starting to change.

One of the common discussions occurring across the nation was the question of what exactly is justice?

Judge Alvin Bridges was the go-to guest on the subject of black justice across the cable news and talk channels. The most common subject was: what was the United States of America going to look like down the road? Was the threat of familial death actually compelling white police officers to stop the wholesale violation of the civil rights of the nation's African American population? Was American culture going to actually see the end of institutional racism, Judge Bridges was asked.

"In a word, no," answered Bridges. "We may well see a halt to the senseless death of blacks, but the impetus of the change is over the barrel of a gun, so-to-speak. Compelling bigoted and racist whites to behave in a certain way is not going to change their fundamental nature. The fear of reprisal is no substitute for self-determination in personal development. Given the nature of whites since the first black foot set on the sands of the east coast, and their history in the preceding centuries throughout Europe, what has really been accomplished here? What change has really occurred? I would hazard to say that nothing has changed.

"Someone has beaten certain kinds of racist acts into momentary submission, but the historical dictates of white privilege in this country will not have whites denied anything. So, it will be interesting how this country changes, if at all. Some of my colleagues on the bench anticipate wholesale resignations of white police officers across the country because they can no longer bully or shoot nonwhites without consequence. Some will resign to avoid an accidental shooting, or one where it was necessary to actually save lives. But why take a chance on one's family being done harm over a trigger-happy mistake?

NO JUSTICE, NO PEACE

"So, when you ask me what do I think this country will look like in the near term, or many years down the road? I truly don't know. There are a lot of questions going begging for answers. Can this change be sustainable? What will happen if the people behind these killings are identified and caught? Will there be an immediate backlash against African Americans? If so, what form will it take?

"This is what America's blacks are wondering: what punishment is going to meted out on them because someone had the nerve to call out the centuries-old murderous tradition of white privilege. In just a few years, in the 2040s, whites are going to become a minority in the United States. Not that they will immediately be pushed out of positions of authority and privilege, but the tide will begin to turn."

That clip, when posted to the Internet, garnered over two million views on its first day. Judge Bridges differed over other black leaders of the day in his absolute refusal to pander. Even while serving on the Appeals Court, he was considered a straight shooter by attorneys no matter their race.

There were those who were advocating a Truth and Reconciliation Commission like South Africa instituted upon the abolition of apartheid. However, no white person in government, business, or the clergy would sign onto the idea for fear of being called a race traitor. The majority of whites in the US still refused to acknowledge or believe that white privilege had anything to do with the treatment nonwhites experienced in their lives on a daily basis.

-=#=-

The FBI had all the black graduates from all branches of the military's sniper schools under close surveillance, hoping that they would discover any of them in some sort of compromising activity. The current internal argument was whether or not to let one of them actually commit murder or to reveal their hand ahead of time and pick them up before they had a chance of committing any crime.

This part of the task force operation was top secret, with the information confined to the president, his chief of staff, and Agent Jefferson posted to the White House. The matter was not discussed at the normal afternoon national security briefing. Each agency in the task force was in an off-the-record race to be the one to break this case open. The Family Matters Task Force daily media briefing was terse and devoid of any substantive details. The explanation was to keep those being sought from gleaning any information that would aid them in avoiding discovery and capture.

-=#=

Devon Compton was cruising his favorite online auction site, known to millions of savvy online shoppers. The site had two different areas, the auction part followed the same online model of countless other sites since the 1990s when the World Wide Web saw its initial explosive growth. The second part of the site was more of an online swap shop where people offered up their unwanted items, looking for a match with someone who had what they might be willing to part with making a no-cash trade.

Today he was scanning the book section of the swap shop, seeing what he could find. As he went down the list, an unusual item caught his eye. Someone was offering up an autographed first edition of AfroFuturism: The World of Black Sci-Fi and Fantasy Culture.

He clicked on the item and looked at the description. Having not read the book, what caught his eye was the online ID of the trader, Vitamin B12. He clicked on the "More Information" button and read the description. Satisfied he'd remember what he needed, he left the site.

He then logged onto the dispatch site where he got short and long-haul assignments to bid on for his independent trucking business. He owned two medium-sized hybrid haulers with four times the battery storage than most comparable haulers. That made the longer trips more profitable than usual. His other driver, Matt Mason, who Devon had all kinds of good natured fun teasing him about having the same name as a 1960s action figure, also had the extended battery capacity. His rig had a slightly larger cab because he often traveled with his girlfriend on some of the longer trips. She had some kind of online business as a short story author and could work on the road. He scanned through the loads looking for transport, remembering the cities for pickup and delivery. He logged off hoping he'd catch a long distance haul. Devon liked the quiet, the travel and if he were to be entirely honest, he didn't mind the solitude at all.

Devon checked the time and decided to take a ride down to the Minneapolis Central Library. Taking public transportation, leaving the driving up to someone else, was no problem for him. Devon was a people watcher.

When he got to the library, he checked one of the terminals to find the book he was looking for. He went to the Fiction section and then located his section of interest, following the Dewey Decimal numbers until he found what he was looking for: a copy of AfroFuturism. He reached under the metal shelf below the book. Out of sight, behind the lip of the shelf was an object taped to the underside beneath the book.

Devon carefully peeled the object and the tape from under the shelf and pocketed both in his pocket. He browsed down along the shelves, picking up several books along the way, then replacing them where he found them. He then went downstairs to the periodicals department and looked through several newspapers from New York, Los Angeles, and Chicago for over an hour. He then left, took public transportation near his home stopping off to pick up some groceries.

Once home, he quickly put the groceries away. He went into the second bedroom he used as his home office. Sitting down at the desk, he manually turned off the Wi-Fi transceiver switch on his laptop, unplugged his broadband router from the outlet strip, and then powered up the computer. Once it was booted, Devon removed the object from his pocket, carefully peeled the tape off what was crystal memory card.

He inserted the card into the laptop's slot and clicked it home. Seconds later, he ran a program that wasn't listed anywhere on the various menus that decrypted the card after he put in a full sentence for the password. Once decrypted, the directory of the card popped up on the screen. Devon started reading through the listed files, taking no notes, or saving any of the files to his laptop. He read all the information on the card, looking carefully at all of the images stored, as well. He read through several suggested scenarios at the end of the files.

After he was confident he remembered the relevant details, he closed all the files and ejected the memory card and restarted the laptop. He then plugged his router back in and reconnected his Wi-Fi to the network. He returned to the online swap shop and saw he had an answer to his query. When he clicked on the message, he was presented with a picture of the cover and the inner page where author Ytasha Womack had autographed the book.

He replied that he was interested but wanted to know what the owner was interested in receiving in return. But his answer to the query was "yes."

When he logged off, he returned to the long-haul dispatch board looking for any runs to Kansas City. Finding two, one originating from Milwaukee and one in Chicago, he entered a couple of low-ball bids for each consignment, hoping to win both. In moments, he had one bid accepted. He decided to make something to eat, hoping his bid for the second run would come through shortly.

Devon brought his sandwich and a cup of coffee to the study to await an answer on the second load. Fortunately, forty-five minutes later his bid was accepted. He logged into his tablet, downloaded the information to his trucking app, and sent an acknowledgment that he'd pick up both loads first thing in the morning.

He decided that he would pack up and set off for Milwaukee and stay the night there, pick up the load, then head to Chicago to get the other. He sent a message to his partner, letting him know his itinerary, and then packed a bag, and took a ride out to the garage where he stored both trucks when they were idle or needed service. He owned the two story garage with space on the ground floor for three trucks with the second floor outfitted as combined office space and a small apartment for emergencies.

When he arrived, he performed his normal mechanical check of the truck, topping off the synthetic fuel tank and checking the charge of the batteries fed from the bank of solar cells on the roof. He tossed his bag into the truck on the bunk in the back of the cab. He then got a power screwdriver from the toolbox climbing into the back and unscrewing the steel floor panel.

He lifted the heavy plate, removed several items from the secret compartment, and took them to a hidden closet in the garage. He then grabbed several items from the hidden closet and stowed them in the truck's compartment. He secured the heavy floor plate and the closet in the garage, then drove the truck out onto the street, waiting until the garage door fully closed before setting off for Milwaukee, daylight still in the sky.

Devon hit the road with clear weather ahead, and while he drove, no automatic pilot for his trucks, he listened to Sixties R&B he had loaded into his truck's digital music system. He had a library of ten thousand songs from which to choose so he was kept well entertained on the road.

He arrived in Milwaukee without incident and booked a room a few blocks from the depot. He then went to a local Mexican restaurant and had a great meal. He checked out the news on his tablet while he ate, seeing that nothing had changed around the country. The media outlets were desperately trying to find some kind of new spin on the death spree,; something to draw eyes to their particular coverage. In the most extreme cases, talking heads were obsessed with reporting the most outrageous theories with the more extreme pundits advocating locking up African Americans as they did Japanese Americans during World War II. The hysteria on the cable channels was becoming a bit much Devon thought as he switched between several of the online sites.

When he returned to his room, Devon logged onto the hotel's public broadband and checked the online swap site to see if there were any additional messages from the book owner and found nothing. Knowing he had a fairly long day tomorrow, Devon decided to bag it and hit the sack early.

The next day, both of Devon's pickups went smoothly. And despite the fact that he'd probably only make a hundred dollars' profit from either of the deliveries, his mood was good. Once he left Chicago, Devon had about an eight-hour drive ahead of him. He was scheduled to arrive close to sundown, which suited him fine.

Once he arrived and dropped off both loads, he checked into a hotel near the industrial part of town. He ate a fairly light meal and waited.

At midnight he pulled on a pair of black pants, black t-shirt, and a black jacket over the shirt. He went down to the truck, quietly unscrewed the floor plate of the living area, and took out several items placing them in the various pockets of the jacket. He then closed the secret compartment, locked the truck, and set off walking.

An hour later, he was standing outside of the Kilborn Extended Care Facility. He caught a break with an all-night hotdog stand. There were several outdoor tables scattered around the open counter in front right across the street from the facility.

Devon crossed the street and bought a polish, onion rings, and a drink then sat at a table allowing him to see the front entrance and the side of the building along an alley, serving as an access drive to a parking structure serving the facility.

He ate slowly watching as several employees entered and exited through a service door down the alley. Once he finished his food, Devon started a leisurely walk around the neighborhood, figuring the traffic in and out of the building would slow as it got later.

At 2:00 A.M., Devon quickly picked the alley door's lock and got into the building. Once inside, he immediately went to the basement and found the maintenance personnel locker room. He quickly shed his pants and jacket. Luckily, he found a desk with several ID tags in the top drawer and selected one that looked somewhat like him. When he was ready, he found a stairwell and made his way to the third floor. Cracking open the stairwell door, he saw that the corridor lights were dimmed for the night, and there was no one in sight. He exited the stairwell carrying a bag filled with dirty laundry, with gloves on. Moving quickly, he found room 314, and seeing the lights were out he slipped into the room pulling the door shut behind him.

Devon let his eyes adjust to the dimly lit room, the only illumination coming through the window. He saw that the patient in the bed, Sybil Francis, was unconscious with several intravenous bags hanging at the head of the bed. He approached and saw that the bag containing the sodium and glucose solution was close to being emptied. He pulled a vial and syringe from his pocket and filled the syringe from the vial. He then inserted the needle into the rubber of the shunt in the IV line and emptied the solution into the line.

Once he was done, Devon quickly moved to the door and opened it a crack to look both ways up and down the corridor. Seeing no one about he dashed to the stairwell and ran down to the basement and quickly changed back into his own clothes. Replacing the uniform and the badge, he then slipped out of the building and began the walk back to the hotel.

When he arrived at the hotel, he got back to his room without anyone seeing him. During the walk back he had disposed of the syringe in one sewer, and about half a mile away, he crushed the vial and scraped the glass into another sewer with a newspaper he found to keep the fragments of the vial off his feet.

What he had injected into the IV line was formulation of potassium and chlorine that forced Ms. Francis' heart into a deadly arrhythmia but was broken down quickly enough that the chances of detection during an autopsy would be quite unlikely and nearly impossible. What Devon didn't know was that the compound worked so well that before he was two blocks away from the facility, Ms. Francis was dead.

Sybil Francis was the mother of a twenty-year veteran of the Kansas City Police Department, Art Francis. Officer Francis, in the course of chasing down a black teenage shoplifting suspect, had followed the teen into an apartment building and up to the second floor. He charged out of the stairwell, weapon out and saw a movement out of the corner of his eye. He turned and fired before it registered that the movement was a ten-year-old girl taking trash to the floor's garbage chute.

He fired four shots, hitting her with three, instantly killing her. In the inquest after the shooting, Officer Francis admitted that he hadn't seen her clearly, and that as he entered the apartment building, he was fearful that he could be shot at any moment. He had failed to collar the suspect he was chasing and once reinforcements arrived minutes later, the police kept anyone from entering or exiting the building as they went apartment by apartment, searching for any teen who matched the description of the suspect. No one was found.

The department cleared Officer Francis of failing to follow procedure, and though the department apologized to the girl's family, there was nothing that could compensate for the family's loss.

Devon powered up his tablet, connected to the Internet and returned to the swap meet site. Once there, he clicked on the book entry, made his apologies, and informed the owner that he was no longer interested in the book. He then logged onto the shipping site and looked for any loads nearby that would help increase the profit for the low-ball trip to Kansas City.

Chapter 16

"We're going about this all wrong," SAIC Willis announced at the beginning of the weekly all-agency status meeting. The room was silent as they waited for him to continue.

"We're looking for some super-secret organization like the CIA or the FBI. What if who we're looking for are single citizens who are carrying out all these murders, but aren't coordinated as a huge organization or army? Yes, there had to be a massive recruitment drive in the beginning, and it had to have taken years to pull off, but what if only a handful of people know everyone who has participated in this campaign?" Willis asked the room.

"But that's still got to be hundreds of people. How do you command and control that many people with just a handful?" Sam Dobson from the NSA asked.

"That's the sixty-four-thousand-dollar question, isn't it? We're so accustomed to hierarchical command and control organizational structures that even now, none of us can imagine this kind of massive operation being anything but," Willis pointed out. "We saw how the French resistance broke their organization into cells that prevented the NAZI's from catching one and as a result, grabbing the entire organization. The people we're looking for could be like the resistance, but they could be something entirely different. The proof to me is that with all of our departments having been on overtime for weeks now, we have exactly nothing. That's just not possible."

Sharon asked, "If this is true, how do we find the head so we can stop this?"

"She's right. We have the best minds in the country in law enforcement and anti-insurgency right here in this room," Willis said. He looked at the representative from the CIA and said, "You guys have the most experience in this arena. Isn't this like getting Bin Laden?"

The analyst from the CIA sat up in his chair, being singled out. "In a way. We don't know who any of these people are. We have no idea where they are. We have no idea how they communicate. And it's looking more and more like we're going to have to find someone in the top tier of the organization to get to the people responsible."

Dobson chimed in with, "We have absolutely nothing. No calls, no email, no text messages to even suggest someone is involved with these people. It's more difficult now because so many Americans are jawin' about the killings. But we've been combing everything for the last ten years, and so far there's nothing. And, we've found nothing to suggest we're ever going to find anything. And believe me, almost the entire NSA is on this case. Our enemies around the world are not looking to doing anything that suggests they're in cahoots with the people here."

"So how do we reconfigure to get results?" Sharon asked.

"That's the question. Anyone have any ideas?" Willis asked the room.

"I do," said Attorney General, Simon Thatcher. "It's an idea, not a great idea, as a matter of fact, it's a heinous idea," he said and paused.

When he couldn't stand the silence for another second, Willis banged on the table and said, "What!"

Thatcher said quietly, "We arrange for a cop to kill someone."

The room was silent. It was silent for going on a minute. No one spoke.

Finally, Sharon asked the question on everyone's mind, "Who the hell is going to authorize something like that?"

"That is the question. And if some kind of operation like this was ever approved, no one outside this room can ever know; except of course the operatives involved," Thatcher said. "And the local PD would have to bring us in to run the investigation while we make damn sure the victim's family was covered wall-to-wall."

"You're serious? That we kill someone to try to catch these people? That's the worst example of the ends justifying the means I've ever heard. It's sick is what it is. In short, it's murder," Sharon objected.

"What if we faked the whole thing?" asked one of FBI analysts.

"That's essentially what I was suggesting. Maybe more along the lines of a sting, not actually killing someone. Although if a single life can bring further deaths to an end, that's a value proposition I'm willing to argue at this point," Thatcher said.

"That's somewhat barbaric, isn't it?" Sharon asked.

"No it's not. We make sacrifices all the time," Thatcher simply said. "I would like to formally request that you look into the logistics of planning and executing such an operation," he requested of Willis. "Both options."

"I'll assign someone to it right away. If anyone else wants in, let me know. This group is off-limits to everyone but the Attorney General and myself. Sharon, let POTUS know what was discussed, but please don't write anything down or post it to the network. For damn sure, this is on a need to know basis, and no one needs to know. Understood?" Willis said, meeting the eyes of each person in the room.

As everyone rose to get on with their duties, Willis asked Sharon to stay behind.

Once everyone had left, Willis gestured to the seat next to him.

"How do you think the president is going to take this?" he asked straight away.

"He's never going to formally give the go ahead to kill someone, especially someone innocent of any crime. The whole trigger for these killings were the murders of innocent blacks in the first place. How are you going to choose the sacrificial lamb?" she asked.

"I have no idea. I don't want anyone to die in the service of catching the people who started this killing spree. But I don't know any other way to pull it off. If we fake the death of someone, what do we tell the family of the victim? Can we pull off a fake killing and keep it under wraps? Can we trust our own people?" Willis asked, more to himself than Sharon.

"Sheldon, this is uncharted territory for the FBI. Yes, we've embedded people where they could die if their covers were blown. But this puts some cop's family at risk if the world out there believes a cop has killed another innocent black person," she said, shaking her head.

"Yes, that's the risk. We can't very well replace the cop's wife with an agent if she's to maintain her daily routine. And we for damn sure can't install a couple of FBI midgets in the family as his kids. But maybe, just maybe we can wire up a cop's home, bring him in on the sting, and then fake a killing, an investigation, and hope for the best."

"Hope for the best?" she hissed. "This idea is madness. I'm not bringing this to POTUS."

"So far there's nothing to bring him," Willis said shaking his finger. "Right now it's just exploratory, nothing's been planned. But I would like you to think about it, strictly from a logistics perspective," he requested.

Sharon thought about it. There wouldn't be any harm in keeping an eye on the planning, she might spot something the others might miss. "Fine, but nothing to the president until, if and when, a plan is produced. And no going over my head," she warned.

"I've learned my lesson," Willis said with a laugh. "I'll let you know who I'm having head up the op plan."

Sharon left, returning to the White House. She updated the network files, omitting everything said by the Attorney General and SAIC Willis about the possible sting. It was clearly a measure of desperation that was pushing the task force to even consider such a plan. From the fatigue in Willis' voice, to the abysmal online status reports from every department in the task force, Sharon was fairly certain that it was going to take a miracle for them to find the person or persons pulling the strings.

-=#=

Andrew and his team were finishing up the final plans for San Francisco's proposed desalination complex when he got a text message from Tony that said, "Ck yr 6."

When he was done for the day and drove out of the building's parking garage, Andrew began keeping an eye on his rear view mirror figuring that if they hadn't put a tracker on his car, there would at least be one car on him.

When he thought he had spotted a government sedan trailing him, Andrew's first thought was to try to lose them in traffic. But then he realized that to do so would only cause suspicion. He watched with mild bemusement as the sedan ended up following him to within a block of home.

Once he cleaned up and was relaxing with a drink, he considered texting a thank you to Tony. But he knew that anything he sent would be recorded as would any call he made.

Andrew laughed out loud, assuming his condo was wired for sound as well, as he realized that the whole idea of watching him for what would never come was a pointless game of cat and mouse. The government knew, if they were paying attention, that Tony had alerted him to the probable surveillance. He knew that there was nothing for them to find tailing him round the clock. But that was just going to make them more determined to find what wasn't there. Eventually, there was going to be some kind of a confrontation, especially if their efforts were constantly frustrated by a lack of results. He'd been on enough missions where what was expected was never there. When he returned to base, the analysts always insisted that somehow he screwed up and dropped the ball. Andrew couldn't recall a single instance where military intelligence analysts admitted that their intel or planning was faulty.

Andrew was no fool. He knew with a certainty that the FBI now had him under surveillance, and that there was nothing to be done about it. He was just going to have to endure.

He pulled out his mobile and called Tony.

"Hey brotha, thanks for the warning," he began.

Tony laughed and replied, "Just doin' a buddy a solid."

"You know they're listening in on this call,"

"Of course," Tony said evenly. "Given that about five thousand people have been wasted, the fact that they're wasting time on the two of us and anyone else black out of sniper school, is either stupid, or desperate. Either way, they're not going to get what they're looking for."

"What's that?" Andrew asked, wanting those listening in to hear the answer.

"A lead on who killed all those white folks. The people who are exacting revenge for the FBI's having let white cops kill innocent black folks since the organization came into existence. Fucking stupid white people," Tony said with contempt. "I will say this: if I ever find out who's behind these killings, I'll be damned if they ever get it out of me."

"Dude, don't beat around the bush, tell them how you really feel!" Andrew said, laughing.

"Yeah, well you know. I never was the blabby type," Tony replied, also laughing.

"Anyway, I just wanted to call and thank you for the heads-up."

"No problem, Drew. Just wanted everyone on the same page. Stay frosty. It should be a whole lot easier with the feds watching your six"

"Ain't that the truth," Andrew replied as Tony ended the call.

Andrew started preparing a light dinner, thinking through what round the clock surveillance meant to his life. There wasn't anything he could do about it, nor could he see where it would interfere at all with his work. The following week, he was scheduled to take his team back to San Francisco, and unless any tails were noticed by the two engineers accompanying him, there wasn't anything to be done about it.

His new circumstance, being followed, made him pay a little closer attention to the evening's news, but there was nothing new being reported. Although he was surprised when two different talking heads on two different cable channels mentioned "isolating" the country's African Americans from the general population until the matter could be resolved and those responsible were brought to justice.

Andrew chuckled at the thought of the government planning and executing the logistics the country would face in the internment of fifteen percent of its population. It was interesting how the notion was always mentioned in the case of a nonwhite segment of the country's population. It wouldn't be but a blink of an eye, just a decade until the 2040s, when Latinos overtook whites as the racial majority in the United States.

Andrew decided to drag whomever was tailing him out to the range in White Plains on Saturday just for grins. Maybe if they had the balls to pull into the lot, he would invite them into the range.

The one thing he decided he was going try to avoid was invite scrutiny of his friends. Currently, he wasn't dating anyone exclusively. But the woman he considered more than just a close friend, Bridget Wills, didn't deserve to have her life invaded, but they were bound to find out about her sooner or later if their research hadn't uncovered the relationship already. On the spur of the moment, he called her up to invite her out for drinks, maybe even dinner.

She was pleasantly surprised to hear from him in the middle of the week and accepted the invitation. They decided that Andrew would pick her up, and they'd drop by their favorite jazz club.

When Andrew pulled out of the garage, he was surprised that there were no government sedans parked on either side of the street. As he drove toward Bridget's apartment, he didn't see anyone behind him the whole way there. Once he pulled up to the front of her building, he saw that she was waiting just outside the door. The doorman opened the passenger door and Bridget got in, giving Andrew a kiss before strapping herself in.

"Hey, stranger. I've been missing you. How's California treating you?" she asked as he began to pull away from the building.

"Frisco's fine. The project looks like it's going to be green-lighted. I'm heading back in a few days to see if we can get the work's department to sign off on the plans," he said, glancing at the mirror. There it was, the same gray sedan from earlier.

"I have something to tell you before we get much further into the evening," he began.

"Well that sounds pretty ominous. Something wrong with us?" she asked, concerned.

"Calm down. Not directly," he said, chuckling. "I'm being tailed wherever I go these days."

"And that would be why?" she asked clearly not mollified.

"Because of my training in the service, and those cops shot out in Los Angeles."

"They don't think that was you, do they? You must have an alibi, don't you?" she asked.

"No, they don't think it was me, I wasn't anywhere near L.A. But I think the feds are covering any black face with that kind of training. They're covering my buddy in Texas as well. I think the FBI, or anyone else in the government's law enforcement community, is doing everything they can think of to try to find who killed all those cop families and the cops. And they are proceeding assuming that the person who sniped those cops is with the same people offing cop families," he explained.

"So then they've got nothing, right? Not with you all, but in the whole investigation. If they're barking up the wrong tree like this, then they obviously can't be chasin' the right dog," Bridget said chuckling.

"That's 'bout it. I wanted you to know just in case you look around one day and see the same people or vehicles too many times," Andrew said, as he placed his hand over hers and squeezed. "I have an idea. What are you doing Saturday?"

"Was thinking about going shopping. Why? What are you thinking?" she asked, excited.

"Want to go and fire off a box or two at the range?"

"Hell, yeah. Can we get there kind of early in the morning, then I can still get my shopping done after lunch—you are taking me to lunch, right?" she teased.

"How about the Crab Shack on the way back?"

"Perfect. I'll clean both pistols Friday night and be ready to be picked up by about 7:30 Saturday. I'll pick up bagels and coffee," she offered.

"Deal!"

Chapter 17

Pastor Augustus King was looking forward to the day's sermon. His was the largest Baptist congregation in Washington, D.C. which happened to be quite ethnically mixed. The Third Baptist Church had a good percentage of those not born in the United States among the congregation as well.

This Sunday, he was going to take advantage of the coverage of the vigilante actions of those who killed the families of police officers in his sermon.

King was the son of a tobacco farmer and an elementary school teacher mother. His father's brother was the pastor of the Southern Baptist Convention in Kentucky's Jefferson County. Because his Uncle Stephen, the pastor, had never married, Augustus was often called upon to help him around the church. Their time together gave Augustus an education in ministering to a community and an appreciation for the role of religion within a community.

It was not so much an awakening, it was a revelation about how the church and its pastor provided both lubrication and glue between members of a community. The head of the flock presided over all manner of transitions, celebrating the bringing of new life into the community, counseling the community and bringing it together when a life ended. Augustus soon found himself attending divinity school not so much for the spirituality, but because of the role he wanted to play for a congregation, for an extended family.

His road to Washington, D.C. hadn't been very arduous, and after having been there for seven years, he inherited the position of Pastor when his predecessor passed away from a heart attack.

The title of this Sunday's sermon was, "Vengeance is Mine, Sayeth The Lord." and Pastor King was on a roll. He delivered on a litany of characters from the Old and New Testament who had done others dirt in the name of the Lord, or had killed at the Lord's behest.

When he concluded the service he received a standing ovation from the congregation and a rousing chorus of "Amens."

Sharon and Felicia often attended church when they had a Sunday free together and were known by name by Pastor King.

"Pretty rousing sermon, Pastor," said Felicia as they shook hands outside the church.

"Thank you, my dear. How have the two of you been?" he asked the couple.

"Always busy, Pastor. But the work's fine. Thank you for asking," Felicia replied.

"Busy, but well," Sharon replied. "You can imagine how things are at work."

"Still at the White House, my dear?" King asked.

"I am. It's been a real eye-opening experience seeing behind the scenes how the country is run. There's never a dull moment," she said as she shook Pastor King's hand.

"Keep up the good work, both of you. The two of you set a great example for our young girls to see regular, everyday black women in good jobs with responsibilities. I pray for you two every night. Have a blessed week ahead, ladies," he said as he turned to the next person making their way out of the church.

"He was pretty wound up about something today, don't you think?" Felicia asked as they pulled out of the church parking lot.

"I don't know. What makes you think that?" Sharon asked.

"First of all, he was all over the Old Testament, all fire and brimstone. And his theme seemed to center around vengeance and retribution. He actually said an eye for an eye!" Felicia exclaimed as she negotiated the Sunday traffic.

"And so?"

"What if he meant this stuff you're investigating? That all those families being killed is justification for all the black folks killed over these hundreds of years?"

"Okay, first of all, I don't condone killing in any form. But I recognize that in some cases it's justified, like in war or to save lives," Sharon replied. "But Pastor King is a man of God, a good man. I highly doubt that he was advocating the killing of whites in retaliation for millions of blacks murdered. But just between you and me, if the net result of these white families dying is that no more innocent blacks are killed by cops, it's hard for me to completely condemn the deaths."

"Oh my God! Do you know what you're saying?" Felicia asked, stunned.

"Of course I do! If we decide to go ahead and have children, what if we have a boy? You know as well as I do that he would have a twenty-times higher chance of being killed by a cop than a white boy. How do you feel about that? If these dead white families can ensure our boy is never killed by a rogue cop, how can anyone, me, you, anyone see the result as a negative?" Sharon asked.

"But all that killing, that's—that's barbaric."

"Felicia, I'd kill ten thousand people if it would save the life of my child," Sharon said quietly.

For the rest of the ride to brunch with several of their friends, a weekly ritual they both enjoyed, they were silent. They didn't discuss their conversation in the car at brunch, or once they returned home. Both knew they weren't going to convince the other to change their perspective. It was one of the main reasons they were attracted to each other. They were both principled in their beliefs and not easily swayed by mere emotion, but they were able to respect the views and beliefs of other.

-=#=-

Compton Trucking was turning a tidy profit for the year, despite Devon's occasional side trips. He was very careful, as he imagined anyone in a secret organization carrying out missions to kill would have to be. He had no idea how many were in the organization. He had no idea who else was in the organization. He wouldn't even know there was an organization at all except for the fact that he knew he hadn't arranged for even a fraction of people who had died.

While he was deadheading back to Minneapolis from Texas, not having found any loads going in the right direction for him to make it work financially, Devon let his mind wander back to how he had been recruited. There were still times when he couldn't believe what he had gotten himself involved in.

Devon was a former medic in the US Army with two tours in Afghanistan. When he returned, he wanted nothing more to do with putting people back together, knowing that despite his best efforts they would never really be whole again. For a while, he pulled an odd job or two, driving a cab, even driving for a package delivery company through the holidays for several years, but he was tired of taking orders from anyone, especially civilians.

So with the aid of a government loan, Devon bought a single hybrid truck then begged, borrowed, and practically stole to equip it with four times the standard battery storage. He also covered the cargo box with electric solar cells to keep the batteries charged during daylight hours. And with the newer blends of fuel, Devon's specially modified trucks could get well over one hundred miles to the gallon fully loaded.

He had always been a tinkerer as a teen. Devon had built his own model helicopter from scratch along with computers and any number of cool gadgets. The military, and his training as a medic, was a means to an end for him, ensuring a college education and possibly putting him through medical school.

He'd been an independent trucker for three years when he was contacted by someone claiming to want to offer him a job. Normally, email messages like that he just deleted out of hand, but this one contained information about his time in the service that convinced him there might be something serious to the offer. He knew that anyone could dig up details about his life, nothing was hidden anymore with so many data mining companies collecting, trading and buying consumer information from a nearly infinite number of sources, but he figured what the heck. He hit reply and said essentially, lay it on me, then waited for the offer.

One day later, a package arrived at Devon's office. When he opened the box, there was a cheap, prepaid mobile phone inside with no numbers in the contact list. Very curious, he powered the phone up and waited.

Ten minutes later the phone rang. Devon answered and was greeted by a smooth male voice, obviously belonging to an urbane, black man.

"Mr. Compton, I'm contacting you to offer you an opportunity to make some significant changes to this nation's behavior toward black people, as well as some extra money; cash money. Please don't hang up, I assure you that not only am I serious, but based on what I know about you, this offer just might appeal to you," the voice said.

"Get the fuck out of here! Who is this really?"

"We have never met, Mr. Compton. The reason I'm contacting you is to have a discussion to determine if you and I are a good fit, just like any job interview."

"What if I don't want a job?" Devon replied.

"Did you not answer the email message I sent? Are you in the habit of leading people on?" asked the voice.

"No, I'm not. Your message contained very specific information about me, leading me to believe that it was from someone who knew a good deal about me or knew me personally. That's why I replied. So, what kind of job are you offering?" Devon asked, on the verge of believing the whole affair was going to be a complete waste of time.

"Okay, let me be direct. I want to know if you're interested in stopping, once and for all, police officer killings of innocent blacks?"

Devon was stunned. This was so unexpected, so out of the blue that all he could say was, "What?"

"I said, are you interested in stopping the murder of innocent blacks by white cops once and for all? That's the job I want you to seriously consider taking. The job is not without risk. It requires a level of confidentiality that is absolute. It also requires the ability to take lives in order to reverse a centuries old tradition in this country. Now, I know that's a lot to absorb, but if you have any questions, I'm prepared to answer them without reservation, Mr. Compton."

Devon hesitated, trying to get his thoughts in order, then answered, "My first instinct is to ask a boat load of questions about how you know me, but that's clearly a waste of our time. You sent a prepaid phone making my, or anyone else's, trying to trace you also a waste of time.

"So let's assume you're serious, and you have a way to stop the killing of innocent black folks by cops. You also mentioned that it will take killing to accomplish the task. Are we talking killing cops?" Devon asked.

"No, I'm not. But to accomplish what I'm aiming to do will require a strong stomach and the ability to keep one's eyes firmly on the end result. And please, no clichés about the ends justifying the means. The fact is there is only one way to stop the killing of blacks and that is to kill the families and friends of the cops, district attorneys and judges who have gotten away with murder or facilitated a cop getting away with murder."

Devon was stunned. He never would have considered the murder of family members, essentially innocents, as the cure. The man on the other end of the phone waited patiently for Devon to let the idea pass through the layers of his mind.

"How long have you been thinking about this? Never mind. Let me ask you this, how did you arrive at this—this solution?"

"Let me ask you the same thing: can you think of any other way for it to happen?" the voice countered.

Devon thought about it for a few moments.

"Why won't killing the cops do the trick?" asked Devon.

"Because that will be perceived as the revenge of vigilantes, and only lead to an escalation of such killings in black communities across the nation; revenge for the revenged." the voice replied.

"What's going to keep the killing of the cops' families from resulting in more killings of blacks?"

"It's more of a shock and awe effect. Besides, the cops will have to live with the consequences of their murders in the most extreme way," explained the voice.

Devon was at a loss for a moment and decided to change gears. "So why me?"

"Because there will be instances where the knowledge and skills of someone medically trained will be a necessity. Any deaths deemed necessary must look like an accident, even when it so obviously isn't. You can never leave a clue behind that will point to a deliberate act of murder or to you, specifically, as the agent of death."

"Whoa, this is extreme. I'm assuming that I'm not going to be acting alone. You're going to have a number of people carrying out these killings, calling them exactly what they are. With so many killings going on out there how do you plan to manage everyone not getting caught?"

"You can be sure that I have thought this out extremely carefully. And frankly, Mr. Compton, all you have to worry about is you. Tell you what, this phone will be active for forty-eight hours. I will call you tomorrow at this same time if that's convenient for you. Think about the whole idea, both my offer, and whether you can think of a better way to make the killing stop. On average, a minimum of two innocent blacks are murdered every week and most are not even reported in the news. After over four hundred years, it's long past time for this to stop," the voice said. "Think it over, Mr. Compton. We need to have a serious conversation once you've had time to think out the all the aspects of the job, as well as all the questions you should be asking me. Just know that my position is No More. Until tomorrow, Mr. Compton."

Once the call ended, Devon didn't really know what to think. The whole idea was almost absurd. He was being offered a job killing people; innocent people no less. And stopping the killing of blacks by cops? Would killing their families at long last change their behavior?

Devon spent hours thinking it through. He agreed that killing the actual officers involved in any shooting was a complete waste of time. Too many of them were bullies who really wouldn't care about putting themselves at risk. He also knew the fact that knowing no one else working at the behest of the man on the other end of the phone call was smart. What he didn't know he couldn't tell someone else, no matter how hard they tried to get it out of him were he caught.

But what about killing to stop cops from pulling the trigger on blacks after so many centuries of doing so with absolutely no consequence? Would the knowledge of the inevitable death of their family if they killed an innocent black person, even accidentally, stop them from killing?

Twenty-four hours wasn't a lot of time to consider joining an effort to change American tradition existing long before the inauguration of the republic.

And finally, how was joining this effort going to affect his own inner rage? His simmering anger living just below the surface over the slights, the insults and constant murder of his people. It seemed in the eighteen years since he served in Afghanistan, and the years since, the country had its first African American president, race relations had sadly deteriorated because of white fear and an idiot of a 45th president.

Devon was no scholar, but he knew that having the notion of white exceptionalism destroyed in the decade after the start of the new millennium had thoroughly panicked too many small minded whites. The proof was in the newspapers nearly every day. Devon recalled the many slights he suffered in school, during his medical training and in the service, merely for having dark skin. Every single one of those experiences fed his anger, frustration and rage, and he surely wasn't alone throughout America. What whites had never understood was the amount of rage that existed in the country's black population. They had no concept of going through life the subject of micro-insults and emotional assaults at every turn.

Would he like to give a little payback to Whitey? Damn right he would. But the question was how he felt about killing. When he examined his soul, Devon realized that he had no real qualms about dealing death, he was just concerned what would happen should he get caught. Fortunately, his marriage had died when he went into the service, leaving him with some understandable trust issues. No kids, and the few relatives he had lived in Texas. His exposure was minimal, but for damn sure he was going to find out what protections he was afforded in this line of work. Whether or not Devon joined the cause, white folks were going to be shocked shitless once this took off.

Before he decided to try to get some sleep, he wrote down a few key words that would remind him of questions he had for the man with the mysterious voice.

Devon didn't sleep much that night, he always had a hard time shutting down his mind when he had something big on his plate. The next day he stuck around the garage and serviced his truck, waiting for the call to come in.

When the phone rang, his heart started to beat a little quicker.

"I hope I haven't caught you at a bad time, Mr. Compton."

"Not at all. By the way, what do I call you?" Devon asked, trying to see if he could illicit any personal information about the man behind the voice.

"Frankly, you don't. No matter what you decide today, this is the last time we'll ever speak," the voice replied.

"That's quite cautious, I must say," Devon observed.

"It's a necessity. Now to business. Have you come up with any questions for me to help you make your decision?"

"A few. The first one that occurs to me, given that we will not be speaking again is how do you or your people communicate with me?"

Devon inquired.

"Any number of ways, electronic, dead drops, misdirected online destinations; you'll know more if you decide to join."

"And the relatives of every cop who's murdered one of us are the targets?"

"That's right," the man replied.

"How many is that?"

"Let me worry about that. You only have to worry about your own assignments," he promised.

"What if the cop's wife or girlfriend is black?" asked Devon.

"Good question. I will evaluate any such circumstance on a case-by-case basis. By and large, whites who marry blacks don't sport a mentality of race-based murder," the voice explained.

"I get you. Is there any money in this venture?"

"There is. Your expenses and compensation will be made in cash."

"How?" Devon asked.

"Let's leave those details until you agree to join the cause," the man replied.

"It truly is a cause, isn't it?"

"That is correct. When no more blacks are being murdered then we will have no further need to carry out these missions. The overall mission is to graphically illustrate the sheer numbers of those of use who have been killed, instill the expectation of what happens when a cop commits what has been up until now, state-sanctioned murder, and to provoke national outrage for the murders we have suffered.

"I do not know if you remember back in the mid-teens when an innocent couple was shot at in their car one hundred thirty times; the last fifteen bullets fired through the windshield by an officer standing on the hood. What I am trying to accomplish is the complete elimination of anymore outrageous behavior like that by any white cop for all time. In the process of doing so, I aim to change American culture with your help. So, any more questions I can answer for you?" asked the voice on the phone.

"What happens if I get caught? What contingencies do you have in the event I am caught in the act of doing whatever it is you require?"

"What would you like to happen? There's no super lawyer who'll come to your defense if you are caught. You're completely on your own. You can either twist in the wind, or I can make sure you don't talk, you don't do time, and you don't suffer. You do understand what I'm telling you, do you not?"

"That I can try to fight it out with the authorities on my own, or I can give you permission to make sure I'm taken out so no one would be able to get anything from me," Devon elaborated.

"Exactly. Your targets will be assigned based on your personal expertise. You will be given any unusual or exotic tools or materials needed for each job. There will be instructions on how to carry out the mission, and I will handle all the logistics for each mission.

"Because of your trucking business, you have a rather unique and unquestionable means for traveling around the country. I will make sure all background information you'll need will be conveyed to you in a manner that should be rather difficult to intercept. Do you read books, Mr. Compton?"

"I do. I read a mix of fiction and non-fiction. Sometimes, I get audio books to listen to while I'm on the road," Devon explained.

"That's very good. There are a number of ways for me to communicate with you based on contemporary books," the voice said. "If you're ready to make a decision on whether or not you will work with me, I'd like to hear it before we go any further, Mr. Compton."

Devon didn't answer right away, listening for any lingering warning from his subconscious. Hearing nothing, he finally replied, "I'm in. I warn you though, I have a lot of anger about cops killing us, perhaps not as bad as you, but it's there. I promise that I will carry out any and all—all missions you assign on the assumption that as I go along, all will be revealed to me in due time."

"Indeed, Mr. Compton. I'll be in touch," were the last words Devon ever heard from the unnamed person on the other end of the call.

Through a series of bland, cryptic but misleading email messages that led Devon to the various commercial Web sites to use for communications, he developed a secure means of communicating with the mysterious man behind the curtain. Most of his assignments were conveyed at the Minneapolis Central Library. And once Devon's laptop was outfitted with the tools necessary to decrypt data files relating to each mission, he created his own routine for getting assignments, reading the encrypted specifics of the mission, and destroying all materials received.

Once Devon had begun, he carried out all but one assignment. The missed opportunity was because of a police officer running cross country with his family on his way to Canada. Obviously, Devon saw that his Washington, D.C. target was picked up by someone else when the cop and his family had stopped overnight in Arizona. His expenses for the run to Washington and full payment for the assignment were waiting for him when he returned to Minneapolis.

When Devon inquired whether or not he was to return the payment as he had not completed the mission, he was informed that since he had made a good faith effort, and through no fault of his own missed the target, he had fulfilled the assignment to the satisfaction of the one who booked the assignments. Devon was both satisfied with the compensation for his work, and the work itself. Watching the country spin itself in tight little circles going nowhere was far more satisfying than he ever could have imagined.

In retrospect, Devon was astounded that he went for the deal in the first place. But he came to realize that his anger at a racist American culture was a whole lot deeper than he had ever suspected. For his entire life he had suffered through a nearly continuous anger verging on rage all too often over the murders of blacks by cops with nothing ever happening to them. He had too many black friends who shared his anger and rage over the slights nonwhites received as a matter of course living in America. He agreed wholeheartedly that it was long past time for it to stop.

Chapter 18

"Tragedy struck today in Compton when an L.A. police officer who lost his family, like so many others, to mysterious circumstances went on a shooting spree, killing sixteen and wounding twenty-six. Armed with an assault rifle and several magazines of ammunition, he crashed his SUV into the front doors of the Martin Multiplex Cinema and proceeded to enter one of the theaters, shooting at the patrons.

"Two security guards for the theater caught the officer in a crossfire as he exited the one theater on his way to the next. He was pronounced dead at the scene.

"The L.A.P.D. has put the department on high alert, and the mayor has instituted a 10:00 P.M. curfew for the entire city. She has scheduled a press conference for 9:00 A.M. tomorrow morning.

"You're listening to talk radio KABC-AM, 790 on your AM dial. Stay tuned for up-to-the-minute news, weather and sports updates as they occur. It's 7:18, next up sports."

Los Angeles was in lock down, with the mayor and the chief of police hoping the curfew would keep any protests and violence from breaking out. Two shifts of officers were patrolling the streets, certain that the show of overwhelming manpower would be an effective deterrent to the citizens of Los Angeles.

The first night was peaceful. There were less than twenty arrests for curfew violation. And there were no injuries.

The next morning Mayor Julie Rodriguez began her press conference with a brief statement.

"Thank you all for coming and to those tuning in. First of all, I would like to begin by extending our sincere condolences to those who lost loved ones in yesterday's tragedy and rest assured that we have begun a full investigation into the specific facts of the incident.

"What we have at this time is that Officer Karl Meyers of the Los Angeles Police Department crashed his personal sports utility vehicle through the front doors of the Martin Multiplex Cinema at 6:30 P.M. Witnesses report that he exited the vehicle in the lobby with an AK-47, which was recovered at the scene, and proceeded into theater Number Two. Inside the theater, Mr. Meyers fired over ninety rounds, killing sixteen on the scene with four more dying of their injuries at Temple Medical Center.

"When he exited the theater, two of the theater's security guards shot and killed Mr. Meyers as he came through the door. It was the quick response of the security guards that is credited for keeping the body count much lower than it could have been. Mr. Meyers was carrying ten magazines of thirty rounds each, making a massacre a certainty had the security guards not intervened.

"The names of some of the deceased are being withheld pending family notification. By the way, the names of the two security guards will be released later this afternoon. Now, I will answer questions," she concluded.

The room erupted in shouting as everyone tried to get the mayor to call on them. They quieted as she pointed to one of the reporters in front.

"Madam Mayor, according to the L.A.P.D., Officer Meyers was one of the officers who lost his family in suspicious circumstances five weeks ago. Had he been cleared for duty?"

"I'll let Chief Loeber respond," said the mayor.

Chief Loeber took his place at the podium. "Officer Meyers had not been cleared for patrol and for the last week had been assigned desk duty."

"A follow-up if I may. Can you tell us what Officer Meyers' mental state was once he returned to duty?"

"What do you think?" Chief Loeber shot back testily. "The man had lost his wife and son in a traffic accident five weeks ago. He requested to be returned to duty one week ago and was passed for desk duty by the department psychologist. He was not cleared for patrol and would not have been allowed on the street until our people cleared him."

"Chief, was the weapon Officer Meyers had at the theater registered?"

"It was not. We're investigating its origin."

"Chief Loeber, were all of the deceased African Americans?"

"They were, as were all of the injured but one," the chief replied.

"Madam Mayor, what contingencies are you putting in place to maintain order?"

"You mean besides the curfew? Or are you asking me something else?" she asked, raising an eyebrow.

The reported at least had the gumption to look chagrined for being called out. "Um, either or both would be fine, ma'am."

"The FBI has sent additional agents here to coordinate should there be a response. At this time, neither the FBI nor Chief Loeber know what will happen in the future, but my office is preparing for any possible contingency this city may face. Last night, there were a handful of arrests for curfew violations. The people of the city are cooperating with authorities. I believe that as terrible as this tragedy is, we will meet it as this city always does and come out the other side stronger and more vital than before.

"Now, the Chief and I have to get back to running this city. Thank you very much, ladies and gentlemen," she said, then led her team out of the room.

-=#=-

SAIC Willis hadn't been to sleep since the massacre in Los Angeles. His top team members were juggling agents across the country, scrounging nine additional agents to send to LA. Their job was to try to predict what likely response would manifest itself from the vigilantes.

Eighteen blacks slaughtered by a cop who had killed a sixty-one year old black man in an alley, claiming he was jumped when eye witnesses refuted his story. The entire country was waiting to see what would happen.

Flights in and out of LAX were reduced at night but not all were canceled. Vehicular traffic into and out of the city was almost nonexistent after curfew. The FBI and LAPD. were hoping that with things so quiet at night, anything off-profile would be easy to spot.

The second night of the curfew found more people on the street in violation of it. But if they weren't doing anything suspicious the cops just shooed them along. Things were pretty quiet while the mayor, the chief of police, and many of the rest of the city's department heads were at the police department's command center, watching for trouble. At the stroke of midnight, there were two explosions, and if one had their windows open in the right parts of town, several shots were heard.

The police command center's phones began to ring off the hook. The homes of the mayor and the chief of police had exploded and were burning so hot that when the fire department responded to the calls, water hoses were useless. Several calls were made by citizens reporting that police officers had been shot, most hit with high-velocity bullets that destroyed their heads.

Eighteen officers were assassinated by sniper fire that evening and the Mayor's family perished along with that of the Chief of Police. As soon as the news broke, the streets completely cleared. There wasn't a black face to be seen except for the few officers on the force and several firemen.

The police were frantically crisscrossing the city in an effort to find the snipers who had killed their brothers in blue. Anyone black on the street was going to get rousted at best but more than likely, shot and killed.

SAIC Willis immediately flew to Los Angeles with a dozen additional agents to oversee the federal portion of the investigation. The first thing the FBI did was pick up all the former African American snipers listed living in the area.

When Willis arrived, he immediately went to the local FBI task force command center where he found activity just short of chaos. The task force was housed in a huge warehouse with all the administrative space clustered in one corner of the open floor with the rest of the space given over to two dozen chain link-enclosed pens for holding prisoners, each equipped with a chemical toilet, like those used at music festivals but with the door removed.

The room was hot and humid. The only concession to comfort were a dozen fans blowing the hot air around the desks and computers.

"Could someone scare up a cup of coffee for me, black, decaf if possible?" Willis asked. "When do you expect the targets to start showing up, and how many are we looking at?"

"Any minute, sir, and we have seven. The lab is going to process them all for powder residue as soon as they arrive. Then we're going to detain them until we interview them all. Is there anything special you want us to do with them once they're processed?" asked Special Agent Jacobs.

"Not so far, Marty. Director Ryan gave me a free hand, I'm giving you the same. I'm here mostly to observe. I'm hoping to see something here on the ground that'll jump start the entire task force," Willis explained.

"We're a way past Family Matters now, aren't we? Assassinating cops is as serious as it gets. These vigilantes have crossed a hard line that makes them infinitely more dangerous to cops and to the public," said Jacobs.

"Yeah, well you're half right. There's been no collateral damage, no citizens killed, other than family members and friends of cops. Yes, that's collateral, but it's also a message. And since we have no idea who they are, we can't even rattle their cage to try to provoke them into making a mistake," said Willis, rubbing his eyes in fatigue.

"Man, you look like shit," observed Jacobs.

"Really? Then I'm improving. You have somewhere I can grab a quick nap until the snipers show up?"

"Yeah. We have the mobile command center parked outside. It's got bunks and it's air conditioned. Come on, I'll take you," Jacobs said, grabbing Willis' bag and leading the way.

Agent Jacobs showed Willis the amenities of the specially outfitted mobile home, pointing out the shower and other features. Willis first set his mobile on the wireless charger then threw his bag on an upper bunk.

As he was leaving, Jacobs promised to send someone to get Willis as soon as the snipers started began to arrive.

It seemed like he had just shut his eyes when a hand was shaking him awake. He cracked one eye open to see who it was.

"The first three snipers are here. Agent Jacobs sent me to get you, sir."

"Thanks, Agent?"

"Devereaux, sir. Eddie Devereaux."

"Thank you, Agent Devereaux. I'll be there in a moment, I need to splash some cold water on my face. Tell Jacobs I'm on my way."

"Very good, sir," Devereaux said heading toward the door.

When Willis returned to the warehouse interior, an agent pointed him to the intake area where he could see three African Americans sitting inside one of the chain link cages with their hands secured behind them in plastic cuffs. He walked over to Jacobs who was talking to two other agents. On a desk, next to them, there were piles of orange jump suits and paper slippers.

"SAIC Willis, Agent Pappas, and Dr. Nobel. They're going to do sample collection before the suspects are interviewed," Jacobs explained.

"I take it their clothes are going to the lab?" Willis inquired.

"Down to their skivvies, sir," Jacobs replied.

"I'm thinking that our guests are not going to be very happy with us," said Willis.

Jacobs gave a laugh. "Surprisingly, they gave us no trouble at all. The agents who picked them up all said that they acted like they were expecting us to show up."

"Really? Now that is interesting. I'd like to sit in on the interviews if that's all right with you. I don't want to interfere, but I do want to observe, not so much what's said, but what isn't. That okay with you?" Willis asked.

"No problem at all. Do you want to be introduced?"

"If someone asks. They'll know we're recording video and they'll see the cameras. And, we don't have any interrogation rooms with the mirrors so everything's going to be out in the open. Let's play it by ear," Willis suggested.

It took an hour for the first three suspects to be processed; stripped, swabbed, and their clothes bagged and tagged.

While he was waiting, Willis noted that the entire FBI contingent was white, with all but one agent male. There was no pretending that the FBI didn't have a diversity problem. In years past, Willis knew of the problems women and nonwhites faced competing in the entitled, good ol' white boys network, his mistake with Agent Jefferson a perfect example.

Willis noticed that Agent Jacobs was gesturing him over to the interview area. A metal table had been bolted to the floor, with several metal loops welded to the table to restrain those being questioned. The first suspect was already seated at the table.

Agent Jacobs took the seat across from the suspect as Willis took a chair and placed it to the side of the table so he could see both of their faces. He checked to see that all three cameras were recording; the LEDs below the lenses glowing red.

"Mr. Lawrence, I am Special Agent Marty Jacobs and the reason—"

"I know why I'm here, Agent Jacobs. We all know why we're here. Let's skip the formalities, and why don't you just ask me the question you really want to know," Brandon Lawrence interrupted.

Willis noticed that there was no anger in Lawrence's voice, nor any indication in his face or body language. That in itself was very interesting.

"What is it that you believe you know?" Jacobs asked casually.

Lawrence chuckled and slouched comfortably in his chair. "Really? You really want to play it that way?"

Jacobs was silent.

"Okay, then. I recognize one of the others you brought in; we were both at sniper school together. It's pretty obvious why we're here. As a matter of fact, I took off work to wait for your people to pick me up at home. Just because I'm black doesn't make me stupid," said Lawrence.

"And why were you waiting for us to pick you up?" asked Jacobs.

"Because a bunch of cops were killed by sniper fire last night. Of course, you'd have to interview us. And by us I mean highly trained black snipers. So get on with it."

"Very well. Where were you between the hours of 11:00 P.M. and 1:00 A.M?" Jacobs inquired.

"I was home. I went to bed just after midnight."

"Do you happen to have any witnesses to your whereabouts, Mr. Lawrence?" asked Jacobs.

"My wife was in bed with me. She works at American National Bank, I can give you the number if none of your people have picked her up yet. And I rather suspect you already know that I was home. I think this whole fiasco is a fishing expedition to see if any of us know anything about the people who took out those cops, the mayor's family, and the chief of police's wife and kid.

"Agent Jacobs, the people who graduate from Sniper School are not fools, nor are they the kind of people who make stupid mistakes. You think that because you're white and that you work for the FBI, that you're automatically smarter that I am. Perhaps you, and this fella from

Washington, D.C., should seriously reevaluate your competency.

"You will find no chemical residue on my clothes. Nor on any of our clothes. The people you're looking for are well financed, well trained, and obviously planned out the main operation for years. Anyone can see that. And your pulling me in today proves that you're still floundering around and desperate," Lawrence said, shaking his head.

"Then let me ask you this, do you have any idea who the people behind these killings might be?" Jacobs asked.

"I have an idea what they are, but no idea who. They are African Americans who have decided that enough is enough. They are doing the job you people have failed to do for the last hundred years—" Lawrence began.

Jacobs interrupted and said, "Us? How do you figure the FBI fits in this scenario?"

"If you had done your job, you and the Justice Department, the constant murder of black folks by cops would have been stopped a long time ago. The fact is that to the Federal Government, black lives don't matter. Someone had to step in and do your job."

"So, you think all this killing is our fault?" Jacobs asked.

"Don't you? Do you have the honesty to embrace—no not embrace— just admit that the perspective has validity. If you can't, then you're never going to be able to get close to the people you're seeking."

"Really now? What makes you such an expert on our methods, letting the whole it's our fault argument pass for now?" Jacobs said, losing a measure of his detachment.

"Agent Jacobs, until your profilers can get into the heads of the people you're seeking you're never going to find them, never. Your very method of investigation demands you believe that the people you're chasing have a legitimate issue with you and your organization's failures. Do you have the internal honesty to admit that there's truth to the fact that the FBI and the DOJ failed to protect a whole race of people in this country? If you can't, your investigation is screwed," Lawrence concluded.

Jacobs and Willis exchanged glances,; both seriously considering what the sniper said. When Jacobs raised an eyebrow toward Willis as if to say, do you have anything you'd like to ask? When Willis shook his head, Jacobs continued. "Your perspective is very interesting. Do you have any other observations you'd care to share with us?" asked Jacobs.

"Only that whoever killed those cops last night is long gone. I dare say they were probably gone moments after the shots were fired. That operation was planned just like those we carried out in combat: make the shot then book as soon as possible. The fact that you picked us up, and the few others living in the area, that I'm sure who're incoming should disqualify us from consideration. Yeah, I know that you have to do it. Hell, you might get lucky, but the chances are slim and none, and slim left town last night."

"May I ask you a professional question, Mr. Lawrence?" Jacobs asked.

"Absolutely."

"How would you have planned last night's operation?"

"What? How would I have killed those cops?"

"Just as an academic exercise. I need to understand the kind of mentality someone with your training has, how you plan, how you execute an operation like this one," Jacobs explained.

Lawrence was silent; his face betraying nothing.

"Okay, take these cuffs off and bring me a cup of coffee," he said, holding out his hands. When he saw Jacobs hesitate, Lawrence said, "You have thirty agents here. I'm wearing paper shoes, I'm in an orange jumpsuit best suited for prison, and my fucking knees have been killing me for a few years now; and might I add that so far you've not charged me with a crime. Uncuff me or not, but I ain't saying shit until you do."

Jacobs looked at Willis who just nodded, then gestured to the agent who was standing against the wall behind Lawrence. The agent unlocked the cuffs, but left the shackles in place, then he went to get a cup of coffee.

When he returned, Lawrence took the cup from the agent and took a cautious sip. He then said, "Thank you.

"So, how would I have planned taking out the cops last night? I think first of all I would have set up day before yesterday, or at least found my perch after checking out the routes the cops take in and out of headquarters and patrolling the neighborhoods.

"Once I found my spot, I would have cased out several routes away from the area, as well as several drops where I could leave my weapon if it looked like I could get caught. Obviously, it was more than one shooter. I would guess at least five or six, maybe all the way up to a dozen.

"The time of day was pretty obvious, you have shift change at 11:00 P.M. so there's the maximum traffic in and out of headquarters, patrol cars then heading out on to the street. Plus, it was dark. I'm not sure how far those shots were, but they were pretty damn accurate if the witnesses are to be believed. Did any of the shots miss?" Lawrence asked.

"Not that we found."

"Then you're looking for some of the best of the best. We're a small fraternity, but I have absolutely no idea who you're looking for. And if I did, I wouldn't tell," Lawrence said.

"And why is that?" Jacobs asked.

NO JUSTICE, NO PEACE

"Because I don't disagree with what they're doing."

Chapter 19

Jackson was primarily known as a numbers guy, first with sports, and currently on the JacksonsRealDeal.com Web site. It was through his faculty with numbers that he was able to accurately take the pulse of the nation. And with his work with Judith, backing up her journalistic assertions with some serious research into the numbers behind the polling across America, he was prescient in his ability to know which way the wind would blow well before most everyone else. Jackson hoped that he would be able to figure out the concealed big picture by assembling the parts that he could see. The landscape was getting very interesting.

Police departments across the United States, having observed what transpired in Los Angeles, were quickly implementing new policies about the use of deadly force. In large part, the new policies were superfluous because complaints of police harassment in black communities were way down. African American traffic stops were way down, and the change in overall behavior did not go unnoticed.

Unfortunately, smaller municipalities that relied on traffic stop revenue from African Americans to run their towns were looking at serious shortfalls in operations cash and were desperately looking for some form of financial relief. And, as predicted by some, there was an increase in white police officers resigning from departments across the country. Unfortunately, the wrong kinds of officers were resigning, leaving behind the worst of the bigots, racists and bullies, but they were keeping their weapons holstered.

The Family Matters Task Force still had no leads on any member of the organization that was changing American culture single handed, and the daily briefings were becoming an exercise in both anger and unspoken hopelessness.

In polling published across America, a clear majority of Americans were pleased with the reduction in racially motivated police brutality and killings, but about that same majority, when asked if they believed killing was a viable means of righting a historical wrong, rejected the notion out of hand.

When the polling was broken down by race, nearly all nonwhites, though not favoring killing as a means to an end, agreed that it was well past time for the disproportionate application of force by police officers on nonwhites to stop. There was an undercurrent of fear about the fact that someone, presumably African American, was targeting whites who murdered blacks.

Also in national polling, white Americans universally felt that the killings were unjustified, and that justice was best met out through the legal system. And when asked if they felt that the legal system was biased against African Americans, about three-quarters of whites reported that no such bias existed. Basically, most white Americans still felt no need to compel racial equality in the legal system; this was a serious problem. Whites were in blanket denial that anything resembling white privilege existed, especially those on the political Right.

After all the weeks dealing with the dry statistics of a nation in crisis, for once in a very long time, Jackson was looking forward to something on television besides the distraction of sports.

One of the major, more intriguing African American voices in the news, Judge Alvin Bridges, was slated to go head-to-head with the leading conservative voice on cable television, Malcolm Leads.

"Hello everybody, and welcome to the Leads Report. My special guest tonight is Judge Alvin Bridges, author of the best seller, The Entire System Is Broken: Throw It Away and Start Over, and a leading African American voice of our times. Welcome, Your Honor,"

Malcolm said, opening the show.

"Thank you for having me, it's a pleasure to be here, Mr. Leads."

"Call me Malcolm, please. Given the seriousness of the events of late, let's jump right in, shall we? Given the events of the past few weeks, it appears that the premise of your best seller has been rendered moot, would you agree?"

"I think you're partly right. Since the justice pipeline begins with an arrest and charges filed, the landscape has somewhat changed. However, changing generations of a tilted playing field in the courts isn't going to change overnight," Bridges replied.

"By somewhat changing are you referring to the reduction in police violence complaints by African Americans against white officers?" asked Leads.

"Actually, Malcolm, it's violence perpetrated by officers of all colors. Often Black officers have engaged in the same kind of violence as whites in order to fit in with some departments. There has been a pervasive undercurrent of violence, a policy of violating the civil rights of nonwhites in general and African Americans specifically for hundreds of years in this country. But you're right, complaints are way down."

"And would you agree that it's the threat of violence or killing that is the root cause of the drop in complaints?"

"I would like to believe that there was a realization that the previous prejudicial, racist behavior woven into the fabric of this nation should stop," Bridges said, chuckling.

Even Malcolm laughed at the judge's assertion. "Recent polling shows that a huge majority of whites in this country repudiate the notion that America's legal system is so heavily unbalanced against blacks. What's your response to their beliefs?"

"White America has a long history of denying the existence of white privilege while still benefiting quite well from white entitlement. Whites who are particularly odious are those who insist that programs like Affirmative Action constitute some sort of reverse discrimination. This attitude is the essence of white entitlement," Bridges suggested.

"But shouldn't everyone be judged by their ability rather than to give special privileges to those who don't measure up?" asked Leads.

"In a perfect world, maybe. But Affirmative Action in the United States is a system where those who have been systematically denied the ability to compete are given priority in jobs and education to redress centuries of discrimination. It's only entitled whites, the intellectually weak, and the selfish who claim that Affirmative Action is discriminating to them. In fact, I contend that those whites who believe they are being somehow slighted by a school's admission policies, or an employer's hiring, even after all of the built-in white privilege in today's society, simply haven't measured up," Bridges declared.

"Whoa there, now hold on, Your Honor. What about in the cases where no more whites are considered in those situations where no matter how high their test scores are, or their grade point average, or how well tuned the job experiences on their resume, slots that whites should qualify for are simply not available?"

"I say, try harder. Isn't that what blacks in this country have been told for hundreds of years, even after being freed from the bondage of slavery? Unfortunately, this is an area where whites are completely and hopelessly ignorant. Blacks in this country constantly live with the expectation that in order to get half the credit a white person would get for any task, for any endeavor, they have to do twice the work. I can tell by the look on your face, Malcolm, that even you have no idea how much this too is woven into the fabric of our society. For you—"

"Now wait just a damn minute, Judge," Leads interrupted.

"Please don't interrupt me, it makes your audience wonder what you're afraid of me saying," Bridges said winking at Leads.

"Apologies, but your assertion is absurd," Leads insisted, clearly flustered.

"And your statement just proved my point. The fact that someone as intelligent and worldly as you are would try to repudiate something so patently obvious to the rest of the world, but is little understood by whites in this country, substantiates its existence, Malcolm."

Leads was quiet for a moment. Calming himself, he then said, "Perhaps. But when you take a culture of single parenthood, low test scores, dropout rates that top our nation, aren't African Americans the root cause of their own problems, including high crime statistics?"

"That's what every conservative since Reagan has said. But the truth of the matter is that it's America's institutional racism that's the real cause for everything you just accused an entire race of, Malcolm. When African Americans receive disproportionally longer sentences for drug possession compared to whites, when they receive disproportionately more traffic citations, when they are stopped by police at a rate six or more times greater than whites, and when blacks stopped in traffic by white cops have a sixteen times greater chance of being killed by the cop than any white in similar circumstance, you mean to sit there and deny white privilege has nothing to do with the problems African Americans face in America? This is the problem; you are the problem, Malcolm. If you refuse to see it, and cold hard facts can't compel you to reexamine your erroneous, closely held beliefs, then it's pointless to hold this conversation.

"But let me tell you this: whomever is behind the killing of the officers' families and friends has changed the behavior of white police officers nationwide, and for the first time in the history of this nation. And as much as you rail against it, it's a good thing—the results, not the means," Bridges concluded.

Leads was all-but sputtering by the time Bridges was finished.

"So, you mean to tell me that you approve of what's been going on in this country?" Leads accused.

"Nice try, but I said no such thing," Bridges said waving his finger in Leads' direction. "I personally don't believe in killing, but the United States of America has engaged in killing and murder since its inception. First, with the attempted genocide of the native peoples on this continent, then with the nonwhites your ancestors brought to this country as slave labor. Killing is merely one weapon in its tool chest of foreign policy, and as we have found out with our modern law enforcement apparatus, also in domestic policy.

"You self-righteous conservatives are always quoting Thomas

Jefferson's. The tree of liberty must be refreshed from time to time with the blood of patriots and tyrants. I submit to you that white police officers, and the powers behind them like the courts, and ultimately the federal government, have qualified as tyrants for centuries. And based on the words of the founders of this country, and your own compatriots, Malcolm, aren't those who killed the family members of rogue cops, and the LAPD. officers, the Los Angeles Mayor and Chief of Police's family nothing more than patriots?"

Leads was completely nonplussed, and couldn't form any rebuttal to Judge Bridges assertion. After an uncomfortable moment of silence he said, "We'll be back after these messages."

Leads took the time to visibly calm himself as his makeup artist blotted sweat away from his hairline and applied powder to remove the shine. When she was done, he turned to Bridges, who was sitting calmly as though he hadn't a care in the world and said, "I was warned you were a pistol, your honor." He then chuckled. "I am tempted to pull the plug on you, but it occurs to me that you should have a forum. And frankly, I can't say that I completely disagree with you."

Bridges threw his head back and laughed heartily, startling everyone in the studio. Moments later, he removed his glasses and wiped the tears from his eyes as the makeup woman approached him to touch up his face as well.

"Malcolm, how does it feel to finally understand that you and I are not so far apart as you've believed all your life?" Bridges asked, rather ironically.

"It's a real bite in the nuts if it's really true. Let's get this party started, Your Honor. Stand by, five seconds," Leads cautioned.

Five seconds later, Leads looked into the camera and said, "We're back with Judge Alvin Bridges, author of the New York Times best seller, The Entire System Is Broken: Throw It Away and Start Over, and the leading voice of social justice for African Americans.

"Before the break, you stated that the people behind the mass killings of police officers' families and friends, those police officers gunned down in Los Angeles, and quite possibly the families of the mayor and chief of police of Los Angeles are nothing more than patriots in a Jeffersonian vein. Is that correct, Your Honor?"

"In many ways, yes. The Colonies started a war of independence against the tyranny of Great Britain. That tyranny consisting of economic suppression, taxation without representation and the like. African Americans in this country have suffered murder, rape, abuse, economic suppression, taxation without representation, denial of education, denial of equal access to jobs, equal justice in our court system and a host of other complaints far more egregious than those for which this country sought its freedom from the British Empire.

"The difference today is that African Americans are not looking for their own state or to succeed from the Union, we merely want equal treatment, equal opportunity, the same access to the American Dream that whites have. And it appears that someone out there has decided to begin the process with reversing the tradition of murdering blacks by white cops."

"But, Judge, their methods are barbaric and against the law. I have to characterize those people as little more than vigilantes and murderers. They kill innocents, not those who may have committed the crimes. That's heinous, don't you agree?" Leads asked.

"Before I even try to do the question justice, allow me to ask you a question, first."

"Go ahead."

"Can you think of any other course of action that would have halted the violation of African American's civil rights and their murders by the police in a matter of a few weeks?" Bridges countered.

Leads sat back in his chair, giving the question some serious thought.

"What about better civilian oversight of police departments? That would put citizens directly in both the investigative loop and give them a bigger say in community policing, Judge."

"Then why hasn't it happened, Malcolm? I'll tell you why. No police department wants civilian oversight of their operations. They don't trust civilians to understand," he said making air quotes, "the demands of the cop on the beat. And for several generations now, the Fraternal Orders of the Police and the police unions have degenerated into nothing more than hard core protectors of dirty cops, no matter the evidence of abuse or misconduct. I defy anyone in your audience to point out a time when a Fraternal Order advocated the removal of a bad cop from the force. It just doesn't happen."

"But murder, your honor? Is this what we've become? Don't you feel any sympathy or regret over the families killed?" asked Leads.

"Five thousand whites verses over thirty million blacks?" Bridges asked in turn.

"If whites were pissed at you before, Judge Bridges, they're going to crucify you now," Leads suggested.

"To do so only exposes their indifference to the insults, slights and deaths of millions of dark-skinned Americans throughout history. Remember, it was white Europeans, and then white Americans, who were bent on the genocide of America's native people. How many millions of Native Americans were killed in the name of white expansion across this continent? Europeans, and, later on white Americans, have a sordid history in this area. And those who would point out some other race in the past that also engaged in this kind of behavior are doing nothing more than trying to deflect attention with a childish 'so's your mother' defense," Bridges said, chuckling.

"Perhaps so. But getting back to those responsible for this highly suspicious spate of accidental deaths, the direct murder of the LAPD street cops and the like. Do you have any idea who they are?" asked Leads.

"The FBI asked me the same thing, and I'll give you the same answer I gave them: No I don't, and I'm quite happy with my ignorance because what I don't know I can't tell. I also told the FBI that the killings were the result of a failure on their part, and the Justice Department, the US Marshals and every other arm of America's law enforcement community."

"How the hell is that?" Leads asked, clearly confused.

"If the hundreds of thousands of police murders of blacks had been properly investigated, those cops actually charged, and appropriate consequences assessed, none of those deaths would have occurred. But you have white cops killing blacks all the time with district attorneys, prosecutors, and judges all facilitating murder by never bringing these cops to justice. Cops know that to kill a black man, at worst, will result in them riding a desk for a few days. By the way, every cop in America also knows a dirty cop, but they remain silent making them just as dirty.

"Look at the thousands of demonstrations that have occurred in this century alone when it was so obvious that the killing of an innocent black was no accident.

"Malcolm, if you and I are driving the exact same automobile on nearly any street or highway in America, and we both get pulled over by a white police officer; why is it that I have an almost twenty times greater chance of being shot dead for no reason than you do, merely because of our respective skin colors? Why do you, or any other white man, continue to defend the indefensible?

"Even a tyro, at least an honest one, has to question why I face death in a way that you never will," Bridges concluded.

"And we'll be right back after these brief messages," said Leads. When they were clear, he asked, "Are you ready for the heat this interview is going to lay on you?"

"Of course. It's time to start an honest national conversation about the issue. I want to thank you for allowing me to have this forum on your show," Bridges said sincerely.

"Oh, this has been a barn burner. They'll be talking about this show for years, Judge," said Leads.

"Let me ask you,; what do you think about my thesis?"

"Honestly, at first I thought you were full of shit; pardon my French. But it's hard to argue some of the facts you presented. That doesn't mean I agree with what's going on out there," Leads replied.

"Of course not. No sane or moral person should. But we fight wars and kill people for all kinds of reasons. This time there's so much hatred and fear attached to the conflict, it's going to be interesting to see how the next few years shake out," said Bridges.

"Ten seconds," warned the floor producer.

"Welcome back to the Leads Report with my special guest, Judge Alvin Bridges. And though his assertions are quite controversial, they are also quite interesting. My question to you is this: what do you think the United States is going to look like say ten years down the road?"

Judge Bridges thought about it for a moment, then replied, "I think it all depends on whether or not the people responsible for the accidents to all those police family members are caught. If they manage to continue to operate without getting caught, I think things for African Americans in this country are going to markedly improve."

"By coercion? Threat of death? That's monstrous!" Leads exclaimed.

"Perhaps. But no one can argue the effectiveness of what has transpired. Remember Jefferson's quote. I believe this period in our country's history is merely the refreshing of our country's Tree of Liberty," Bridges concluded. "It is the right of the citizenry to undertake such acts necessary to ensure the liberty of every citizen in the democratic republic, not just whites. It is my belief that what's more galling to the white majority is not the fact that so many whites have died, but that they presumably died at the hands of blacks."

Leads felt compelled to protest. "That's not really fair, Judge. I abhor the killing of anyone—"

"Excuse me for interrupting, Malcolm, but just how many times have you mentioned the murder of African Americans by rogue cops on your show?" Bridges asked not waiting for an answer. "Exactly none. The slow genocide of blacks in this country was never an issue addressed in terms of stopping it; it was just sensational reporting. And when blacks protested, and the militarized police departments provoked a violent response, whites always pointed out that blacks deserved whatever harm befell them for speaking out."

Judge Bridges took a moment to take a leisurely sip of water then continued. "But to return to your original question, I believe that the reduction in violence and murder blacks experience at the hands of police officers will continue as long as those responsible are not caught. Their continued existence will act as a deterrent and will pretty much guarantee the beginning of equal justice in this country. I also think the end result will be a vast reduction in the numbers put through the prison pipeline that has plagued African American men for hundreds of years.

"What I don't see changing much at all is the second-class education urban blacks receive, nor do I see any great change in the lack of job opportunities for blacks coming soon. As a matter of fact, there's bound to be some retaliatory backlash across the country from whites out of anger for being forced to change. The notion of the tail wagging the dog isn't one that whites are able to take with relative equanimity. But the threat of one's family being killed for murdering an innocent black man is one hell of an incentive for keeping one's weapon holstered."

"What about a black man bent on murdering a cop? How the hell is a white police officer supposed to do to address that threat?" Leads asked, somewhat belligerently.

"Treat him like a white man," Bridges immediately replied, shutting Leads down.

Leads pause a moment, checked the clock and then said, "Unfortunately, we've run out of time with Judge Bridges, author of The Entire System Is Broken: Throw It Away and Start Over. And Judge, I'm going to have to have you back to continue our discussion soon; I honestly look forward to it."

"Malcolm, I too would like the opportunity if I live that long."

"From your mouth to God's ear. Tune in tomorrow night when we'll be talking to the Public Information Officer from the Los Angeles Police Department. Until then, this has been the Leads Report. Good night."

Good night, indeed, Jackson thought. This night's Leads Report was going to make for some very interesting conversation across the nation. He couldn't wait to call Judith in the morning.

Chapter 20

The Los Angeles Police Department was loaded for bear. The rank and file officers were determined to break open the nationwide crime spree by catching whomever had killed the mayor and chief's families. The message sent, that those who lead will bear the responsibility for the actions of their minions, was not lost on anyone. The Family Matters Task Force descended on Los Angeles searching for any clue, beginning with the likely locations from which the snipers fired.

The countless man hours of legwork suddenly paid off. In the steeple of a church, a likely perch for one of the snipers. One of the forensics people found a smear of saliva in the corner of the steeple that had not been exposed to the elements.

The sample was collected and analyzed for its DNA content.

Since the United States Armed Forces had been collecting DNA samples from every enlisted soldier for years in order to make identification easier in the case of disfiguring injury or other circumstance that made any other method of identification impossible, SAIC Willis was convinced this just might be the clue that would break the entire case open.

The fact that they had collected the sample was kept secret, especially from the LAPD. There would be no vigilante action from any rogue cops. Willis was a "by the book" agent and wasn't going to let some procedural error compromise this case.

Willis was still in L.A. when the identification of the DNA came through. It belonged to an ex-military specialist discharged eleven years ago and whose last known location was Miami, Florida. Willis reassigned fully twenty agents to assist the Florida office in locating a Vernon Mendes, a half black/half Mexican truck driver. The orders were to locate and observe Mendes, not pick him up.

His bank accounts were accessed and his mobile phone records were downloaded by the task force. Once they determined his email address, his account was accessed by the NSA and all his text messages were copied from his mobile carrier's servers. Everything the task force could unearth was being collected.

The first troubling find was the fact that Mendes had received no sniper training in the armed forces. As a matter of fact, he had never been given any advanced weapons training.

His credit card records showed him spending money at a local shooting range outside of Miami. But other than range time, there were no records showing specific ammo nor any weapons purchases. The analysis of the shots that killed the LAPD officers showed that were he one of the shooters, he had delivered kill shots from over fifteen hundred yards away. That spoke of extensive training, training that Mendes had to have gotten somewhere, unless he was the spotter for another shooter. But he would have had to still be trained in ranging, windage, offsets and a depth of math necessary to support a highly-trained shooter.

The task force investigators traced Mendes' itinerary by hacking into the trucking company's computers. From the data downloaded, they found that he was in the vicinity of Los Angeles the night of the officers' assassinations.

Once they had Mendes' mobile phone number they started tracking his phone's whereabouts in real-time. Currently, the phone was crossing the lower portion of the country on Highway 80, traveling east through Texas. The FBI had two long haul trucks loosely following the rig Mendes was driving, one from behind and one about twenty miles ahead on the same route. There were no marked or unmarked vehicles following the truck's path for two reasons. The first was that unmarked fleet vehicles were easy to spot. The second was that no local authorities knew Mendes was under suspicion. This was a top secret federal operation.

Both the FBI and the NSA were investigating everything they could on Mendes' background, his friends and family. He was divorced, so the FBI was following up on his ex-wife and his current girlfriend. The NSA downloaded all of his routing and delivery history in the trucking company's systems.

The FBI broke into the man's home while his girlfriend was at work and inspected it from attic to basement, cloning the hard drive of a laptop they found in the dining room and shooting pictures of every room and closet. Then the data team began to compile a list of all the places they could find that Mendes visited or frequented based on his credit card usage.

The suspect's banking records had already been obtained by a team now looking for any unusual cash deposits or disbursements. The FBI was busy uncovering known associates of the suspect in an effort to try to uncover more of the members of the shadow organization.

This is where the FBI shined, in the tedium of tracking down even the most remote clues in an investigation. In less than forty-eight hours the task force knew almost every aspect of the man's life. And unless someone screwed up, Mendes was unlikely to know he was under surveillance.

-=#=-

"Mr. President," Sharon said as his secretary led her into the office.

"Agent Jefferson. So glad to see you. You mentioned on the phone you have some news for me?" President Temple asked excitedly.

"Yes sir. It looks like we have located one of the target group's members. He's either a non-military trained sniper or spotter. His DNA matches DNA found at the likely location from which one of the snipers killed one or more LAPD officers," Sharon explained. "The suspect is currently driving cross country through Texas, presumably back to his home base in Miami."

"When is he going to be picked up?" Temple asked, excitedly.

"I'm not sure. Right now, SAIC Willis has the man covered six ways from Sunday, hoping that he will lead us to others in the organization," she explained.

"Really? What if he gets away from us?"

"We are compiling a complete profile of the suspect, including everything we can find on his family, friends, associates, his daily routine, the works. SAIC Willis is keeping this informa-tion very close. Nothing is being released to local authorities, especially the LAPD. Willis doesn't want anyone butting in and messing up the first solid lead since the Task Force was empaneled, Mr. President."

"This sounds like real progress, Agent Jefferson."

"Mr. President, SAIC Willis has a request to make of you," Sharon said.

"And that is?"

"That you keep this information confidential and not mention it in the afternoon briefing until he deems it the appropriate time."

"I can do that. But the American people are going to want to see signs of progress as soon as possible. This has been a nightmare. Exactly where is the investigation into this suspect?"

"Currently, Mr. President, the suspect is on his way back to his home base in Miami. He lives there and the trucking company he works for is headquartered there. He's being shadowed by FBI agents driving trucks undercover. His phone's being tapped, as are all other forms of communication. He'll be tailed closely once he's home. If he contacts anyone else, we're going to find them, sir." she replied.

"Very well. Thank you for the briefing, Agent Jefferson. Please keep me in the loop. Is there anything else?"

"No sir. For the time being SAIC Willis requests only face-to-face briefings, nothing online or even by email. I hope that meets with your approval, sir. Otherwise I will convey your objections."

"No, that's fine. Please pass along my congratulations to SAIC Willis on all his hard work and to his team as well. Thank you, Agent Jefferson," he said getting to his feet, shaking her hand and leading her out of the office.

-=#=

Once Vernon Mendes returned to Miami, dropped the long-haul truck off at the garage and drove home, all he wanted to do was get a home cooked meal with his girlfriend then sleep around the clock. He was covered by four rotating cars during the drive from the trucking garage to his home. Once there, every word spoken in the house was recorded and transmitted to an FBI motor coach parked in the driveway of a house behind the Mendes home.

All Internet traffic in and out of the home was being monitored by the NSA, as were calls, and text messages on both mobile phones. A government tracer and a radio transmitter had been attached to Mendes' car while it was parked in the shipping company's outdoor lot. The FBI was now capable of monitoring the exact location of the car as well as any conversation taking place inside.

SAIC Willis had flown to Miami as soon as Mendes arrived back from the west coast, wanting to keep a close eye on the surveillance. After so many weeks of no leads at all, Willis couldn't wait to break open the case.

By the time he arrived at the Miami FBI office it was getting toward dark. The first thing Willis did was to review the scope of the surveillance on Mendes. The second was to make sure their NSA liaison had them receiving real-time capture of the communications taps on phones and the home's laptop.

When Willis checked on what was going on in the house, the agent monitoring the audio feeds merely said that Mendes and his girlfriend were "getting reacquainted."

"Good for him, I guess. Where's the photos from their house?" Willis asked. The agent pointed to a workstation then went over and pulled up a folder full of pictures for Willis to go through. The house furnishings were fairly unremarkable, middle class with all the usual networked kitchen appliances and home entertainment system components. Nothing in the bedroom out of character. There was what looked like a study containing a lot of sports memorabilia displayed on the walls and on two book shelves.

"Where's the inspection report?" Willis asked the agent monitoring the audio feeds.

"Scroll down, there's a bunch of text files containing the investigators' reports."

"Thanks," Willis said already opening and scanning the first report.

Nothing stood out as he scanned the first file. There was nothing hidden found, no safe, hidey holes, nothing in the basement walls or in the floors. Nothing unusual in the fridge or freezer.

Looking over the report on the home's laptop, it appeared like they both shared it. No specific sign of tablet ownership, but if Mendes took it on the road with him it'll be difficult to get hold of it. The laptop was used to access social media, sports memorabilia and run-of-the-mill sports sites. The disk was cloned, with the clone sent off to the FBI CERT folks for analysis.

Willis spent the entire night reading every report filed on Mendes, as well as what was dug up on the girlfriend. Not much on her, she worked for a nonprofit specializing in foster care. Not much else filed so far. He then went through all the files containing everything they had on Mendes to date.

No recent military or law enforcement service since his discharge. Had been driving cross-country for eleven years. Divorced, no children, and two siblings. One, a sister, alive and living in Mobile, Alabama. His younger brother had died in jail of a ruptured kidney that went untreated after several police officers beat him during, of all things, a jaywalking offense in Mobile.

Fuck, he thought, if the people in this organization are enlisted from the ranks of those who had a relative killed by the cops, they have several million potential recruits out there.

No sign of a church affiliation. No pets. No weapons found in the home. Checked the bank, a checking and two savings accounts in Mendes' name; a total $281,000 in assets. No safety deposit box. Willis made a note to have all the banks in the area canvassed for any other accounts belonging to Mendes.

His credit card statements showed purchases from a local sports memorabilia store about every other month. Mendes also frequented a local comic book store, but the receipts showed no details of what was purchased.

Mendes had a very healthy homeowners insurance policy and

what looked like a detailed inventory of the collectibles he had on hand. Willis made another note to have someone from the IRS take a look at the valuation of the listed items. Just doing some cursory calculations, Mendes and his girlfriend weren't living beyond their collective means. If Mendes was being compensated for his work as a killer, it didn't show financially in his daily activities.

Willis then turned his attention to the mobile phone records. Looking at the detail of the bill, Willis saw Mendes had both smart phone and tablet. Unless they could get hold of the tablet and plant an app that monitored network use, it would be difficult to keep track of where Mendes went on the net, especially if he was using someone else's Wi-Fi connection. He made another note to try to get a surveillance app on that tablet.

Then Willis turned his attention to the tedious task of going through Mendes' email, trying to see a pattern that might lead him to the next link in the command chain. He knew the NSA was doing the same thing with far more sophisticated tools than just his eyeballing the messages, but it gave him something to do.

Engrossed in going through several years of email, by the time Willis looked up from his studies, agents were trickling in to start their day. He greeted a couple he knew by name, and thanked one he didn't know when the agent set a cup of coffee down by his elbow. Willis got up, stretched, and gave his notes to the Miami Section Chief. He then wandered around the command center chatting with a number of agents until the agent monitoring the home announced that the girlfriend had gotten up and was getting ready to go to work.

"What about Mendes?" Willis asked.

"Looks like he's sleeping in. Don't worry, if he leaves the house we have him covered," the agent assured Willis.

"Just be damn sure he doesn't get a whiff of our people. We can't afford to lose the only lead we have so far," cautioned Willis. He then left word to be contacted if anything cropped up, and that he was going to go get some shuteye.

-=#=-

Just when the nation thought it was safe to relax, a new spate of families, et cetera were dying. It didn't take very long to figure out that they were related to police officers and private prison staff members who were implicated in the deaths of blacks killed in custody. Those responsible for suspicious hangings, injuries from beatings, untreated wounds, and the torture of confinement to chairs for hours, sometimes even days at a time, were being punished.

The shock of the killings had somewhat worn off; now the country was angry. Some of the anger was turning toward the country's collective law enforcement apparatus for having let the murders of so many blacks at the hands of cops slide. The most vocal anger was now directed at that same law enforcement fraternity for not having caught or killed the vigilantes responsible for the collateral deaths of families and friends, leaving the cops who committed killings alive.

The anthem of America's urban communities was, "Payback's a bitch!" uttered without response. And though there was every expectation that the vigilantes responsible were eventually going to be caught, very few were convinced that the temporary moratorium on the traditional violation of the civil rights of America's darker-skinned citizens was permanent. Even the Justice Department knew that once the threat of retaliation was over, it would be business as usual, with an unhealthy helping of revenge added.

-=#=-

Andrew was keeping close watch over the news reports, especially the talking heads on cable and the Sunday interview shows. He also kept an eye on the surveillance the FBI appeared to have permanently saddled him with both in New York and in San Francisco. On occasion, Andrew sat with his tail on the flight out to the west coast or returning home and they took advantage of the opportunity to discuss their perspectives on the vigilante situation, though neither gave up their true feelings on the situation—more of an abstract, academic discussion.

What was worrying Andrew was that he had lost touch with Tony. When he called OpFor and spoke to Michelle, she informed him that Tony was on a sabbatical. She didn't know if he was in-country or on a mission overseas, but it was all very hush-hush.

Andrew texted Tony merely asking for a call when the chance permitted and left it at that. He wondered if his friend had taken up the offer he was so mysteriously extended. If so, he wasn't going to breathe a word of it to anyone not even to Tony's friends at OpFor.

Andrew had memorized the address Tony gave him of his safe house, but he wasn't going to go anywhere near the place unless he had no other recourse. For now, he was content to go on with his daily routine, dragging his government tail behind him.

One thing Andrew noticed was that a quote from Judge Bridges' last appearance on the Leads Report was becoming a very common meme across the country, appearing on T-shirts, buttons, hats, and even in everyday conversation with blacks. Everywhere the phrase "treat me like a white man" was co-opted by African Americans, and exceeded the popularity of the original headliner from 2015, "hands up, don't shoot" in no time at all.

Chapter 21

Several leaders of various police reform organizations started a nationwide tour of demonstrations, beginning in New York, culminating in a massive rally scheduled for Labor Day in Washington, D.C.

The organizers had managed to snag Judge Alvin Bridges as the event's headliner. Andrew was interested to hear the speakers, and more important, judge the mood of the crowd. He decided to attend alone, also wanting to mess with the FBI detail shadowing him as he mingled with the crowd in Central Park.

The mayor of New York was taking no chances on any problems occurring before, during, and especially after the Central Park rally. He had the chief of police pull in everyone he could for patrol during the day, and double coverage for the evening and the next day. There was also a concern about the weather ramping up peoples' ire with temperatures predicted to be in the high eighties to low nineties that afternoon with humidity to match.

On the Saturday of the rally, the city set up water stations and had a number of EMS stations set up around the periphery of the park. The police and medical staff were circulating through the crowd on the lookout for anyone in heat-related distress.

Protestors and spectators began filling Central Park in the early morning even though the official program didn't begin until 11:00 A.M.

Saturday morning, Andrew went into work deciding to get some time in before the rally started. He got several hours in on the San Francisco project before he went downstairs and hailed a cab which dropped him off several blocks from Central Park. He actually laughed out loud when he stepped out of the cab and saw a government vehicle pulling to the curb half a block back. He took his time meandering toward the temporary stage set up for the event, purchasing a pretzel from a street vendor to eat along the way.

Once he reached the park, Andrew strolled toward the gathering, hearing people speaking over the public address system but not really able to understand the words. As he drew closer, he was able to understand what was being said.

A woman was talking about the historical basis of cops killing

African Americans. How the first Africans brought to this country barely made the crossing of the Atlantic, stacked like cord wood, barely fed, if fed at all. And how the worth of dark skinned people was measured in how much money they made for their white masters. And that those same capitalist cash cows, once they rebelled, or their worth to their masters fell below what the resources to keep them alive cost, then their lives were forfeit.

What surprised Andrew was when the woman claimed that north of forty million blacks had been killed from the time the first slave ship was loaded in Africa until the present. The number was staggering, it was so large that it couldn't be encompassed by rational thought. Hell yes, it was long past time for the slow, continuous genocide to stop.

When the woman concluded with, "When will enough be enough?" the crowd's roar of approval rose to a deafening level. It was a physical force that pressed upon Andrew's body, squeezing him like twenty atmospheres of pressure. He stood and carefully looked around for any sign of trouble, for any attendee getting out of hand in anger. The police officers posted nearby looked alert, maybe a touch nervous, but none exhibited any aggressive posture. The shouting slowly blended into clapping as the Mistress of Ceremonies returned to the podium.

"Ladies and gentlemen, our next speaker really needs little introduction today. He has been the most visible voice talking about the inequities of America's justice system. His best seller is entitled, The Entire System Is Broken: Throw It Away and Start Over. In the last few months, he has appeared on several talk shows throughout the broadcast spectrum. Everyone give a warm New York welcome for the Honorable Alvin Bridges!" she said making way for Bridges to take his place at the podium.

The ovation was long, loud, and sustained. Judge Bridges nodded to the crowd, waving his hands in a gesture of thanks, and then motioning for quiet.

When the clapping died down, Bridges jumped right in. "Very quickly, I would like to thank The Violence Project for inviting me to speak at today's event. I applaud any organization carrying out the good work of trying to reverse a several century tradition in this country.

"But let us take a few moments and track just how this whole killing of nonwhites got started. We begin with the continent's original peoples. The first thing the white man did upon arrival was to systematically murder the people already living here. As a matter of fact, it is widely believed that a white men used biological warfare against the native peoples employing infected blankets given as gifts.

NO JUSTICE, NO PEACE

"Originally, historians estimate that the population of the North American continent was around fifty million although that could be a number of convenience to conceal the savagery of the original settlers. Between the 1490s and end of the nineteenth century, that population dwindled down to just under two million. And although much of that decline is attributed to diseases that white Europeans brought to this country, we must remember that history is written by the victors.

"So, at least forty million Native North Americans were murdered by Europeans in the birth of this nation. The United States of America was born of the attempted genocide of those native people who were already living here. Some even say that the original count was closer to eighty million whittled down to less than half a million. Regardless of the actual numbers, the intent was still the same: the genocide of the native people on this land.

"Then, slavers in Europe and along the western corridor of Africa sent millions of Africans to North, Central and South American, most agree that the number was in the neighborhood of twelve million, perhaps only ten million actually surviving the trip over here. I'll readily admit that the enormous number probably only came to half a million or so showing up in what is now North America. But looking at the fact that half a million original slaves have become over fifteen million African Americans today, it's not hard to imagine at all why low information, racist whites throughout America's history are terrified of racial equality. Why we might get the notion to want to have equal access to the American dream for example. We might want to be able to live anywhere we want. We might want our kids to sit next to theirs in school. Or we just might want to determine our own path in life without the slights, insults, injuries, and death that whites seem to feel is their due."

The crowd was cheering Bridges along, all roused at the litany against the tyranny of a bloodthirsty beginning of the nation. Andrew looked around at the various police officers within eyesight. He also noticed that of all the officers he could see, all but one were white, the other appeared Hispanic. Many were standing nervously, hands on the butts of their still-holstered weapons.

It occurred to Andrew that he would have loved to be a fly on the wall of the New York Police Department's squad room when instructions were given on what to do if the crowd turned ugly.

"This country was designed to foster and protect white privilege as the basic underpinning of American society. Nothing is to be denied whites. And when anyone dares mention white privilege, you can't find nary a one who will admit any such thing exists.

MYRON MacHUTCHENS

"So now, we get down to it. Police officers or their ilk have been killing blacks without consequence since we first arrived on the continent. Tens of millions unjustly jailed, beaten, and murdered for no better reason than their skin color, men and women, boys and girls. The stories are too many to count, and even with nearly everyone having the capability to film confrontations, how many police officers have been charged and jailed for the crime of murdering an innocent black man in the last thirty years, one generation? Six! And how many blacks have been killed in that same period of time? Just short of thirty-thousand."

The crowd responded with cries of disbelief. In the momentary lull, someone shouted, "Kill the pigs!"

Judge Bridges immediately responded, "No! Killing cops only leads to more dead civilians. We need do nothing, for at long last someone has taken it upon themselves to change the landscape of justice in this country. And though I abhor the fact that nearly five-thousand people have died in the name of social justice." Several in the crowd cried out in dismay at the judge's characterization of the death of the families. "Now, now, I know how that sounds. But what we are seeing is that for the first time in the history of the Republic, we have experienced eleven weeks where not a single African American has been murdered by a white police officer."

The crowd went silent.

"That's right," Bridges continued. "How many times have you heard that on television or talk radio? I haven't heard it from anyone else at all. And why is that? Because to even say it calls into account the actions of hundreds of years previous. Never in recorded history has there been a time in the United States where the murder of blacks ceased for this length of time. This is change, this has never happened before in the history of this country.

"So, let us examine the issue of the killings, although the authorities have found no evidence to suggest that any one of those people who died from anything but accidental death. We do have the deaths of the LAPD cops who fired into a crowd of demonstrators to prove murderous intent, I'll give you that.

"But let us set aside those people for now. Let us focus on the nearly five thousand others who died under, so far, accidental circumstances. On the whole, they died as patriots serving a higher cause in this country's current history. Their deaths have led to a more equitable United States of America. It was Thomas Jefferson who said, the tree of liberty must be refreshed from time to time with the blood of patriots and tyrants. What most people leave off is the next sentence from that letter he wrote to British diplomat, William Smith, and that is, It is its natural manure, Jefferson stated. We cannot overstate the importance of those thousands who have died fertilizing the Tree of Liberty. Make no mistake, they died in the service of righting a heinous wrong that has existed since before the inception of our democratic republic. For that we must be grateful to this freshening of our nation's Tree of Liberty. Let us not forget that though they were presumably blameless for the murders, beatings, and imprisonment of innocent blacks, they too benefited from white entitlement's status quo."

Andrew was impressed with the way Bridges was presenting his case as well as his manipulation of the crowd. Scanning those nearby, he couldn't see anyone familiar from the FBI detail that normally tailed him. Just for grins, he made his way to the opposite end of the park, quickly going behind the stage, and burying himself in the crowd. It wasn't long before he arrived at the west side of the park boundary. Just as he was going to step into the street to hail a cab, someone tapped him on the shoulder. Assuming it was his tail, Andrew whipped around ready to knock the man's lights out only to find it was Tony.

"My man!" Tony said, hugging Andrew in an unbreakable grip.

At that moment, a nondescript sedan pulled to the curb and Tony said, "Get in, I'll explain everything to you on the way."

"On the way where?"

"Get in," Tony said opening the front door and gesturing for Andrew to get in. "The FBI is eventually going to figure out where you went, brother."

Deciding, what the hell, Andrew got in the front seat, receiving a nod of greeting from the driver. The car smoothly pulled into traffic as Tony patted his shoulder from behind. "Just wanted to grab a bite to eat with you without dragging the feds along with us. Anyone following, Jim?"

"Doesn't look like it. I'm James Pendleton," the driver said, shaking Andrew's hand.

"I'm—"

"I know who you are, sir. I came up a couple of classes behind you. Your reputation precedes you," he said, chuckling. "I'm a spotter."

"One of the best," Tony added.

"Okay, I'm not stupid. What are you here for? Trying to recruit me for something I'll regret for the rest of my life?" asked Andrew.

"Can't. The heat's on you like stink on shit. I wanted to give you the heads up; the FBI is still convinced you're involved in these killings, somehow. Frankly, they're getting desperate, almost to the point where they might cobble up some kind of false evidence so they can parade someone in front of the press. I'm here to warn you to keep your nose clean," said Tony.

"And you? What are you up to? Michelle said you were on sabbatical and that no one at OpFor knew where you were. Talk about making one's self a prime target," Andrew pointed out.

"Yeah, well it can't be helped. I had shit to do."

"In L.A.?" Andrew asked, seeing Jim glance at Tony in the mirror.

"Let's just say I didn't pull any triggers out there and leave it at that. Don't you want some plausible deniability?" said Tony, smiling broadly.

"I gotcha. Where are we going?" Andrew asked.

"I know a great place in Harlem. If soul food is all right with you, One Shot?" Jim asked. "By the way, would you remove the battery from your mobile? The old tricks are still the best."

Andrew pulled the back off his phone and pulled the battery out, slipping it into his shirt pocket. The three then drove in silence to the restaurant.

Jim pulled in front of a small storefront, finding rock star parking just steps from the door. Surprisingly, the air conditioning held the temperature inside very comfortably, and the smells of the restaurant's signature cuisine immediately made Andrew's mouth water.

When they were settled and menus passed out, Jim said, "There's nothing on the menu that isn't simply exquisite."

"Been here often?" Andrew inquired.

Jim laughed and said, "I live six blocks from here, my man!"

Just then the waitress arrived to take their order.

"Hey, Jim. Who're your friends?" she asked.

"Buddies from the service, Pearl. This is Tony, and this here is Andy."

"Pleased to meet you, gentlemen. What can we fix for you?" she asked.

The three ordered a mix of traditional fare; red beans and rice, greens, chicken, ribs and home-made cornbread.

"So, I was asked to give you a warning about not giving the FBI any reason to pick you up. I know, snatching you off the street isn't going to help, but with so many people at the rally they may just figure they lost you in the crowd," Tony said.

"Exactly who was it that told you to warn me?"

"Really?" Tony asked. Even Jim had a bemused look on his face.

"Fuck both of you," Andrew said with a laugh.

"Yeah, you may be able to shoot the wings off a fly a mile away, but sometimes your elevator ain't going all the way to the top," declared Tony, setting off a table full of laughter. When they calmed down, Tony lowered his voice and said, "I don't want you anywhere near this thing. And I'm being totally selfish about this. If the shit really hits the fan, folks like Jim and me are going to need the best of the best helping out."

"Helping out with what? Are you all really with the people behind— fuck it, I don't want to know. Wait, tell me this, how many of you are there?" asked Andrew, also keeping his voice low.

"No one knows. And other than Jim, I have no idea who else is involved, and I like it that way. No one can get something I don't know about out of me," said Tony.

"Holy shit! Then it's real!"

"Of course it's real! You were the one telling me exactly what an op like this would take. And you were right. Given how much Jim and I have seen of the operation, the people behind it are well funded and organized better than anything in the armed forces or the CIA," Tony declared. "But for damn sure you better watch your six. The government is out for bear. The only thing keeping them off of guys like you is the fear of reprisal."

"Not to mention, even if they catch a few of us, they are never going to find the brains of the outfit," Jim added.

"So what are your plans?" Andrew asked.

"I'm heading back to OpFor, just like nothing ever happened," Tony replied. "I'm flying cargo out of here through New Jersey."

Jim shrugged his shoulders and said, "Me? Back to driving a hack. How's the food, fellas?"

"This is my new favorite place," Andrew replied, grinning.

"I miss this. Nothing like it down in cowboy cracker territory. Although they do do 'Q' right, down there."

"He's right. They know a thing or two about grilling of all kinds," agreed Andrew. "So, what's next?" he asked Tony.

"Keeping your ass out of custody. Jim's going to transfer us to his cab, drop me off at the train station, and then drop you off in front of wherever you want to go; and don't forget to tip!"

Jim laughed then explained, "There's no way they know about me. And all my info is legit. When they run the bar code on the cab, it'll come up just fine."

The three spent the rest of the meal swapping mission stories, ending up closing the restaurant. Then they all rode to Jim's house, swapped the sedan for the cab, and then headed back south. Tony hugged Andrew before he got out to go catch a train. And when he closed the door, Jim said, "Battery, One Shot."

"What?"

"Your phone."

"Right!"

Andrew pulled out his mobile, reinserted the battery, and watched as it booted back onto the network. It wasn't but a few more minutes until Jim had him in front of Andrew's office building, which had an unmarked car out front with government tags. Andrew figured, what the hell. And knocked on their window as Jim drove off, telling the feds he'd be right out, laughing all the way into the garage.

Chapter 22

Agent Willis arrived at the Miami office of the FBI bright and early the morning after Labor Day. Drawing a cup of coffee from the common urn, he then checked the overnight report on Mendes and his girlfriend. Seeing nothing of note, he then went over to the electronics monitoring agent.

"Anything yet?" he asked.

"Nothing, sir. It sounds like they're sleeping in," the agent replied.

"It's almost seven, time's a wasting!"

It had been several weeks since the beginning of close surveillance on Mendes. So far, the coverage of the man's communications had produced nothing of note. However, the NSA was analyzing everything they captured with the same intensity and secrecy as the British employed solving the mystery of Germany's Enigma coding machine.

The two runs Mendes made away from Miami in that time were to Oklahoma and Detroit. The FBI lojacked the truck at the first stop Mendes made for food on the way to Oklahoma while the task force scrambled to try to find any white cop who had killed an innocent black in the past decade in the area. Nothing was found, but the FBI was taking no chances. Fortunately, that trip was made without incident. That was not so for the trip to Chicago.

Mendes left Miami, loaded up in Orlando and began his trip north. Agents planted another homing device on the truck when he stopped for the night, and then trailed him all the way north. What made this trip different was the fact that in Chicago there were so many possible targets; cops who killed, cops who had beaten suspects or lied in court. The FBI identified sixteen preliminary targets, leading SAIC Willis to remark, "This is just bullshit. How many of these corrupt cocksuckers are still floating around out there still unidentified? These vigilantes are relentless; the families of the cops in Chicago are all at risk. Do we have anyone covering them?"

"I'll call the Chicago office and send the list. We may catch a break if the vigilantes try to arrange an accident for one of them," said the electronics intelligence agent. "I'll get right on it."

There were no less than twenty-two agents responsible for direct coverage of Mendes in the Windy City. He dropped off his load and checked into a hotel just north of the downtown area. The FBI parked an electronics surveillance van outside the hotel, hooked into the hotel's phone system while they scanned the Internet traffic on the tablet Mendes carried.

They watched as Mendes logged into the trucking company's server, looking for a load to bring back south. They watched as he went through his personal email. They watched as he surfed a dozen sports memorabilia sites. They watched most carefully as Mendes stopped on Jackson's Real Deal Web site and scanned the database for Chicago-based shooting incidents. Interesting enough, the two shooting incidents they had found on their own were also in Jackson's database.

The FBI was covering the families of the two officers, and assuming that Mendes was a spotter not a shooter, there was a deadly loose end somewhere in the city. Though they could have used the manpower, the FBI did not inform the Chicago Police Department of the operation being conducted right under their noses.

When Mendes only stayed in Chicago for two days, then started his return journey Willis was of two minds. He was relieved there was no loss of life, but he was further frustrated that they had no further leads. Since then, there was nothing, even after Mendes arrived back home.

"Hey, are they still in bed over there?" Willis asked the morning after Mendes arrived home.

The agent pulled on headphones and cranked up the gain of the microphones throughout the house. "I've got nothing. No one's in the bathroom, and I can't even hear Mendes snoring," he reported.

"How about the girlfriend? What time does she usually get up?" Willis asked, beginning to worry.

The agent pulled up the log on his workstation screen and replied, "6:45 when she's scheduled to work."

"Get a couple of agents in gas utility uniforms to get over there and knock on the door! Now!"

Less than forty-five minutes later a couple of men dressed as Florida Gas and Coke workers, with an official utility truck, were knocking on the front door of the house. Agents were visually covering the entire house, making sure no one slipped away.

After five minutes of knocking, while the two disguised utility workers appeared to be looking over the gas feed from the street and the meter, an agent picked the lock on the patio door then several agents slipped into the house. Two minutes later they reported the house empty; Mendes and his girlfriend were gone.

"Son of a bitch!" Willis shouted, slamming down the phone. "Who was on watch last night? Wake them up and get their ass in here right now!"

The FBI team checked the garage, both cars were still there. Then when they began to sweep the house, they found both mobile phones sitting on the kitchen table with a sticky note on one saying, "Later, Pigs!"

"Get up!" Willis said to the monitoring agent. He sat down and pulled up the audio from the night before. He began when he heard a TV broadcast of the baseball game in the living room. He fast forwarded until the game was over. He then heard the nightly news. The girlfriend could be heard saying she was going to go to bed because she had to get up early for work; Mendes said good night and that he'd be up shortly. Willis heard the end of the news and Mendes switching over to one of the sports channels doing the recap of the day's games around the country. Then he heard the television go off and in a moment, Mendes washing up in the bathroom upstairs. When the water shut off there were sounds like someone getting ready for bed, then silence. He fast-forwarded through the recording looking for any ambient sounds that would suggest the two got up in the middle of the night. There was nothing, no rustling, no bumps, no sound of any doors opening or shutting. "Fuck!" Willis exclaimed, throwing down the headphones in frustration.

"Should we put out an APB for the Miami area?" another agent asked.

"Yeah. Pictures, the whole nine yards. Say they are persons of interest in a cargo theft ring. It's probably a waste of time. But who knows, we may get lucky. Someone or something tipped them off—they're obviously gone. Do me a favor, check the camera footage on the street. See if anyone stopped on the block. It's a long shot, but that's all we're left with. I'm going to head over to the house," Willis announced. "Someone pull everything we have on file about that Jackson guy and his Web site. I want to go through it when I get back."

-=#=-

"Good morning, Mr. President."

"Good morning, Agent Jefferson. You told my Chief of Staff that you had something important to report?"

"Yes, sir. SAIC Willis wanted me to brief you on the latest in the investigation. The Miami office has lost the person of interest down there. They slipped out of their house in the middle of the night, the subject and his girlfriend, sir," she explained.

"Son of a bitch! Are there any other leads, Agent Jefferson?" the president asked, clearly displeased, angry even.

"He didn't mention any over the phone, sir. I can convey that you would like to be completely briefed on the investigation upon his return. He's flying in later today," she suggested.

"I believe it's time for me to see everything on the investigation. Please give Agent Willis my compliments, and that I would like to see him as soon as possible."

"Right away, Mr. President. Will there be anything else, sir?"

"That will be all, Agent Jefferson. Thank you."

-=#=

Jackson was at his desk in his home office when the door system announced he had guests. Seeing the badge in the camera's view, he clicked on the desktop icon to release the door.

Out in the hallway were a man and a woman, both holding up their identification for Jackson to see.

"Agent Conley, Agent Norman, what can I do for you today?" he asked.

"Mr. Richards, we'd like to ask you some questions about your Real Deal Web site," Agent Conley answered, her smile well practiced.

"Come in," Jackson said, leading into the living room. "Please, have a seat. Coffee?" he asked.

Conley said, "No thank you, Mr. Richards." Agent Norman merely shook his head.

"So, what would you like to know about my site?" he asked.

"When did you start gathering data on officer-involved shootings?" Conley asked.

"About nine years ago. It took about a year's worth of development time to actually go live with it."

"And exactly what was it that made you want to keep statistics on officer-involved shootings?" she asked.

"Officer-involved shootings of innocent black people, Agent Conley. And the reason should be patently obvious to you especially," Jackson said, nodding to both agents.

"And why is that?" Conley asked, her voice tightening.

Jackson chuckled, then said, "Because as Judge Bridges says, it is a graphic example of the systemic failure of the Justice Department, and the FBI, to have ignored the slow genocide of black folks since the first white man landed on this continent. Actually, it was born of anger about killings that went unpunished, millions of them in under five hundred years.

"Look how batshit crazy this country went when a couple of thousand whites were killed, along with a handful of nonwhites in the 9/11 attacks. A couple of thousand! We almost hit that number of innocent blacks killed in little more than one year after that. But it's not a priority with you, with the whole government. Remember fifteen or so years ago when the phrase black lives matter and I can't breathe started to resonate across the country? What did the anger and social networking get us? Nothing!

"So, I started to count all those lives hoping that it would be a daily reminder of just how this country has failed the race that built it. Does that answer your question, Agent Conley?"

"Who else is involved in maintaining the site?"

"No one. Do you know that I'm helping out the White House in trying to locate the so-called vigilantes killing the cops' families?" Jackson asked.

"Yes, the FBI is aware of your participation in the investigation. We also know you visited the White House recently although there was no information concerning who you may have met with. We also know about your collaboration with independent journalist, Judith Spencer. What we don't know is whether or not you're collaborating with the vigilantes."

Jackson snickered. "Really? That's why you're here? Then should I be calling my lawyer?"

The two agents looked at each other, then Agent Norman shrugged.

"Do we really have to get lawyers involved, Mr. Richards? Then we have to take you downtown, book and hold you. You are aware that we can hold you for up to seventy-two hours without charging you, are you not?" Conley informed him.

"Let's cut the crap. You can hold me indefinitely if you want. The problem for you is I'm a black man of means. I can hire the best attorney in town, hell in the country. And along with that attorney I can also hire the best publicist to spread the word that I was detained without cause. And you know why that will work so well for me, agents? Because there's not a thing you have on me relating to the vigilantes. Oh, I've speculated that they may be using my data for their operations, but again, it's you guys who made that possible. If no innocent blacks had been murdered by rogue white cops, there'd be no dead families out there. That's on you. I wonder if Judge Bridges would consent to representing me?" Jackson wondered.

"There's no reason to make this hostile," said Conley.

"Perhaps, perhaps not. That's all up to you. You see, even if they're using my data for their crimes, that doesn't make me complicit and coincidence is not causality. Now, do you have any more questions for me?"

"As a matter of fact I do. For the record, do you know anyone who is a member of the vigilante group responsible for the deaths of police officer family members?" Conley formally asked.

"I do not."

"And what specifically are your responsibilities in this investigation, the ones for the president?" she asked.

"You'll have to ask him that. It's obviously above your pay grade. I think this interview is over," Jackson said.

Agent Norman spoke for the first time. "The interview is over when we say it's over. I think that we should take you back to headquarters so you can cool your heels in a cell for a few days. How do you feel about that, Mr. Richards?"

"Lawyer. That's all I have to say," Jackson said, holding out his arms, waiting for handcuffs.

Agent Norman looked over to Conley, waiting for a response. After a few moments of silence, Conley said, "We're finished here." She stood up without a word, along with Norman, turned and made her way to the door. Jackson didn't get up until the door closed.

Pulling out his mobile phone he made a call to Judith. "Hello, Jackson. This is an unexpected pleasure. What's up?" she asked.

"I just had a visit by the FBI sniffing around for a connection between me, and the people we're looking for. Do you know anything about that?"

"Did they ask about your Web site?"

"They did."

"So, what did you expect? Your data could be the road map for the killings, didn't you expect you'd come under scrutiny?" she asked.

"Of course, I did. But when President Temple asked me to work with you, I thought they'd leave me alone."

Judith laughed. "Brace yourself. It won't be the last time you have someone question you. Chalk it up to the usual bureaucratic efficiency of the government. My only advice is to not lose your temper with them. They have the upper hand, always. Thanks for the heads up about that case in Arizona. That cop on the run had the right idea, but obviously didn't know the capabilities of the organization pursuing him. Carbon monoxide poisoning was brilliant. These people could have made a fortune hiring themselves out to the government."

"After today's visitors, I really want to meet them. I'd love to be able to talk philosophy with their command and control people," Jackson said, chuckling. "Although, I imagine that there's a ton of people who want the same thing."

"In any case, keep your nose clean. I'd hate to lose the best damn research assistant I've ever had."

"Doin' my best, ma'am," Jackson said laughing.

Chapter 23

The national conversation was obsessed with the theme of social justice. The most vocal deniers of the fact that institutional racism was part of the fabric of America, held on to claims of blacks being congenital criminals using crime statistics as proof. The rest of the world was able to look upon the preponderance of evidence with more dispassionate eyes and saw differently.

The top members of the Family Matters Task Force were demoralized over the loss of their prime suspect. No trace of Vernon Mendes was found anywhere. Surveillance of his family and friends turned up nothing. No phone calls, no electronic communications to anyone in his past were found. The trucking company he worked for had no idea where he was, or that he had even quit. SAIC Willis and the rest of the domestic law enforcement department heads had to endure a ninety-minute tirade from President Temple about the loss of their only suspect. And since Mendes and his girlfriend disappeared right under the FBI's nose, an internal investigation was launched to try to find the presumed mole or leak that tipped Mendes off.

The irony of the internal investigation was that it placed black agents at the top of the list of suspects, thereby proving, by extension, every notion the vigilantes exposed to the nation's consciousness. SAIC Willis was aware of how the leak investigation looked, but the entire FBI agreed that the likely culprit, if there was one, was probably black. More than likely, someone slipped up in Miami, but there was no way to tell unless they caught Mendes, and he spilled how he found out.

Agent Jefferson and SAIC Willis were having a very early breakfast in a small, hole-in-the-wall restaurant several blocks from the White House, engaged in an informal chat about the task force.

"That was a pretty ugly display yesterday. Did you get a chance to talk to anyone after the meeting broke up?" Sharon asked.

"Yeah, spoke to Dobson at NSA, he said that POTUS has been riding them every day, screaming about how with the legal and extralegal collection of emails and phone records, and the actual calls themselves, there was no sign of anyone putting together an organization like this. Dobson said that they have over three hundred keywords their sniffing software's using, and they have nothing but millions of false positives for calls and email messages; I guess that means SMS messages too. The chief of staff called after lunch to try to smooth things over, but fuck that. I'm no pussy who needs stroking after being chewed out for not doing my job," Sheldon said bitterly.

"He's been a bear in the White House, too. I think the questions about the investigation, especially those about what our response will be when we find them, are really grinding his gears," she said.

"What about the whole race thing? You getting any shit about that?"

"No. Everyone thinks that once you get to this level, you're above reproach; even someone like me. I earned my post and everyone knows it."

Sheldon sardonically replied "Yeah, because I was an asshole."

Sharon laughed, "Well, there was that! But I should really be thanking you. I'm now posted to the White House because of you."

"Whatever. But the thing that's really draggin' me down is that the people we're looking for are infinitely better than we are," Sheldon said morosely.

"Yes, they are. What did this country think would happen if they oppressed an entire race of people for hundreds of years? Yes, we got a number of malcontents bent on mischief or crime, but you also create an over class of hyper competent people who kick ass at the far right end of the IQ distribution curve," Sharon explained.

"You almost sound like you're on their side," he accused.

"No, not at all. But what Judge Bridges has been preaching about this situation being the result of the Justice Department's failure to protect a race from genocide is right on the money. Why have whites, and more specifically, cops been able to kill so many innocents and get away with it? Because black lives have never mattered. Knowing that was one of the primary reasons I joined up, to maybe change things a little from the inside. But I simply can't argue with the success of what these vigilantes have managed to pull off," said Sharon.

"No shit. If I wasn't hunting them I'd almost be admiring them."

"Now who's sympathizing with the enemy?"

"There's no shame in admitting when we're outclassed. All that American exceptional-ism crap is one of the reasons we come in second, or worse, all the time," Sheldon said, bitterly.

"How's that?"

"Because we always assume we're better. Not because we try harder or work harder, but simply because we say we are. And white exceptionalism isn't doing jack in this investigation," said Sheldon.

"You can't give up. You aren't thinking about pulling out, are you?" she asked.

Sheldon looked at her with a haunted expression on his face, the hopelessness clear in his eyes. "I don't really know. I have a lot on my mind."

"You talked to anyone about how you feel?"

"I thought I was talking to you," he replied.

"What about your wife. What does she say?"

"All she says is that she supports me whatever I decide to do. Not really helpful, is it? I guess it's my fault though. I don't really discuss anything detailed or confidential about the task force with her. But I can't afford to give up the task force or the FBI. I'm in way too deep now."

"So, what's next? What are you going to do?"

"After the ass-chewing the president handed out? Unless something breaks real soon, I'm fucked," Sheldon declared. "Obviously, I'm going to hang on for the sake of my wife and kids. I'm a little too long in the tooth to be looking for another job with the same salary and benefits."

"And what if we never find out who's behind those thousands of deaths? There hasn't been an officer-involved shooting of an unarmed black for months. This is the first time in the history of the country there's been a moratorium on the senseless killing of my people. Do you know how significant this is?" Sharon asked.

"Of course, I do. But at what cost?"

"As agents of the bureau, we're supposed to abhor crime of any kind. But the death of five thousand people compared to the tens of millions of blacks murdered in this country seems like a bargain."

Sheldon looked hard at her, trying to understand exactly what Sharon meant. "Is there a loyalty problem here, Sharon? Are you pulling for the other side?"

"Has anything I've done even hinted at that? Sheldon, you've known me for over a decade now. Are you questioning my commitment to my oath?" Sharon asked pausing for a moment. "Don't you think I'm intensely aware of what my posting to the White House means?"

"I didn't really mean it, of course you are. What's going to happen to you if we don't get hold of these people?" asked Sheldon.

"Good question. My being there makes the president look good. And I'm not above being a token black woman on staff. We'll see. So, what's next?"

"We have some leads from Mendes, the way his job was integrated into his missions, well at least one. So, we're doing the grunt work looking for other truckers, package delivery people, any job that calls for travel.

Also, cross-reference for former military service, and we're bound to get at least a few hits. Mendes gave us more than a thin hit, I have a team going over possible jobs these men might have," explained Sheldon.

"No women?"

"We've been hashing that out amongst us. It's obviously possible, but we're so conditioned against the idea that it's been difficult wrapping our minds around it. But I have two female agents looking into it, building psych profiles and such."

"Good thinking," she said, looking at her watch. "I've got to run. I have a meeting first thing."

Sheldon checked his watch, then drank down the rest of his coffee. "Me too. Need a lift?"

"I'm good. I'll see you tomorrow afternoon at the regular meeting."

-=#=

A man is sitting in a basement somewhere in the United States. He has several computers in this basement, all connect via fiber optic cable to the Internet in a manner that cannot be traced. The room in this basement is shielded from any electromagnetic signals, incoming or outgoing. The entire room is surrounded by the strongest neodymium core electromagnets ever produced on the planet, ready to activate in microseconds should the room be breached. And finally, each of the computers were equipped with nanomachines that, once activated, will destroy the solid-state storage devices in moments, making recovery of the data they hold impossible.

This secret room has been hidden within the building under which it sits for over a decade. The room's protections against detection and recovery of the information held in those computers were in place even before the computers were installed. And, those protections were updated and refined as new technologies were developed, tested, and deployed.

This man, this black man, had despaired of a United States of America where every member of an entire race was at risk for murder twenty-four hours a day, every day, ever changing on its own. He watched as on average, over a thousand innocent African Americans a year were shot and killed with no consequences ever suffered by the killers.

In the beginning, he sought a way to change the culture, to, somehow, stop the killing nonviolently. But a racist America lacked the will to change the casual killing of African Americans that had been going on for centuries. So, he researched, he studied, and in the process, he discovered the only strategy that would make racist, white cops in

America hesitate to pull the trigger when they had a black person in their sites. For too long, it had been this way, it was going to take something completely unexpected, something groundbreaking, to change this hard-wired traditional response in American culture.

Once he was committed to this path, there was no turning back once the first operation was executed. But before he began the campaign, he had to recruit an army.

This, not the execution of so many, was the most difficult task in the entire plan. Finding the necessarily people with the required skills and the commitment to see the plan through was the next step.

Surprisingly, there were African Americans everywhere, from all walks of life, willing to work for the cause. Most of them were researchers, locating the thousands upon thousands in the last one-hundred-thirty years killed by cops because they were black. Jackson's Real Deal Web site was a brilliant beginning for their own data collection; the thousands of recorded killings comprised nearly eighty percent of the total number of blacks murders across the country. The man was tempted to send Jackson Richards data on the cases he had missed in his singular research, but the risk was too great.

This man recruited carefully, never letting anyone he deemed loyal enough to join the cause know who he was. And contrary to FBI estimates, his group numbered less than three hundred people, three hundred extremely dedicated, extremely deadly people.

-=#=

As if to punctuate the intent of the vigilante's killing, the friends and relatives of rogue, murdering cops, now the family members and friends of whites who murdered African Americans, and got off with no more than a virtual slap on the wrist, if that, were the newest offenders to receive retribution. Even the families of those in jail or prison for other crimes weren't immune from deadly consequence.

America was seeing a clean sweep of every class of racist murderer being punished. And in response, African Americans were not only taking it in stride, but they were given to taunting police officers. The shout of treat me like a white man was the new anthem of a people long the victims of an inequity whites so often refused to believe.

Andrew watched the coverage of the new spate in accidental deaths reported. The FBI was taking heat for not having anticipated this new trend and prevented the new round of deaths.

As usual, last place in the ratings CNN was letting social media direct their coverage, marking trends, and even reading the ridiculous comments and suggestions the low brow public were posting. They even got sucked into a several hour discussion about interning African Americans just as the government did Japanese Americans during World War II.

Apparently whites with guilty consciences were terrified that they would never know if a black person passing them in the street was going to kill them. If ignorant, racist whites were fearful of anyone with a dark skin before, they were absolutely completely out of their minds now. And worst of all, they couldn't just kill a black person with their accustomed privilege anymore.

As he turned off the television, there was a knock at Andrew's door. When he answered, he was surprised to see Agents Greer and Carson back for a visit. "I don't suppose I can tell you I don't want any and shut the door?" he said.

Agent Carson laughed. "Letting us in is probably a lot more convenient than hauling you down to the office for a three-day stay, wouldn't you say, Mr. Simmons?"

"Fine, grab Grumpy, and come on in. Coffee?"

"We're fine, Mr. Simmons. Thank you," Carson replied as they followed Andrew into the living room.

"So, what brings you back? I thought I had made my position clear about how pointless it was to look me up in the first place. And by the way, before you ask, I was nowhere near L.A. when those cops were shot."

"Obviously, otherwise we'd be having this interview with bars between us. But we are interested to know the whereabouts of Anthony Dawson. He was on a leave of absence from OpFor, returned two weeks later, then disappeared again. When was the last time you had contact with Mr. Dawson, Mr. Simmons?" asked Carson.

"Not long ago. I had dinner with him here in town when your detail lost me at the rally. You did lose me, didn't you? I found your boys camped out at the garage downtown waiting for me to pick up my car," Andrew said baiting the agents. "Sorry about disabling my phone, but the old tricks are the best!"

"Real funny. How about we roust you every week? Let you spend half the week behind bars? Would that be funny to you too, asshole?" Greer said rising to the bait.

"Really? Even you can't be that stupid," said Andrew as Greer started to rise from his chair.

"Knock it off, both of you. Unless you just want to whip them out and throw down on the table, let's just call it a draw, shall we? Now, Mr.

Simmons, I believe you were going to tell us about the last time you saw Dawson. Something about during the recent Central Park rally if I'm not mistaken," Carson reminded.

"That's right. Tony was here to warn me about this visit, and the pressure the Bureau is under to find the people responsible for fucking up the status quo."

"How's that? He somehow knew we were coming here?" Carson asked, clearly alarmed.

"Not in so many words. But he did say that your surveillance was going to be kicked up a notch in an effort to find someone, anyone, who's responsible for the killings. He said that the FBI wouldn't be above framing someone just to show that progress is being made. And since I'm a better shot than just about anyone, it might just as well be me. So, what say you, Agent Carson? Are you here to take me in, manufacture some bogus evidence, destroy my reputation in the media and then whisper that the FBI was mistaken several months down the road when no one is listening?" Andrew said holding out his hands to be handcuffed.

"Of course not," Carson said, pushing Andrew's hands down. "We're here to find out about your friend Dawson. When the two of you had dinner, did he discuss at all where he'd been lately, or what he was doing?"

"He said he was laying low for the same reason I just told you. He said that a lack of progress by your task force and desperation were going to force you all to do some snaky shit and for me to watch my back," said Andrew, chuckling. "And presto, here you are!"

"Again, Mr. Simmons, we're not here for you. We know you have nothing to do with the killings. But you may know someone who does."

"I would check with his friends at OpFor. Mercenaries like OpFor do the government's dirty work all the time. Did you ever consider that he may be off overthrowing some third world government to make the world safer for our corporatist democracy?" Andrew suggested.

"Unfortunately, much of the work OpFor does for the government is above our pay grade," Carson said frankly. "But it was worth a shot. By the way, do you have way to contact Mr. Dawson that we don't have?"

Andrew threw his head back in uncontrollable laughter. When he calmed, he said, "Really? You have my phone tapped so you have his mobile number. You have undoubtedly compromised the OpFor email server, you or the NSA, so you have his email accounts. You have more ways of getting hold of him than I do. Good luck with that."

"And can we count on you to let us know if he contacts you?" asked Carson.

"Nope. You're going to have to do your own footwork on this one,"

Andrew said, speaking plainly.

"Don't make us have to haul you in—" began Greer then Carson cut him off.

"I think we're through here for today," Carson said, getting to her feet.

Leading them to the door, Andrew said, "Hey, next time you stop by, leave Grumpy here in the car. Or maybe I need to have some doggy treats in the house, just in case."

Agent Greer, to his credit, and much to Andrew's surprise, didn't rise to the bait and softly pulled the door shut behind him.

Just to spite Agent Carson and anyone else privy to his text messages and email, Andrew texted to Tony, "FBI wants you. Peep ur 6." He then put the visit out of his mind, grabbed his keys, and left for work.

Chapter 24

The country was awaiting a widely-announced press conference scheduled by the U.S. Attorney General's office. AG Thatcher called the televised event to address sweeping changes in the department's handling of police-involved shootings, arrests, and prosecution of African Americans across the country.

AG Thatcher was being carried live across the country on all but the most conservative television and talk radio stations. After Thatcher introduced his colleagues behind him, he wasted no time.

"This country has a race problem as we have been graphically shown, specifically with racist white police officers. Up until now, these officers operated with little oversight, and practically no accountability since before the inception of this country.

"The United States has never reconciled with its racist past, nor has much been done to eradicate it either. A recent as sixteen years ago, the U.S. Supreme Court handed down a ruling that gutted the Voting Rights Act which served to disenfranchise millions of African American voters, and five years ago, rolled back protections against Redlining across this country as well.

"Ignoring these racist practices has brought us to this precipice of lawlessness we're facing today. The FBI's task force is going after one symptom of America's institutional racism; the United States Department of Justice is going after the other. Beginning today, every killing of an unarmed, innocent African American will be prosecuted as a federal capital crime," he announced, causing an upwelling of outcry from those in the room.

"Say what you will about the severity of this action. However, it is far better than watching the deaths of family members, colleagues and friends of police officers, judges, district attorneys, and politicians. No amount of regulation, training, or administrative punishment has made the least amount of difference in the behavior of far too many white police officers over the past several generations in this country.

"The guidelines for this new focus of the Justice Department are being published online as I speak. It's long past time for the United States of America to live up to the ideals it was supposed to stand for, even while being made by slave-owning founding fathers.

"White privilege is a sickness that has festered the soul of our country. The Department of Justice is supposed to protect all Americans equally, and until today, we have failed miserably. So today that sentiment becomes a reality as we begin to right the centuries-old wrongs of our society.

"If anyone wants any further information, please make your inquiries through the DOJ Web site. We all have work to do. Thank you," Thatcher said, immediately grabbing his notes and left the room.

The reaction was equal parts outrage and surprise. The media talking heads were caught completely off guard, believing that there would be a Q&A session following the statement. Online, the number of people trying to access the DOJ Web site numbered in the millions just in the first five minutes after the AG made the announcement and nearly crashed the site.

It was only on Progressive media outlets where the announcement was met with bemused irony as there had been no such incidents in several months. The speculation discussed on those stations was whether or not the current change in police behavior was permanent. Should those behind the killings be caught, would there be an immediate backlash by whatever racists still remained in police departments across the country?

When he returned to his office, the AG peeled away from his assistants, shut the door, and picked up the phone to call the president.

When he informed the switchboard who he was, they immediately connected him to the president.

"That was epic, Simon! They're still sputtering on all the channels. The conservatives are screaming special treatment while the progressives are claiming your new initiative moot. They aren't far from wrong, the progressives I mean. If we don't get some traction with the task force soon, I'm seriously wondering if we're ever going to catch the leadership of the vigilantes. I suggest you begin formulating a contingency plan in the event we don't," President Temple directed.

"How the hell do we do that?" Thatcher asked, clearly confused.

"Hell if I know. The people we're hunting are like ghosts. The only lead we had so far disappeared without a trace. How the hell do you pull that off in today's America? We're monitoring everyone in this country every which way but loose. In the last ten years, identity theft is almost nonexistent because we're digging into American lives so deeply. And no one, not you, not the FBI, no one, has the first clue about these people."

"Yes, Mr. President. But to expect to never find them? I've never considered the possibility, sir."

"I know, Simon. But let's face facts, we have nearly five thousand murders, and make no mistake, that's what they were, committed by an unknown agency operating without limit in this country. We have no idea how they pulled it off. And, I'm sick and tired of having the American people, in the form of feckless media hacks, asking what am I going to about those killings? It'd shock the shit out of them if I told them, nothing. Not because I don't care that lawlessness is going to go unanswered, but because the entire country's law enforcement apparatus can't find anyone responsible for the mass murder of thousands of Americans," Temple said, annoyance creeping into his voice.

"Understood, Mr. President."

"Good, I'll be in touch," Thatcher said, then hung up.

-=#=-

"We have a breaking news story outside of Atlanta. The New World Baptist Church in Druid Hills has been the site of a mass shooting. There are twelve reported dead and twenty-one injured in what local police are calling a racially-motivated act. A man described as white, between twenty and thirty years of age, entered the church during choir rehearsal and started firing. He fled the scene in a late model pickup truck and was cornered several miles away from the scene of the crime.

"When police took him into custody, bystanders reported that he was shouting that all, and he used the "N" word, deserved to die for the crime of murder in the killings of police officers' families. He was taken into custody and transported to an undisclosed location. The man has been identified as twenty-four year-old Lawrence Daryl Becker.

"Stay tuned for updates as they happen"

-=#=-

"Shit!" SAIC Willis exclaimed, watching the national news.

"What's up, sir?" asked his wife, Beth.

At the same time, Sheldon's mobile rang and a series of text messages arrived.

"Willis. Yes, just saw the coverage on the news. Good. I'll be in the office in half an hour," he said, ending the call.

"Some nut job went and shot up a church in Atlanta. About thirty were shot,; a third of them dead," he replied. "I gotta go."

"You need a bag packed, honey?" she asked.

"Good idea. You know what I need. And let the kids know in the morning that I had to jet," he said, dashing up the stairs to get dressed.

She followed him into the bedroom and packed his overnight bag, then gave him a kiss en passant as he dashed out of the bathroom and out the door.

On his way to the office, he called the Atlanta Field Office asking for the case officer for the church killings.

"Do me a favor and put full protective coverage around this asshole's family, if you haven't already thought about it."

"Yeah, we offered, but his folks declined, Shelly. We have three men on them anyway. We're also covering his sister. There's no wife or identified girlfriend, and we have cordoned off his shitty little apartment, too. Local PD is being quite cooperative on this for a change. You coming down?"

"Not sure. What do you think? I'm hoping someone takes a shot at his family—sorry, you know what I mean. We definitely need to catch a break if something does happen. Anyway, I have a bag in the car just in case I need to head your way. I'm on my way into the office now. I'll probably be there all night. Keep me updated, will you?"

"No problem, Sheldon. Let me know if you do decide to come down, I'll have someone meet you at the airport."

"Good enough, check in later."

-=#=

"This is car one. The family car is pulling out of the driveway, heading east. Father and mother inside. Cars two and three take up parallel tracks."

"Roger, car two rolling."

"Roger, car three on the move."

"Stand by, subject is approaching the corner, signaling a right—holy shit! The car has exploded; call for fire and rescue. All cars converge," the astonished agent radioed as he pulled up about thirty feet from the rear of the car, now completely engulfed in flame.

He jumped out and quickly opened the trunk, pulling out what he now saw was an inadequate fire extinguisher. He still ran to the flaming car and emptied the extinguisher of its powdered retardant on the driver's door, unable to get closer than five or six feet away because of the heat. He peered into the already obscured window and saw the two occupants were masses of flaming flesh, neither appearing to be moving on their own.

The other two surveillance cars rolled up to the flaming wreck, and the agent warned them back. "They're dead already!" he shouted over the noise of the fire, as they all heard the sound of approaching sirens.

Seconds later, the first fire truck arrived. The firemen jumped out, connected a hose, and had water pouring on the car in a matter of moments. After a second hose was deployed, and the firemen were confident that there would be no secondary explosions, two fire fighters began to pry open the driver's door as they were being doused with water to protect them from the heat. When the door was pulled fully open, smoke roiled out of the interior. The agents could plainly see that both occupants were dead, burned into unrecognizable, smoking lumps of charred flesh.

"I'll call it in," the first agent on the scene said as an EMT tore open his sleeve and proceeded to spread salve on his hand and arm. "Don't let anyone touch that car once the fire is out," he ordered. "This is a federal crime scene."

Two hundred miles away, the small family home belonging to the older sister of Lawrence Daryl Becker exploded completely destroying the wooden frame house. Neighbors running outside to see what caused the tremendous, window-breaking noise were greeted to a jet of flame shooting thirty feet into the sky being fed by a broken gas line.

Police and fire fighters arrived minutes later only to find nothing but flame in the wreckage and had to wait until the gas to the home was shut off before inspecting the debris.

Once the commander of the fire brigade gave the all clear, they quickly began the task of sifting through the destroyed home. It was only a matter of minutes before five bodies were discovered. Lawrence Daryl Becker's sister's entire family was dead.

-=#=

The outcry was immediate and harsh. Though now the voices calling for gun control and mental health screening for gun owners completely overrode the NRA's usual sound bites. Fear was a powerful motivator, and the entire country was scared. Knowing that any crime against an African American would be met with deadly retribution had changed the culture of America. Those who still harbored resentment or hatred against blacks were not tolerated in public. Even conservative talk radio was dialing back their usual rhetoric, mostly in fear of instigating an incident that would bring horrific retribution down on their own heads. Although the communications mega-conglomerates had been propping up the spate of conservative voices across the country for a generation at a loss, the ratings had fallen to such ludicrous levels that the pouring of more dollars down the drain was seriously in question.

The American people were swinging the cultural pendulum back toward the progressive; conservative values having decimated the ideals the country had stood for so many years after its inauguration with Reagan's election.

Malcolm Leads invited Judge Bridges back to his show to discuss the state of affairs in America and pulled in his highest ratings in the history of the show. Portions of the show were immediately posted to social media almost as they aired.

"Welcome back to the Lead's Report, your honor. It's a pleasure to have you back. Thank you for stopping by," said Malcolm by introduction.

"It's a pleasure to be here, Malcolm."

"A lot has happened since you were last here, is there somewhere specific you'd like to start?" Malcolm asked.

"First of all, my heart and prayers go out to the families of those gunned down at the church in Atlanta. America has experienced far too many of these mass murders. It's long past time for them to end," Bridges began. "This country's legislators have let a tiny organization, that has all the traits of a terrorist organization by FBI definition, rule their actions in the area of gun control."

"But the Second Amendment—"

"Let me interrupt you here, Malcolm so you don't make a fool of yourself. What you and all of your conservative ilk believe the Constitution's Second Amendment says is completely fallacious; that means wrong."

Malcolm began to sputter, trying to control the discussion, but Judge Bridges continued on talking over Malcolm's objections.

"Here is the entire text of the amendment: A well-regulated Militia, being necessary to the security of a free State, the right of the people to keep and bear Arms, shall not be infringed," Bridges recited from memory. "And what conservative idiots want to ignore are the first four words, a well-regulated Militia.

"Now what reasonably intelligent people understand about the Second Amendment is that the right to gun ownership shall not be abridged, but that regulating such ownership is what the founding fathers intended."

"Let me finish because I truly would like to hear your rebuttal. So, the requirement that all firearms be secured with a lock, or that they be kept in a locked case or container, or that gun owners must register their weapons, or that gun owner insurance be mandatory, or that pediatricians inquiring about family gun ownership to assess the dangers a child will face in the home are merely well regulation. How say you, Malcolm?"

"The Supreme Court did not agree with that interpretation of the Second Amendment, your honor."

"A Supreme Court, populated by demonstrably conservative political hacks back in the day, Malcolm. History has been quite clear on that," interrupted Bridges.

"Perhaps so, but their interpretation has stood for almost twenty years."

"What you say is true. And look where we are today after over a generation of the NRA's posturing. This country is out of control. The only hope we have is that they're so scared of black folks with guns killing white folks and getting away with it that something finally gets done in the area of gun control.

"You're probably too young to remember when Ronald Reagan was governor of California. He signed legislation allowing open carry of weapons back in the 1970s on a Monday. The Black Panther Party members began openly carrying their weapons on Tuesday, and the law was repealed on Thursday.

"Perhaps, for once, this country's psychotic fear of blacks will yield some good in the area of gun control. We'll see. The Department of Justice's new initiative of classifying the murder of African American's as a capital crime is a beginning. And for those whites out there listening, just think of this new initiative as the ultimate execution of affirmative action. That should make a bunch of your viewers' heads explode, Malcolm," Bridges said chuckling.

"And just what makes that idea so amusing, Judge? You seem to be wallowing in the fact that many in this country are going to find the reclassification of crimes against African Americans as capital crimes prejudicial. That hardly speaks for an America of equality, where everyone gets treated the same regardless of color, gender or religion. Can you admit that doing so is patently unfair?" Malcolm asked, thinking he had the judge trapped in a paradox.

"Absolutely not. Over the life of this country, we have made concessions for circumstances that combated maintaining an unfair status quo to try to promote a more level playing field.

"In some cases we had quotas, in others we had set-asides, and overall, the most successful were the various implementations of Affirmative Action. These programs were designed to right systemic wrongs based on white privilege, pure and simple—excuse me, white male privilege. Many were designed to allow more women to participate in business to compensate for the good old boys' network, or what is commonly called the glass ceiling. Or to allow more minorities to have a better chance of competing in a whites-only economy.

"And now, we have, presumably, an end to the murdering of African Americans by whites without consequence for all time—I hope. But your assertion that we should treat everyone the same regardless of circumstance is absurd. Had everyone started in the same place, at the same time, perhaps. But that didn't happen, did it? Conservative whites are now going to have to get used to sharing. It'll be hard at first," Bridges said with a twinkle in his eye and a huge grin. "But sooner or later, the pie's going to be sliced equally for everyone. And that's what small-minded, conservative whites are terrified of. How say you, Malcolm?"

Chapter 25

America's most vocal bigots were being silenced at every turn. Their calls for wholesale restrictions on gun sales to African Americans, restricting their travel, and claims that the Department of Justice was engaged in reverse racism fell on deaf years. The guilt of a nation, along with the zero tolerance of an invisible, deadly force was finally beginning to overcome hundreds of years of white privilege. That is, at least where police brutality toward blacks was concerned.

Blacks had taken to taunting white police officers at the beginning of the wave of family deaths. But realizing that the change in American culture was unprecedented, even the angriest understood that they were better than bigoted, racist whites. They also knew that what they endured as a race would have driven whites to leave the country.

Surprisingly, when the Department of Justice took a look at the recent statistics of police-involved shootings since the initial batch of office family deaths began, there was no increase in civilians shooting officers during traffic stops or officers responding to domestic violence calls at homes. This gave lie to any notion that cops, by shooting and killing suspects, had been saving their own lives. Traditional claims of self-defense were completely repudiated by the number of stops made, and the statistically insignificant incidents of police officers attacked in the last few months.

The worst offender in police brutality was the Los Angeles Police Department, followed closely by the New York City Police Department, both leading in the number of violence complaints for generations. The reality of America's deadly institutional racism was starkly on display everywhere one cared to look.

Predictions of a surge in black crime didn't materialize. As a matter of fact, without white officers singling out blacks for harassment, unnecessary traffic stops, and racially motivated searches on the street without cause, African American crime statistics dropped over ninety percent. Even black protestors around the country had left off taunting the police during demonstrations, ever mindful of the dire consequences should the vigilantes be caught. And the rest of America was mindful of the certainty of what they faced should the vigilantes remain free.

-=#=

A man sat in a basement, considering whether or not to publish a manifesto for the movement he created. Something that spelled out why he chose to do what he had done to America. Leaving the decision whether to release such a document for later, he contemplated what to say in such a document.

His issues with the country were many, seemingly too many to codify any such document. He was determined that there would be no hint of apology for what he had done; none was due in his opinion. Five thousand lives balanced against millions were beneath mention as far as he was concerned.

But the change in American culture was extraordinary. With whites on track to become a minority over the next decade, and police officers no longer willing to chance deadly retribution murdering blacks; single handed he had changed American culture in a matter of a few months. His challenge now was how to sustain the efforts for the long haul.

At the top of his to-do list was not getting caught. And it was time to plan for his successor or replacement for continuity should something go wrong. But who?

-=#=

The FBI Task Force department heads debated whether or not to put out a national bulletin on Vernon Mendes and his girlfriend. They definitely could use as many eyes possible looking for the fugitive couple. But identifying them as people of interest with the Family Matters Task Force could only serve to make them targets for vigilante-minded citizens on the street. It was also of concern that local police officers just might engineer some sort of fatal accident in the process of apprehending either or both of the pair.

In the end, the argument to release the information was chosen by the majority of the heads of the various departments. The thinking was that with the extra help, they multiplied their chances of finding Mendes. And if he did succumb to some sort of police retaliation, it would put the task force no further behind than they were presently.

"We got the bulletin and the memo this morning," Sharon announced when she breezed into Willis' office.

"Yeah, you missed the big debate yesterday. Someone even argued that to put out the bulletin would alert Mendes to the fact that we were after him," Willis said laughing and miming a faceplant. "Sometimes, it's hard not to believe that the majority of the people working at the Bureau are just here for the paycheck."

Sharon plopped herself down in a chair and said, "It's got to be ten times worse at the White House. Most of the mopes over there only plan their lives four years at a time. So, what do you expect to happen?"

Willis grunted. "Hell if I know! If by chance he gets caught, then we find out everything he knows; his girlfriend, too. Just knowing the logistics of how he operated should help break the investigation wide open. Learn the operation; look for the patterns. Whomever is the mind behind this operation surely knows exactly that. That's why Mendes bugged out when he did."

"Any idea how he was tipped off?" Sharon asked.

"The best guess is that he saw something. Someone got careless, and Mendes saw something he didn't like. Probably someone on one of the surveillance teams got careless," Willis speculated, shaking his head.

"They have to know, I mean every damn one of them must know that they're the subject of the biggest manhunt in history," Sharon observed.

"No doubt. And I'll be the first to admit they've done a damn good job keeping out of sight. Better than anything the Bureau has seen in its entire existence. We have north of fifty-thousand people working at the Bureau. It's just a matter of time until we catch the next mistake these vigilantes make," Willis promised.

"One last question, and I'll let you get on with your day."

"Sure."

"What if we're looking for someone who has offshore assets that are working against us?" Sharon asked.

Willis was quiet for a few moments. "Then that would change the landscape considerably. I can see several paths to a possible declaration of war if another government is involved. And that opens up a whole new set of complications. Why do you ask? You have a hunch about something?" asked Willis.

"No—nothing like that. But it's pretty damn hard for someone to hide out in this country. We have access to far too many cameras, email, phone, and text records. You can't even use any of the third party communications apps without raising a red flag. And we have drones and cell tower spoofers everywhere. So how the hell does someone just disappear? How did Mendes get out of that house, presumably away from Miami and somewhere else in the country without being seen?" Sharon asked, a trace of irony in her voice. "We have people in this country conditioned to avoid using cash unless they're doing something wrong;

or if not wrong, then borderline shady. I can't believe that Mendes was some kind of black super spy—with extra driver's licenses and credit cards under other names—just in case."

"Even if he did, we're tapped into too many surveillance cameras at stores, gas stations, and city streets everywhere to not catch any single person's face somewhere. Face recognition software has been looking out for him from before he disappeared into the wind. Eventually, we'll catch up with him if he's still in the country. And thanks, by the way, for sticking that thought in my head," he said, wagging his finger at her.

Sharon laughed and rose from the chair. "I'm outta here. I'm heading back to the White House. Let me know if anything drops; otherwise, I'll see you next week. Have a good weekend if you can."

"Yeah, sure," he replied wryly. "Hey, thanks for stopping in."

Several hours later an agent rushed into Willis' office. "We just caught a break! Mendes has been spotted in Seattle, sir."

"No shit? Where?"

"Getting off an Amtrak train. His girlfriend cut and dyed her hair. He lost his mustache and beard. No telling where they got on the train. We have an agent who caught up with them at a restaurant. We aren't taking any chances, chief. AirTac has two drones on them in stealth mode in high orbit. And we should have a dozen additional covert agents in town within the hour," the agent informed Willis.

"Good. Watch and see where they go to ground. I'll decide whether we're going to ghost 'em or pick 'em up. See if we can get an acoustical pick up on them. I want to know every word they say especially if they meet up with anyone else. And get the drones' video piped in here and any other CCTV or surveillance camera feeds that catch them as well," he ordered.

"Right away, sir."

Willis picked up the phone and dialed Agent Jefferson's mobile number. "Yeah, it's me. Remember telling me to call you when something happened? Well we just spotted Mendes in Seattle!"

"Seriously?" she said, excited.

"Damn right. We've got him covered with drones, and I have a dozen agents due there within the hour. We're going to watch him for a moment then we have to decide whether to pick him up or not."

"Should I inform the president?" she inquired.

Willis thought about it for a few moments before answering.

"Not yet. I'm tending toward picking him up and squeezing him. For damn sure, I don't want him slipping away again. Wait until this afternoon, I'll call you to let you know what we're going to do," Willis promised.

"Sure thing. That's good work. Thanks for the heads up!" Sharon replied, disconnecting the call.

-=#=

A man gets a single beep of notification on his specially-modified smart phone. He makes his way to a room hidden away in a basement. He disarms security measures seen and unseen. Once he arrives at the inner sanctuary of the hidden room, he changes the root Internet Protocol address of the network, then logs onto a global warming discussion site.

Once logged in he begins to scan the messages in the unusual weather forum. Finding the terse message no one would notice, he then logged off the site.

He sat and thought for a few moments, then he logged onto several other sites, left ordinary but cryptic messages, then logged of the Internet altogether. The man then left the room, resetting the various traps undone that allow him access to the room.

-=#=

"Agent Willis, are you seeing the drones' video feeds?" asked one of the agents on the ground in Seattle. The image on Sheldon's computer monitor was focused on a frame house on a residential street from overhead. The image from the second drone showed a wider angle view of the immediate neighborhood, including all streets in a two-block radius around the house.

"I do. How long have they been inside?" Willis inquired.

"About ninety minutes. We managed to place two bugs outside windows. We can hear the two of them talking. No one else seems to be inside the place. But we have no idea who or what was in there before they arrived. A title search shows it belongs to a real estate holding company that buys these places, renovates them, then rents them out.

"The lease is under another holding company that we're trying to pierce as we speak. The house was provided furnished. There's no way to know if they're armed. But we're hanging back until you give the word."

"Does local PD know we're there?" Willis asked, shuffling through the papers on his desk, looking for the list of names of the agents on location. "Bring one of those portable cell simulators over there and monitor any calls or text messages in or out. If they slip out from under us again, I'm not going to be happy at all."

"Uh, got you, chief. By the way, we've kept the entire operation on the down low. The FAA only knows that we're flying a couple of drones in the area, but not why. You have any special instructions for the crew?"

"No, if we decide to pick them up, I'll let you know," said Willis.

"Got you, chief. If anything happens, we'll call you immediately."

-=#=-

FBI Agent Lewis Parker was the electronic communications technician on the scene a half block away from the house where Vernon Mendes and his girlfriend Eva Jensen were closeted inside. He controlled the cell tower-spoofing device that Mendes' phone connected to. So far, nothing but handshaking between the two devices had occurred.

All of a sudden, a SMS message was sent to the phone. Parker saw the contents of the message but could make nothing of it. It was a link to a YouTube video of an oldie by the Bee Gees, Tragedy. The first thing Parker did was initiate a back trace to find out where the message originated.

Parker immediately got on the phone to Washington, D.C. and was put directly through to Agent Willis in his car, on the way home.

"Sir, Mendes received a message on the mobile he's carrying."

"What was it?" Willis said, pulling over to the curb.

"It's a link to a YouTube video from the old disco group The Bee Gees. The song is Tragedy. That's the whole message, sir," Parker reported.

"Son of a bitch. It's got to be some kind of code. Have they left the house at all?"

"Not since they arrived. They did stop for some groceries, but they haven't stepped outside. We can hear a television inside tuned to a movie channel and some light conversation. That's it."

"What about when the message came in? Anything then?" Willis asked, becoming worried over what the message actually meant.

Parker went back over the audio from the bugs. He heard the phone ding with the announcement of the incoming message, but there was no real break in the conversation about what to have for dinner. "Nothing. They were talking about doing dinner, the message came in, and they just kept on talking. Hang on—they're discussing ordering a pizza.

"Mendes is looking up local pizza parlors in the area," Parker said, watching the mirror of what Mendes was doing on his mobile on the screen before him.

"Do they have a car, any kind of transport?"

"No, the garage is empty. They arrived in a cab."

"When he decides which pizza place, get your youngest looking agent over there so they can deliver the pizza. He might get a look inside that house. I'm flying out in the next hour," Willis announced.

"Got it. I'll send someone to the airport to pick you up," said Parker.

Willis detoured directly toward Andrews Air Force Base as he got on the phone and called logistics at the FBI. He arranged for priority, military transport to Seattle.

When he arrived and was cleared on to the base, Willis was directed to base barracks and given a flight suit and was fitted for a helmet. He was then driven out to a hanger on the edge of the airfield by jeep, taken inside, and strapped into a long, black two-seater aircraft with no markings at all.

The pilot introduced himself as Colonel Pritchett, who warned Willis not to touch any of the controls. "We will be in Seattle airspace in under two hours, Agent Willis. By the way, this aircraft doesn't really exist, sir. Because it doesn't exist, I have to have you down on the ground, and be on my way back so that I return before daylight. Consider yourself lucky, only twelve people have ever been airborne in this aircraft."

The hanger lights went out as Pritchett fired up the engines then the doors began to open. They quickly taxied directly to the end of the runway and moments later they were climbing almost straight up into the sky. Willis felt his ears pop as the air pressure reduced. In less than a minute, the aircraft tipped over and they were flying horizontally.

"If you don't mind me saying, you must be doing some mighty important work if they gave you this bird as a taxi, Agent Willis," Pritchett said once they leveled off.

"You could say that. Probably not as important than what this bird is used for," Willis replied.

Colonel Pritchett laughed. "Yeah, a lot of secrets, and an even bigger pot of money to keep them. From what I hear, they spent about one hundred and eighty billion on the design and construction of this bird. Hang on sir," Pritchett said as he throttled up the engines. Seconds later, Willis saw a doughnut of clouds surround the fuselage of the aircraft, then disappear as it passed through the sound barrier.

"How fast are we going to be traveling, Colonel?"

"Sorry, sir. But I can't really say."

"I get it. No problem."

"Look at it this way: total flight time from D.C. to Seattle is just over an hour. I'm sure you can do the math," Pritchett said, laughing. "But I never said a word about how fast we're traveling!"

Willis chuckled. "Got it!"

"And you don't have to tell me anything about your mission, but it's also not hard to guess. I think between the two of us, yours is the harder job to do. I'm guessing that you might be chasing down a lead, a damned important one," said Pritchett.

"Interesting guess. Remember the old film Sneakers with Redford and Poitier?"

"Too many secrets?" Pritchett replied.

"Exactly. Hey, is it okay if I snooze a while?"

"It's going to be a pretty short nap. I'll wake you when we're on approach to land."

"Thanks Colonel."

The flight was as quick as it was uneventful. And Willis was quietly amused when after landing at Lewis-McChord Field, instead of taxiing toward the terminal, Pritchett rolled to a turnout and stopped in the darkness.

Pritchett opened the canopy and deployed the built-in steps. He exited the aircraft, engine still running, then guided Willis to the ground. He popped a small hatch and pulled the bag containing Willis' clothes from the compartment and re-secured the hatch.

"There's a car coming to pick you up after I take off, sir. Leave the suit and helmet at the admin building. Good luck and happy hunting," Pritchett said, shaking hands with Willis.

"Thank you, Colonel. It's been a blast, this whole non-experience I never had!" Willis said as they both laughed.

"Do me a favor when I get into the cockpit. When I shout, make sure both of these pull back into the fuselage," Pritchett said, pointing to the twin ladders.

"No problem. Hey, don't you need to fill 'er up?"

"Already taken care of, I'm meeting a tanker once I'm airborne." he said, climbing back into the cockpit. Seconds later, the ladders pulled back into the body of the aircraft.

"All clear," Willis shouted giving a thumbs-up, then quickly moved to the grass along the turnout.

The black jet began to turn in a tight circle, washing hot exhaust over Willis momentarily. Apparently, Pritchett had direct clearance to depart because the jet immediately accelerated down the runway and leapt into the sky. Moments later a sedan with a blinking blue light on the roof pulled up.

"I take it you're the FBI guy?" the uniformed driver asked, chuckling at the absurdity of the question. Once Willis got inside, they shook hands, the driver then said, "You must live in a very rarefied stratum, sir. I wasn't able to come near you until the special left."

"Just lucky I guess. I'm supposed to go to the admin building and change clothes. These are yours," said Willis, gesturing to the flight suit.

"We'll have you squared away in no time. Do you have a ride?" the airman asked.

"I will but thanks. Has that aircraft ever been here before," Willis asked, curious.

"What aircraft? Can't say I know what you're talking about, sir," the airman replied winking.

Chapter 26

Darkness was falling overhead of OpFor's headquarters. Interestingly enough, when Tony Dawson entered from the shooting range entrance, Michelle was in the armory turning high-precision shells on a lathe.

"Whoa there, pardner! What's up with the creeping in like a thief in the night?" she asked, surprised to see him. "Does it have anything to do with the FBI looking for you? Because no one here said a damn thing!"

Answering with surprising candor, Tony replied, "Probably. They want to see if I have anything to do with all those deaths even when the only people shot were those L.A. cops. It's a fucked-up fishing expedition, and I'm not takin' the bait. What the hell are you doing here? Your car's not in the lot. I thought no one was here."

"Jim gave me a ride in. I wanted to reload some of my brass, just in case."

Tony picked one of the finished bullets. "Nice! How many are you doing?"

"Probably fifty, all told. And don't think I didn't notice you change the subject. Look, Tony. I really don't care what you do in your spare time. I'm not some southern cracker who thinks blacks are some kind of evil subspecies. We didn't have that kind of crap in Connecticut, at least my parents weren't like that. And Wellesley was pretty cosmopolitan. I'm not a fan of killing anyone, even in my work. But I recognize the need when it occurs," she said.

"And?"

"And nothing. It's pissed me off all my life that you and your people could be killed by cops without any consequences at all. So a few thousand whites get killed, and all of a sudden the equation changes. You'd have to be a fool to not recognize the value proposition in the killing of a few thousand to balance and change what was a killing streak of millions," explained Michelle.

"I didn't know you thought like that. And Connecticut? How the hell did you end up here?" Tony said in surprise.

"I like the precision of being a sniper. I like the fact that I can change bad to good, most times, with a single shot. I like shooting at better than Olympic competitive level. I like the juice, the thrill. I like working with the best of the best, or, since One Shot ain't here, next to the best," she said, making Tony laugh. "There's only two other women in this country who come anywhere close to my ability. And I like competing as an equal to any male shooter around."

"You certainly do that! Okay, to answer your question, I've been scoping out the lay of the land. Trying to see how this organization planned and executed all those killings with such precision. Not a single one, as far as I can tell, can be attributed to anything more than a tragic accident. That's skill! That's better than even we could ever pull off and they did it to several thousand people.

"I know the FBI wants to have a chat with me because I've been out-of-pocket over the last few weeks. But I haven't shot anyone or arranged any convenient accidents," Tony said.

"May I ask you a personal question?"

"Anything you want to know, just ask."

"Would you join those people if asked?"

Tony was silent, mulling over his answer. "That's hard to say. I believe in the cause, no doubt about it. But until I found out what the organization was like, what the expectations were, and especially how I would be protected in case I got caught, I can't say."

"But you wouldn't automatically say no?" she asked.

"No, I wouldn't. I would have to hear the offer. Does this change things with us?" he asked her in return.

"Not at all. Who knows, maybe they'll ask me because no one would ever suspect me," she said grinning broadly.

"Not a bad idea at that. If I ever meet them, you want me to put in a good word for you?"

"Hey, if the money's right, who knows?"

"Yeah, right. Anyway, I'm here to pick up a few things then I'm heading out. Need a ride home?" asked Tony.

"Sure. I'll polish up this bad boy, tidy up, and be ready in a few minutes. Thanks."

Tony went to his office and unlocked the safe. He pulled out a box about the size of a deck of cards and opened it. He emptied the contents in his hand and sorted through them. They were mobile phone SIM cards, each with its own unique number stenciled on the back. He selected three, put the rest back in the box, and returned the box to the safe.

When they left, they exited through the range and hiked about half a mile to Tony's rental car. Michelle let it go without comment. But when they were in the car she said, "I don't want to get in your business, Tony. But if you ever needed my, or anyone else's on the team's help, we're there for you. So, if there's anything I should know in the service of keeping you safe, tell me now so we can work out the best plan possible. Even if it's just a word that will let us know you're in trouble. Maybe even what to do if we need Drew's help to bust you out of someplace."

Tony glanced at her and smiled. "I should be fine. My vacation is over Monday; I'll officially be back then."

"What if the FBI picks you up?" she asked clearly worried for her comrade in arms.

Tony laughed, and said, "Let's take it one thing at a time. If they do, they don't have anything on me other than I don't like people trailing me. That's hardly an admission of any kind of guilt." He reached over and patted her hand reassuringly. "Don't sweat it, kiddo, I'll be fine. But keep in practice, just in case."

On the way back to Michelle's, they stopped and grabbed a bite to eat. When they arrived at the house, Michelle leaned over and gave Tony a hug, saying, "You take care now. Don't be afraid to call for help, and as you guys say, watch your six." Tony assured her he was no hero, watched until she was safely inside, and then drove off.

Tony drove to a small airfield outside of town. When he arrived he saw a Gulfstream jet parked under an awning that concealed it from overhead view. He parked next to a small building next to the awning with a single window through which a warm glow of light spilled out onto the ground.

He parked a little ways away from the building, and as he exited the rental car, the light went out and the silhouette of a man was seen outside the door. The man waited until Tony made his way to the building.

"You the shooter?" he asked. When Tony said he was, the man stuck out his hand and said, "I'm Archie. I've got your gear on board. You have anything you need to load up?"

"Nope, it's all right here," Tony said, patting his jacket pocket.

"Right, then we'd better get a move on."

Archie led them to the door of the sleek aircraft, opened it, and the two climbed aboard.

"Make yourself at home and strap in, it's just us tonight. If you want anything to eat or drink, go ahead and hit the galley once we're airborne."

Tony chose a plush seat by a window. The engines started, and moments later the Gulfstream began to taxi. Tony watched as the jet made its way to a darker line not far off. Moments later, the engines throttled up and in no time the jet was in a steep climb into the night sky.

Once the jet leveled off, Archie came back into the cabin, hooking his thumb over his shoulder and said, "Autopilot."

He went back to the well-appointed galley to get a bottle of water. "You want something?" he asked.

"Sure, I'll have one of those," Tony said, pointing to the water.

Archie grabbed a second bottle and handed it to Tony. He then went to a storage bin and pulled out a nice piece of rolling luggage. "Here's your gear. Take a look and make sure everything's there. If you need something, there might be a chance to get it once we land, but I wouldn't count on it."

"Thanks, man. You know what I'm supposed to be doing when we arrive?" asked Tony.

"No idea. That's how things are. All I know is the name Tony and where to drop you off. Everything is compartmentalized so we keep risk of discovery as low as possible."

"I get that," Tony said as he opened the case and began to check out the equipment inside.

Archie pointed to the side pocket of the bag and said, "There's a card in there with a phone number you're supposed to call once you're on the ground. No rush though, call when you're secure. In the other pocket, is a clean smartphone that's unregistered by any carrier. You're supposed to know what to do with it."

"Thank you kindly, Archie. You put this together?" Tony asked, opening the bag and gesturing to the equipment inside.

"Can't take any credit for it."

"Not really knowing the Op, I can't really say either. But all the parts for all the pieces are here. I notice a digital radio with headset. I'm guessing that you have no idea who might be on the other end?" Tony inquired, checking the batteries and their charge before returning it to the foam cutout in the bag.

"Labor, not management. I'm heading back to the cockpit, don't want to bump into anything. Come on up if you want to chat a while," Archie invited.

"In a bit."

"By the way," Archie said, reaching into his pocket. "You got the word on this, right?" he said, throwing something to Tony.

Tony took one look at the object and began to laugh. "Yeah, I know what AND why."

"Toilet's in the back," said Archie, pointing.

Tony repacked the bag, carefully stowing all the equipment in its proper spot. Then he went into the jet's bathroom, the lights coming on as soon as he closed the door. He looked around not believing that he was thousands of feet in the sky. It was like any powder room you would find in a home or condo.

He took off his jacket and shirt and hung them on hooks by the door. He then smiled at himself in the mirror as he draped a towel over his shoulders and turned on the shaver Archie had tossed him. His instructions included him shaving his face clean and cropping the hair on his head as close as possible.

Fifteen minutes later, after he wiped all the stray hairs from his head and torso he looked twenty years younger.

It was going to take him a while to get used to the person looking back at him in the mirror. When he was dressed again, Tony went to the galley to see what else there was to drink. He passed over the fully-stocked bar and settled for another bottle of water. He then made his way to the cockpit, taking the right hand seat. "Nice jet. I know I shouldn't ask, but is it yours?" Tony inquired.

First, Archie did a double take at Tony's appearance, then he laughed and said, "Unfortunately no. It's a corporate rental. I'm just a pilot for hire. I've been doing this since I was discharged from the Navy. It's a living—a pretty good one. And it gives me some flexibility to do other things, if you know what I mean," said Archie, cutting Tony a glance.

"Like now?" said Tony.

"Like now."

"Let me ask you a question that doesn't put us both at risk," Tony put out there.

"Go ahead."

"What do you think about the big picture of this movement?"

"It was long overdue."

"I agree, but what specifically do you think about that?" Tony prodded.

"The thing that I lie awake and think about sometimes is what it would be like today if we did this right after the Emancipation Proclamation. If we stopped white folks from killing us in 1863, what would this country be like? Hell, what would my life be like. We let it go on for too long, long enough for the cops to feel like they could kill anyone without a care in the world. That's what I think about most. As for what we're doing? It's what's necessary, necessary for my kids, yours too if you have any, and anyone else's," Archie replied. "What about you?"

Tony snorted. "At first, I looked at it as an opportunity to kill whitey; like a revenge or vengeance thing. Then I looked at it in a bigger context, without my own ego, anger and prejudice in it, and I saw it from a desperate need perspective. That this is the only way to change something that's so ingrained that no one thinks twice about it; like you said about the kids. How do we ensure they live without the constant threat of dying in a state-sanctioned killing?"

"Whew! You don't pull any punches, do you?" asked Archie.

"I guess not. But when you sign on to something like this, it's even deeper than joining the service, or in my case, the CIA. I will die before I give anything away to the authorities," Tony said seriously.

"I think we're all like that. And the fact that none of us have been caught says something about both planning and execution. This is only the second time I've been called in to transport someone from here to there. But both times there's been no risk, no fuss, no muss," he said, raising an eyebrow in inquiry.

Tony laughed, with Archie joining in a moment later. "Ask me no questions—" began Tony.

"—and I'll tell you no lies!" Archie finished, sending them both into gales of laughter.

Tony drained the bottle of water he'd brought into the cockpit and asked if he could bring Archie something from the galley.

"How 'bout a ginger ale? I kind of want to stay up here just in case the weather ahead is topping out above thirty-thousand. If you're hungry, go ahead and take what you want," Archie offered. "It's covered," he assured Tony.

"I'll take a look around. Be right back."

Tony first brought Archie his ginger ale, then he looked around the cupboards to see what they stocked in a jet like that. He finally settled on a corned beef sandwich, Swiss cheese, brown mustard, and poked around in the cabinets and fridge for everything he could imagine to add.

When he returned to the cockpit and asked if he could eat forward, Archie had no objections. While Tony ate, the two chatted about whatever came to mind, sports, entertainment, even a couple of movies they had in common on their personal favorite's list. They talked until the jet entered the Seattle airspace.

Tony stayed in the copilot seat all the way to the ground, watching how Archie handled the aircraft and the radio traffic, admiring the skill displayed.

Once they were on the ground, Archie informed Tony that there would be no baggage screening when they arrived at the executive terminal and to call the number in the mobile phone's contacts for further information. When the Gulfstream parked in the slot the ground team directed, Archie shut down the engines, opened the door and followed Tony down to the tarmac.

Shaking Tony's hand, Archie said, "Good luck, whatever your

mission is, man. It was good meeting you."

"You too, man. Safe travels," Tony said, then disappeared into the dark as headed for the terminal.

Chapter 27

When Willis arrived at the Seattle Command Center, he quickly brought himself up-to-date on the surveillance of Vernon Mendes. The local agent in charge introduced himself as soon as Willis arrived.

"Terry Daniels, great to meet you Agent Willis," he said, shaking Willis' hand, then handed him a cup of coffee.

"A pleasure. I'm not going to jog your elbow. I just want to make sure he doesn't slip away again. Well, not exactly make sure, just want to help. Anything you think you need I'll have here A.S.A.P.," Willis promised.

"Thank you very much, sir. This break has been a long time coming. When Mendes leads us to someone higher in the food chain, we'll follow them, and to the next step, and the next. It's just a matter of time," Daniels said, smiling. "By the way, the two of them went shopping last night. Paid cash for everything, brought groceries and some beer back to the house."

"Any idea what they're up to?" Willis asked.

Daniels shrugged his shoulders. "To me it looks like they're holing up. I just don't see how they think staying here for the duration is a real option."

"Could be it's like the Underground Railroad, they're waiting to be taken to the next stop. And based on their ending up here, coming all the way from Miami, I wouldn't be surprised if they're going to make a run for the border. Vancouver is pretty cosmopolitan, they wouldn't have much trouble blending in. And you know as well as I do, getting across the border isn't going to be hard to do at all," Daniels pointed out.

"We just have to make sure that doesn't happen," Willis said, draining his coffee. "Any chance I can take a quick tour around the neighborhood? I don't want to get any closer than a block or two to the house, though."

"Sure thing. We have a pickup truck out back, no cop plates, no antenna. As a matter of fact, lose the jacket and tie and I'll get you a hat," Daniels suggested.

-=#=-

Sharon was busy reading through the task force updates from all the departments other than the FBI. She was especially interested in how the NSA was getting along, what specific strategies they were employing since the usual methods of filtering content didn't appear to be working.

Her encyclopedic mind sucked in every detail, especially the current filtering and digital markers the NSA was sifting for. Being Friday, she wanted to get completely caught up on the weeks' worth of data and analysis before the weekend. It was to be Felicia's and her fifth anniversary living together, though not married, and they had plans for a nice evening out Saturday, church on Sunday with brunch to follow with Pastor King and friends.

She concentrated on the various channels the NSA covered in electronic communications across the United States. There really was no means of privately communicating between parties in the United States. All email was collected, all text messages, and telephone calls were routinely recorded. It was truly as if the Fourth Amendment didn't exist. The United States government was completely in control of the nation's communications. There was nothing that was transmitted from one person to another that wasn't monitored and recorded. All file transfers, including the illegal ones, were completely compromised. And the few encrypted networks still available were fully compromised by the NSA.

The only communications that neither the NSA nor the FBI could divine were those that consisted of messages transmitted that contained no hint of their real purpose. For example, if someone sent a colleague a recipe for chocolate chip cookies. The recipe itself could be the message that indicated some sort of action was going to be taken, or that a directive to act on previously-made plans was imminent. Everyone had caught on to this method of transmitting short messages no matter that both parties had to have a key of some sort to know what was actually being transmitted.

So, all manner of messages were undoubtedly being passed back and forth with no way of the authorities knowing. Additionally, with the millions upon millions of Web sites where people were able to directly converse back and forth, anyone who was seriously interested in concealing dialogue from those monitoring the country's electronic communications had an almost infinite number of opportunities available to them.

The fact that nothing suspicious had been found with tens of thousands of hours already devoted to electronic surveillance and analysis showed just how formidable those the task force sought were in their organization's command and control procedures.

It was going to be interesting to see how the situation in Seattle was going to play out. Sharon had a hard time being completely on the sidelines. But being at the hub of the government's response team was really the best place to be in terms of monitoring the task force's progress and any breakthroughs that might occur. And even though her posting was the result of an initial conflict with SAIC Willis, the position was an enviable one; one normally filled by someone more senior at the Bureau. So, she had no intention of squandering her good fortune. To that end, she was going to continue to prove that she was still the best agent for the job.

-=#=-

"Sweetheart, you want to go to a movie tonight?" Vernon Mendes asked Sylvia, presumably unaware that his every word spoken inside the house was being recorded.

"Aren't we supposed to stay in as much as possible?" she replied.

"Sort of. We have been shopping. Besides, I'm getting cabin fever just sitting around watching TV all day and night," he complained.

"If you think it's okay, look up what's playing nearby; hopefully within walking distance," she was heard saying.

Agent Daniels, alerted by the monitoring agent on duty, called Agent Willis at his hotel.

"Sorry to disturb you, but it looks like Mendes and the girlfriend are going to see a movie at a theater," said Daniels.

"Do we know which one, what time?" Willis asked.

"Not so far. We're listening in to see what's up. I wanted to call you right away to keep you informed."

"Thanks. I'll be right in," Willis said, then disconnected the call.

Twenty-five minutes later, he arrived at the command center.

Rushing in the door, he greeted Agent Daniels with a nod, asking, "What's the latest?"

"They're going to a movie!" Daniels replied, laughing.

Willis was incredulous. "He knows he's the subject of a nationwide manhunt, and he's going to a movie? What's he going to go see?"

"Some chick flick, It's Great When You Find One That Fits." Daniels said, laughing. "We already have three people inside the theater he looked up. The management is being very cooperative. We still have the two drones all fueled up and on station. If you can think of anything else, let's get it before they leave the house."

"Terry, I'm not here to boss anyone around or take over. So far your work is top notch, some of the best I've seen. Let's just keep on top of them, Mendes is undoubtedly going to be in communication with someone, sometime. Has he been doing anything on his mobile?" Willis inquired.

"Just checking sports memorabilia sites, the news and such. But no email and the one SMS message about that song. There's no phone in the house, and if they had another phone, the spoofer would have picked it up," Daniels replied. "You saw the video from when we delivered the pizza. There's not much in the way of furnishings that we saw."

"How are the two of them getting along?"

"A hell of a lot better than my marriage," Daniels ruefully replied.

"They ever talk about being on the run?" asked Willis.

"Not really. Stuff about staying inside. But nothing about how they got there, nothing about if they were tipped off in Miami, and especially nothing about what Mendes was into. If they're sure no one knows they're there, they're some mighty cool customers. They've let nothing slip. Frankly, they're pretty amazing," Daniels grudgingly admitted.

"I think our biggest mistake will be underestimating the intelligence and capabilities of these people. They've killed thousands without leaving any trace of their actions. No one has ever done anything like this in America, operated unseen, unknown, and with such effect before. Truth be told, I envy their operation. If we had to do the same thing in this, or any other country, I doubt we or the CIA could do as well. The situation and the threat is unprecedented, and it's up to us to find them, and eliminate the threat of further deaths," Willis said soberly. "So, what's next?"

"We have a mobile command center, looks like a regular Winnebago. We can leave shortly and park near the theater. Come on, take a look at it and make sure you don't see anything that might tip them off," Daniels suggested.

Daniels took Willis out back and showed him the vehicle. Willis walked around the dirty, tan camper, then laughed when he saw the dozen bumper stickers from various tourist venues stuck all over the back of the unit. He noted that the camper even had a Baby On Board placard in the rear window.

"Outstanding," Willis said, chuckling.

"I even have protective camouflage for an agent couple so we can have groceries and such brought in. We even have a grill, some patio furniture, and a fold-up table inside. There's a grocery store and laundry in the strip mall across the street from the theater. I've got a couple of loads of laundry being brought in so we can have at least one agent outside on the street. We're going to have the drones overhead, two cars circulating within a block or two of the theater, and the command center. We're also bringing the spoofer so we can see if anything comes into his phone. Did I miss anything?" Daniels said, grinning.

"Hell no! Can we go inside?"

Daniels unlocked the door and gestured for Willis to enter first. Inside, Willis saw that where there would be cabinets, a kitchen table and the like, there were multiple consoles and displays. There were displays above displays and a rack of communications equipment that ran along the ceiling. The rear of the vehicle was curtained off. When he parted the curtain, Willis saw four bunks. He also noted that the shower and toilet cabinet appeared to be standard issue.

"Holy crap! How much juice does this beast draw?"

"A lot. But we have one of those hybrid generators; it's practically silent. We have enough fuel to run it for seventy-two hours without having to gas up again with the spare tank stored underneath. That's where we have the grill and picnic stuff stored, too. The AC unit on the roof is also hybrid powered. When we set up, we try to get under some trees even though we can't recharge the batteries. That saves on power needed for the AC unit and helps conceal someone slipping in or out." Daniels was obviously proud of the command center and its capabilities. "We receive the drone video directly on these screens, and we have cameras pointing in all four directions poking through just below the roof line."

"Your design?" Willis asked, parting the curtain to see the driver's console.

"We took the standard layout and just added a few improvements," Daniels replied.

"You have specs on the design? If so, send them to me and I'll make sure our electronics intel people see what you've done," Willis promised. "Now, when are you planning to take off for the theater?"

"Not sure, the two most likely shows ate 8:00 and 10:20 P.M. I figure we head out about 7:00 and get set up in the strip mall. We'll have six agents in here, including you, three in the theater and one in the Laundromat. Two cars circulating with both drones completing the package," Daniels tallied.

"Okay, I'm running back to the hotel and getting into something more casual. How many women are on the detail?"

"One outside and two in here."

"Okay, have one of them dress casually, jeans and a jacket, just in case we decide to go inside the theater with Mendes," Willis instructed.

"No problem. We also have a full complement of FBI windbreakers in the closet if we have to go public."

"Good deal. All right then, I'll be back in an hour," said Willis, turning toward the door. The two exited the vehicle, Daniels locking the door, and parted ways for the time being.

-=#=

Jackson was in Washington, D.C. for the weekend, meeting with Judith. They were having a working weekend to go over all the leads they had uncovered in their confidential investigation. Spencer was also a member of Augustus King's congregation and invited Jackson to accompany her to this Sunday's service. Having only seen and heard clips of Pastor King's sermons on the Web, Jackson was looking forward to attending the service.

When he arrived, he rented a car and drove into Georgetown to his favorite hotel and checked in. He sent a text message to Judith inviting her to dinner and got a response a few minutes later. Not fond of back and forth texting when a quick call would do, he phoned to settle on a place to eat. Judith had some things she wanted to share with Jackson right away so they decided to eat at the hotel's restaurant.

When Judith arrived, she and Jackson spotted each other at the same time. Jackson rose and gave her a hug and then held her chair. Once seated, Judith inquired after Jackson's parents as well as his flight to Washington.

They made small talk until they both had drinks before them.

Once the waiter left, after taking their food orders, the both started speaking at once, then laughed.

"You go ahead," Jackson offered.

"Thanks. So here's what I found. I looked at the dates of the family members who died, and guess what?" she asked.

"The majority of them follow the chronological order of the records of my database," Jackson replied, smiling broadly.

"They—what? You already knew?" she said, surprised.

"I did. I found out by accident. But it was clear to me that my database was being used by whomever is behind the killings. And, whomever is behind the killings collected data on at least eighty officer-involved killings that I didn't have data on. I added them in as soon as I discovered the information. In most cases, I had to go into archives of local newspapers to make sure I had the facts straight. And when the FBI sent agents to interview me, I had a pretty good idea why," he explained.

"I have a contact inside the FBI. I normally don't get anything top secret, but I do get a heads up before much of the media does, so I asked about your possible connection. And they thought that you may have accumulated the data for the express purpose of someone using it to carry out the killings—by the way, they still haven't uncovered any clues that point to anything but those people dying by accident. Let me amend that, obviously the deaths were killings, but not a one had been proven to be from deliberate action," she explained.

Jackson just shook his head. "I'm thinking that what's got everyone terrified is that we're behind it all. They never thought black folks could do something like this, let alone do it in a way that no white man can figure out."

"No doubt about it. But look what else I found out. Do you have your tablet?" she asked.

Jackson pulled a tablet out of the folio on the seat beside him and held it out so Judith could tap it with hers and transfer over the files.

Once the files were transferred, Jackson opened the first in the group.

"Okay, what am I looking at?" he asked, not sure what he should be concentrating on.

"Look at the race of the wife in that first file," Judith directed.

Jackson read through the info on the wife, then opened the next file, and the next, and the next. In every single case the family member, relative, lover or friend was black, and they escaped death. Though anomalous, the overall numbers weren't statistically significant.

"Now, I can't say that no one else has noticed. I'm going to assume the FBI is on it. I can't imagine they missed something like that, but it's not been mentioned in the news in all this time, and there's been a boatload of whining and gnashing of teeth over the law's inability to find the people responsible."

"That's an understatement," Jackson said, distracted as he paged through the files Judith gave him.

"Here's one more thing I have for you. The FBI thinks they might have spotted one of the people behind the killings, a member of the vigilantes," she said excitedly.

That caught Jackson's attention. "Get out! Where, how? I mean how close are they? How did they identify them?" he asked in rapid-fire.

Judith laughed. "Slow down there, pardner! I didn't get any real details, but it was something in L.A. that tipped them off. Someone having to do with killing those cops, that's all I got, though."

"Any chance of getting more info?" Jackson asked.

"I don't know. My contact was playing it pretty coy. I'll call Wednesday and see if I can get anything else out of her," Judith promised. "How long are you sticking around D.C.?"

"Not sure. I am really looking forward to hearing Pastor King. Thanks for the invite. I brought proper attire so I don't put you to shame for inviting me," he said chuckling. "Have you spoken to the president lately?"

"No. I spoke to his chief of staff. He said the president was interested in our idea to publish a historical retrospective on what the country's gone through. I want to see if we can get him to do a forward for the book."

"That would be excellent! Oh yeah, hold out your tablet," Jackson said, quickly tapping on his own screen. He tapped tablets with Judith, saying, "Here's the outline you asked me to do. Take a look and see if I missed anything."

At that moment their food arrived, and they put away their work. The conversation turned to more mundane things with Jackson inquiring into Pastor King's background. Judith had been a member of his congregation for several years and told stories about sermons to entertain Jackson. When they had both finished dinner and were chatting over dessert, Judith went over the things she wanted them to concentrate on in the morning. She invited Jackson to her place so they could both go through all the project files together. She even promised to have breakfast ready for him when he arrived. "After all," she said, "it's the most important meal of the day!"

Chapter 28

"You've got a great mobile command center here, Terry. I can't even hear the AC," Willis marveled.

"These hybrids are getting better and better every year. And look at the drones, they can stay aloft for over a day without refueling or recharging the batteries. If we're careful and don't jinx them around a lot, the solar cells keep the units charged during the day, and we only have to use fuel and the batteries at night. The batteries run the cameras, too. There's a little more drain on them so we carry spares. All we have to is land them, swap batteries, top off the tank, and in five minutes it's back in the air," Daniels bragged. "Don't be fooled, this ship gets great mileage, too. But the damn thing's always parked when we're using it. The fuel cells power the AC and all this for up to three days without having to run the engine to recharge them," he said, pointing to all the electronics gear.

"You still thinking about going inside with Yvette here," Daniels asked, flashing a wink at the attractive agent. "When was the last time you were out at a movie?"

"My wife and I went out a few weeks back," Willis said, emphasizing the word wife.

"It wouldn't be a date, Agent Willis," Yvette chimed in not having been introduced formally yet.

Flustered, Willis said, "Sorry, I didn't mean anything by it. What is your last name?"

Laughing, she replied, "Bailor, Yvette Bailor. The one on the screens is Matt Allen." Willis shook their hands.

"But to answer your question, we have the theater locked up tight. We have eyes on every door, plus the night sight on these drones is fantastic. You think we should grab them when Mendes gets here?" Willis asked all around.

Everyone shrugged their shoulders, quite willing for Willis to make the call.

"Let's play it by ear."

"Attention, wake up everyone. They just left the house," came over the radio.

"Cars one and two on the move."

"Got them on the drone?" Daniels asked.

"Yep! There they are," the electronic intel agent said, pointing to the monitor. He then switched on the larger screen overhead so everyone could see without leaving their seats.

The one drone was focused directly on the couple. The second drone had a much wider shot that covered a couple of blocks around the couple. Willis was surprised to see their chaser cars had numbers that showed brightly on the monitor.

Pointing, he asked, "Can anyone see those numbers?"

"Absolutely not. Not during the day or in the dark," the agent on the drone console said, pointing.

"The drones are painting the area in a frequency not visible to the human eye, and our cars have a special reflective paint that bounces the beam back. You should really get out in the field more, Agent Willis. Some of the equipment I have is like science fiction, even to me," said the agent. "Sometimes, if we can pull it off. We'll spray a suspect's car so it shows up better."

"Tell him what you did last fall?" Daniels prompted.

The agent laughed. "That was epic. I sent an agent into a bar a drug trafficking suspect hung out at, and when the suspect went to the can, our guy sprayed his jacket. When he left the bar, he lit up like a road flare on the display!"

Willis busted out laughing along with the others. "You make the job really sound like fun!"

"We try. But we're all business where the work is concerned," Daniels said, just a tad defensively.

Willis was quick to reassure him, saying, "I didn't mean it in a bad way. Sometimes even the best of what we do is pretty f-ed up. It's good that you all can hang loose and keep your heads in the game."

"Hey! There they are!" Matt said, pointing to a screen displaying the output of the hidden cameras mounted on the command center. Mendes and his girlfriend were walking toward the theater the next block over. They were holding hands and ambling along like they didn't have a care in the world.

Everyone was silent as they watched the only Family Matters Task Force suspect discovered to date. Willis forced himself to relax, noticing he'd tensed his shoulders and was nearly holding his breath.

"One," came through the radio, announcing that the agent selling tickets had spotted Mendes. Moments later, those in the motor home heard, "Two," as the agent behind the concession counter announced that the couple was inside.

They waited a few minutes, then heard, "They're in the theater sitting a little to the left of dead center, ten rows from the back wall. The lights are up and it looks like the place is about half full so far. The projectionist says we have about eight minutes before the lights go down."

Daniels unclipped the mic from the radio's and replied, "Good job. Will you be able to watch them through the movie?"

"I think so. I tried the night vision goggles, and the damn screen is too bright; they're useless. Also, where they are I can just see her arm, they're a little too high up for me to see them both from the booth," the agent reported.

"Do your best. We've got the outside covered. And if they come back through the lobby, we'll see them. Keep us posted," said Daniels, then he hung up the mic.

The three agents made light conversation in the mobile command center, mostly talking about past cases and other investigations they were privy to. They were interrupted once by the female agent who was doing the laundry, dropping off a neatly-folded load and taking another load to wash and fold.

The surveillance team watched disinterestedly as a soda syrup delivery was made to the theater, along with several CO_2 tanks. One of the cameras on the vehicle was focused on the entrance to the theater, recording the faces of those entering just in case someone made contact with Mendes inside.

The agent stationed in the projection booth periodically left to patrol up and down the hallway, checking out any late arrivals to the specific theater the couple were in, picking up trash, and sweeping up spilled popcorn in his disguise.

The evening passed uneventfully for the surveillance team. But they were all old hands at staking out subjects. As the movie approached the end, the team perked up.

Once the credits began to roll, the agent in the booth went downstairs and grabbed one of the huge plastic trash cans and wheeled it into the theater. When the seats came into view, the first thing he saw was that the couple were not in their seats.

"Hey! Anyone got eyes on the suspects?" he radioed, barely moving his lips in case he was being watched.

Daniels grabbed the radio mic and shouted, "What in the hell do you mean? Look around, they have to be there!"

The agent behind the concession counter quickly came around and moved into the exiting crowd, scanning for either of the couple. "Stand by—checking. Maybe they're in the washrooms."

NO JUSTICE, NO PEACE

"Stay here," Willis ordered, as he grabbed Yvette's hand, pulling her out of the vehicle. "Just act cool, we're just two people going to a movie," he said as they sauntered toward the multiplex entrance. They both scanned the crowd exiting through the front entrance. "We got eyes on the other exits?" he radioed.

"Yeah, one of the cars is parking, the other circulating the route back to the house," Daniels replied.

"Son of a bitch! The last thing I wanted was a hard target search in a public venue. Make sure all the exits are covered. Matt call Seattle PD and tell them we need at least a dozen officers, immediately. Let's lock down this theater," Willis said, as the agent from the laundromat came running toward the theater. "One of you inside get the manager, make him understand we need to seal the building."

Seconds later, Willis and Bailor reached the front entrance. Willis pulled his badge and pistol and shouted for everyone to get back inside, that their lives were in danger. Most complied, though several complained that they were leaving. Bailor also drew her weapon and began corralling the stragglers.

The agent in the car sent to check the street drove up to the entrance to the multiplex, driving up on the sidewalk right outside the door. When he exited the car he waved Willis inside, saying "Go! I got the door."

Seconds later, several Seattle Police Department squad cars rolled up. The agent covering the door dispatched them around the building to cover the other exits. More Seattle PD officers arrived and in minutes the building was secured.

Inside, the crowd was getting restless, with some even trying to push themselves past the officers blocking the exits. Half a dozen patrons had to be restrained in plastic cuffs and pushed to the ground before the rest of the crowd got the idea and settled down.

Each theater was emptied with the authorities moving everyone into the broad hallway in the center of the multiplex. As each theater was cleared, an officer was posted to keep anyone from reentering. Next came the restrooms. Once everyone was moved into the common area, Willis posted several police officers and two of his agents at the main door.

Agent Allen had printed a number of copies of photos of Mendes and his companion and handed them out to all of the officers. The Seattle PD sent twenty-five officers to the theater, with more on the way.

The theater complex and the adjoining parking structure were quickly sealed off. And once the complex was under control, Agent Willis allowed people to leave in single file through the front door after being photographed. Those who had driven vehicles to the venue had them searched before they were allowed out of the parking garage.

After checking over eight hundred men, women and children through the exit, Agent Willis gathered up all the officers and agents not covering exits, and along with the theater's manager, began the search through the entire structure. Searchers worked through the building in pairs, with all lights turned up full. The restroom stalls, any HVAC ducts large enough for a person to get into, all the utility closets and corridors were searched.

Agent Allen returned to the mobile command center and reran all the surveillance video, trying to see where and how anyone could have exited the theater right under their very noses.

A number of people had left as their movies ended, and he didn't have high enough resolution to completely rule out the fact that the two escaped in disguise.

Agent Willis dispatched two agents to cover the house on the off chance that the two might return there, but in his heart of hearts, he believed that the couple had given them the slip once again.

Someone of considerable means was helping them, that was clear. What wasn't clear was whether or not the task force had been compromised. That way be dragons, Willis thought. In order to pursue that kind of investigation, anyone black in the bureau would have to be a suspect.

The search was turning up empty. "Matt, what have you got?" Willis radioed.

"Nothing, really. They could have walked right out the front door, but our guys would have seen them. The drones didn't pick up anyone heading back to the house. The only vehicle that was anywhere near the building was the soda distributor's van."

"Can you track it?"

"It's been too long, chief," Allen said with regret. "It drove out of the drone's view a couple of hours ago."

"Then we are truly screwed. We've found nothing inside the building. We're going to sweep through one more time then I'm calling it a night," Willis said. "There's gonna be hell to pay for this night," he said, ruefully. "Over and out."

-=#=-

The syrup company's van was stopped under an awning in the company's parking lot, rows of identical vans filling the small lot.

"Just hang on for a second. I want to have a look around to make sure we weren't followed," Anthony Dawson said to the couple seated on the deck of the cargo space inside the van. He returned five minutes later, now out of the company coveralls and in his own clothes.

"Okay, let's get you to my car, and I'll get you on your way," he promised.

After the couple got out of the van, Dawson locked the doors and returned the keys to the lock box hanging on the wall just outside of the loading dock door. He led them through a narrow walkway between the buildings, stopping them before they could be seen from the street.

"Wait here until I signal."

Mendes and his companion waited, watching as Dawson went to a limousine parked at the curb about twenty-five feet down the sidewalk. He entered the limo and reached back to unlock the back door and open it. He had removed the bulbs from the interior lights so there would be no telltale light when he opened any of the doors. Looking up and down the street, Dawson gestured for the two to get in the car.

He immediately pulled away from the curb and set off directly for the airport. "Okay, you have luxury travel accommodations if we get to the airport before they think to lock it down. When was the movie scheduled to be over?"

"In about forty-five minutes," she replied.

"I'm Tony," he said, reaching back to shake hands with the pair.

"I'm Vernon and this is Sylvia. Thanks for doing this," he said.

"Service with a smile," Dawson said, tipping an imaginary hat. "Let me ask you this, any idea how they copped to you so quick?"

"No idea. I thought we were home free until I got the message. And the whole time after I got it, there was no sign of anyone watching us."

"You remember the pizza guy? That was an FBI agent, and that kid filmed the two of you and the interior of the house. I was supposed to tell you that they picked you up at the train station. That's all I know," Dawson said.

"You have anything else for us?" Mendes asked.

"Nope. How are you holding up?" Dawson asked.

The couple both laughed. "This is the first time Vernon's taken a vacation in three years," Sylvia said.

"Speaking of which. These are for you," said Dawson, handing Mendes a new SIMM card for his phone and a bundle of cash wrapped in plain, brown paper. "That's forty-thousand bucks, there."

"We still have over half of what we got in Miami," said Sylvia.

"No worries. It's for when you may need it. You have to be careful. I'm also supposed to warn you that if I wasn't able to extract you, I was supposed to kill you," Dawson said soberly.

"We know. We half expect to be shot, or worse, most every second of the day," said Mendes.

"That's not how we operate. Something like that would only happen in a case where the authorities grabbed you, or were about to get you and we couldn't prevent it from happening. As you see, we have our ways of preventing something like that from happening.

"Anyway, here's what's going to happen next. I'm going to drive you onto the field to a private jet. The pilot is a guy named Archie, and he'll take it from there. Here we are, both of you sit back like VIPs," Dawson said as he turned onto the access road to the private terminal. He navigated through the parked aircraft, pulling up to the Gulfstream that had brought him to Seattle. When the car came to a stop, Tony got out and opened the door closest to the jet.

Archie was just letting down the combined door-stairway as Dawson led the pair to the aircraft.

"Archie, Vernon and Sylvia," he introduced.

"Perfect timing. Come on everybody, let's get a move on. I have clearance for departure in fifteen minutes. Tony, good to see you again, obviously everything went well," he said bumping fists with Tony and taking the offered bag of unneeded equipment he'd had given Tony when they had arrived.

"Damn, skippy. I'm out of here before the shit hits the fan," Tony said.

"Me too. There's bound to be an alert out on them in no time. Hopefully I'll catch you soon."

"My feeling as well, Archie. Safe travels."

Both men turned to enter their respective vehicles and in no time Tony was on his way off the field as Archie started the Gulfstream's engines, contacting the tower for clearance to taxi. By the time the Gulfstream's wheels left the ground, Tony was already a mile away, heading for the bus terminal. Locating the CCTV cameras outside and inside the terminal, Tony kept his head down as he bought his ticket and waited for the bus to depart.

Chapter 29

Pastor King's 11:00 A.M. Sunday service was just about full, those attending filling nearly every pew all the way to the door at the back of the church. Sharon and Felicia had arrived early enough that they were six pews from the front. Judith and Jackson were sitting about midway between the alter and the doors in the rear.

From conversations and greetings before the service started, many of those in the congregation knew each other. There were a number of conversations going on with people updating their friends and acquaintances with what went on the week before.

Sharon and Felicia were sitting with a dozen or so of their friends, a few who were going to be attending their brunch after the service. At five minutes until the service was to start, organ music began playing, signaling for everyone to take their seats and settle down.

When Pastor King came out and took his place, the music stopped, and he led the congregation in the opening prayer. When he finished, he said, "Everyone, please be seated."

Once everyone had taken their seat, he began.

"In large measure I wanted to talk about the differences between God's relationship with man, and man's relationship with man. What brought this to mind were the interesting times we are living in right now.

"It's no secret that much killing in the name of historical wrongs committed over the last four centuries has visited the specter of death on many thousands of family members, friends, and colleagues. And for that there can be no excuse. No excuse forgives the taking of innocent life in the name of vengeance, in the name of retribution, nor even in the name of justice. For modern man, the notion of an eye for an eye is one that we struggle to overcome every day.

"The killing by the state is no more right than the murder in the street; both are heinous, and both are above the pay grade of man. But man's laws must be obeyed, that is until they are discarded and/or replaced.

"No one will argue that the behavior of the nation has changed in a very short period of time. That the killings of late have graphically illustrated an evil woven into the fabric of this country's history, but a history that extended into the present. It appears that those historical ills are no more. But at what cost? The families of rogue police officers who committed no crimes have paid the ultimate price for the sins of their spouse, their parent, their son, or daughter; and is that right? Is that just? Do we make the calculation that the ends justifies the means? Is there any more cheap, distasteful—no, not distasteful—disgustingly hateful calculation that kills children in the name of cultural change, even though it may be righting a wrong that stood for hundreds of years?

"It is not man's place to make such a calculation, and I certainly cannot believe that a just and righteous God would demand such squandering of life."

Pastor King continued on that vein, questioning the morality of anyone who would kill in the name of justice. But he took everyone by surprise when he asked, "However, we have to ask the question, how else was the killing of innocent blacks in this country going to stop? Millions of innocent blacks have been killed since the first African slaves were brought to our shores. Equal justice under the law has never applied to nonwhites in this country, nor has it applied to anyone except white men; at least the justice part. There is still no equality in this country, women still do not receive equal pay for equal work unless they take their employer to court, and then what's the outcome? A settlement and the necessity for searching for a new job.

"Far too many in this country have gone searching for equality and justice only to find that those notions are the stuff that dreams are made of, ethereal and unreachable. And now we have someone who has halted, for now, the murder of innocent blacks. That, is significant. And what I think about is: why did it take so long? Not the killing, but the extension of justice to African Americans? The cries of treat me like a white man have resonated with more than the country's African Americans. You hear the same refrain from women, too."

Pastor King paused a moment to take a sip of water in the silent church, then he continued. "If God makes the final judgment of all of us when our time comes, and as it says in the Bible, vengeance is mine sayeth the Lord. Then I want to ask this question, is it our place to punish those who have transgressed against God's laws?

"It hurts my heart weighing every perspective in our current circumstances. I weep over the loss of life, but I have great difficulty calling it senseless given the result. I do not personally enjoy the perfection of our Lord, nor can I judge others in His stead. All I can do is to live my life in His grace to the best of my ability. No man can do better. But we must ask ourselves, what is the pinnacle of man's existence? What must we strive to leave behind for our children and our children's children?

"I believe it is a world where they can live free, having every opportunity for the American dream, and to live without persecution because of their skin color, the language they speak, or the person they love.

"We are one third the way through the 21st Century, and we still settle our differences with violence, with killing, with economics that feed corporate concerns but let people starve. We must be better than this, we are all the family of man."

Pastor King continued on with more standard Biblical fare, winding up with community announcements. When he concluded with the closing prayer, several of the congregation enthusiastically clapped.

Pastor King made his way to his accustomed spot just outside the church doors. When Judith introduced Jackson to Pastor King, he expressed his excitement at meeting the young man.

"Do you have time to chat, young man? It would be an honor to get to know you better," King asked.

"The honor would be mine, Pastor," Jackson replied, shaking the man's hand.

At that moment, Sharon and Felicia were exiting the church. Pastor King said, "I am so glad to see the two of you! And right on time. Let me introduce you to Jackson Richards, the Web Master of Jackson's Real Deal Web site. Mr. Richards, this is Sharon Jefferson and Felicia Davenport, we were going to brunch together shortly. Would it be all right if Mr. Richards and Judith here joined us?" he asked, knowing the two were acquainted with the journalist.

The two women looked at the other, checking to see what the other thought. "We'd be honored and delighted for the two of you to join us," Sharon offered.

The four of them moved off away from the entrance so Felicia could give directions to the restaurant. Everyone then disbursed to their cars and headed off to the restaurant.

Sharon and Felicia arrived first with Sharon dropping Felicia off out front and then driving off to park. When she went inside and let the hostess know who she was, Felicia was escorted to a private room set up for their use.

Sharon entered the room a few minutes later, followed by another couple, long-time friends of theirs dating back to when the two met.

"Sit anywhere," Felicia offered. "Just save the seat at the head of the table for Pastor King."

The rest of those invited to the small celebration trickled in with

Pastor King the last to arrive. He arranged to have Jackson sit on his immediate right, with Judith next to him, and Sharon and Felicia on his other side.

Pastor King got everyone's attention, and as the assembled quieted down, he made introductions all around. When he explained who Jackson was, a number of the guests immediately started to ask questions, but stopped when Pastor asked for all questions and the lively art of conversation be held until after the introductions. Surprisingly, of the nearly twenty people in the room, nearly every one was a notable in one Washington circle or another.

And just when everyone thought he was done, King raised his glass and said, "As you all know, we're here to celebrate the official fifth anniversary between these two crazy kids here, and I certainly hope that one day I have the honor of making honest women of them both. To Felicia and Sharon, may they find life, love and affection for each other for all of their days; Felicia and Sharon!" Everyone repeated Felicia and Sharon's names, clinked glasses all around and drank the toast.

The venue was an upscale restaurant and the party room was set up buffet style, giving everyone further chance to talk and circulate around the long table. For the first fifteen minutes, Sharon and Felicia circulated around the table, thanking everyone for coming and finding out what was going on in their lives. Meanwhile, Pastor King was in close conversation with Jackson.

"...and because of your love of sports statistics, this is how you came up with the idea for the Real Deal web site?" Pastor King asked, somewhat amazed.

"Sort of, Pastor—"

"Please, call me Augustus. I'm not much for standing on ceremony. But you were saying?"

"What drove me to start gathering the stats and details of cop-involved killings, murder if you will, was anger. I was tired of reading about cops killing us for no reason but convenience. It always looked like the cops were committing murder because it was inconvenient to have to investigate or determine if deadly force was warranted. And that bullshit, sorry, Pastor—Augustus, about all of them fearing for their life was crap. Like Judge Bridges says, that excuse, up until just recently, was the universal get out of jail free card for anyone white who murdered anyone black. It was like African Americans were some kind of super monsters, even our children, that threatened the very existence of a cop."

"There is a very serious moral discussion about the ends justifying the means. Killing has never been proscribed, even though it is codified in the Ten Commandments it is the commandment that has been least followed. Governments use killing to secure political mastery over other countries. War is a woven into the existence of man like life itself," said King.

"Is that kind of what you were getting at in your sermon?" Jackson asked.

"It is a difficult subject. As a man of God, I abhor the taking of a life as against all the preachings of Jesus Christ. But as a black man who has lived over six decades in the United States, my personal perspective is often at odds with my religious teachings.

"I admire how you have chosen to deal with this cultural crisis. Pointing out the inequities of a system that places no real value on the lives of blacks is the best first step in trying to change the paradigm. Please excuse the impertinence of the question," King said, lowering his voice, "but are you at all associated with the party or parties who are behind all these killings?"

Jackson laughed. He then pointed to where Sharon was standing and said, "That's what her people wanted to know when they came to my house and questioned me. My answer then hasn't changed; I am not helping anyone. Judith and I have determined that group extensively used my site's data. The FBI interviewed me, asking if I had knowledge of the fact that my data was used in carrying out the killings of the cop families, and I said that it was obvious that anyone could."

At that moment Sharon returned to the table with a plate of food and sat.

"Just in time," King said. "I was just about to get into the weighty discussion of current events with young Mr. Richards, here. Sharon is posted at the White House, that's all right to discuss, isn't it, dear?"

"No problem. I'm the FBI liaison to the White House. I'm working on the Family Matters Task Force," she explained.

"Holy crap!" Jackson exclaimed. "Right in the thick of it, so to speak. Making any progress?" he asked, with a sly grin.

King laughed as did Sharon.

"Nothing I can discuss," she answered.

"Well can I ask you this? And please, let me know if this is too personal, but how do you feel about chasing down the people who, after centuries, have managed to stop cop killings of innocent blacks? It's what Pastor here was getting at in his sermon, if I'm not mistaken, right Pas—Augustus?" Jackson asked, nodding toward King.

Sharon took a few moments to think about her reply. "It's complicated because there's a definite conflict between having sworn an oath to uphold the Constitution and the laws of the land, and what I know about social justice and the historical track record of law enforcement in the United States."

"That's what I mean. How do you deal?" Jackson asked, intently. "That would be extremely hard for me to do."

"It's not easy. I don't think anyone of color could avoid an internal debate on their obligation and oath to the law, and what is right," Sharon replied.

"That is the crux of the issue," King said. "As blacks, blacks old enough to know what the culture of America has been since the first settlers came over from Europe, I see two dynamics of thinking prevailing. The first is the deliberate loss of life."

"Shouldn't that be the main consideration?" Jackson asked.

"Perhaps. But context is everything," King replied. "Okay, let's look at it from the perspective of a country that has a disagreement with another country where both parties have exhausted every other course of action. When diplomacy, trade, or even the use of proxies to try to sway events has failed and one party feels pushed into a corner and that the situation is completely untenable, war all too often is the inevitable result. Killing has become the tool of state in order to resolve conflict; as counter-intuitive as that situation is.

"Now let's take our situation in this country. A case can be made for there having been an undeclared war between whites and blacks since President Lincoln signed the Emancipation Proclamation, as far too many whites refused to cease owning slaves, and furthermore, failing to treat the former slaves as equals under the law. Therefore, since January 1, 1863, the treatment of former slaves being untenable to the life of black men, women and children, and being systemic to the culture and custom of the United States of America, a de facto state of war has existed for the last hundred-seventy years or so."

Jackson was speechless, King's declaration catching him completely by surprise.

King continued as both Judith and Sharon leaned in to hear more. "And unlike stupid, white men who claim their unfettered gun ownership will save them from a government intent on subjugating them, blacks know only too well exactly how easy it is to be persecuted. We cannot change our skin color which makes us such easy targets for slights, insults, violence, or death.

"And after all this time, the consideration that whites get in this country is still to be denied us, it appears that someone has decided to prosecute this de facto war. What wasn't ever expected was that this would ever happen. Whites assumed that since they held all the power in this country, they would remain invulnerable to the slings and arrows of outrageous fortune," he said, smiling. "Judging by the data you've accumulated on your site, young man, it appears that the last straw was the murders of so many children killed by white police officers.

"Since the families of rogue police officers began to die, not a single black child has attacked, hurt, or killed a police officer. Since these families started to die, not a single police officer has been attacked, hurt, or killed during a traffic stop of a black man or woman. Or am I mistaken, Sharon?"

"No, you're right. Reports of crime are down everywhere. I believe it's because of a lack of provocation by white cops toward blacks. Even my white colleagues in the Bureau are forced to agree. It has given lie to all notions that blacks are prone to higher rates of crime in this country. But don't hold your breath waiting for any admission of the fact," she said, bitterly.

"You don't sound very happy with your colleagues, my dear," King observed.

"It's complicated," she said, as Felicia put a comforting arm over her shoulders, obviously eavesdropping.

The others in the room, seeing that something wasn't right quieted. Hearing the sudden silence, Pastor King looked around and said, "Nothing to see here, everyone move along!" breaking the tension of the moment and getting laughs from everyone as they resumed their conversations.

Judith said, "Are you allowed to talk about what the White House is thinking about what to do when these people are caught?"

"Nothing out of the ordinary has been discussed, I can tell you that. We have discussed what the likely reaction from the public will be. In all likelihood, the backlash against African Americans by police and racist civilians is going to be horrific. Deep down, I'm hoping that they never get caught, and I know how that sounds. I'm just happy that I'm the liaison with the White House, not running the task force," said Sharon.

"Judith and I talk about the what ifs all the time. I'm afraid you're right, this isn't going to bode well for us. I think the only thing that will ensure that the status quo becomes the de facto condition in this country is if the people behind the killings remain undiscovered and with the Sword of Damocles constantly held over the collective heads of this country," stated Jackson.

"Nice classical education there, young man" King said, chuckling. "But you're right, I'm afraid. Whites are vindictive; they're scared; and we all know what scared people do when they're backed into a corner. I will never preach this, but—the only way forward for this country, in my belief, is for those people to never be caught. I hope that doesn't upset you, dear," he said, patting Sharon's hand.

"Not at all. I'd be less than honest if I said I hadn't thought the same," she said; Felicia nodding her head in agreement.

"Now that's a conversation I'd love to continue with the four of you," King said. "But this really isn't the place."

Chapter 30

Andrew was hard at work when the receptionist buzzed and informed him that there were a couple of people from the FBI on their way to his office. When he looked up, he saw it was the seemingly ever present Agents Greer and Carson.

He stood waiting, and when they reached his glassed-in office space, he offered them seats as he took his place behind his desk.

"So, what is it today? More questions about my feelings on being free at last, free at last, Thank God almighty we are free at last?" he said, chuckling when he finished the Martin Luther King, Jr. quote.

"You really can't help yourself, can you?" Greer said, sneering.

"It's just that you two bring out the best in me. Tell me, what is it today that it was so important to roust me here at work? Trying to make me look bad, Agent Carson?"

"Not at all. This is only peripherally about you. We still want to know where Anthony Dawson is, he has become a person of interest in our investigation. Have you had any contact with him since we saw you last, Mr. Simmons?" Carson inquired.

"I have not."

"Would you tell us if you had?" Greer asked belligerently.

Andrew snickered. "Honestly, if it would piss you off, I definitely wouldn't. It's just so fun watching you fume over the fact that you can't punch this nigga in the nose!"

Greer started to get out of his seat when Andrew said very quietly, "If you take one step toward me, I will break you in half. And lady, there wouldn't be a damn thing you could do to stop me." he paused a beat, then said, "Think it over Whitey. I am better trained than you are, and I have an inner rage that just might lead me to throw your ass out the window. But I will take no more of your bullshit. You hear me?" Andrew said, standing up and leaning both fists on his desk.

Carson put her hand on Greer's arm, not holding him in check, but as a reminder that they were not there to get into a fight.

"That won't be necessary, Mr. Simmons," she said as Greer sat back down. "But nonetheless, the whereabouts of Mr. Dawson are very important to us and any assistance you can give us would be appreciated."

"I don't know where Tony is. And I doubt he has anything to do with your investigation. And unless I'm misinformed, and you know I'm not, no one has been shot, no one white, in relationship to your investigation, and you know it. It would be all over the news. So why do you really want him?" Andrew asked, a mocking tone in his voice.

"Not everything about this investigation is about someone getting shot, or dying, Mr. Simmons. If you haven't heard from Mr. Dawson, then we'll be on our way," Agent Carson said, getting to her feet, Greer following suit, still with a scowl on his face.

"Thank you for the visit," Andrew said, following them to the door. And as the two agents walked down the hallway toward the exit, Andrew shouted at their backs just before they turned out of sight, "You think this kind of harassment might possibly have something to do with black folks being pissed off at you law enforcement types?"

Andrew heard more than one laugh down the hall as he returned to his desk to try to get back to work.

Since he knew the authorities were monitoring his mobile phone, he pulled it out and texted to Tony, "Shit's getting deep, don't lose your paddle." He figured that if they couldn't find Tony by his phone, the message would be harmless, and just might piss off Agent Greer even more should he see it.

-=#=-

Agent Willis was leading the post mortem in Seattle, hoping they would discover something they could recoup from the loss of Mendes and his companion. Currently, they were back at the command center going over all the surveillance footage from the cameras and drones.

He was also going through stills capturing anyone remotely resembling the couple at the bus station, train station, the airport and any ferries on the way to Vancouver, and CCTV images from around the city. They were pre-screened by face recognition software operating at 99% efficiency. Those images flagged by software were shunted aside until a person could review them.

Agent Allen was going over the drone footage frame by frame and had been for the previous four hours, listening to the rest of the proceedings with only half of his attention.

He was concentrating his attention on the beverage company's truck at the delivery entrance when he announced, "Hey guys, I think I found something!"

Everyone gathered around to see what he was talking about. "Take a look here. This is that syrup and CO2 delivery truck. Watch as the delivery guy goes in, this is right after he parked."

They watched as the driver got out of the truck, went to the back doors, facing the delivery entrance of the building. In the eerie green tinted night vision picture, they watched as he put several boxes of syrup on the hand truck and rolled it over to the door. When he opened the door, there was a flare of light that overloaded the night vision camera for a brief moment, obscuring the immediate area. Then a black blotch covered the same area from the door to van as the camera overcompensated for the flare of light.

"Damn! Do you think?" Agent Daniels asked.

Allen shrugged his shoulders. "Unless they separated, were wearing disguises, and then walked right past us out the door, it's the only thing I can find."

"What about the wide-angle drone? Any idea where that truck went?" Daniels asked.

"No, but here's the address of the company," Allen said, pointing to another screen.

"Yvette, grab someone and go over there. Find out—Matt, can you get a tag number on the truck?" Daniels asked.

"Nope, I thought of that. It pulled out of the lot on the far side, away from our cameras. And as you can see, they don't put numbers on the roof," Allen replied.

"Okay, Yvette, see if you can locate which truck it was and seal it up. Tell the company it's evidence in the commission of a crime," Daniels ordered.

"Got it. If I find out which one it is, I'll call forensics to get their butt over there," she promised.

"Anything else, Matt?" Willis asked.

"I'm afraid not. The drones didn't catch anyone heading back to the house and our bugs haven't picked up any sounds from inside."

"Okay, would you send a team over there, Terry. I doubt we'll find anything, but I still want your people to scour the place top to bottom," Willis requested.

"Right away," Daniels said, leaving the room to dispatch a team to the house.

"Good work, Matt. You are the best!" Willis said, clapping the younger agent on the shoulder. "And don't forget the photos and specs on the mobile command center. That thing is amazing!"

"Thank you, sir. As soon as I finish going through the rest of the video, I'll send you the complete packet."

Agent Willis left the room, on his way to check in with Daniels before he headed to the hotel to pack. Fortunately, he wasn't going to have to fly commercially; one of the Bureau's jets was already on its way to pick him up. It was hard to believe anything but the fact that the FBI was completely outclassed by those they sought. What he would give anything to find out was whether the couple fled because that was their original plan; or if they were tipped off by someone inside the agency; or something they might have seen of the surveillance crew.

-=#=-

The Los Angeles Police Department was still stinging over the officers shot and killed, though most conveniently forgot that the officers fired into a crowd of peaceful demonstrators first. The street cops were still keeping their weapons holstered, but several African Americans were roughed up or held without processing for several days. Unfortunately, there was little that could be done about that level of misconduct, the cops relied on it.

What black residents of Los Angeles took to doing was traveling outside their homes in groups of two or more where possible. And if one or the other was being harassed, the other filmed. And where such incidents were observed by others, people would rush to record video of the incident.

When cops tried to confiscate the cameras of citizens, that effort was met with a level of resistance few were willing to challenge; but the guns stayed in their holsters.

Small towns that relied on working class African Americans paying bogus traffic citations were in a world of hurt. Blacks were no longer putting up with questionable citations. The meme of "treat me like a white man" had spread even to the smallest towns. And though years of institutional racism didn't disappear overnight, beginning with the worst of what America handed its former slaves by eliminating their senseless murder was a damn good start.

Culture and society did not move forward at the same rate as technological advances. It had been that way since the beginning of the Industrial Revolution. And, there were recognizable good and bad aspects to the proliferation of new advances in communications, in data storage, in social networking, and in electronic surveillance of a nation's citizens.

The FBI, the CIA, the NSA, and all the other arms of the Department of Homeland Security were accustomed to knowing everything possible about those living in the United States and in many cases, overseas too. The only organizations with superior knowledge of Americans at large were the mega-conglomerates such as Google and Amazon. Their data collection techniques were superior to those employed by the federal government because they specialized in developing algorithms that predicted, and to a slightly lesser extent, controlled a consumer's behavior.

Since the second decade of the 21st Century, online information gathering corporate concerns had grown further and further away from cooperating with federal law enforcement. Privacy was a growing concern as Americans began to fully realize just how intrusive the government was in monitoring their behavior.

Cameras were everywhere, exponentially growing in number in the name of security. Constitutional rights were, for all practical purposes, nonexistent. People could be spirited off the street or even out of their homes without explanation.

But slowly the people were fighting back. Personal mobile devices were encrypted with algorithms so powerful even the fastest, most powerful computers would take years to break.

Open source encryption software for computers, for Web servers and cloud storage services for those tech savvy enough, made them virtually unbreakable. The only weak point was the actual wiring between points on the network. The Bureau had spent the last fifteen years lobbying for back doors in commercially available encryption applications that would enable them to break into any system they wanted to at will. But even though Congress passed legislation regulating the retention and storage of encryption keys by American software publishers, the Open Source Community stepped up, created unbreakable operating systems, and gave them away for free. This forced the NSA to design and build faster and faster computers whose sole purpose was the real-time decryption of weakly protected electronic communications. And with so many people using encryption apps to secure their phones and tablets, and the remote disabling capabilities of the units themselves, not only was a person's data protected from scrutiny, but theft of the devices had dropped to practically zero.

The biggest unspoken challenge that the entire United States law enforcement apparatus faced, the one insurmountable problem that no one could figure out how to overcome, was the fact that virtually any black in the country could be associated with or belong to the vigilante group, including those working in America's law enforcement community. The possibility was giving the highest levels of all branches of the United States Government fits. Even though the senior members of the Family

Matters Task Force never openly discussed the matter, every single one of them was unwilling to give voice to the fears they harbored.

Agent Willis was secretly relieved that Sharon Jefferson was stationed in the White House out from under his direct supervision. Many of the other African American agents and assets working for the Bureau were in sensitive positions, but Willis believed he would know if something untoward were to occur. If there was a mole in the agency, he was certain he would find them.

When he returned to Washington, D.C., the first thing Willis did was review the distribution list of the task force online database to see exactly who had access to the network. He also initiated a full Information Technologies audit across the entire agency. This included assets from all the other agencies. To have lost Mendes twice was too suspicious, and Willis wasn't about to take any chances overlooking something critical.

Willis called over to the NSA to speak to his opposite number.

"Hey! How's it hanging over there," he greeted Oscar Pelcheck, one of the assistant Directors of Operations.

"Sheldon. To what do I owe the honor?" Pelcheck inquired.

"How about I take you to lunch?"

"Does the Bureau know you're not feeling well? And that you're making them pick up the tab?" Pelcheck asked.

"It's the agency's take an unfortunate at NSA to lunch program."

Pelcheck laughed. "Then what are we waiting for? When and where?" he asked.

"You pick."

"How about The Dog House?" Pelcheck suggested. "11:30 okay with you?"

"See you there," Willis promised.

Willis was already seated, a cup of coffee already in front of him when Pelcheck arrived. He stood and shook hands then the two sat. Willis had taken a booth away from the rest of the patrons there.

"Okay, Sheldon, spill. What's up?"

Lowering his voice, Willis asked, "How many African Americans are in your group? No, check that. How many are in your entire Ops department?"

"I don't know, fifteen or so. Why—wait, you're not suggesting what I think you're suggesting?"

"Oscar, I just had our only lead to the vigilantes disappear out from under what normally would be characterized as air-tight surveillance, twice! I have to consider the possibility. I was wondering if you have given it any thought yourself?" asked Willis.

"Yeah, we did. But they keep such a tight lid on our people that it would be impossible for any one of them to be working at cross purposes," explained Pelcheck. "Hell, most of them who came here from out of state almost never get home, even for the holidays. So, what are you thinking?"

"Shit if I know. I guess I wanted to know if you're on top of monitoring the members of the task force?"

Pelcheck gave Willis a hard look, silent for the moment. "Sheldon, you know you can't even ask me that question."

"Dammit, Oscar! You don't think I know that? But what if we've all been compromised? I mean how do you kill thousands of people in a matter of weeks and do it without anyone twigging to it ahead of time? I know you don't have a clue either. And to manage that size organization, with the assets to kill without trace? We're all sucking hind teat in this investigation, the NSA most of all," Willis said, holding up his hand to forestall rebuttal. "It's not just you, it's the FBI, it's every local law enforcement department, it's Homeland Security, it's the Marshals—it's all of us! We don't have a fucking clue!"

"God damn it, Sheldon! You think I don't know that? We have sifted through one and a half trillion telephone calls, countless billions of SMS messages; metadata up the ass. And do you know how many email messages? More than the calls and text messages added together. And there's not even a whiff of anything suspicious. This is fucking embarrassing, Sheldon," Pelcheck hissed, looking around to make sure no one was close enough to eavesdrop. "Other than more brute-force efforts, I'm tapped out. What about the possibility of finding the guy who got away?"

"What? Third time's the charm? Doubtful. The team in Seattle is checking every possibility. We originally tracked him from Miami to Seattle. I think the chances are pretty good he's over the border," Willis explained.

"You pass along his description to the Mounties?"

Willis reluctantly replied, "Yeah, we listed him and his girlfriend as persons of interest in the task force investigation."

"You don't sound hopeful."

"Would you be if someone fell through your fingers twice? Sorry, I'm just trying to figure all this out. Your people are monitored; my people are too. And if absolutely nothing shows up, then that scares the living crap out of me," said Willis, his voice full of fatigue.

"How's that?"

"Because that would mean that however they are doing all that they're doing, it's all so far above our best that we honestly have no chance of catching them," Willis said, holding up his cup toward the waitress. "What looks good on the menu?"

Pelcheck opened the menu, looking at the sheet with the specials. "Soup and sandwich looks good. Chicken noodle and corned beef with a slice of Swiss and brown mustard. You?"

"Tuna salad," said Willis as he put the menu aside. "So back to my problem. Do I have to treat every African American in the Bureau as a possible leak?"

Pelcheck shook his head. "If you want my advice, forget about it."

"What!?" Willis almost yelped.

"There's nothing you can do about it. If we can't find them with our assets, you certainly won't. So if you have no control over the situation, ignore it. Trying to do anything else is just going to give you a stroke, so concentrate on something else," Pelcheck advised. "Let me ask you this, how long have your core investigators, the black ones, been with the Bureau?"

"I think the newest one has been there six or seven years," Willis replied.

"So, let's say he or she is a plant. If they haven't tipped you off so far, what makes you think they ever will? And how the hell would you know?" asked Pelcheck.

"That's why I'm buying lunch. I thought you had all the answers."

"Yeah, at one time I thought so, too. So, tell me what happened in Seattle," Pelcheck asked.

Willis recounted what happened over the rest of lunch. When they were through, they walked out together. Just as Willis was going to head to his car, Pelcheck reached out and stopped him.

"I know you're worried about the possibility of a mole in the Bureau, and I advise moving forward cautiously. But concentrate on the things you do best, it's all anyone, even you, should expect," Pelcheck said, clapping Willis on the shoulder in reassurance.

Chapter 31

Pastor King couldn't arrange his dinner gathering until the Tuesday following Sharon and Felicia's brunch celebration. He invited everyone over to his house, preferring the comfort of home to a restaurant.

Unfortunately, Felicia wasn't feeling very well, but she insisted that Sharon join Jackson and Judith at Pastor King's home anyway. King had a housekeeper who helped him with the upkeep of his modest home and usually cooked dinner before she left for the day.

She had prepared grilled salmon, butternut squash, and salad with sherbet for dessert. She was just leaving when Jackson and Judith arrived; Judith having picked up Jackson from his hotel. Pastor King introduced them to the housekeeper then conducted them to the study.

"Sharon just called, she should be here in a few minutes. Felicia isn't feeling well so it's just the four of us. In the meantime, may I get you something to drink?" King offered.

"I'm fine," replied Jackson.

"Water would be nice," she said.

"Bottled?" King asked.

"Perfect."

When he returned with the bottle of water and a glass, King started to sit when the door entry system announced that Sharon was there. King went to let her in with the two returning moments later.

As he led her into the study, he said, "Let's go ahead and sit down to eat. I don't want the salmon to dry out. That okay with you guys?"

He led them to the dining room, making everyone sit while he brought in the various serving dishes and set them on the table. Once seated, he said grace, and they began to serve themselves then pass everything around.

It was quiet for a few minutes, except for the occasional compliments on the food. After everyone was well into their meal, Pastor King said, "I suppose you're all wondering why I called you all here tonight," drawing chuckles from the others. "But the purpose is serious. The three of you are all extremely bright, and you all have proven capabilities in your fields. What I want to discuss is what it takes for a person, a black person, to join a secret group that has done what's been done in this country.

"It is important to understand the overall dynamic of this phase in the country's history," he said, looking at everyone around the table. "Because I fear that if the people who have undertaken to end the murder of blacks in this country are caught, the resulting fear and hatred born of vengeance will end up destroying our race."

"Those are some pretty strong words, Pastor," Sharon said, somewhat taken aback.

"Please, call me Augustus, or Augie, because what we discuss tonight is not the province of a man of God."

"Are you suggesting that we discuss some sort of permanent insurrection? That we somehow decide to become as lawless as those we're discussing?" asked Sharon. "Because if that's what you're suggesting, you put me in a very awkward position."

"I know. But all we're doing is talking. I would never counsel anyone doing that which they did not approve. But what is going on is unprecedented. And the resulting changes in American culture cannot be allowed to revert. We have experienced more progress in equality than at any other time in the history of this country, and that includes Lincoln's signing of the Emancipation Proclamation. We as black Americans cannot let the opportunity to continue winning these strides in equality be squandered."

"So what do you want us to do Pas—Augustus?" asked Judith.

"I don't know. But it's going to be clear very soon that the lack of murder is only the first step for us. The backlash so far has been an increase of peripheral violence toward blacks in police custody. I think police departments are going to keep escalating until they find the threshold of exactly where the vigilantes, for lack of a better term, are going to retaliate. What I think we need to be prepared for is what it's going to take to keep the movement going forward. There must be some support system for pushing for full equality above and beyond the terror of a family being killed," King explained.

He saw that the others were interested. "As a race, we have never had a better opportunity than now to change American culture, and we need a social movement to go along with what the threat of killings has provided. And it cannot mimic the civil rights movement of the Sixties either. It has to be relentless and unforgiving. Whites are a minority in several states now, and that will spread to the entire country in the next few years. It's time to stamp out white entitlement once and for all. Everyone will benefit, nonwhites, women—everyone, including white men," King said emphatically.

"This is like a bad joke: a cop, a journalist and a Web site owner walk into a bar," Jackson said in a lame attempt to make a joke.

"Not so at all. Movements are born of opportunity, message, and timing. The fact that the three of you do such different jobs is deliberate on my part," King reassured.

"But what about me? I can't get involved with something like that, for one thing I'd lose my job!" Sharon said.

"Maybe so, but your insight as a—a consultant or advisory board member will be invaluable. The task force is one thing. I know you cannot violate your oath. But what about Department of Justice directives that go out to local police departments, or even their own changes in protocols and what they monitor on a local level? Making sure that any movement doesn't violate new protocols is important. It's not like the corporate media would be on our side, and any conflict that results in injuries or death will be marked against us, not create sympathy for us.

"Judith, your work regularly appears in Rolling Stone, Mother Jones and dozens of well-trafficked Web sites. By carefully slanting articles about such a movement, you'll be reaching those who would be most likely to support a change in the status quo. For example, if you do a piece on violence against certain groups, you can draw parallels between the unrelenting violence against women since organized religion was invented by man, making women property and the tradition of ownership whites had over blacks. And yes, I know how that sounds coming from a Pastor, but I am not so ignorant as to deny the truth," King said, smiling.

"That's not much different from what I've been doing for years," Judith replied. "But I get it. You're talking about a much more deliberate effort."

"As for you," King said, nodding toward Jackson. "There are ways of writing things that can be provocative, compelling in certain directions on a subconscious level. It's like subliminal propaganda. Instead of calling someone an aggressor, you call them a victim in the case of a police-involved killing in your database. Deliberately doing so when you add a new killing to your Web site will definitely work on peoples' perceptions, again at a mostly subconscious level. But believe me, all this effort will slowly have a profound effect."

King paused a moment, waiting for anyone else to speak. When the others were silent, he continued. "Sharon, in the meetings you've attended on the task force, which emotion dominates the discussion, fear, or anger?"

She thought about it for a moment, then said, "The anger is what's driving most everyone. Anger over being manipulated, anger over the arrogance, anger at the casual killing of so many. I think the fear component is more so at the local level with the local police departments. And you're right. That anger is going to translate into some pretty vicious behavior directed at us if the people responsible for the killings are caught."

"We have to think of ways to keep that from happening. White folks do not forgive, let alone forget. They're running scared already worrying about being overrun by Hispanics. They have watched the southern states' demographics changing since the turn of the century. We're looking at a very desperate race, angry, scared, and having the power to do practically anything to anyone without much consequence, until now.

"They can't stand not being in control. And they can't stand being denied whatever they want. They're still pissed as hell that they can't use the word nigger without consequences anymore. They're small-minded, petty people because they never have to care about how evil their actions are. White entitlement rules this country. Make no mistake, what we're planning, assuming you're all in, is going to be the struggle of a lifetime," King concluded. He sat back and waited, letting the others think through his proposal.

Seeing that no one was going to speak up any time soon, King began to clear the dishes with the others lending a hand, bringing everything into the kitchen with little conversation. King dished up dessert for them all, and they returned to the dining room.

The conversation resumed slowly, everyone tossing ideas back a forth, seeing what generated the most traction. And after dessert came coffee, then after coffee, some stronger libations. The conversation became a planning session, with Jackson keeping notes on his ever-present tablet, but only after he was able to reassure the others that his device's security was absolutely unbreakable.

They also began to compile a list of people around the country, blacks who they were going to approach to recruit for the cause. The list contained people from media, musical culture, some members of the NBA and NFL, politicians, though not many of them, and academics.

They continued on into the night. They finally decided to call a halt to the evening just a few hours short of morning. By the time they were leaving King's home, what started out as an insurmountable task, had been whittled down to manageable steps. Jackson promised to set up a private server for them to keep track of the team's efforts and keep their data secure from even rigorous attempts at unauthorized access.

They had a good beginning of a plan, now all they had to do was put it in motion.

-=#=

Agent Willis had been having a bad few weeks, and the events of the past few days did nothing to improve his streak. He was entering all the separate reports and notes from his trip to Seattle when a call came in from Agent Daniels.

"Sheldon! Hope your trip back was uneventful," greeted Daniels.

"No problems at all. To what do I owe the call? Please tell me you found something."

"We actually found a lot. Yvette located the truck that made the deliveries to the theater that night. It was parked in a different place than the night before, so we were able to get the forensics folks in there right away. The steering wheel was wiped, or the driver used gloves, so nothing there, or on the door handles. But inside we hit the jackpot. We found Mendes and his companion's prints all over the place. They also matched prints we found all over the house. What we didn't find were any clues to where they went. Another thing, the mobile phone they were using dropped off the grid just a few minutes after they entered the theater. Their getaway had to have been planned well in advance, but hell if I know if they were on to us or not," Daniels said.

"How's that?"

"Well look at it this way: if they had been tipped off, how did they signal that they needed extraction? There's no land line in the house, and the snooper was tapped into their phones the whole time. If they sent or received anything from someone else, a call, text message or even accessed an email account, it went through us. There was nothing," explained Daniels.

"So, if they weren't in contact with anyone else, that suggests that their escape route was already set up," said Willis.

"Exactly. You have to wonder, if their exit strategy was preplanned, they may not know we were on to them after all."

Willis thought about if for a few seconds, then asked, "What about that truck? Did your people check out the owner? And was the truck hot-wired?"

"I know where you're going with this. The owner of the distributor is white, been in business for sixteen years. He doesn't exactly fit the profile of a sympathizer. The keys for the truck were in one of those locked key cases outside the building's loading dock. The truck lot was locked with fourteen-foot-high, razor wire topped fences with no easy way into the yard.

But here's where we got lucky," Daniels said, making Willis sit up to listen. "Across the street is a home and garden store, one of those kind of superstores. They had two cameras out front; one on the door and one on the lumber yard driveway. The one pointed toward the driveway caught three people getting into a limousine that was parked on the street. The limo had been parked out in front of the distributor's since just before dark. None of the video recorded from the security camera is good enough for us to identify the driver of the limo, though.

"According to the time stamp on the camera feed, three people came out from a gangway next to the distributor's building about thirty minutes before the movie ended, got in the limo, and drove off. So far we don't know where the limo went, we couldn't get tag numbers from that cheap security camera. We're trying to run down every limo that was out on the streets that night," Daniels reported. "Sorry, that's all I have."

"That's some great work, Terry. Outstanding, work. Please convey my praise to your team," Willis said.

"We're also looking into flights out of Sea-Tac, both commercial and private," Daniels added. "I've got someone looking into the railway and bus terminals too. But we're thinking that they were probably headed into Canada judging by their route here from Miami. The Mounties have their description and a bunch of photos. They're looking at anything commercial and private coming into Vancouver. I'm a little hopeful there because they have a shitload more CCTV cameras spread around the city than we do. If they went that way, we have a decent chance of spotting them."

"That's really solid work, Terry. Send me a list of outgoing flights out of Sea-Tac,; I want to alert the destination cities to keep an eye out. We got damn close, it could happen again. FYI: we haven't gotten anything else from L.A. The pieces of the rounds we recovered are useless, no way to trace them, they're all off the shelf. I'd forgotten what a .50 caliber round can do to a head," Willis said distractedly, shaking his head.

"No doubt. Let's just hope no one else decides to go stupid and fire on anyone dark-skinned. As much as I hate these people killing civilians, it's pretty telling how crime stats have gone down. Shows me just how fucked up local law enforcement has been jacking black folks around forever," Daniels said with a sick laugh.

"Maybe so, but we have a group of people who have killed several thousand Americans on American soil. That's more than on 9/11. We have to catch them; there's no two ways about it."

"If President Temple had been a Republican, he would have invaded Scandinavia by now in retaliation!" Daniels said, busting out laughing.

Willis snorted, a bark of laughter breaking out despite his effort not to laugh. "Very funny, Terry."

"Sorry. If I could have my cake and eat it too, I would love to see the status quo maintained, with crime down and all, and I want us to catch these people. But we can't have both. Anyway, just wanted to bring you up to date personally. I hope there's not too much fallout from the Op here, Shel. I'll keep you posted on any new developments in this neck of the woods," Daniels promised.

"Thanks for everything, Terry. I'll be in touch," Willis said, then hung up.

-=#=-

President Temple was in the private quarters of the White House, thankful to be done for the day. His wife Sylvia was curled up on the couch, reading the newspaper. They had no difficulty sitting around in companionable silence, they were very happy together. She knew exactly what kind of stress his days carried, and to a lesser extent, being First Lady had its baggage too. So their custom was to spend some quiet time together, then have a light dinner where they talked about their day. With their only daughter away at school, it was just the two of them most evenings.

Sensing that Temple was unusually unsettled, Sylvia broke the silence and asked, "What is it, Marcus? Something's on your mind tonight. Want to talk about it before dinner?"

"Only if it's okay with you. This one is getting more worrisome as each day goes by," he replied.

She put down the newspaper and patted the couch next to her. He got up, slipped off his jacket, and tossed it over the arm of a chair, and sat down beside Sylvia. She put her arm behind his shoulders and began toying with his hair.

"So tell me. What is it?" she asked softly.

"The Family Matters Task Force. They are exactly where they were as the day they formed it. They almost had a person of interest, but the man slipped out from under their fingers twice. I'm really afraid that we may not catch any of the vigilantes before the campaign for the next election. Then it's the soft on crime nonsense that's going to rear its ugly head," he revealed.

"I don't want to be cold blooded, hon, but isn't crime down significantly?" she asked, twining her fingers in his hair.

"Yes, but—"

"And for the moment, aren't killings of African Americans by police officers down?"

She held up her other hand to stop him from replying. "And don't you have the entire law enforcement arm of the government looking for the people behind the killings?"

"Yes."

"And, given the need for secrecy so that the government's hand isn't revealed, don't you have no comment on an ongoing investigation? And isn't it a fact that anyone who tries to pry information about the investigation from you or any of the department heads on the task force is working for the people you're seeking?" she asked rhetorically.

The president laughed, and said, "Why aren't you president instead of me?"

"Because I'm not nearly as diplomatic as you are. I would no more put up with the crap that congress pulls than I would an errant child, Marcus. But back to your problem. What happens if the FBI or whomever doesn't get hold of the people they're looking for?" she asked.

"I suppose they keep looking. It's unconscionable that someone who killed thousands of Americans gets to remain free."

"But for the sake of argument, what if?"

"Then for the next few generations, Americans will know what happens if an innocent African American is murdered by the police or anyone else, I suppose," he replied. "But really long term I suppose the country gets a start on truly living up to the equal protections of the 14th Amendment."

"Maybe. But the course of this country has changed under your watch, and despite the thousands killed, all for the better. Pragmatically speaking, the changes were long-past due. And that's a legacy worthy of a good man," said Sylvia. "I'm hungry. Let see what the chef came up with tonight."

Chapter 32

Augustus King was leaving the doctor's office in a very subdued mood. His lab results from his latest physical were troubling. Even more so up against the progress of the effort he, Judith, Jackson, and Sharon had set in motion several weeks back.

With no officer-involved shootings of any African Americans and no announced progress in the search for those responsible for the thousands of killings, there was nothing to disrupt the quiet doings in their formulating and slanting public opinion. At the very least, the changes in Jackson's reporting, Judith's essays, and other publications were being carried over into other media. They had put together a very effective group who were editing various articles in the venerable online encyclopedia Wikipedia. The changes were subtle, but their influence would be most felt in the halls of academia by those doing online research. Students, younger minds, and even those who wrote news copy were being exposed to the nuanced descriptions and definitions the clandestine organization was producing.

King was grateful that his idea was bearing fruit, that the carrot, for lack of better term, was appearing to be equally as successful as the stick. King was quite the fan of one of Architect Daniel Burnham's quotes: Make no small plans; they have no magic to stir men's blood. What he set in motion was nothing short of miraculous, even though made easy by the ease with which people communicated and received communications from others, from media sites on the Internet and via social networking.

But the success of his endeavor was blunted by the diagnosis he just received from his physician, one of pancreatic cancer. It wasn't very advanced but it was aggressive. The prognosis for surgical treatment was not good, and several of the other treatments were not any better in their expected efficacy.

But King was not a man to dwell on the negatives life threw him. His immediate concern was making sure the things he set in motion would continue on past the end of his life. He had so much to do and perhaps nine months to do it. Unfortunately, much of it he had to do, he had to do alone, so there was no time to waste.

-=#=

Felicia was as excited as Sharon was, watching how the group was helping to mold the way information was disseminated to the world. They both reveled in seeing Jackson's or Judith's handiwork on television or in print. Sharon didn't have any direct media-related work to do, and she was not revealing anything that violated her oath as an FBI agent. But her frequent discussions with Pastor King about how the world was looking at the Family Matters Task Force's lack of progress were uplifting her soul. Felicia saw the sense of accomplishment in Sharon and was very happy that the FBI's demands on her were not bringing her down nearly as much these days.

King had not revealed the condition of his health to anyone, yet. He wanted to continue the work they were now making so much progress on without the distraction of how people would treat him once they knew about his illness. He looked at Sharon as someone to mentor, perhaps even to groom to take his place when he no longer could work. As for the church, King also started looking for a successor, at least someone to name as his preferred replacement.

Jackson consolidated all the data he and Judith accumulated and began to construct the manuscript. It was a chronicle of the crimes perpetrated against America's blacks, starting from the signing of the Emancipation Proclamation through the killing of Robert Wilson in Tampa, Florida.

He felt that to include the families killed in retaliation was nothing but a distraction, even though Judith believed that including those deaths punctuated the cultural change. But since Jackson was only in the outlining stage, they tabled that discussion until later.

-=#=

It was bound to happen. The entire country was ripe for it.

On Chicago's west side a black teenage boy was exiting a mini-mart in the Homan Square community; an area that had come up quite a bit since the turn of the century. There was a technology corridor with several schools, a youth center, and a social service facility in the community just off one of Chicago's major expressways.

This seventeen-year-old had just put money down on his mobile phone account at the shop, purchased a bag of chips and a soda. He exited the shop and had started the walk home when a Chicago Police Department patrol car pulled onto the sidewalk blocking his way. The young man raised both hands, one holding a can of soda, the other the chips.

Two white officers jumped out of the car, the closest one knocking the can and chips out of the teen's hands and shoved him face first against a chain link fence. Bystanders could hear the young man shouting, "What did I do? What did I do?" as he was then thrown across the hood of the patrol car and handcuffed, the one officer was holding him down as the other started turning out pockets. Suddenly, the teen wiggled free and started to run away, hands cuffed behind him.

Both officers pulled their weapons and pointed them at the fleeing boy. They exchanged a look between them and then began to fire. After several shots, the boy was hit and fell heavily to the ground, rolling from the inertia of his running.

The officers approached the obviously lifeless body, looking around to see who might have been watching and saw half a dozen people were filming them with their phones. They had a quick conversation and one began to walk over to the crowd gathered in front of the mini-mart, the other standing over the body talking into his radio.

One man from the crowd approached the body on the ground, and was warned away by the officer. He slowed, but didn't stop. The other officer approaching the crowd started shouting for everyone to hand over their phones as evidence. Seconds later, two shots rang out. Both officers fell to the ground with fatal head wounds as the crowd went silent.

The man who shot the officer near the crowd, announced, "Never again." The other checked to make sure the young man in handcuffs was dead, then checked the officer. He came back to the crowd and said, "All the video that doesn't show our faces, turn over to the media."

He paused, seeing those with phones nodding. "And when the cops get here," he added as sirens could be heard approaching, "you tell them, never again."

The two men cut through a gangway to the alley behind the mini-mart and disappeared. People started checking the video they had just taken. Two women had recorded everything from when the police car hopped the curb to trap the young man, until the one man shot the cop standing over the dead youth. The shooter's face was not visible in either video. Everyone else who had recorded what happened started to walk away from the scene as the first patrol car arrived.

As the first patrol car pulled up and stopped, the officers saw the bodies in the street and immediately called in for backup. They drew their weapons and first checked the fallen cops. The small knot of bystanders had moved away from the dead cop on the sidewalk outside the store, but they held their ground when the officer, gun drawn, approached them.

"What happened here?" he asked belligerently. "God damn it, what the fuck happened here?"

"Stop waving that gun around, and I'll tell you," a black woman in her seventies replied.

The officer didn't holster the gun, but he did point it toward the ground. "Well?" he said.

"The young man on the ground in the handcuffs had just left the store with a pop and a bag of chips. Those two cops handcuffed him for no reason and shot him in the back when he tried to run away," she said.

"I don't give a shit about him! What happened to these cops?" he said, his gun rising slightly.

"After they shot that boy over there, they each got shot in the head," she replied, still holding her ground. As she finished explaining, four more patrol cars arrived, sirens blaring.

"Who shot them? Did you see who it was? Where did they go? Does anyone here know who they were?" the officer fired the questions at the woman, clearly wanting an answer from anyone who would answer.

By now, there were a dozen officers on the scene, some grabbing onlookers demanding answers to their questions, but the crowd wasn't having any of it. The chant of "never again," began quietly, and grew as more people from the neighborhood arrived to see what the commotion was all about. The chant grew louder, halting the manhandling of the people in the crowd. More officers arrived, as did more people from the neighborhood. And all of a sudden, a remote truck from the ABC News affiliate arrived.

The police tried to keep the news crew from talking to the crowd, telling them that it was an active crime scene and that officers had to interview everyone present before anyone could be allowed to talk to the press. Unfortunately for the police, neither the news team nor the people in the crowd were having any of that.

The crowd control tape went up as an evidence technician began to photograph the scene. The police were circulating through the bystanders, trying to find anyone who witnessed what had happened. While the cops were otherwise occupied, one of the women who captured the entire incident on her phone approached the technician in the news truck, and while the chant of never again continued, she allowed the technician to download the phone's video. Moments later the video was transmitted to the television station and in no time at all a special bulletin was broadcast out to the world.

Once word went out that the footage had been broadcast, the

crowd began to melt away, except for the dead boy's mother and several family members supporting her. The local ABC newscaster in the crew immediately interviewed the mother, and tried to get the officer in charge of the scene on camera as well.

The police were completely outmanuevered, seeing their own on the street, one next to the now clearly innocent young man, and one in the gutter. With the cops clearly loaded for bear, no one on the street wanted to become the focus of that anger and frustration. When the officers learned that video of the incident had already been broadcast, they nearly lost their minds.

The footage clearly showed that the young man, of slight build and not wearing any concealing clothing, was no threat to the officers. Furthermore, the footage showed that they clearly hesitated, then decided together to gun the teen down. The video was devastating.

An hour later, the Mayor held an emergency press conference. The first thing he did was to extend condolances to the family of the teen. He then stated that a full investigation was going to be conducted into why the officers chose to shoot the teen, and who executed the officers. He promised the investigation would be complete and transparent.

"Now, I have time for a few questions," he said, pointing to a reporter in the front.

"Thank you, Mayor Blackwell. Does the killing of the officers execution style signal a new phase in the retaliation against the murder of innocent blacks in this country?"

"How can I answer that? There's been no manifesto, no communique from the people we presume are responsible for the deaths of officer family members. I will not speculate," he answered, and then pointed to another reporter.

"Mr. Mayor, if the video is showing exactly what it seems to represent, that two of your officers decided to shoot that teen in the back a total of eleven times as best we can tell from the footage, isn't that vindication for the revenge killings of officer families? And as an African American, how do you feel about such street justice being handed out."

"Really? You believe that the killing of innocent people is somehow justified by what looks like a barbaric shooting? And that I would rejoice in murder? That's pretty screwed up thinking. No murder, even in an eye for an eye context, is justified in our society. And it's against the damn law!" he testily responded. "Before we go any further let me say this. On the surface of it, those two officers murdered that young man in cold blood. Make no mistake, there is no policy or procedure in the Chicago Police Department that calls for any such action to be taken. And absent some sort of action that wasn't captured on video, and I admit that I cannot imagine what the hell it could be, there is never justification for shooting anyone unarmed in handcuffs. One more question."

Everyone shouted at once, trying to get their question heard. Finally, the mayor pointed to a reporter and they all quieted down.

"Mayor Blackwell, the act of killing those two officers, though barbaric and heinous, may have saved the lives of their families, if they have any— "

"Is there a question there?" the mayor interrupted peevishly.

"My question to you is this, if the men who killed the officers are caught, what is your intention toward them; how will the state's attorney proceed?"

"They will be changed with capital murder. That is the act they committed, that's what they will be charged with. And God willing, they will be found guilty and punished to the full extent of the law."

"I'm sorry, a quick follow-up," the woman reporter asked. "And what if those who prosecute the two men become a target for those who killed all those police officer families?"

Mayor Blackwell was silent for a few moments, as everyone waited for his answer. Then he quietly said, "We will cross that bridge when we come to it. Thank you for coming." He then quickly left the room. As he was walking back to his office, Mayor Blackwell allowed himself a private sliver of hope that the men who killed the cops were never identified.

-=#=

Andrew turned off the television coverage of the Chicago Mayor's press conference. He had caught the bulletin on his mobile's news feed and decided to check it out before he headed home from work. Things were getting very interesting in America. Having people on the street assassinate cops in the act of murder was a completely new, and hopefully scary, development for beat cops everywhere.

He checked his email to see if there was anything he had to deal with before he left for the day. Finding nothing, he grabbed his briefcase and headed for the elevator, saying good night to the receptionist as he breezed past her.

He took the elevator to the lower level garage. When the elevator opened he saw a teenage girl waiting to get on, and has he passed her she said, "This is for you, Andrew," and handed him a small piece of folded paper. He unfolded it and saw the name of the restaurant he had eaten in Harlem the day of the rally and informing him a cab was waiting out back. He looked around for someplace to get rid of the piece of paper, knowing he had no matches, and he simply wasn't going to indulge in the drama of eating it.

Andrew quickly went to his car, got in the driver's side, and popped open the glove box. Fumbling around, he found the original cigarette lighter that came with the car which had never been used. He pulled the decorative plastic cap off the console receptacle and pushed home the lighter. When it popped out he carefully burned the paper and dropped the ash on the garage floor and then twisted it into dust with his shoe. He then pulled out his mobile and removed the battery. He locked his briefcase in the car and took the stairs to ground level. He slipped into the receiving room for the building and exited via the loading dock door. Once he was outside he saw a cab waiting and wasn't too surprised to find James behind the wheel.

"Get down," said James as he began to drive out of the dock area.

Andrew waited a few minutes before he asked, "Talking distract you?"

"Not at all. What's up?"

"Dinner? Is this a date?"

James laughed. "No, but your best friend invited you to dinner. You disabled your phone I take it? I'm just about to head north."

"We're good."

The trip took about forty-five minutes, and when James parked, it was at the side door to the restaurant. They walked in through the kitchen with James leading him to a seating area not visible through the front window, and there was Tony. He was sitting slouched in the chair, eyes closed, looking like he was asleep.

James pointed to Tony and then went to some other part of the restaurant, leaving the two friends alone.

Andrew's footsteps alerted Tony that he had arrived. Tony opened one eye, saw Andrew and smiled. The two hugged, clapping each other on the back.

"Still out on the street I see. I'm getting right friendly with the local law here trying to find you. So what's up?" asked Andrew, taking his seat.

"Busy, busy, busy! They leaning on you?"

"Not really. They did come visit me at work, but that was actually fun. Should I be asking you what have you been up to lately?" said Andrew, smiling.

"Planning for retirement. But I invited you to dinner to give you a present," said Tony, holding out something small between his fingers.

"What the hell's this?" Andrew said, taking it from Tony's grip.

"It's a new SIMM chip for your phone. It won't change anything that your phone already does, or change the number. When you get back home, put this chip in and turn on the phone. Follow the directions on the screen, it's going to download an app that won't show up on the screen anywhere, then it's going to have you shut down, and replace the original chip. Once the phone reboots everything should look normal. When you get the message, upgrade complete, destroy the chip I gave you."

"And what is the bottom line here?"

"Anytime you want to call, text or email me, the feds won't see the traffic," explained Tony.

"How the fu— "

"Man, I have no idea. I'm thinking that the entire cellular network has been compromised in a way that the carriers and the authorities don't know anything about. The fact that I can leave my phone on all the time now and not be traced is a miracle. Yours isn't like that, otherwise they'd know something was up," Tony said. "It just lets us stay in touch."

Andrew tucked the chip into a flap in his wallet. "We eating? I'm starved."

Tony slid the menu across the table. Seconds later, Andrew slid it back. Tony said, "Hang on," as he got up and waved to someone in the next room.

Seconds later the waitress entered the room, beaming a huge smile at Tony. She took their orders and quickly left.

"How deep are you into this?" Andrew asked.

"Not very. Just some errands here and there. I stop in at OpFor about once a week, mostly at night, to get my mail, check out who came by looking for me. I don't want to get caught 'cause I'm sure they're gonna squeeze me. I don't know much, but my days of freedom would definitely be over. I am kind of tired; been on the move for a while. I could definitely use a little R&R," Tony said.

"You see what happened in Chicago?" Andrew asked.

"No shit. Cops shot the kid; someone took out the cops. That's all I know."

"That's all anyone knows according to the mayor."

Tony leaned back, putting his hands behind his head. "You know, if that's the way we reacted back in the 1800s, things would be a whole lot different today."

"Yeah, but how?"

"That's always the question. You never know how one little change is going to effect the whole system—the butterfly effect, I mean," said Tony.

"You all need any help? I'm almost there with all this shit happening.

I have money squirreled away, I could take some time off."

"Not yet. It may come to that," said Tony "But not yet. But enough about me, what's up with you?"

"The San Francisco desalinization plant is a go. We should have it up and have phase one done in about fourteen months after we break ground. Not sure what I'll tackle next; maybe something outside the country."

"Hey, man. I'm really sorry for all the trouble I'm causing you. The FBI is a pain in the ass, I'll bet."

"A little. But the pair they send after me are fun to fuck with. The woman's all right, but I get a hard-on baiting the guy. He obviously doesn't like niggas, and he ain't as smart or capable as I am. When they came to the office I offered to throw his ass out the window. I'm damn certain he knew not only was I serious, but that I could do it! Ain't no thang, brotha," he said, slapping five with Tony.

The food came a few minutes later, and they both set to. About ten minutes later, James stuck his head in and asked if he could join them. Tony hooked another chair at the next table over and gestured for the man to have a seat.

The three swapped stories for a couple of hours over ice cold bottles of beer. And when Andrew figured he had pissed off the FBI long enough for having given them the slip again, he had James drive him to within a half mile of his office and drop him off. He walked the rest of the way. As he used his key card to enter the building, Andrew laughed out loud when he saw the government car parked across the street from the garage entrance.

Chapter 33

No one was talking to the police on Chicago's west side about the three murders that took place. The police had copies of the two videos given to the press, but they didn't show either of the men who shot the officers dead in clear enough detail. The police canvassed the neighborhood in an attempt to get any witnesses to give a statement, but all of a sudden, no one had seen a damn thing except for a couple of cops murdering a kid in handcuffs.

The DOJ was in flux. Shooting police officers, even rogue cops, was a habit that no one wanted to see get started. In a perfect world, one wouldn't see bad cops on the street. They should have been weeded out in the academy, or at least, after poor departmental performance reviews. But the police unions and fraternal orders had a knee-jerk defense of any officer accused of any criminal activity. The Illinois Fraternal Order of Police sprang to the defense of the dead officers, first praising their action in killing the teen, and then dug the hole deeper by demanding the rousting of every household in the Homan Square community until the killers of the officers were found.

At a subsequent press conference, Mayor Blackwell stated publicly that he refused to meet with representatives of the union or the FOP if the best they could do was defend the indefensible. And although the mayor drew unrelenting criticism from police unions across the nation, the public was firmly on his side. All he had to do was ask publicly when the last time the FOP ever recommended the removal of a corrupt officer from the force closely followed by him quoting the number of officers found guilty of corruption and sentenced to prison. He was quick to point out that the various police unions and FOPs across the country had never issued a press release of condemnation for any convicted officer. Mayor Blackwell also stated unequivocally that rogue police officers will not be tolerated in the Chicago Police Department.

He said, "Aren't you people getting the message? Someone has determined that murdering innocent African Americans is no longer going to be tolerated. Doesn't self-interest and the safety of a cop's family at least give one pause when they draw their weapon? Do we have such small minded racists on police forces across this country and right here in Chicago care so little for their families that their need to murder a black person overrides their love of family and friends? If that's the case, I am at a loss as to how to deal with these sick people. But the coddling of racist murderers is over in the Chicago Police Department."

That clip was uploaded to the Internet and garnered several million views in less than twenty-four hours.

-=#=-

In Los Angeles, Franklin Thomas was crossing the street at dusk, carrying a large bag of groceries for his grandmother. Two cars back from the corner was a marked police sedan with one officer inside. When the light changed the squad car began to pull forward until it reached the corner. Officer Davis looked down the street and saw Thomas walking, carrying the groceries and turned the corner to drive parallel with Thomas.

Thomas was wearing earbuds, listening to music. When Officer Davis honked his horn to get the black man's attention, the honk was not heard and Thomas kept walking. It was only when Officer Davis pulled ahead of Thomas and turned sharply to the curb that Thomas saw the police car. He waited, his hands clutched around the large paper grocery bag, both in full view of the officer.

Officer Davis got out of the car and called for Thomas to raise his hands. Thomas turned his head to show the officer the earbuds, but Davis either didn't take note of the gesture, or ignored it.

When Davis shouted, "Show me your hands," Franklin Thomas wiggled his fingers to show both hands were holding the bag.

By this time, several onlookers had pulled out their phones and were recording the white police officer shouting to the black man to show his hands.

Franklin Thomas slowly lowered the bag to the ground, and when he began to straighten up, his hands in front of him, both empty and in full sight of Davis. Davis quickly pulled his weapon from its holster and shouted one more time for the man before him to show his hands, even as the man's hands were clearly in view, palms toward the officer.

In that instant, Officer Davis fired a double-tap directly into the chest of Thomas, who immediately dropped to the ground.

A group of bystanders, phones held in front of them began to approach Officer Davis, even as he warned them back. A second later, a shot rang out catching Davis in the neck. A geyser of blood spurted out several feet. As he began to crumple to the ground holding his neck, two more shots rang out, one catching the top edge of his protective vest, the other penetrating the upper right side of his forehead, knocking his hat flying.

Everyone looked toward the shooter, but not a single person recording the incident pointed their phone in his direction. The man with the gun said, "Never again," tucked his gun into the back of his waistband and took off down the street. Once he was out of sight, the crowd started to melt away. It was only then that one of the onlookers called 911, warning the crowd she was doing so. Several of those who recorded video of the cop shooting Thomas stuck around as others hurried home to upload their video to the Internet.

Moments later, a dozen police cars arrived, coming from all directions. All the officers jumped out with guns drawn, fanning out all around the area. Everyone in the crowd held their hands up above their heads, not wanting to be shot by some angry, overzealous cop bent on revenge. In no time at all, the officers confiscated two phones containing video of the killing, even cuffing the owners of the phones and putting them in the back seats of two separate squad cars.

Again, the police were frustrated in their effort to get a description of the shooter. The street was condoned off from traffic a block in both directions as the police began a house-to-house search up and down the street for someone they didn't even have a description for.

As in Chicago, the video of the murder was broadcast on all the L.A. local television stations less than an hour after the shooting, inflaming a city already rife with racial tension. As soon as the video footage was broadcast, tens of thousands of people left their homes to surround Police Headquarters chanting "No more!"

An hour later, the crowd was estimated at over a hundred thousand and still growing. By 10:00 P.M. the crowd swelled to half a million demonstrators. Chief of Police Loeber called in all off duty officers to reinforce the perimeter of the station. The crowd was pushed across the street from the building on all sides. Traffic was diverted away from the area for two blocks around the building. By midnight the crowd was estimated at over a million. The chant of "No more!" had continued unabated for hours with no sign of flagging.

Shortly after midnight, the crowd would not let police vehicles in or out of the immediate area around the headquarters. News helicopters were jockeying for space above the crowd, reporting live on the demonstration. By 2:00 A.M., the building was effectively under siege, the only officers able to enter or leave the building were those on picket duty around the outside of the building. No police officer was willing to try to cross the crowd so Mayor Rodriguez was brought to the building by helicopter to meet with the chief.

"You really screwed the pooch this time, Chief. Consider this your 30-day notice. They aren't going to be satisfied with anything but raw meat this time. Too bad the cop was killed, I'd throw him to the crowd if I thought it would save this city," Mayor Rodriguez said. "What's your plan for fixing this, Stanley?"

"In thirty days?" he replied ironically.

"No, I mean right now," she said in exasperation. "Jesus Christ, haven't we both suffered enough? I've been barely holding on as it is. You have no idea how many times I started to resign. Losing my family nearly killed me. If it wasn't for the rage in my heart towards these people, I would have left this whole fucking job behind. How the hell do you do it?"

"None of your God damned business. I was cleared by the department shrink and I'm dealing with it; that's all you need to know," he growled. A moment later, he continued. "For your information, my officers have orders to keep their weapons holstered unless directly threatened with deadly force. Hopefully the crowd will get tired and go home in the morning. Have you thought about going on television and calling for calm?" he asked, changing the subject.

"Of course I have!" she almost screeched. "But what in the living hell can I say that's going to calm everyone down with that fucking video being played continuously on every channel?"

"I'm sorry. I am truly sorry. This isn't what I wanted either," said the chief. "All I want to do is catch the cocksucker who killed my wife and my little girl," he said bitterly.

"We're quite the pair. After this is over, I may just go through with it and leave this all behind. But for now, get into your dress uniform. You're coming back with me to City Hall to apologize to the people of this city for failing its citizens."

-=#=-

Americans were striking back. Black Americans were striking back at murdering white cops. Most considered what was happening was a long time coming.

The United States Department of Justice was seriously concerned about a breakdown in law enforcement should the general public decide to take the law into its own hands, especially killing police officers, rogue or not. So far the officers killed had murdered blacks demonstrably innocent and were recorded in the act of doing so.

The public's attitude was that if those officers were allowed to continue to serve on the police force with their obvious racist attitudes, they would have murdered no matter what, their absence was a welcome relief. Coincidentally, white men were resigning from police forces at an unusually high rate. Fortunately, the frivolous rousting of nonwhites had abated so much, crime statistics remained much lower compared to the same period the previous year.

In Texas, the total losses on all the police forces across the state reached a nationwide high of thirteen percent. But none of the departments were in any hurry to replace the lost officers with nonwhites. Even people of color graduated from various police academies or trained by the FBI at Quantico were rejected to fill open slots in these and other southern police departments. With no clear way forward, and no sign of who was behind the officer family killings, there was no consistent response going forward. And the direct killings of officers by sniper fire, and now by citizens in the street, all unpunished, left police officers feeling cut loose and unsupported.

Judge Bridges, when interviewed for a progressive radio network show, expressed his surprise over the citizen killings of the police officers.

"What's surprising to me is that we have come to the point in our nation's history where seemingly ordinary people are so fed up with the racist, criminal corruption of police officers that they are handing out street justice out of hand. This is an unexpected manifestation of a larger revolution. Or, if one doesn't like calling it that, the undeclared war between white and black in this country just became a shooting war. No one wants to see a full-blown outbreak of hostilities. And the only way to keep that from happening is to rid every law enforcement organization in this country of trigger-happy racists," said Bridges.

"And how likely is that to happen, Your Honor?" asked Gretchen, the host.

"Obviously not very. Or at least not anytime soon. But what is at work now as a deterrent has been injected into the equation that the Department of Justice, the FBI, and all these local police departments have no response for. The fact that each of the citizen-involved shootings were of police officers who plainly committed murder has neutered any indignation and anger that everyone could be distracted by. Proven killer cops who have been immediately struck down should give everyone pause."

"Your Honor, it almost sounds like you approve of the killing of these officers."

"Not at all. I abhor the killing of anyone. However, I welcome the change in the social dynamic. Look at it from this perspective: for hundreds of years, blacks were killed without much thought or outcry. And in the last couple of generations there was some focus on white officers killing African Americans, but it was almost universally discounted as black hysteria. We've seen those shot running away from the police; African Americans with their hands raised shot, mentally ill backs shot, children shot, black women shot, and an ignorant white America finally got a glimpse of what we as a race have faced in this country for centuries. For the first time in history, when a white officer pulls his weapon from its holster, they are presented with a serious incentive to not pull the trigger just because it's easier."

"How many whites have we seen paraded across television screens in the last thirty years claiming that we are living in a post-racial America? Utter nonsense. It's a ridiculous notion and illustrates just how out of touch most white Americans are about the reality of the experiences of nonwhites and foreigners in this country. Although, I have to admit a number of those who repudiated those claims had political motivations for doing so. That level of cynicism is practically criminal when it's thrown up as cover for some extremely heinous racist policies in this country," he said.

"Then given the revenge killings of family members of officers who shot innocent African Americans, do you think white America has achieved a better understanding of at least the numbers of police shootings over the past couple of decades? That the veil of ignorance has been pulled from their eyes?" asked Gretchen.

"I doubt very many have had any revelation about the true nature of the numbers of African Americans who have suffered from racist police habits or policies. Since their experience doesn't come anywhere near what the average black man, woman or child in the street experiences, there's a cognitive disconnect between reality and their steadfast beliefs," Bridges explained. "What we're seeing is the only way that the tradition of senseless and unpunished murder of African Americans by white cops could be stopped."

"That can't be! You mean to tell us that the deaths of all those family members was the only way to have stopped the murder of African Americans by white police officers? There's no other way it could have happened?" Gretchen asked incredulously.

"Take a breath, Gretchen. Obviously it was the only way this change could have happened."

"That's preposterous, your honor!"

"If you say so. But answer a question for me: after over four hundred years, why didn't white police officers stop killing innocent blacks before now?" Bridges asked.

Gretchen was stunned silent. Then struggling to formulate any answer, she desperately threw out, "Weak laws? A continuous string of corrupt, racist cops?"

"You're making my point for me, Gretchen."

"How do you figure?"

"Until a few short weeks ago, nothing done in this country addressed the issue whatsoever in a manner that made any difference at all. And that is my entire argument. Nothing, until the killing of officers' families, stopped the murders by cops over the entire history of this country. Nothing done until now has even slowed the rate of police murders of black folks in this country. White America lacked the will, nay the desire, to do a damn thing about the murder of nonwhites by members of the law enforcement community; in fact, they wanted it. If a cop killed someone in this country, until just recently, everyone was conditioned to believe no matter the circumstances that the killing was justified. It is only recently that a minuscule number of grand juries have indicted police officers for misconduct. Even in those cases, juries are manipulated and conditioned to believe a police officer over any testimony offered against them. Police officers have enjoyed endless, and often unearned, support from the public. Do you remember the FBI's bogus hair identification fraud uncovered in the mid-twenty-teens that had sent hundreds of innocent people to prison; sometimes for life? This is what every nonwhite has arrayed against them, especially the innocent. So, to get back to your original question, yes, killing the families of corrupt, murderous officers was the only means of even beginning to achieve social and criminal justice in this country," said Bridges. "And it's working quite well. We're seeing potential murderous white cops leaving departments across the country, and the reason why is that they know to stay on the force is to put their families and friends at risk if they succumb to their baser instincts."

"So what happens next? And what if the people behind the families being killed are caught?"

"Gretchen, the backlash against African Americans will be horrendous. Even now many of those cops leaving their departments are joining armed white supremacist groups, most likely planning revenge killings of African Americans as we speak. And here's the upcoming trap, if the federal authorities don't go after those groups with every investigative tool at their command, this country is going to see a race war the likes of which no one wants."

Gretchen was silent, stunned at the picture Judge Bridges painted.

"Here's what the DOJ, the FBI, and all the other lettered agencies had better be paying attention to: the killers of cop families and the LAPD officers have demonstrated a skill and determination that no one in this country can equal. From my sources inside the DOJ, not one of the family member killings could be proven to be anything more than an unfortunate accident. And the skill demonstrated by whomever killed those LAPD officers was superior to that of most any SWAT team sniper in the country. A race war will see whites in this country, and the power structure standing behind them, come out a distant second inless the government seriously considers genocide.

"The government will not be able to lock up all African Americans in this country in concentration camps like they did with Japanese Americans in World War II. And no one white in this country will know if the black face they're passing on the street could be someone who is bent on harming them. I would remind your listeners that five thousand whites have already been killed. And there's been no clue as to who arranged those deaths. I would counsel everyone listening to your program to seriously consider just what would happen if the government decided to go to war against an enemy that no one can find."

"Excuse me for saying so, Judge, but it sounds like you want that kind of war to be declared," Gretchen observed.

"No, Gretchen. At long last, I want justice."

Chapter 34

A man walks into a basement after disarming a host of anti-intrusion devices designed to protect the contents of a room. He secures the door and then takes his seat in front of a console full of monitors displaying countless details of events happening around the United States.

The man types in his access code and then executes a seldom-used command.

"Good morning, sir. How may I be of assistance today?" a well-modulated male voice announces.

"Prepare for reorientation protocol Sigma Juliet," the man said.

"Affirmative."

"Execute."

"Working. . ."

"Estimated time of completion?"

"Forty-eight hours until complete."

"Thank you," the man said, logging out of the system.

He then left the room, restoring the numerous protections disarmed when he arrived.

-=#=-

The promise of quantum computing had yet to be realized in 2032. However the work various online search companies had done with voice recognition, along with steady advances in artificial intelligence gave people remarkable conversational interfaces for their computers, tablets, mobile phones, automobiles, and even many of their household appliances.

Changes in culture though were incremental. However, the one constant was that governments will do anything they believe they can get away with. Control of the media was ceded to corporate interests whose focus, more often than not, coincided with government's. But what was not easily controlled was the flow of information via social media. Videos of police brutality were propelled into the forefront of the consciousness of the United States, and across the world, instantaneously and unfiltered. When people saw police misconduct on the streets these days, the first thing they were doing now was pulling out their phones and recording the action.

Those states and municipalities that had passed legislation criminalizing the act of recording police officers found their laws directly challenged by those arrested for filming officers in action and more often than not, organizations like the American Civil Liberties Union. The truth was that most people filming were either avoiding capture by immediately getting away from the scene or protected by mob rule. The public was becoming less and less intimidated by belligerent officers. The accustomed supremacy of police officers was seriously on the decline. And Judge Alvin Bridges said it best in a brief sound bite captured as he left a rally for racial justice, "Respects is earned, not automatically bestowed," replying to someone shouting that everyone must respect the uniform of officers of the law.

Corruption was a constant in police culture,; a sad sickness born of an "us versus them" mentality and an unmitigated feeling of entitlement and dominion over everyone else. And after having owned the judgment of life or death for anyone they chose, now having to face the fact that they risked deadly consequences for either bad judgment, or murderous intent, the equation had changed their encounters with America's blacks.

Police officers across the nation debated America's new normal. Many were angry, but just as many were relieved. And the stonewalling by officers protecting the bad in their ranks was receding, even the fraternal orders were quieting their knee-jerk defense of obviously bad cops. But as much as the dynamic in law enforcement was changing, old habits were extremely hard to break. African Americans who did manage to be arrested suffered beatings, water, food, and sleep deprivation, or worse, in custody. Privately, police departments across the country were holding their collective breaths to see what repercussions or consequences might be waiting just around the corner as a result of their treatment of blacks in custody.

President Temple condemned the killing of the police officers, but came up short of characterizing the killings as unwarranted. He focused on the possibility of lawlessness in the streets, and what would happen if police officers were absent their role in preventing criminal acts just by their presence. Temple's dissatisfaction with the lack of progress of the Family Matters Task Force was no secret, and he had almost completely lost confidence in the FBI catching any member of the group. This was not because of a lack of expertise on the part of the FBI, but because of the obviously expert operations of those they sought. To imagine anywhere from two hundred to a thousand black hyper achievers wasn't a stretch in his mind. An entire race of people who had endured the worst of what a nation had to hand out would in turn be able to operate quite well under the most demanding circumstances and right under everyone's nose as the unseen underclass relegated to them. Temple didn't see too much difference between what African Americans had to endure and what black South Africans suffered under apartheid, and probably neither did America's blacks, he imagined.

Temple decided that there had to be a contingency plan in case the Family Matters Task Force failed to produce results, so he summoned the Director of the FBI, David Ryan, and U.S. Attorney General, Simon Thatcher, to his office.

"Gentlemen, let me cut to the chase. We need a contingency plan should we not find and capture these people," Temple began. "I know that we may find that single lead that ultimately brings us to finding them, but if things drag out much longer, we have to be prepared."

"Mr. President, I can't say that I agree. It's only a matter of time—" began Ryan.

"I'm sorry, David. But I just can't count on the possibility of some unpredictable future event. From a sociological and political standpoint we have an opportunity here, but we have to determine exactly what kind of opportunity it is. Let me play Devil's Advocate for a second. What do the two think would happen in this country if we don't catch the murderers of all those people?" he asked.

Thatcher didn't hesitate a moment before he replied, "A race war!"

"And one that's liable to have us come in a distant second if it comes to a shooting war," Ryan added. "You can't kill what you can't find and you can't kill everyone with black skin."

"Exactly. Above all else, I want to avoid any kind of armed insurrection. We simply can't isolate fifty million Americans merely because of their skin color. Besides, I doubt the people you all are looking for will stand for that kind of nonsense. We have armed insurgents operating in this country who we cannot identify, essentially hiding in plain site. I'm not accusing your department of any incompetence, Ryan. However, this Mendes guy slipped through your fingers twice!" Temple held up his hand to forestall any comment. "I'm not criticizing you and the Bureau; I'm well aware that you've focused every resource on catching these people, but let's stick to the facts. We have to be prepared to implement a backup plan should we fail to find them."

Thatcher paused, cleared his throat, then said, "I get where both of you are coming from. And I agree that we should have a contingency plan just in case we make no headway with the task force, but what if we did nothing? Not say that we're doing nothing, carry on like we are now, and just keep plugging away and let events go on as they are? Yes, we're going to take some heat for not making progress, and there's going to be plenty of political fallout come election time."

"I'm planning to respond with the old 'I don't comment on investigations in progress.' You may want to do the same, David. And let Agent Willis know that I said to do the same damn thing. As for you," Temple began, gesturing to the AG, "I would concentrate on weeding out corrupt cops everywhere. This problem has been around for hundreds of years. And since Lincoln signed the Emancipation Proclamation it's been a national disgrace. Every black person killed by a cop is validation of what these people are rightly pissed off about. Unless we get a handle on that, white families are going to keep dying. And as long as cops fire on demonstrators, they will keep on dying. And as long as gun nut crazies shoot up civilians in theaters, shopping centers, schools and the like, prosecutors, judges and I dare say politicians are likely to keep getting killed too.

"We haven't been doing our jobs. That damn Judge Bridges is right. This entire fiasco lays full responsibility right at our collective feet. Until we level the playing field in this country as far as race is concerned, the Republic is ultimately at risk," the president concluded.

"I want you to concentrate your attention on race-based crime at the DOJ. It's long past time, and an ironclad case can be made for doing so. Making killing innocent blacks a capital crime is a good example no matter who it pisses off, let's see what kind of framework we can build on that. And if anyone tries to give you shit, ask them to their face why they condone race crimes in this country, and why are they so racist that the murder of millions of blacks are just fine with them. It'll work with most; some you won't be able to get away with that tactic, but it'll definitely put a lot of them on the defensive," Temple pointed out.

Ryan let out a sick chuckle. "That's one way of getting these people on our side," he said sarcastically.

"I know it's an old refrain, but black lives do matter. We have failed to protect African Americans the same as we do whites for far too long. And though it took a literal gun to the head for things to change in this country, let's see what we can do to keep them that way," Temple said. "This is not a movie where sworn adversaries all of a sudden become bosom buddies. They know who and where we are, and we have no idea even who they are. And we can't for a minute forget their grievance is real. Let's see what we can do to leave a legacy better than the country we started with when I took office."

"I have to say that it sounds like capitulation, and that's a bitter pill to swallow," admitted Ryan. "I still believe that I have a sworn duty to find these people."

"I'm not suggesting that you stop trying. But for damn sure, I don't want any more cops committing murder on blacks, whites, Hispanics—whomever! I don't care what the press says, or what the unions say, or anyone else, I want it to stop!" Temple said, banging his fist on the table.

"Hey, easy, Marcus. No one is suggesting that we don't. I'll get on it as soon as I get back to the office. We should have a draft plan for you in a couple of days. Look, we go way back, and I do understand where you're coming from," Thatcher assured President Temple.

"Let me ask you both, aren't you tired of Judge Bridges and a host of others laying this at your departments' feet? And damned if I can argue with the son of a bitch! Not you two, but what this country has allowed to go on for years, decades, centuries even. It's stopped for the time being, let's see if we can keep it that way. Okay, gentlemen? Please, let's just get it done."

-=#=

America's media outlets made much of the civilian killings of police officers, conservatives calling for vicious crackdowns on citizens who lived in troubled communities, and progressives pointing out that the lawless should expect nothing less. The outliers in conservative politics, having been slowly shut out of national offices over the last two decades, were hysterical about gangs of lawless African Americans running around the country unchecked. Although, that wasn't what they were really calling blacks. Accusations of raiding parties of roving blacks raping and pillaging like in days of old were flooding the email boxes of the dumbed-down faithful on the Right.

Andrew listened to the television coverage when his stomach could take it, even some conservative talk radio and seriously wondered exactly how long was it going to be until some gang of white supremacists decided to try to impose some street justice on someone black.

He had taken to going out to the range every weekend, and was now practicing with a vintage Smith & Wesson Model 5904 and a newer Glock G55ES. Andrew wasn't stupid, he applied for and received a concealed-carry permit, thanks to the lax gun ownership laws in the state of New York.

When they were the only two on the range and he could safely lock the front door, Matt helped Andrew with his technique until he was equally proficient with the heavier Smith and the much lighter Glock.

Matt teased Andrew one day about his desire to gain proficiency with a pistol given the fact that he could hit a quarter from a mile away with a rifle.

His reply was, "What if someone sneaks up on me, and they get close enough to try to bash me on the head?"

Matt laughed. "You're just going to have to hole up somewhere where you can see them coming from a long way off, my man!"

He hit the switch to bring the target up to them to check out Andrew's groupings. Once it came to a stop, Andrew was surprised at how tight the holes in the target were grouped together. In the center of the torso silhouette were ten bullet holes a tea cup saucer could easily cover. The five to the head were grouped even tighter.

Matt took the target down and produced a red marker. "Sign here, please," he said to Andrew, pointing along the side of the silhouette.

"Why's that?"

"Because I said so. When you get caught doing something notorious, I'm going to put this up for bid in the Internet," Matt replied, chuckling as Andrew signed with a flourish. "You know, you shoot in the top two percent of all law enforcement officers with a handgun now."

"How in the hell do you know that?"

"The guy who runs the range over at Quantico is a pretty good friend of mine. We swap stories and stats all the time. You're good, Drew. Damn good."

"You didn't mention me by name, did you?" Andrew asked, more than a bit concerned.

"Hell, naw! I just know how you rank against the entire FBI and the cops they train. I'll say this, if a bunch of folks sneaked up on me in the dark, I hope and pray it's when we're out together. I'm good. Matter of fact, I'm damn good. But with you it's like you and a gun have been lovers for life. Here, take these," Matt said, sliding ten boxes of ammo across the counter to Andrew. "It's a gift just in case you can't get by here any time soon."

"I can't accept these," Andrew said, reaching for his wallet.

"Stop! Whatever is going on in your life, and I don't wanna know what, I got your six." Gesturing Andrew in closer so he could whisper in his ear, Matt said, "Drew, if you're becoming a part of this, I'm behind you and anyone else helping you out a hundred percent." He then clasped hands with Andrew then made a shooing motion. "Now, get the hell out of my shop so I can get something productive done today."

As he drove back into the city, Andrew couldn't shake what Matt said out of his mind. On the one hand, changing the shape of social justice in America was a righteous cause, and one that was even more worthy of his talents than what the Army normally had assigned him. With the FBI all over him even trailing him back into the city a couple of hundred feet behind him, he wondered exactly how it could happen. He'd been able to give the surveillance team the slip whenever he really wanted, but abandoning everything in his life to take up a cause, a cause that could get him killed, called for some serious thought.

If he pulled all his investments, taking losses on some of them, he was sure the fact of doing so would be flagged immediately. It could be done, but once he did so he had to be ready to run that very moment. His condo, his car, everything material that he couldn't carry was forfeit. It was definitely a lot to think about.

-=#=

Sharon was curious about Pastor King's call to her office with an invitation to lunch. King sounded all right on the phone, but there was an ominous subtext to the call that she couldn't put her finger on. In any case, she was looking forward to seeing him and finding out what the mystery was. She let everyone know in a quick email that she would be off campus for lunch.

They met at a crowded café with the noise inside making eavesdropping nearly impossible. When Sharon arrived, King was already seated so she breezed by the hostess pointing to the table.

King stood and gave her a hug, held her chair for her, then sat.

Sharon gave him a look as to say, "Well?" making King laugh.

"Okay, it may have sounded kind of ominous, and maybe it sort of is. But I have some news that's taken me a while to digest," he said then paused a beat. "Sharon, I have cancer."

"What— Pastor, I'm so sorry. How can I help? Is it serious—Jesus, of course it's serious. Are you under treatment?" she asked, glancing at his full head of white hair.

King laughed knowing exactly what she meant. "Not really. There's really no treatment yet that will help me with this type of pancreatic cancer. The new protocols in stem cell therapy can't help this far along. There's too much tissue involved. So far, it's not spread to any other organs according to the lab tests. It is what it is, dear."

Tears came unbidden to Sharon's eyes. "I'm so sorry. How do you feel?"

"Other than a little tired, I'm doing well."

"For how long?"

"No telling. A few months at minimum. Given how much work I have to do, I am wondering if you might be willing to lend a hand?" he asked.

"Of course, anything!"

"No, you're going to have to seriously think about what you're committing to. And I'm not talking about within the church, I'll have a replacement lined up, introduced to the congregation, and handling Sunday service long before I check out. God has been good to me. He gave me a good life, introduced me to great friends along the way, brought me and Vivian together and gave us many great years until he called her home, so I have no complaints. But I have unfinished business that must continue, and the work you, Mr. Richards and Ms. Spencer are heading up is just the tip of the iceberg." King reached over to hold Sharon's hands and looked her in the eye and continued, "Some of what I need done may be outside of what your oath to the FBI requires of you. But it's so important if we are ever to achieve equality in America and protect our children and their children. So before we go any further, I think you should think about which is the more important priority to you."

"But—" she started to say.

"No, really," he interrupted. "You are destined to do great things for this country; I have seen it. But it's still your life to choose. Someone has to continue to direct the effort to change the underlying racial dynamic in America. That's why I brought the three of you together at my home. So, think about it, and let's have something to eat. And while we're eating, I want to know if and when you and Felicia might be tying the knot. It would do my heart good to officiate the ceremony before I'm gone," he said. But when he saw the look on Sharon's face, he quickly added, "But no pressure! I'm not trying to have you all do anything you don't want to. Admittedly, the two of you seem perfect for each other,; and if it's at all in your future, keep your old pastor in mind."

"Of course we will. We talk about it, and obviously there's no stigma attached to us getting married like there was just a few short years ago. But it's still a lingering question where I wonder if marrying Felicia will effect either of our careers," she explained.

"Why that's nonsense! Look at how even the church has adapted. I perform marriages for gay and lesbian couples all the time," he said, smiling.

"I know, Augustus. We're just not there yet. But we've both agreed that if it comes to pass, you're the one. Is it all right if I tell Felicia about your cancer?"

"Go right ahead. It's not like it's a real secret. I just haven't mentioned it to anyone but you so far. I needed time to put it in proper perspective; come to grips with it myself. "

For the rest of the meal, Sharon told Pastor how the task force was coming along. He definitely perked up when she mentioned that there was a secondary focus on cleaning out corrupt police officers across the nation. He saw this as a direct result of their efforts to slant the conversations on race taking place in the media. His carefully conceived plan of subliminal propaganda appeared to be working, and for that, he was grateful.

Chapter 35

A white University of Cincinnati police officer pulled a black man over for not having a front license plate and ended up shooting the driver in the head, killing him instantly. Three motorists driving by stopped and immediately started filming. The video showed the officer shouting for the driver to get out of the vehicle. After less than a minute of shouted discussion, the officer reached inside the car and tried to pull the man through the window. Seconds later, a single shot rang out and the video showed the officer stepping back, weapon in hand as the driver slumped out of sight.

The officer was seen on his radio as the motorists continued recording the scene. Moments later two additional patrol cars rush to the scene, sirens blaring and stopped on either side of the car, obscuring it from the street.

Again, those who recorded the killing immediately uploaded the footage to the Web and at least one of them called local media to inform them of its availability.

The officer's family was rushed into protective custody as soon as the video started airing on the local Cincinnati television stations, and police headquarters went on lockdown; guards at every door. As the video started to make the rounds of the national cable news stations, the nation held its breath waiting to see what the fallout from the killing would be.

In a mistaken attempt to try to placate those who saw the killing as just another example of a racist white cop committing the murder of a black man and destined to get off, the Cincinnati Chief of Police made a statement explaining that campus police had the same powers as those on the Cincinnati Police Force, even when away from the campus. He sidestepped the question of why a campus cop was making traffic stops off campus instead of calling for backup from the actual Cincinnati PD which only inflamed the situation.

The campus officer was being held at police department headquarters "for questioning" overnight, although a department official who insisted on remaining anonymous stated to one local reporter that the officer was in protective custody in the event someone wanted to take revenge on him. The press was camped out around the headquarters building looking for the opportunity to interview the chief or the officer who killed the motorist.

The University was holding tight with a "no comment on an ongoing investigation" line, stating the officer was on administrative leave, with pay, for the duration.

As in Los Angeles, it didn't take long for the department's headquarters to be besieged by demonstrators. The police tried to keep a perimeter a block away from the building but that wasn't working very well. When the media dug up the officer's name, Owen Stickle, there was a frenzy to uncover every detail about his and his family's life.

At the same time, across town, there was a prayer vigil held outside the hospital where the driver, Levi Brown, was being held pending autopsy. Levi's wife was there briefly until her brother took her home when she became overcome by her loss. Her departure spurred anger in the crowd as she left, and the angrier members of the crowd started an impromptu march down the middle of the street on their way to police headquarters. By the time the police caught up with them, the crowd numbered nearly two hundred.

Social media was blowing up, informing vast numbers of Americans that the march was taking place. Scores of marchers activated broadcast apps on their mobile phones that showed their progress in real-time, giving the Cincinnati police force plenty of time to call for reinforcements at headquarters. The spread of online coverage of the march drew a huge influx of protestors at the march's destination. Chief Darren was tempted to collect all ammunition from the patrol officers guarding headquarters, but stopped short of doing so in case the crowd seriously got out of hand.

By the time the marchers arrived at Police Headquarters, the crowd numbered in the tens of thousands. Their chanting demanded that the chief or Officer Stickle come out and face them. The media was already on hand, thanks to the crowd broadcasting the march and demonstration live.

It was quickly apparent that the Police Department was shielding Officer Stickle from not only the crowd, but from media scrutiny as well. Despite Chief Darren's promises of transparency in the investigation, keeping Officer Stickle under wraps repudiated his word to the public and press to everyone present.

Meanwhile, Stickle's wife and daughter were in protective custody in Cleveland, spirited away from their home less than an hour after the shooting of Brown was reported. They were in a downtown hotel under an assumed name with officers stationed in the rooms on either side of the family's.

Hidden cameras were mounted in the hotel hallway, looking in both directions as the protective detail took turns watching, never leaving the monitors unguarded. All prepared food was monitored by an officer in the kitchen, stupidly alerting the entire hotel staff that there was some sort of protected VIP in room 805. And though many of the hotel's staff were African American, none of the protective detail, all white, appeared seriously concerned about that fact. They were sure that they had given everyone in Cincinnati the slip and no one knew who they were, so they were looking forward to an easy detail.

Both television sets in the details' rooms were tuned to national coverage of the events back home. They watched the demonstration, then the march as it happened, then the growing crowd circling headquarters. The crowd was getting loud, chanting "black lives matter" and "never again." They began to worry how their fellow officers were going to make out with an angry crowd shown on the news.

The coverage quickly became repetitious when nothing of note happened. No one came out to be interviewed and there was no sign of Stickle leaving the building. However, the crowd of demonstrators remained, growing steadily through the night.

At 2:00 A.M., all the doors in the building burst open as police officers and civilian employees fled the building, thick, dense smoke also poured from the doors, billowing out around those leaving. The demonstrators moved farther away from the building, fearing the unknown.

The staff and officers all gathered in the parking lot, well away from the demonstrators. Several of those isolated in the area and under guard were obviously prisoners as evidenced by the leg shackles.

Sirens were heard off in the distance signaling the imminent arrival of fire fighters. But before they arrived, fire started to shoot through the roof of the building looking like the flame from a blowtorch. The crowd, well across the street, could feel the heat from the fierce flame. The heat was so intense that the roof disappeared; the tar disintegrating into a wispy haze driven upward into the sky.

The extent of the flame widened until everyone could see that it had spread throughout the entire building. Its growth was all being captured and broadcast live on several television channels. The police began to push everyone farther from the building as the intense heat began to ignite banners on streetlights and the tops of several trees.

When the fire engines arrived, the fire fighters' focus became saving everything around the fully engulfed building. They sprayed down trees and vehicles in an attempt to keep them cool.

People in the crowd screamed and several officers pulled their weapons at the sound of a loud report. Fortunately, it was only a tire bursting on a squad car parked too close to the building. Moments later an outer wall of the building began to collapse into itself. Shortly after, the other three walls collapsed to the ground, all three floors fell into a heap with the intense flame subsiding into a heap of the heated glow of molten brick and metal. The temperature of the middle of the rubble was hot enough to melt steel making the whole building and its contents a complete loss. One of the firemen measured the temperature of the melted materials at the edge of the rubble and it registered over 2500°F, surprising the battalion commander and everyone else. Their hoses were all pointed toward the middle of the yellow-hot pile of rubble, the heat turning the water immediately into clouds of steam.

One of the local reporters, obviously well known to the Battalion Chief, managed to get him to go on record about the fire.

"We're here with Battalion Chief Jeffery Todd of the Cincinnati Fire Department. Could you tell us the likely source of the fire that has completely destroyed Police Headquarters?" she asked.

"It's the strangest thing, Heather. This fire is hotter than melted steel, something I've never experienced before. The building is a total loss. You'll have to get an estimate from the Chief on what the losses are for the department," he replied.

"Have you even heard of such a fire anywhere else, Chief?"

"Never in my twenty-one years. This is like a blast furnace at a steel plant; it's that hot. All we can do now is make sure that the fire is contained, and that the surroundings are kept watered down until the heat dissipates," the chief explained.

"Were there any casualties, Chief?"

"Not according to the Chief of Police. He said everyone was safely evacuated. We're going to have to maintain a perimeter around the block for several days until the rubble cools down. About all we can do right now is keep hosing it down. I'm looking forward to getting in there once it cools down to see how the fire got started and how it burned so hot—hopefully what remains will give us a clue."

"Thank you, Chief. This is Heather Thomas with Chief Todd for Eyewitness News. Now back to the studio."

-=#=

"Get the local office to quarantine that site and send a dozen agents to back them up. Make sure our top people in arson are included," Agent Willis ordered then hung up the phone. He had been watching multiple channels covering the march and demonstration in Cincinnati. He hit "record" on every channel when the fire started and watched something he'd never seen before. He called the Bureau's top expert in arson, waking her up, and told her to turn on the news. When she called him back after the fire chief's interview, she excitedly told him that she'd never seen anything like it either. Even thermite couldn't have done what they saw, except maybe a couple of tons of it, she explained.

This was something new. This was definitely retribution for the killing committed by Officer Stickle and the Cincinnati Police Department shielding him from the public. Willis estimated the cost of losing that police station in the tens of millions, probably fifty million dollars or more; he really had no exact idea. Now, on top of killing the families of rogue cops, the vigilantes were going to cost the police department, and maybe others, millions. This might be even more effective than the killings because nothing gets institutions and governments to change policies faster than costing them money.

Willis sent out an email message to the department heads of the task force, calling for a meeting first thing the next morning. He also began to draft a preliminary status report for the White House. Checking the clock, and seeing it was 4:30 A.M., Willis decided to get an early start for the office knowing he was never going to get back to sleep.

When agents arrived at the operations center, they were surprised to see Willis already on site. He was online looking up accelerants that could fuel a file as hot as 2500°F and rerunning the news footage of the fire. When the lab tech he had sent an email to meet him in Ops arrived, the two of them started down the road of simple chemistry, then ending up all the way to war munitions designed to create a veritable fire storm with little or no oxygen present.

Willis was also in constant contact with the investigative lead in Cincinnati, but it was much too soon for any findings from the still-molten rubble. Some atmospheric samples were collected and run through a gas chromatograph in an effort to find any exotic substances at the molecular level. But nothing unusual had been found so far.

The local police had cordoned off their former headquarters, keeping the streets around the site clear of traffic. The fire department had four hoses directed toward the middle of the molten rubble, clamped to small weighted stands saving the need for anyone manning them. The cloud of steam rising above the rubble was as opaque as smoke but quickly dissipated ten stories up. The temperature was still stifling close to the rubble. No one wanted to venture close to the scene for fear of possible toxicity though the fire chief was convinced that they were reasonably safe. Whatever had started and fueled the fire had most likely either burned off or dissipated. He was extremely interested to get into the wreckage to try to determine exactly what had fed the impossibly hot fire.

Agent Willis opened the department head meeting by announcing, "We have now moved into a very dangerous phase in this, this—insurgency is exactly what it is. These people are not only capable of killing with impunity, they have proven capable of casual destruction on a frightening level."

"Yes, but it appears that they did so with no loss of life," said the representative of the Department of Homeland Security.

"Luck or deliberate action?" Willis tossed back.

"From the news video it looked like the smoke drove everyone out of the building quite a bit before that hellfire began," Sharon observed. "To me it looked like destruction of the building was the intent, not killing."

"Anyone know if the shooter's family is still safe?" Willis asked.

"I called the Cincinnati Chief, and he said they were. But he wouldn't say anything more," Willis' assistant replied.

"Smart. Here's what I want all of you to be thinking about, to take back to your people. We now have proof that the vigilantes have shifted to a new track. They just destroyed an entire building to make a point. And destroyed it so thoroughly that nothing could be recovered; the destruction was complete. Preliminary estimates of the damages total over a hundred and ten million," Willis said, as several of those present gasped. "That's just the preliminary cost of that asshole campus cop shooting a man in the head. Make no mistake, we were sent a message last night. They can kill, and they can cost us millions, billions even for murdering black people."

Willis paused, then everyone stood when Director Ryan entered the room.

"Please be seated. This won't take but a minute," he said as he went to stand at the empty head of the conference table. "We are shifting the focus of the Department of Justice and the FBI. Not this task force, but certainly the other departments. We are now about the business of rooting out racist, untrained, and incompetent cops from every police force in this country, and I guess that includes the DOJ, the FBI and DHS as well. This is a mission that is long past due. And make no mistake about it; last night's destruction of the Cincinnati police headquarters was a clear message to us. As long as there are murdering, racist cops on the job, it's going to cost this country in lives and cold, hard cash. The problem is not the vigilantes, if corrupt cops weren't on the job, there would be no killings, nor this level of punitive destruction. Get these cops off the streets. That is all. Sorry to interrupt; thank you for your time," Ryan said, nodding to everyone then leaving.

"Whew, just what you said," Sharon said to Willis.

"He's right. If we had been more concerned with rogue, racist, killer cops, this task force wouldn't exist. We're still going to be hunting for the people who killed the families and cops. No one gets away with murder, no matter how justified anyone thinks it is. And if we do find one or more of them, we're not going to have another Mendes fiasco on our hands; we grab them before they know what hit them," said Willis. "Look, you all know what to do. There's nothing more we need to cover unless someone has something else to add?" he said, looking around the table.

"Fine. Check with your superiors and see if there's anything like what Director Ryan had for the FBI. If you are reassigned or there's any organizational changes in your department, document it and send it to the distribution list. Thank you all for coming."

Everyone gathered their things and departed with Sharon staying behind.

"I can't say that I disagree with anything the Director said," Sharon announced.

"Me neither. And he's right. With no killer cops, there would have been no task force. You think the changes in the country are going to last?" Willis asked.

"They'd better. With the vigilantes on the loose, they're probably going to be a pretty good deterrent."

"Just between you and me, do you ever hope they don't get caught?" Willis asked cautiously.

"Honestly? I sometimes think about it. But it's pretty grim knowing that there's people out there who kill with scarcely any remorse—well, I think they have no remorse. But changing four hundred years of tradition in a matter of months is a rather unbelievable feat," she replied. "When I listen to Judge Bridges talk about the numbers, balancing a few thousand compared to millions, even I get it. In terms of social justice, I sometimes look at the ends justifying the means as something hard to argue."

"I can't know and understand what you go through on a daily basis, hopefully not too much bullshit to contend with. But over your lifetime, and your family's lifetime, it's impossible to fathom. I don't think I could have done it," Willis said with unaccustomed candor.

"No one should have to go through life with an entire country's slights marshaled against them for something like skin color or who you chose to love. It colors, pardon the term, everything in life," she said, getting up and patting him on the shoulder. "I'll see if the president is behind this new focus. If I do find out anything, I'll call you later."

"Thanks."

Chapter 36

"Good afternoon, everyone. Welcome to Issues on the Hill, I'm your host Peter Hartman. Joining me today is Judge Alvin Bridges, author of the bestselling, The Entire System Is Broken: Throw It Away and Start Over. But today, he's here to discuss the latest issues of race facing this country. Good afternoon, your honor. Thank you for stopping by."

"A pleasure, Peter. Glad to be here."

"Let us begin with the events in Cincinnati. It's all over the news and on everyone's mind. Another senseless African American death at the hands of a white police officer, and now it appears that the retribution for that killing was the total destruction of the Cincinnati Police Headquarters in a most spectacular manner. Your thoughts, your honor?"

"First off, the country was treated to a very different response to a police officer killing a black civilian. Police headquarters in that city was completely destroyed in, as you characterized it, spectacular fashion. Estimates of the resulting losses number in the hundreds of millions of dollars and have robbed the Cincinnati Police Department of their headquarters.

"What is most frightening to this country is the fact that all the actions of those in opposition to police departments who have rogue officers on their force is the complete absence of any communique or manifesto. And, their actions invoke a completely unambiguous message to law enforcement across the nation. What makes me curious is exactly how this new message is being considered by the President, the DOJ, and the FBI. What do they think about this new response?" Bridges speculated.

"There's no doubt that the complete destruction of the headquarters sends a message, judge. But what is it?" asked Hartman.

"Probably that they will punish those who harbor rogue cops, or allow those same officers to remain on the force, on a financial level that is unsustainable for any municipal police department. It also begs the question, what else can and will they do in response to an officer killing an innocent black man, woman, teen or worse, a child. They just escalated the game," Bridges replied.

"Do you think this new facet of their retribution will spur law enforcement to change their tactics in searching for those responsible?"

"When you start costing white folks money, the general reaction is a redoubling of effort to make whatever's causing it to stop. According to reports from the Cincinnati Police Chief, Officer—Stickle, that's his name, is still unharmed as is his family, otherwise we would have heard differently. So, what we now face is millions of dollars in destruction for a black life. Now black lives really matter, hundreds of millions of dollars in this case.

"What's a damn shame is that the necessity for vengeance still exists. I abhor the deaths that beset the officers who killed before, but I think costing police departments millions of dollars for each murder of an innocent African American is brilliant in its simplicity. This is something that will resonate with white America. We live in a culture where cash has more value than the lives of most everyone who lives in this country; this hits America where it hurts," Bridges concluded.

Hartman gave a wry chuckle. "It really does sound like you admire what these killers have done. How can you sit there and laud those who have killed thousands of whites, and have cost the City of Cincinnati hundreds of millions of dollars?"

"How can you sit there and insult an entire race of people by ignoring what brought us to this point? It sounds to me like to you only white lives matter."

Hartman sputtered. "That's not what—"

"How dare you fail to mention the millions of black lives ended in the name of white entitlement?" Bridges said, interrupting. "See, it's that kind of attitude that brought us here. You have the unmitigated gall to sit there and hold the white lives lost in some higher value than the millions of black lives lost. One can make a case of those paltry thousands of white lives lost as a pittance of collateral damage to repair American society and put it on the path to truly color blind justice for the first time in half a millennium. I'm curious how you defend your apparent lack of concern for black lives lost?" Bridges challenged.

"I in no way feel that the countless black lives lost in this country are without worth or even have less value than whites lives. We were discussing the so-called vigilantes, that's the only reason I hadn't gotten to the others," Hartman said defensively.

"Then I apologize for the implication, Peter. But your apparent reaction, the one I mistakenly attributed to you, is not uncommon in our society. Since the death of thousands of white family members did little to rid the country of racist, murdering officers let's see if the loss of millions of dollars in real estate and equipment convinces America's law enforcement community to finally rid its self of those unfit for duty. Long term, equal justice under the law is essential for the country. It costs less in law enforcement resources, in the prison system, and in the courtrooms of America. The only way to maintain the status quo is unadulterated racism designed to maintain white entitlement as long as possible. Whites are a minority in over a dozen states now, and it's a terrifying prospect for the smallest-minded of them."

"Why is that?"

"Because it's common psychology that people will imagine that others will do to them whatever dirt they themselves would have done. So, given all the horrific acts that whites have committed against nonwhites, today's white people believe will be committed against them a thousand-fold. So, a lot of what drives violence against blacks is simple fear; fear and the tradition of violence against blacks going unpunished. Well things are different now, at least for police officers, and now whole departments. And once the law enforcement community finally applies the law equally across all races, whether or not the vigilantes are caught is irrelevant."

"Your Honor, really! Are you advocating that these people not be brought to justice? That's not only preposterous, but it's a heinous perspective!" Hartman declared.

"How so, Peter?"

Hartman sputtered. "Be—because to let people who have killed thousands go free is unacceptable. They have to be punished. They should not be given what's essentially a free pass for murder!"

"But isn't that what thousands upon thousands of white officers and civilians have been given for hundreds of years? Where's the justice for African Americans whose killers were never charged or simply given a pass by law enforcement and the legal system? How do you propose we answer for their crimes of murder today? Those still alive, if they went through the legal system, can't be tried again unless we suspend laws concerning double jeopardy, and that's playing hard and fast with the constitution and hundreds of laws already on the books.

"Why should the people behind the family killings be subject to justice all those whites who did the same thing were not?" Bridges asked. When Hartman was silent the judge continued. "The only reason to punish these, presumably African American killers is because they're black. And isn't that another example of what brought us here?"

"I'll admit there's merit in what you say. But America is not going to sit well with the possibility that those people will not face justice. And you're right, a lot of that is based on racism and prejudice. But as much as

I'm going to catch heat for saying so, the changes in America's landscape in crime, law and order, and the equal application of justice have been a long time coming," Hartman admitted. "Anyone with an ounce of integrity has to admit that this country has been tilted away from equality for all ever since whites came from Europe and tried to exterminate the native peoples. You have people in this country who think the Bible was written in English here in the United States. Who are so misinformed that they believe that this country was created as a Christian nation. The defining characteristics of America to those who live elsewhere are a love of guns and nearly terminal stupidity. And in terms of race, your honor, these are the most interesting times since the 1960s."

"There's nothing I can argue with, Peter. Though I daresay that a host of ignorant, prejudiced folks out there are quite upset with you for what you just said. And the fact is, they're what holds this country back, keeping it from greatness.

"The forty-five percent or so of conservatives in this country are the only thing preventing the US from not only living up to the promise of that extraordinary document, the United States Constitution, but they're destroying any chance of us moving the country fully into the promise of the 21st Century.

"Let's take the time when the Affordable Care Act was passed for example. Before the law passed American automakers were forced to add an extra $2,200 to the cost of each automobile they sold here and abroad to cover the cost of company-provided healthcare. And yet, captains of industry did everything they could to keep a public option from being offered because it would have inched up taxes a bit.

"Conservatives are still trying to control women culturally through inequitable treatment in today's society. Look at the constant assault on women's healthcare. Until they were driven from congressional leadership, conservatives were constantly trying to take healthcare away from women, chipping away at the guarantees of the 14th Amendment in terms of abortion or the cadre of white, male politicians who worked tirelessly to decriminalize rape. And, tireless efforts against marriage equality came to naught. But it's been over seventy years since the Civil Rights Act was passed, and we've only seen tiny, incremental advances. Banks and real estate companies still redline neighborhoods. Candidates for jobs are still rejected out of hand for their skin color. And up until a few months ago, African Americans innocent of any crime were still being executed by police officers," Bridges concluded.

"If you could ask the President of the United States one question about this issue, Your Honor, what would it be?" Hartman asked.

"Now that's a good question," Bridges said, thinking. "I suppose I would want to know if he would devote the efforts of his administration to getting corrupt people out of all levels of government and law enforcement? Because the whole reason evil is allowed to be done in this country is because far too many people in positions of power are allowed to violate the public trust without consequence. You have corrupt people in congress—and yes I can admit that progressives sometimes act outside their constituent's best interests—bought and sold every day.

"But I would like the people who are tuned into this show to consider a proposal I have. What if we forced the government, our own legislators, to make violating the public trust a capital crime? So any government worker, from those in city hall all the way up to the US Congress and the presidency, if convicted of corruption would be put to death. How long do you think it will take to return the government and the law to the people? And here it is, 2032, and we still haven't taken the money out of political campaigns or instituted term limits. Government is not particularly functional and look what it took to force equality on this country. This is a great example of a true grass roots movement," Bridges said, chuckling.

"As you've said in other interviews, a rather Jeffersonian movement," Peter said.

Bridges quoted, "The tree of liberty must be refreshed from time to time with the blood of patriots and tyrants is what Thomas Jefferson is credited with saying. And although the quote's definition has to be stretched somewhat to cover what has been going on today, the idea is still sound. The question that we should all be debating is why it took the death of all those family members to finally bring us to equal treatment under the law? Perhaps it was because they were white.

"What took place, and has now been escalated, is anathema to me. But governments use killing to enforce doctrine, and most often, diplomatic failures. The promise of the Civil Rights Act was an abject failure until now. Racists should never have jobs with power over others; neither should misogynists, or those who are cruel to animals, anyone not reasonably well adjusted for that matter. But white entitlement is so deeply ingrained in the underpinnings of this country that nothing could be even remotely fair. It will be interesting what kind of response you get from your viewers, Peter. I'm willing to bet that the responses are going to be evenly split between conservative and progressive political outlook. But the fact of the matter is that this country cannot move forward, or live up to the promises of the founding fathers, until the conservatives in this country are driven completely out of power—everywhere," Bridges said soberly. "By the way, half of your viewers are losing their minds right now."

Hartman laughed. "No doubt. But we have proof going all the way back to Eisenhower that conservatives have evolved into some kind of parasitic, selfish beast of one-percenter promoters and sad sacks who have demonstrated beyond a shadow of doubt that they simply cannot govern. No matter how good a person is in their own life, if they lack compassion, and are determined to remain willfully ignorant, they are a blight on this country's potential. There are still a majority of conservative talking heads on television and talk radio, but progressives are making gains all the time."

Seeing that they were running out of time, Judge Bridges hurried to get in his last point. "The upshot of what we're experiencing in this country is the further dismantling of white privilege. Not everyone is going to be happy to see that happens. What everyone is overlooking is the fact that taking down white privilege in this country is good for everyone. We have had whites whining about affirmative action being unfair to them as some sort of reverse discrimination. Once a few generations of a level playing field have passed, there will be no need for those sorts of programs to right traditional wrongs. Let your angry viewers chew on that, Peter."

"Thank you for your time, Judge Bridges. It was a pleasure to have you in studio."

"Thank you, Peter, for the invitation. I hope we can do this again soon."

-=#=

The president turned off the TV with the remote and turned to Attorney General Thatcher and said, "And so it goes."

"The guy's turned into the voice of his people, maybe even the voice for a generation. There's not a damn thing we can debate him on. It's like he was listening in when you gave your directive about racist cops being flushed from the system," said Thatcher.

"It's pretty obvious that it's the only thing that will begin to change racial justice in this country. What's interesting to me is his notion of making violations of the public trust a capital offense. Privately, I hope the notion picks up some serious steam."

"What?" Thatcher exclaimed, shocked.

"Bridges is right. The one thing that has destroyed fairness in this country is corruption. Selective enforcement of the law, passing legislation that singles out people for special consideration, passing laws that screws the majority of citizens in this country for a narrow slice of the populace. The whole system is completely fucked up, and you know it. How many bankers has your department prosecuted since the start of this century, Simon?"

"You're preaching to the choir, Marcus. But political necessity has always raised its ugly head."

"And we still haven't taken the money out of the game," the president said ruefully.

"You never would have been elected if it had been. As it was you barely made it," Thatcher observed.

"Do me a favor, take a look at the judge's proposal. I'll bet it could get the next president elected by public acclaim. Anyone campaigning against the notion could get buried—should get buried. Anyone who campaigned against it would automatically be branded a crook, especially if someone gave it just a little push. Maybe I should invite Judge Bridges here for a one-on-one?"

"It couldn't hurt. But the press is going to have a field day if they find out," Thatcher cautioned. "Have you given any thought to paneling a commission on race? It's the right time, and there's a good chance something substantive could come out of it."

"I've been giving it some thought. I just don't want the press to jump on the notion that doing so is in any way capitulation to the vigilantes."

"Spin it as a way to gather information that could get us closer to understanding and locating those people," the AG suggested.

"Perhaps. I'll give it some thought. And thank you for this," he said, holding up a bound report. "I'll take a look at it tonight. Ridding America of bad cops is long overdue."

Chapter 37

Officer Stickle had been whisked away from the burning police headquarters building in an unmarked police car, crouched down in the back seat to be taken to a hotel just outside of Cincinnati. He arrived while it was still dark outside and he settled into his room, watching the coverage of the fire until well-past dawn.

His wife woke up to see the news coverage of the fire and was frantic with worry until one of the protective detail knocked on her door after inspecting the breakfast cart and informed her that her husband was safe. Betty and Chloe were a little restless, not allowed out of their room except to go to one of the detail's rooms while housekeeping tidied up their room.

Eight-year-old Chloe was distracted by Betty's tablet with its many games and all the movies they could ever want, but she still got cranky having to remain in the room. The protective detail would not let them go to the pool or the mini-arcade in the hotel. They were determined to make sure nothing happened to Officer Stickle's family. They were also hoping for the opportunity to catch someone in the act of trying to harm them and perhaps solving America's greatest mystery in the process.

Betty watched the news while Chloe played games on the tablet. Updates on the local Cincinnati stations were frequent, and all the location shots showed a still-smoldering pile of rubble. Even in the daylight, the center of the pile was still yellow hot. Reporters were interviewing scientists and firefighting officials across the country trying to find out what could have set the fire and gotten it so hot for so long. The experts were baffled even with samples of gas and molten debris from the edge of the pile being analyzed.

Unfortunately for Betty, her husband was forbidden to contact her in case anyone was monitoring his communications. Both knew the necessity, but it especially galled Owen because he didn't really believe that there was any real danger. Chief of Police Darren didn't agree nor did the FBI liaison in Cincinnati. In a face-to-face conversation, Chief Darren disclosed the whereabouts to the lead FBI agent, asking for additional, covert coverage for Stickle's wife and child. He, along with the FBI, was hoping to take advantage of the circumstances though he would never deliberately put a civilian's life at risk as bait. But the chief and the bureau both saw an opportunity to add an additional layer of security around the Stickles and lay a trap for anyone trying to get near the family.

The FBI took a room on the same floor, and one floor above and one floor below. An FBI command vehicle was parked in the adjacent parking structure, monitoring the FBI assets, and providing logistical support for the Cincinnati detail as well. Their combined around-the-clock coverage was the best they could come up with. Now, it was just a matter of waiting to see if anyone tried to get to the family.

-=#=-

Anthony Dawson flew into Wilkes-Barre International Airport in Scranton, Pennsylvania under false credentials and rented a car right at the terminal. He immediately set out for Cleveland. He calculated he had about a six-hour drive ahead of him traveling at the posted speed limit. There was no hurry; there was plenty of time.

The drive was quiet, and after a stop for fuel and a bite to eat, Dawson made it to Cleveland right on time. He had reservations at a hotel a little more than half a mile from where the Stickles were staying. But before he checked in, Dawson stopped at the train station, retrieved two rolling suitcases from a long-term locker, and put them in the trunk. He also changed into a suit and tie in the washroom and returned to the car to drive to the hotel.

When he checked in, the desk clerk asked if Dawson—not the name he was using—was in town for one of the conventions. When Dawson admitted he was, she handed him a map of the area and circled three venues currently holding conventions. He thanked her then followed the bellman pushing his bags on a cart to the elevator and on up to his room. Once he was inside the room, the bellman tipped, Dawson laid the two bags he retrieved from the train station on one of the beds. He opened them both and took inventory of the equipment within.

He checked the inner pocket and found several sheets of paper and an eight by ten picture of a hotel with two windows circled and an "X" on the window between the two.

Dawson went to the window with a scope from one of the bags and looked out toward the hotel in the distance. The picture exactly matched the building with the other buildings around it matching the photo confirming that the right side of the target faced him. He then inspected the window before him and saw that even though it would open, when it was tilted all the way into the room, there was no way he could shoot through it. He looked at the arms that prevented it from opening it any farther and saw all he had to do was remove four screws to get it to open completely. He chuckled when he saw that one case contained an electric screwdriver. Nothing was left to chance with these operations.

The instructions informed him that the scheduled time for the operation was. 5:00 A.M. the coming morning. Dawson pulled the drapes closed and then proceeded to assemble and load his weapon. Once he was done, he slid the rifle under the bed closest to the window and then put the bags in the closet.

Since he was in for the duration, Dawson ordered dinner from room service, grabbed a beer from the mini-bar, and turned on the television to see what was going on around the country. He watched the segments on the Cincinnati police department's destroyed headquarters. There was nothing new being reported, but speculation from the talking heads was laughable. Dawson didn't know who pulled off that operation, but his admiration was sky high for the execution and effect the fire had on the media. He could only imagine what the FBI was thinking. He also wondered what the FBI, or even the president, thought about what Judge Bridges was saying in all the interviews being broadcast on the cable channels. Dawson hadn't met only four other operatives, no one who he could point to at or near the top of the organization chart and he liked it that way.

He knew the cause was righteous. Had he felt any doubt, seeing the results would have convinced him of the need for the work he did. What impressed him most was the quality of the intelligence on every operation, as well as the equipment he was always provided. The logistics were perfect, his documentation—phony credentials, tickets, everything—was also perfect.

This operation was the biggest in terms of personnel Dawson had ever participated in. He almost made it to Los Angeles when the officers were gunned down, but missed because the logistics just weren't right. From the briefing for this mission, Dawson saw that he was one of four shooters and at least two spotters. He didn't know if any of the other shooters were in the same hotel, or stationed in or on top of any of the buildings he could see out the window.

After his food was brought to the room and he ate, Dawson watched a movie. When he began to get sleepy, he put the cart in hallway, then set his mobile to wake him at 4:30 A.M. and undressed for bed.

Moments before his alarm was about to chime, Dawson woke on his own shuting the alarm off. He dressed and retrieved the powered screwdriver from the bag. He quickly opened the window and removed the screws securing the brackets preventing the window from opening all the way. He quickly set up the spotters scope and the rifle, both aimed at the distant hotel, and laid a bedspread over the barrel of the rifle to slightly deaden the sound. The last thing Dawson removed from one of the bags was a walkie with a headset. He donned the headset, turned the unit on and clicked the transmit key five times. He then heard two clicks in response.

Ten minutes until the hour he heard, "Spotter one." Then, "Spotter two." Dawson held the transmit key and announced, "Shooter one." He heard shooters two through four announce themselves.

"Spotter one. Wind from left to right at eight. Shooter one, distance seven hundred eighteen meters. Shooter two, six hundred twelve. Shooter three, six hundred fifty-six, sixteen meters down. Shooter four, four hundred seventy. Shooters one and four, right target, shooters two and three, take left."

"One, roger."

"Two."

"Three."

"Four."

"Spotter two. Stand by, ten minutes."

"Spotter one, wind left to right, six mph."

Dawson could see two people moving around in the room assigned to him. Fortunately, the curtains in both rooms were open. The range was dialed in as he tracked the movement.

"Shooter one, taking target on the right," Dawson announce.

"Roger that. Shooter four taking target on the left."

Seconds later Dawson heard shooters two and three announced their target assignments.

The team waited as Spotter One counted down the minutes.

"Sixty seconds, wind eleven, left to right."

"Thirty seconds"

"Ten seconds."

And on the mark, Dawson fired, chambering another round should it be necessary. The upper half of the window was shattered, but Dawson could see his man was down. He sent another shot to blast a hole in the lower window, then sent a third round into the head of the police officer lying on the floor. He panned the rifle to the right to survey the officers in the other room, both were hard-down.

Dawson got up and grabbed the screwdriver, the brackets and the screws and quickly reassembled the window. He then broke down the rifle, stowed it back in the bag and replaced the bedspread; all the time listening for any unusual noise in the hallway.

Hearing nothing, Dawson dressed in shirt and tie and pulled on his suit coat. He looked into the corridor and saw a luggage cart sitting by the elevators. He wheeled the cart into his room and loaded his bags on to it, then left for the elevator.

He pulled on his fake, black-rimmed glasses. And when the elevator opened into the lobby, he saw everything looking normal. He went past the desk and out to the front of the hotel, handing the doorman his valet ticket.

"Checking out?" asked the doorman.

"Not at all. I'm taking samples and literature to the convention," Dawson replied.

"Got any freebies you're handing out?"

Dawson laughed. "Yeah, if you like medical bags and such. They're not even sterile, no fun at all," Dawson offered.

"Never mind, I'm good," said the doorman as the car hiker pulled up with Dawson's rental.

They each grabbed one of Dawson's bags and put them in the trunk. He tipped them both and then smoothly pulled into traffic. He returned to the Amtrak station and replaced the two bags of equipment in the same locker from which he retrieved them since he had kept the key. He took out his personal carry on, then proceeded to board a train departing west with a ticket pre-purchased a few days ago.

He found his compartment, quickly entered, and pulled the shades. He tossed the fake glasses on to the seat next to his bag then went into the tiny bathroom. Looking in the mirror, he peeled off the fake mustache and goatee, then washed all traces of adhesive off his face. He then peeled the sideburns and partial wig that made him look years older and rinsed off his head.

He dried off and then changed clothes, removing the suit and pulling on a Morehouse hoodie, he didn't look anything like the man who checked into the hotel the night before. Moments later the conductor knocked on the door to see Dawson's ticket. The two chit-chatted for a few moments and the conductor moved on. Once the train pulled out of the station, Dawson began dropping pieces of his disguise out of the window every few minutes until everything was gone. Once he was through, he pulled his tablet out of his bag and continued to read a novel he had begun a few days back.

-=#=-

NO JUSTICE, NO PEACE

The FBI agents heard the noise of the windows shattering and rushed from their rooms to the stairs. Getting no response from their frantic knocking, they kicked in the doors on all three rooms. The carnage in the details' rooms was horrific. The curtains were blowing in the breeze of the shattered windows, all four officers dead. In Stickle's wife's room, both occupants were still in bed and unresponsive to the agents calling their names. When an agent turned Betty's face up toward the light, her face and skin were cherry red,; and when the agent checked her neck, there was no pulse.

Another agent checked the girl and found her to be unresponsive as well and couldn't find a pulse, either. The agent quickly opened the window to try to flush out what he knew to be a deadly amount of carbon monoxide. The lead agent first called the Cincinnati Chief of Police to let him know his men were down and that the Stickles were also deceased. He then called in a forensics team and the Cleveland police department to secure the floor of the hotel. The agents on site tried to figure out sight lines from which the shots had been fired, but there were too many possibilities to choose merely by looking out of the windows.

The Cleveland Police Department showed up en mass, setting up a perimeter around the hotel. They kept the media at bay and helped isolate the floor the rooms were on. The hotel relocated guests on that floor to other floors or booked them in other area hotels if the guest requested.

Chief of Police Darren rushed to the hotel where Officer Stickle was holed up. He also called the University to let the Head of Security there know what had happened in Cleveland. When he arrived, Stickle was just waking up and hadn't yet seen any news coverage.

He took the news hard as the chief expected. The University sent over two officers and their staff psychologist. Chief Darren waited until the University people arrived and turned Stickle over to them.

Darren then visited the families of two of the officers slain in Cleveland and informed them of their losses. He called in and arranged for grief counselors to visit them as soon as possible, and for the department's human resources to do whatever they could for the families and Officer Stickle. His department was struggling under the handicap of not having a headquarters and the loss of millions of dollars of equipment and all the paper records stored in the building when it burned to the ground. Fortunately, many of the department's records were stored on the City Hall network so payroll and benefits were still being calculated and disbursed without interruption. But the city of Cincinnati was hard hit by the loss of police headquarters. Not only was it going to take several hundred million dollars to replace all the equipment lost, disbursing officers to the other district offices and several underused city properties was straining resources. The city struggled with the shortages as well as possible, but the administration had not forgotten how they got there. The City Council had at the top of its agenda discussion of revocation of police powers for the University's Security Officers in the wake of the tremendous losses Officer Stickle's killing had wrought.

Across the country, African Americans were becoming a defacto protected class of American citizen. There were those who tried to take advantage of the new normal, but those caught committing legitimate crimes were still being processed and held.

A few were subjected to some roughing up, but with the threat of severe retribution always apparent, those incidents were becoming fewer and far between.

America's sociological and racial landscape was changing. And those most angry about it were getting less and less traction with their hysterical claims of preferential treatment of the nation's blacks.

Fear is a great motivator. Fear; and now for America's institutions, the loss of money. And the so-called vigilantes had demonstrated their command of both. From the president on down, the entire apparatus of the Federal Government was painfully aware of their impotence against those determined to change policy and practice in America vis-a-vis racial politics.

When word got out about the killings of the detail protecting Officer Stickle's wife and daughter, there was a demand for the FBI to find the cop killers often forgetting that Stickle's wife and daughter perished, as well. Cincinnati was reaping the whirlwind from the killing of a black motorist by a campus cop, no less. The citizens of the city were very vocal about their displeasure with the police and city hall. They knew where the money to replace the police station was going to come from, and they decried the unnecessary loss of lives because of the police department's shielding of campus cop Stickler.

The tide was turning. No one but the terminally stupid in America was willing to risk the kind of retribution already experienced. Experts in social psychology noted the changes and were having a field day speculating on the extent of the effects that the country was experiencing, what was likely in the short term and the kinds of long lasting alterations the acts of the vigilantes would produce.

Racism was still apparent in many whites, especially those who lived in the South. It simply wasn't going to disappear for generations. White fears about the growing majorities in the Hispanic population were just as pronounced as their centuries old hatred of blacks. Their reign was ending, and their influence on society declining. Many publicly threatened a racial crusade against blacks, but few were brave enough to chance the kind of consequences already seen.

Chapter 38

When Felicia arrived home she was surprised to see Sharon's car already in the garage, unusually early, especially for a Friday night. She hurried inside, thinking something was wrong only to find Sharon cooking Italian for dinner.

"You're home early, any particular reason?" Felicia said, stopping in the kitchen to give Sharon a kiss.

"No, not especially. I just cut out early while everyone sorts out what went on in Ohio. This time there was a clean sweep of the family of that campus cop as well as all the members of the protective detail guarding them. Each instance of retribution is more and more pointed in demonstrating two things. The first is that all murders of blacks will be avenged. The second is that there's nothing we can do to prevent them from carrying out that retribution. Go on and grab a shower, dinner will be in about half an hour," said Sharon.

"Thanks, babe," Felicia said, heading off to the bedroom.

"Everything smells great," she said as she came back into the kitchen.

"Perfect timing," Sharon said, pointing to a covered basket with twin mini French loaves still warm from the oven. She brought a pan of lasagna to the table, already set.

They sat, then said grace. Sharon cut a square of lasagna from the pan and put it on Felicia's plate then did the same for herself. Felicia dished out salad in both their bowls, then poured the wine.

"You know this is my favorite meal, what's up?" asked Felicia. "You have some bad news to lay on me?"

"Sort of," she replied. "Pastor King has terminal cancer."

"Oh no! How's he doing? Is he in a lot of distress?"

"Easy, it's serious, but not that bad," Sharon said, laying a comforting hand on Felicia's arm. "He has a few months before he says he won't be able to function; it's pancreatic cancer," Sharon explained.

Felicia's appetite was gone. She drained her glass of wine and then poured a healthy refill. She gave a wan smile the said, "Did he give you the ol' I want to marry you before I'm gone line?"

Sharon laughed. "How'd you guess?"

"Really? How many times has he hit you up with the idea?"

"You're right. But he had a request of me that I need to discuss with you," Sharon said.

"That sounds pretty ominous. What's this all about?"

Sharon began with an overview of the work she, Jackson, and Judith had been doing for the last few months that Felicia didn't know details about, some of the deeper specifics of their efforts to sway public opinion and to combat slanted news stories. Then she went on to explain what Pastor King had been doing on his own.

Felicia's appetite slowly returned as they discussed the extent of what Pastor was asking of Sharon.

They talked through the meal, cleanup and another bottle of wine. It was well past 2:00 A.M. when they prepared for bed, still discussing all the implications of King's request of Sharon.

Even in bed they talked past 5:00 A.M., going over every aspect of the what Pastor King wanted. What surprised Sharon was how easily Felicia accepted the idea. By the time they fell asleep, the sky was just brightening off in the east.

When they woke up, luxuriating in a late morning start, the first words Felicia said once she finished brushing her teeth and freshening up was, "I think you should do it. It sounds like you can still work at the Bureau and help out the cause. It's fine with me, you have my complete support."

"You're sure?"

"Yes. It needs to be done, and he picked you." Felicia said.

"And what about the wedding?"

"If it's okay with you, I'm okay with it. It will be a fine farewell for Pastor King," Felicia said, hugging Sharon and giving her a heartfelt kiss.

-=#=

Andrew had been waiting to hear back from Tony for several weeks, constantly wondering what his buddy was up to. He had quietly converted a good portion of his investments to cash, ostensibly to purchase a new condo in downtown Manhattan. He even went so far as to engage a real estate agent to help him find something he might like. He looked at a couple of units, both in the two-million-dollar range. But what he was really doing was waiting for Tony to get back in touch.

One afternoon, while he was in the office, he received a text that simply said, "Alley."

Andrew removed the battery from his mobile phone and dropped both pieces in his jacket pocket. He took the elevator down to the garage and exited through the loading dock. As usual, James was waiting for him in the cab.

Andrew got into the back seat and crouched down out of sight. About ten minutes later, James let him know it was all right to sit up. He leaned forward and slapped five with James.

"How've you been," Andrew asked.

"Stayin' frosty. You?"

"Same shit, different day. Tony put you up to this?"

"Yep, he must be hungry again. This time we're going to a different place. The food's still good, though," James explained.

"You haven't steered me wrong yet," said Andrew. He sat back and watched the streets go by as they headed toward Harlem again. Every now and then both James and Andrew checked behind then to see if they could spot anyone trailing them. James even periodically checked the sky.

After a fifty-minute drive, James pulled up to a restaurant and told Andrew to go on inside.

Andrew exited the cab and went inside looking around for Tony in the dimly lit room. All of a sudden he saw Tony wave near the back of the room.

He made his way to the table and hugged Tony who stood, clapping Andrew on the back.

"Good to see you, my man," Tony said as they sat down.

"You're a sight for sore eyes as well. Nice haircut. I'm almost afraid to ask what have you been up to," said Andrew.

"Don't ask. You'll be better off with the plausible deniability. Let's just say it ain't been pretty out there."

"Does that have anything to do with your clean-shavin' puss?" Andrew said, chuckling.

Tony rubbed his close-cropped head, also laughing. "Exactly. It is easier to keep up. But you didn't contact me for grooming advice. What's up?"

Andrew lowered his voice and said, "I've been thinking about what you're doing, and I'm prepared to do my part."

Tony was silent for a few moments, looking at Andrew's face trying to read what was going on inside. "You serious? To be honest, it looks like things are winding down. The heavy lifting is just about over. You would be better off if you kept to your regular gig and held yourself in reserve, honestly."

"What's that supposed to mean?"

"Hey, cool out, Drew. I only meant that once you jump in everything changes. And since operations are winding down, you would be best held in reserve. Look, the FBI is all over you already. Let them tie themselves in knots chasing after you and leaving my snaky ass alone. That's all I'm sayin,' nothing on you."

"Okay I get you. So what's it like?" he asked, mollified.

"A lot better than the CIA. We're much more organized, and believe it or not, it seems like we're better funded on the ops end. Hey, how's that San Francisco project going?"

Andrew chuckled at the naked attempt to change the subject. "It's fine. The first phase will be completed in a few months. Full construction to commence after that. Seriously though, I'd love to be out there giving you a hand."

"I know. Just let it be for the time being. I'll be the first one to get in touch if you're needed."

"All right. Kind of hard to watch your six when I have no idea where it is," said Andrew. "Is there anything you can tell me?"

"It's just as rough as back in the day. You saw what happened in Los Angeles and Cleveland. This is a shooting war," Tony said soberly.

"Answer me this, how did they do that fire in Cincinnati? That was epic, and not a single life lost!"

"I don't exactly know. But our braniacs figured out how to get a burn hot enough to melt steel and let it loose. White folks don't respect nothin' but money. I guess when you stand to lose hundreds of millions of dollars for every black life ended, that's gonna give them pause," Tony explained.

"We both know it's going to have to be done more than once so they don't think Cincinnati was a one-off. That means something like it is necessary, and that means seeing another black life extinguished."

"True-dat, Drew. But what happened in Cleveland is making them think, too. The message that no one is safe anywhere in the country was sent loud and clear," Tony said. "But enough about that, you going shooting this coming weekend? I could slip in and join you."

"Not hardly. Every time I head out to the range the feds trail my ass there and back," Andrew explained.

"They come in?"

"No, but I have to believe that they're keeping an eye on me outside by drone or satellite. Let's not risk it. With my phone jiggered up with that stealth program, just give me a heads up if you're in the area. And keep bringing me to places like this with great food." He looked Tony in the eye and said, "And it goes without saying, if you need me, I'm there."

They two ordered and ate, talking about all manner of things, skirting around the work Tony was involved in. By the time they were finished chatting, it was well past the time Andrew normally left work.

MYRON MacHUTCHENS

Tony texted a message to James who arrived half an hour later to take Andrew back downtown. On the way back to the office, Andrew was still curious what Tony had been up to, but he was glad he knew nothing just in case someone wanted to vigorously question him.

-=#=-

What frightened America most was the silence. No one took credit for the deaths or even the property damage in Cincinnati. It had been months since the first family members died, and there was still no manifesto published. There was no communique, statement of purpose, or warning.

Whomever was behind the killings was an unseen boogeyman striking fear into the people of the United States from the President on down to the relatives of every white police officer who could end up killing an African American. With no organization, or even a person to point a finger at, the nation had no traction on locating a target.

FBI Profilers and psychological warfare experts had nothing but admiration for the efficacy of the vigilantes' tactics. There were many who believed that African Americans couldn't pull off the tasks that had already occurred. But when the FBI crunched the numbers the computers estimated that it could take as few as two hundred well-trained, highly motivated professionals in intelligence, insurgency, warfare and logistics. Out of fifty million African Americans living in the United States, gathering two hundred with the requisite skills would have been child's play.

This made locating those associated with or working for the group in a population of four hundred and twenty-two million US citizens worse than the proverbial needle in a haystack. The FBI was convinced that Anthony Dawson was now working for the group, and they had forensic evidence that Vernon Mendes was as well. But locating either man was nearly hopeless, especially since Mendes was certain to know that every asset the FBI had at hand was focused on finding him. As for Dawson, the authorities were hoping that someone at OpFor would lead them to the man, or barring that, his buddy from sniper school might slip up and do the same.

Neither the FBI nor the NSA, the two lead agencies trying to locate the command and control structure of the organization, had found any pattern or clue indicating how members of the group communicated with each other.

The arrogance of white men was the weakness of the investigative agencies. The conscious and unconscious bigotry handicapped the wider investigation because in their heart of hearts, whites couldn't wrap their heads around the fact that African Americans were smarter than they were and beating them at their own game. Far too many times, in the course of the investigation, the proposal for clearing the agencies of blacks, and in some cases all nonwhites, was floated. SAIC Willis, still stinging from the rebuke he received for his treatment of Agent Jefferson, a woman he even called friend, resisted such calls knowing what a minefield to do so would be.

White entitlement and an imaginary notion of white exceptionalism were preventing the task force department heads from getting into the mind set of those they sought, and not a single department head was willing to invite black participation at the highest levels of the investigation. Their lack of trust in blacks was hoisting the task force by its own petard.

Chapter 39

Harlan Peebles was driving cross country from Spokane, Washington, to Minneapolis, Minnesota, taking I-90 west, crossing through Idaho as dusk approached when he pulled into a service station in Wallace, Idaho. While he was quick-charging his car, several locals hanging out at the station started shouting insults at him.

"Nice car, boy. I bet you think you're something, don't you?" a white man in his mid-twenties shouted.

Harlan didn't respond, waiting for the car to charge.

"What? I'm not good enough for you to talk to? Am I too white for you?"

Harlan still didn't respond. He decided that he could get several hundred miles on the fuel and battery charge the car already received. He unplugged the charger and prepared to leave, angering those with the man who had shouted at him. He pulled onto the road and headed back toward the interstate in the gathering darkness.

He had gotten a few miles down the road when he saw headlights coming up fast behind him. He knew if he tried to accelerate, attempting to get away, not only was he liable to get into an accident, his mileage was going to suffer. He just hoped that whomever was behind him was just trying the scare him and wouldn't really try to do him harm. Harlan was wrong.

The headlights came right up to his bumper and what looked like a pickup truck gave him a pretty rough smack. He sped up to about eighty miles per hour, trying to keep from getting hit again, but to no avail. The truck struck him again, and he could hear whooping and shouts over the sound of the impact.

The truck approached a third time, but instead of striking him from the rear, the truck pulled alongside the car, driving in the oncoming traffic lane. Harlan could easily hear their shouts and taunts. All of a sudden the truck slammed into the side of the car and drove it onto the shoulder. When Harlan tried to stop the car, the truck drove him off the shoulder and into the ditch along the road. The car bounced twice, then tipped over sideways on top of the passenger door and came to an abrupt stop. The airbags had deployed, protecting Harlan from serious injury, but the steering wheel bag prevented him from seeing the brake lights of the truck as it stopped, then backed up to where the hybrid was laying on its side.

Once he regained his senses, Harlan triggered the car's emergency service beacon, then he pulled his phone out of his pocket and dialed 911, then tucked it into his sock. He had no weapon so he stayed put, hoping someone would come in time, responding to his emergency calls.

The four men left the truck and scampered into the ditch, quickly surrounding the car.

"Hey boy, you all right in there?" said one, kicking at the windshield and cracking it.

Harlan closed his eyes to mere slits, hoping they would think he was unconscious.

"Hey boy! I'm talking to you," the same man said, as two of the others were climbing over the car to try to open the driver's door. Getting the door part way open, they pulled against the bent frame until they got the door completely opened. Pulling harder, they snapped the hinges and were able to tear it completely off.

"Hey boy," one of the others said, reaching down to slap at Harlan's head.

Harlan automatically tried to bat away the offending hands, drawing hoots of excitement from the men outside.

"Come on, boy. Let's get you out of that car and make sure yer all right."

Harlan said nothing. He just continued to watch the antics of the men without comment.

Getting frustrated at the lack of desired response, two of them reached in and cut away the shoulder harness and tried lifting Harlan out of the car, but he resisted. Then one of them picked up a good-sized rock and began to break out the entire windshield. The others jumped down and when the glass was largely gone, then reached in and pulled Harlan from the car. As they did, Harlan could tell that his right leg and left arm were injured and he couldn't stand on his own. When he fell to the ground, the others lifted him, dragging him up the side of the ditch to the truck. They lifted him into the cargo bed and two of them jumped in to sit on him while the other two got in the cab. They then turned the truck around and quickly sped away from the wrecked car.

As the truck was bouncing down the road, Harlan slightly moved his leg and touched his hidden phone with the toe of the other shoe, making sure it was still in place. He hoped that the GPS transmitter would alert anyone who came to investigate the car's beacon and would follow to where he was being taken.

In about twenty minutes, the pickup turned off the highway onto a dirt road. They drove for another ten minutes in the wilderness until they came to some kind of compound. The truck took a couple of turns and then parked.

"Don't let him up, I got to get something," one of the men said.

Moments later, the gate of the truck was let down and a bag was pulled over Harlan's head as his hands were tightly tied behind his back. They dragged him to the ground and tried to stand him up, but Harlan's right leg wouldn't hold his weight, so two of the men dragged him about a hundred feet and inside a building with rough wooden floors. They dropped him into a chair and tied him down.

"How's that, nigger? Not too tight I hope," a man said, laughing along with several others.

"Where'd you find him?" someone asked.

"He ran off the road outside Wallace. Apparently this nigger here cain't drive so good! Ain't that right, boy?"

"What'cha wanna do with 'im?"

"Good question. He thought he was too good to talk to the likes of me, right boy? So maybe we teach him some manners before we bury his black ass."

"Anyone gonna come lookin' for him?"

"Fuck no! Why you askin'?"

"You fuckin' stupid? You see what's been goin' on everywhere?"

"No one even knows he's here. Quit worryin'. Besides, ain't none of us cops."

"Yeah, but the whole town knows where we are. If he comes up missin' they're gonna figure we had somethin' to do with it."

"Bullshit. We bury him, and no one's gonna know."

Harlan was beginning to panic. If no one traced his phone soon, he was a dead man. He started to move and flex his wrists, trying to see if there was some slack in the ropes. He could immediately tell that he wasn't going to get out, whoever tied him up knew what they were doing.

"So what do you think, boy? Anyone comin' lookin' for ya?" someone said, slapping him in the side of the head hard enough to make Harlan see stars.

"What'cha doin' out this way, boy?"

Harlan figured, what the hell. "I was driving home. I was visiting my mother in Spokane. I live in Minnesota."

The men were startled at Harlan answering and didn't say anything for a few seconds.

"Is that so, boy? You was visitin' your mama. Now isn't that sweet, fellas? You got any money on you boy?" Harlan could feel hands checking his pockets, then pulling his wallet out of his pants pocket.

"Well lookie here! Four hundred dollars and change. Where'd you git all this money, boy?"

"Actually, I got it out of an ATM in Spokane. There's plenty more where that came from if you want cash," Harlan offered. "I have over seven thousand in the account."

"We ain't stupid. You cain't get seven thousand dollars out of an ATM."

"No, but you can from the bank in the morning," Harlan offered. He heard some muttering between them, but couldn't make out what was said. Then he heard, "That's bullshit. He cain't even walk."

"Well, fuck it then. Let's just have some fun and then bury him out back."

"Whatever. I'm out," said one of the men.

"Hear that, boy? We're gonna have a little fun with you. How's that sound?"

"Frankly, it doesn't sound so good for me," said Harlan, making the unseen others laugh.

"You got that right, boy."

"Let me ask you this, is there anything I can say, or offer, that would stop you at this point?" Harlan asked.

The others laughed. "Fraid not, boy. I bet you wish you'd been polite to me at the station now, don't'cha?"

Harlan was silent, steeling himself for what was to come. One of the men removed the hood, the lights momentarily blinding him. When his eyes adjusted he saw three of the men from the pickup truck. The room was sparsely furnished, almost like a storage space. The walls were rough hewn wood, and the room was lit by a single fluorescent bulb hanging down from the ceiling.

Seeing the feral grins on the faces of the men before him, Harlan knew his only recourse was to play for time, hoping against hope that someone was trying to track him down.

The three men took turns savagely beating Harlan, first concentrating on his face and head. But when it looked like he was going to pass out, they began to rain pounding blows to his chest and stomach, laughing when Harlan vomited from the pain his abdomen suffered.

They would periodically give him a moment's rest, throwing buckets of freezing cold water on Harlan to revive him when he was in danger of passing out. Harlan held out, praying that they wouldn't find his lifeline still tucked into his sock.

After they had been working him over for almost three hours, one of the men drove a fist into Harlan's chest so hard that it broke a rib whose jagged end nicked a small vein leaking blood into his left lung. They laughed when Harlan coughed, wincing from the pain of the ends of the broken rib grinding together, and blood spewed from his mouth.

"It ain't gonna be long now!" one said, laughing at Harlan's pain. Then they all quieted as they heard a helicopter off in the distance.

"Who the hell's out this late at night?"

"You think maybe they're looking for this son of a bitch here?

"How?"

"Did you check to see if he has a phone on him?"

"Hell yeah, when I checked for his wallet," he replied, as the helicopter was coming closer. In moments, it was directly overhead.

The fourth man from the truck came running into the room shouting, "Someone's coming!"

"We know, retard. We hear the chopper."

"No asshole, I mean someone's coming up the driveway. I saw the headlights."

"More than one?"

"Hell yeah."

"Fuck. We need to get this nigger out of here."

"Too late for that, asshole. Everyone put your hands up!" a state patrol officer said, kicking in the door from the outside. Three other officers entered, flanking the first officer, guns drawn.

"Move away from him and line up against the wall, hands on the wall and feet spread. Cut him loose and see to him," the officer said. Outside, they could hear the chopper fly over the building, then land not too far away.

Outside, a dozen officers were rounding up all the people in the compound, laying them on the ground in front of the headlights of the patrol cars. Two tried to run and were shot, both injuries non life-threatening. Everyone else got the idea and decided to cooperate. Inside the room a medic was examining Harlan.

"Lieutenant, he's bleeding out internally. We need to get him to the hospital."

"Is he going to make it?"

"Hard to say," the medic replied, pulling an oxygen mask over Harlan's face. He then started an IV as two officers came inside carrying a stretcher.

"Let's get him on the chopper and out of here."

"Yes, sir."

They gently lifted Harlan onto the stretcher, but when they laid him flat he vomited dark blood.

"Let's move," the medic shouted, holding Harlan's head turned to the side.

The Lieutenant turned back to the four men on their knees with their hands secured behind their backs.

"You know you sons of bitches are going to die, don't you? I'm not going to have to do a damn thing. It's a sure bet your lives are forfeit, especially if that man dies. You boys have set me a poser. If I take you, and the rest of the scum outside, and lock you in my jail, that's putting my boys at risk. But if I leave you out here, someone has to watch to make sure none of you run. Again, that's also putting my boys at risk." He told several of the officers in the room, "Get their names before you drag them outside. They're going to be charged with attempted murder. Then someone radio for a truck to haul them all into town."

"You sure you want to do that, Lieutenant? Like you said, they're all liable to be killed. What if—you know?"

"This is my responsibility. Let's get them in town and locked up, then everyone goes home."

One of the local sheriff's deputies ran inside, looking for the Lieutenant. "Um, sir?"

"What is it, son?"

"The guy they were beating died in the chopper. They radioed me to tell you pronto. You know, just in case."

"Thank you, deputy. As soon as the trucks get here, you and your men take off. We'll take them into town and lock them up. Radio and tell the sheriff we're coming. Also tell him that when we get there, I want him to clear out of the building. You understand?"

"Yes, sir."

When transport arrived, the nineteen from the compound, and the four from the pickup truck were all driven to the Wallace sheriff's office and distributed into the four cells in the building, the four to be charged with murder all in one cell together. A crowd had gathered to see the known white supremacists being brought in. Many in the town of Wallace knew the men, had even done business with them, and some thought it was about time. The crowd quickly dispersed once the prisoners were brought inside.

The residents of the town of Wallace had coexisted with the supremacists' compound for close to twenty years. It was no mystery who lived in the compound, and what their philosophy was; the complete annihilation of the black race and Jews in America. Their capture and torture of Harlan Peebles wasn't the first time they had snatched an African American to torture and kill, it was just that no one was ever able to find any evidence of their crimes. This time was different.

Once everyone was locked up, the Lieutenant sent everyone home. He called the FBI and asked to speak with anyone on the task force. He was connected to the duty officer to whom he explained exactly what had happened. The agent took down all the information and promised someone would contact him shortly. When he disconnected the call, he phoned Willis, waking him up.

When Willis was brought up to speed about the incident, he immediately called the lieutenant back. Once he identified himself, he ordered the lieutenant to leave the building, fearful of what might happen to the prisoners and anyone else who might be injured or killed as collateral damage. The lieutenant informed Willis that he had to stay, and that he'd be quite careful until morning.

Willis dressed and was in his office in less than an hour, he assigned two agents to travel to Wallace first thing that morning. He also tasked the overnight staff with finding out everything they could about Harlan Peebles.

When morning came, Willis made the call to the sheriff's office checking in with the lieutenant and found that the night had been uneventful. Unexpectedly, the state patrolman had emailed Willis a copy of the incident report, the arrest report, and the charges pending against each member of the supremacist group. He packaged the documents into one encrypted file and sent it to the task force distribution list, adding that the incident might present them with an opportunity to find one of their target group if they approached the town and acted against the jailed supremacists.

When the charges were announced in the morning, the story, carried on local television, was quickly picked up by national media and spread across the country. Everyone was speculating about what kind of response was coming over the torture death of Peebles. The four who had originally run Peebles off the road were charged with multiple counts of attempted first degree murder, aggravated first degree murder, and held without bail. The other nineteen were charged as co-conspirators and various other charges with each being held on one million dollars' bail.

Oddly enough, no one from the national media showed up in Wallace to cover the story, letting local media cover the arraignment, and an interview with the Idaho State Police public information officer. There was a sense of anticipation surrounding the crime and all the players involved, even President Temple, were waiting to see what would happen. It was only the residents of Wallace, Idaho who seemed oblivious to the danger they faced, or at least what those who inhabited the compound were facing. By evening, Willis had two agents in place undercover posing as a couple going camping in the nearby wilds of Idaho, stocking up on supplies for a five-day camp out.

Willis had been in touch with the sheriff's office several times throughout the day, but everything was quiet in Wallace. By the time evening rolled around, he was exhausted from the stress of waiting, from trying to imagine and cover every possible contingency. When he returned home, his wife could see exactly what kind of day he had and made a simple dinner for him to eat before he fell into bed, praying nothing would interrupt his sleep.

Thankfully, nothing did interrupted his sleep. When he woke the next morning, Willis felt like he had been drugged. It took two cups of coffee before he felt sharp enough to go into work.

Once he arrived at the office, he checked to see if anyone from Wallace had called, apparently they had just as quiet a night as he had. When he called to check with his two agents, neither answered their phone. That was nearly impossible. Neither would have been away from their phones, and since the camping story was a ruse, there was little chance they were both out of cellular range. Something was wrong.

When he called the sheriff's office there was no answer except the office's automated attendant. He called city hall, checking the time. Surely someone should have been there by 9:00 A.M. local time. Looking up the number online, Willis called the Idaho State Police headquarters.

"This is Agent Willis at the FBI calling to find out if anyone has been in touch with your men in Wallace."

"And this would be for what purpose, Agent Willis?"

"I was in touch with him late last night about logistical support and no one is answering the phones at the sheriff's office. Do you have anyone close enough to check on them there?" Willis requested.

"Agent Willis, is this the best number to use to get back in touch with you?"

"It is. If I'm not in the office, you'll be routed to me no matter where I am. I really appreciate it."

"No problem. You'll be hearing from us shortly."

Willis hung up the phone and called the Seattle FBI office to see if they could get a chopper in the air and got a promise that one would be airborne in thirty minutes. While he waited, the tension in the task force staff present in the command center wound tighter and tighter, imagining all sorts of disaster befalling Wallace.

Forty minutes later, Willis' mobile phone rang.

"Willis."

"Chief, you have a problem here in Wallace," the Seattle FBI bureau chief announced.

"Why? What the hell happened?"

"We're hovering about a thousand feet over the center of town and there's not a soul on the streets that we can see who is alive. There's about a dozen cars and trucks run off the road. There's three people who were obviously walking their dogs laying dead in the street, along with their dogs—dead too. We're not dropping any lower. But if you know anyone on their way here, you'd better warn them off unless they have full BL4 hazmat protection; something rolled through here like instant death."

Willis was stunned. "Are we talking about a biological attack? On the whole town? What the fuck?"

"Sorry to say, that's exactly what it looks like. I already called the state patrol and have the major roads into town being blocked off. They're spooked just from seeing the shit load of dead birds on the ground everywhere. No one's touching anything. But if my guess is correct, we're looking at a quick dispersing agent. There's already scavengers nosing about. Still, anyone sent in here should be wearing protection, whatever nerve agent tore this place up could be lingering in enclosed spaces. Sheldon, I've got to go. I want to check the roadblocks they're setting up and see if we missed any roads in the back way. I'll call with an update in an hour."

"Thanks a lot. I'll be awaiting your call," said a stunned Willis. He left his office and announced to the room, "We have a level 3 or 4 hazmat situation in Wallace. The head of the Seattle office took a chopper and found folks lying dead in the street. I need someone to coordinate a hazmat team to get their asses on the ground there ASAP! We have to assume that our two agents are down, someone has to lead a search for them to make sure. I have to make some calls, let's go; I need answers yesterday, people."

Willis returned to his office and closed the door. He then put in a call to the White House and got Sharon on the line. "We have a situation. It appears that the entire town of Wallace, where those stupid racists killed that motorist, has been taken out by some kind of nerve toxin."

"Holy shit! Who knows about this?" Sharon asked, alarmed.

"Just the head of the Seattle office and the state police, but everyone's too shook up to be spilling the beans—so far. The roads into town are blocked off, and we're getting a hazmat team on the ground as soon as we can. But you have to inform the president as soon as you hang up. I'm not transmitting anything electronically until we know for sure."

"Okay, I'm on it. Keep me posted, if I'm not in the office, call my mobile," she said.

"I definitely will."

Chapter 40

"Is Willis absolutely sure, Agent Jefferson?" asked the president.

"So far, there's nothing to suggest otherwise, Mr. President. A hazmat crew is en route and should be there within the hour. Our people are supervising the situation in cooperation with the Idaho state police. We have the area around Wallace cordoned off and have, so far, kept the press in the dark. If it weren't for the reports of Mr. Peebles having been tortured to death by those white supremacists, no one would have been the wiser except maybe out-of-town family members or vendors making deliveries," Sharon explained.

"Okay, explain this: what if it was a chemical weapon attack? That raises the stakes with these people to a level that's unthinkable," Temple said quietly.

"I think the message is unambiguous as well, Mr. President."

"And what do you think the message is, Agent Jefferson?"

"That those who allow the lawless to exist are just as likely to suffer the same fate as those who committed the crime?"

"My thought exactly. What's the population of Wallace?"

"Somewhere between twelve and fourteen hundred residents with some vacationing in the area. We have on file eleven white supremacist compounds numbering somewhere in the neighborhood of eight to ten thousand people spread throughout the area. We have not checked to see if any of the other compounds suffered the same fate as the people of Wallace."

"How many blacks live in Wallace?"

"The latest census shows less than two tenths of one percent. Anecdotal information we've uncovered so far suggests that any blacks who are in the area are employed in Wallace but live elsewhere nearby. When we get our teams in there, one of the things they're going to be looking for are any deceased nonwhites. We had two FBI agents there undercover, a male and female team posing as campers. So far we've heard nothing from them. Our teams are going to be searching for them as well, Mr. President. At the top of our list of priorities is determining exactly how everyone died and precisely what agent was used to kill that whole town."

"And what about the torture victim? Has an exact cause of death been determined?"

"According to our own forensics people in Seattle, Mr. Peebles bled out from a punctured vein in his chest. A broken rib nicked the vein as near as she was able to tell. Based on the time the driver triggered the emergency beacon on his car, and the time the authorities showed up, Mr. Peebles was probably tortured for several hours," she replied.

"This afternoon's meeting is going to be very interesting. If they can manufacture nerve toxins, or even steal it right from under our noses, no one is safe. This was a huge warning, if we don't get our collective shit together on race in this country, no one is safe. This is definitely a national security matter," Temple said, exhausted from trying to work out how to steer the country through tortured waters. "There's nothing to stop these people from committing the same kind of attack here or anywhere."

"That is correct, Mr. President. And the only place you and your family would be safe is inside the PEOC."

"I'm not cooling my ass in the bunker for the duration just because they used nerve gas in Wallace. It's not that easy to gas the capitol and cripple the nation, Agent Jefferson. But this attack in Wallace has given me pause. As soon as we're done here, I'm alerting the Secret Service and dividing the government for continuity. The Vice President is going to the alternative command shelter along with a core group of congressmen. I want all the department heads from the task force at this afternoon's meeting. Inform SAIC Willis for me," said Temple.

"Yes, sir," she said immediately getting to her feet.

"Thank you, Agent Jefferson," he said, watching her leave.

-=#=

It only took four hours for the national media to go public with the details of the attack in Wallace; somebody talked. The country was at a standstill, especially when it was leaked that the nerve agent that killed fourteen hundred people was sarin gas. Sarin gas was just one of the nerve agents stockpiled by the US government and a host of other country's militaries as well. The use of nerve gas is forbidden by numerous United Nation's international treaties but that didn't stop folks from keeping it around. Since it was stored all over the US, it was going to take some doing to see if the sarin used in Wallace was stolen or manufactured; either prospect was chilling.

Whomever was behind the movement to completely stop the murder of blacks in the United States of America had drawn a line in the sand. The message was clear, from now on the country was under a zero tolerance policy as far as the murder of even one African American was concerned. And no consequence was too harsh. It was particularly frightening from the first explosion in Orlando that children were not immune from suffering the same consequences as their parents.

Malcolm Leads paid for a private jet to pick up Judge Bridges in Denver to get him into the studio as soon as possible to discuss the latest developments in Wallace, and they wasted no time getting started.

"Your honor, welcome back to the show. Thank you for gracing us with your presence, once again. Let's get started. Can you describe your take on the events in Wallace, Idaho? It appears to me that the repercussions and consequences for murdering an African American have hit a new low," Malcolm began.

"Thank you for having me, Malcolm. I believe you're right. If the death of all the residents of Wallace Idaho was retribution for the torture and death of Mr. Peebles, then we have reached a definite turning point in this country. But before we go any further, I would like to extend my sincere sympathies to the relatives of those who died in Wallace," Bridges replied.

"What do you have to say about the indiscriminate deaths of everyone in that town? That includes men, women, children, and even pets. What kind of barbaric response is that to the death of one man, your honor?"

"If I had to guess, I would chalk it up to a town full of people who knew what kind of white supremacists lived nearby and did nothing whatsoever about their criminal behavior. But that's just a guess," Bridges said soberly. "I have absolutely no knowledge of the thoughts in the minds of those who precipitated the deaths in Wallace. Sometimes I wish I did, then I could warn the country about what kinds of behavior will trigger what kind of response. I think the psychological effect of not knowing is heightening the fears in the public and is probably exactly what's wanted."

"But children? I know that children have died, cops' children before now. But this is a bridge too far, you have to agree," said Malcolm.

"I agree with nothing of the sort. Do you have any idea how many innocent black children have died since this century was colonized, Malcolm? Thousands, tens, maybe hundreds of thousands. And yes, it's troubling that the sins of the parents are visited on the children, but if the senseless murder of African Americans in this country is going to stop, then everyone has to shoulder the responsibility for making that happen. If a town does business with white supremacists who feel they can kidnap, torture and kill someone black any time they feel like it, the town is equally responsible for the crime or crimes committed I believe is the message that's being put out there."

"Do you feel that a small group of people have the right to dictate the behavior of the entire country, your honor? That any minority should be given that kind of power? These people are not elected, they aren't even known. How dare they hide in the shadows and dictate terms to the greatest nation in the world!"

"You aren't referring to the three hundred wealthy white families that essentially control this country, are you, Malcolm?" Bridges said, chuckling, seeing his point was not lost on anyone in the studio. "But I digress. Blacks were subjected to the tyranny of the majority for hundreds of years; they still are. They were enslaved, indentured, slighted, cheated, beaten, maimed, and killed with no one saying anything about the inequity and nothing really changed until now, Malcolm. The thing you've let upset you isn't feces on a fly's butt in the totality of the evil done to those with dark skin. And your whining about a minuscule number of whites who have died in the service of stopping the greatest evil done in this country is sad. Who do you think you are trying to equate a few children who were collateral damage in righting the greatest evil in this country as unreasonable? We've been here before. How many times did you lament the senseless death of an African American on this show before you invited me to join you? Exactly never!"

Malcolm was sputtering, not even able to get out an intelligible word in rebuttal.

"Malcolm, I like you. And I understand the positions you take in the name of conservative politics. But to pretend that what's being done in this country isn't long overdue is sophistry," accused Bridges.

"I admit that prejudice, and even racism, have no place in an enlightened society. But to force their elimination is still coercion. Changes like these have to be done with the will of the people engaged—
"

"Let me stop you right there, Malcolm. I have to call bullshit, sorry, on your will of the people notion. Why do nonwhites in this country have to bend to the will of the white majority in a twenty-first century already a third over? How long do we have to wait for white people to get around to giving us our due? How long are you white folks going to ignore the fourteenth amendment of the founding document of this great land, and I quote: No State shall make or enforce any law which shall abridge the privileges or immunities of citizens of the United States; nor shall any State deprive any person of life, liberty, or property, without due process of law; nor deny to any person within its jurisdiction the equal protection of the laws.

"You conservatives worship your twisted, almost retarded, incorrect interpretation of the second amendment like the word of God, but have never said a word about any other amendment, especially the fourteenth I just quoted. The bottom line is that someone has decided that they're tired of waiting for white people to get around to granting African Americans equal treatment under the law, and you will either live up to the United States Constitution, or suffer deadly consequences. Deal with it, they appear to be saying."

Leads was clearly not happy with the way things were going on his show. Judge Bridges clearly had taken control.

"So, if I understand you correctly, killing people to right a historical wrong is fully justified—"

"Malcolm, stop trying to put words in my mouth. I have always stated that I abhor the loss of life. However, to respond to your accusation, you can't argue with success," Bridges stated then was silent.

Malcolm didn't have a rebuttal. "We'll be right back after these messages." When the floor director signaled they were clear, Malcolm chuckled and said, "Obviously you've been eating raw meat since we last spoke."

"No, I'm just weary of your conservative cohort ignoring what got all this started. Tens of millions of senseless deaths of colored people in this country going unanswered," Bridges said wearily, taking a drink of water. "I apologize that I have to do this on your show, Malcolm. As I have said, I really think we're more alike than different. But I am grateful that you continue to invite me on."

Malcolm laughed heartily. "No matter how you try to verbally beat me into submission, I have to say that I haven't enjoyed trying to debate anyone like this in a long time. And no matter that I may think differently than you; I truly believe that the country needs to hear what you have to say."

"Not to mention the ratings you get when I'm on, eh?" Bridges said chuckling.

"Did I say that?" Malcolm said with a wink. "Five seconds." When they were live he asked, "Judge Bridges, I agree that it has been long past due that the promise of equality be the rule, not the exception. But killing is killing and must be punished, wouldn't you agree?"

"I do agree. But until someone is caught, the question is essentially moot. If law enforcement can't find those responsible, there's nothing that will put those people in check. So while we can all agree that those responsible for killing the residents of Wallace, Idaho, must be brought to pay for their actions, until someone is caught there's nothing to stop more killings except the halt of the murder of blacks in this country."

"We have ample evidence that white police officers have stopped killing blacks all across the country. And I know what you're going to say, that every killing must stop. If you look at the statistics, the killing of whites by cops is also down, so there's been a collateral benefit all the way around," Malcolm pointed out.

"That's true, Malcolm. And urban crime is also down significantly. When the police are forced to stop behaving like some sort of lawless vigilantes, the whole criminal justice system benefits. I think what happened in Wallace has had a net positive effect on this country—"

"What? How the hell do you figure that?"

"If you'd let me finish I'll tell you. Just before the events in Wallace were reported, we saw several incidents where civilians killed officers who had killed presumed innocent African Americans on the street. In the last few days, we have seen neither blacks nor police officers shot. Maybe Wallace was the wake-up call for the whole nation. If you're the head of a police department, and you see that a whole town was exposed to nerve gas in retribution for the torture and killing of a black man, what are you going to tell your officers? Are you going to let some hothead on your force put your entire town at risk?" asked Bridges.

"But isn't that simply extortion? Or maybe it's blackmail—hell, I don't know what to call it. But a threat like that is monstrous!"

"I agree. But again I have to ask, what's it going to take for this country to finally treat blacks just like whites?" Bridges asked.

"Whites get the short end of the stick too, your honor. You should know that. White people have their civil rights violated all the time."

"That's true, but they don't get killed for their skin color. The irony of the cry of treat me like a white man can't be lost on you. No matter how bad a white man or woman is treated in this country, it's infinitely better than that of a black person. For all of the phony protestations about how blacks have it made with affirmative action, quotas and set asides in business, education and the like, there isn't a white person in this country who would trade their life for that of a black person's. Would you, Malcolm? Would you trade your privileged existence for random searches at the airport, police searches on the street for no better reason than having dark skin, being pulled over with a twenty-times higher chance of being killed than a white man just because you have black skin? Is that the paradise you're craving because it works out so well for blacks? Of course not, the entire notion is absurd and all the bigoted, racist whites who lie about how good blacks have it in this country wouldn't spend five minutes taking the insults, abuse, violence, and risk of death every black man, woman and child faces every minute of every day. Let's get down to it, would you give up this show and all the perks you get for being a white broadcast celebrity for the life I lead? And I've got my own minor celebrity, Malcolm. Would you trade your life for the twenty times greater risk of being murdered because you have a taillight out on your car? Or being denied a mortgage because of skin color or because of the neighborhood you choose to live? Let me save you the trouble for having to come up with an answer full of crap, of course you wouldn't. No sane white man would, and admittedly, I have it pretty good. I have a good job; I'll be getting a pension soon, and my home is paid off. But that doesn't cut the mustard when it comes to life on the streets."

"Admittedly, I'm quite comfortable with my life of white privilege as you call it, your honor. However, that's the hand that I was dealt, just as you have yours. I have admitted that there's so many places where improvements can be made in our society, but is it right to have to make these changes over the barrel of a gun?"

"In a perfect world, absolutely not. But the last time I was here I characterized what the country is going through as a Jeffersonian solution to a problem that has existed since Europeans arrived on the continent. In this case, the tyrants are the white police officers and white civilians for whom blacks lives don't matter. As a matter of fact, not only don't they matter, but they can be extinguished at will without consequence; that was until now. I would hope that the chilling events in Wallace would give us all pause. The people behind this movement have obviously thought their strategy through for any and every contingency. If I were the president, I would give considerable thought to what comes next if, heaven forbid, another black man, woman or child is killed. I would also think that the civilians who killed the police officers in Chicago and Los Angeles should also be a wake-up call for everyone in law enforcement. There's been an undeclared war between the police and the people they're supposed to serve for generations now. The police in this country have had the unquestioned power of life and death, with the citizens going along because initially they trusted what they were told. But for decades now, that trust has evaporated. What is the most galling aspect of the situation we're in for whites is the fact that it's most likely blacks who are calling the shots, and there's nothing anyone has been able to do about it. Gassing a whole town with proscribed biological weapons because of the torture killing of one, mind you one, black man should scare the living hell out of the whole country. Imagine what's going to happen the next time a cop kills a black child."

Leads paused, letting the idea sink in, a moment later he said, "That's a sobering thought, and debating the morality of killing is pointless at this time. The people behind all this killing have demonstrated their resolve in a most frightening manner. I guess the question now is, what can be done to minimize any further killing?"

"It's simple, Malcolm: stop the murder of African Americans in this country."

Malcolm had nothing to say in response. He let the silence hold for a few seconds, then said, "And we'll be right back." When they were clear, he said, "Whew! This one's a barn burner, judge. How much shit do you figure you'll be catching for this one?"

Bridges laughed easily. "Remember the ancient Chinese curse?"

"May you live in interesting times? That one?"

"Exactly. We're all in the soup now," Bridges said, going quiet while his makeup was touched up.

"And we're back. We just have a few minutes left, your honor. Do you have any final thoughts on the subject?" Leads asked.

"Just one. I believe the only thing the DOJ can do now is to strip the nation's police forces of dirty cops, otherwise the consequences are just too horrific to consider, just as I imagine those people planned. Once you've demonstrated that you're willing to kill on a horrific scale, everyone knows the score, everyone knows what to expect. Imagine what a sarin gas attack on the New York subway system would have been like? Can the city of New York afford to allow bad cops to roam the streets anymore, choking people to death for selling cigarettes as in the past? Some would say that the citizens of Chicago and LosAngeles who gunned down those cops are doing their part to clean up their police forces, but a paltry handful of killings are not the kind of remediation we should be looking for; you still have unjustified shootings and murders. You want to eliminate every instance of that kind of crime committed by our country's policemen regardless of the color of the skin of the victims."

"And we're going to have to end it here, your honor. Many thanks to Judge Alvin Bridges, author of The Entire System Is Broken: Throw It Away and Start Over, for stopping by again, you never fail to give our viewers plenty of food for thought. On behalf of everyone here at The Leads Report, we wish you a good night."

"And we're clear," said the floor director.

"Think anyone was listening?" asked Malcolm. "I mean anyone in power?"

"I can't believe that I'm the only one thinking about this. The president's liable to have some of the finest minds on race at his beck and call, nothing I said should be a surprise to him by now."

"Well, your honor, as always, it's been an honor and a pleasure. Where are you off to now?" Leads asked.

"Back home to Georgetown, I get to sleep in my own bed for a couple of days, and then I'm off to LosAngeles. And thanks for the quick flight in, Malcolm."

"It was my pleasure, your honor. Now, I get to look at all the hate messages about the show posted on the Web site. Take care," Leads said, shaking the judge's hand, chuckling.

Chapter 41

Special Agent in Charge Sheldon Willis was trying extremely hard not to show the despair and frustration he felt in his heart. On top of the heartbreak of losing two agents in Wallace, he was now responsible for leading the investigation into the source of the sarin gas that killed the residents of the town. His request for the location of all stores of sarin gas held by the military was tied up in a seemingly infinite supply of red tape. Getting an inventory was going to be impossible as he wasn't vetted by the armed forces, and any order allowing him access to the information coming from the Commander in Chief was sure to be resented. And chances were that any demand for information he would make was sure to be met with an endless supply of "classified" roadblocks.

The entire country was terrified, now knowing that no one was safe from such brutal, heinous retribution for the murder of an African American. Those in bigger cities feared any closed-in location, smaller towns, even those with largely bigoted residents, were terrified that some racist nut in their ranks could get the whole town killed. And though there were those blacks who tried to take advantage of fearful whites, the incidence of such attempts were few.

When the body count in Wallace was completed, not a single black person had been killed by the gas. The only two black families living in town were found unconscious in a motel halfway to Spokane, drugged and presumably spirited away from their homes in the middle of the night before the gas had been dispersed. Such an opportunity to remove African Americans from harm's way wouldn't happen in the New York subway system or a major mall across the country. Perhaps there was safety in the presence of nonwhites, but no one knew for sure, nor was anyone interested in testing the theory.

-=#=-

"Pastor King, we're so glad you've consented to officiate our wedding," Felicia said.

"It is I who is honored. I have loved and respected the two of you ever since you found each other. You do an old man proud to have the opportunity to officiate the service. Thank you both," Pastor King said, smiling broadly, the joy in his face obviously genuine.

"Excuse me for saying, but you're looking well, Pastor. I hope you're also feeling well," said Felicia.

"I am, indeed. I don't really know what to expect from this wretched disease. I have good days and bad days, but the bad days are nothing more than a greater measure of fatigue so far. I'm well, that's all both of you need know," he said.

Sharon reached over and clasped King's hand, "Whatever you need, don't hesitate to ask."

"Thank you, dear. So, when's the date? Have you two made a decision on when we're going to perform the service?" he asked.

"We're wondering if Saturday, six weeks down the road is okay with you?" Felicia asked.

King looked at the calendar on the wall and asked, pointing, "Do you mean the nineteenth?"

"Exactly, how's that weekend for you?" asked Sharon.

"It's perfect. I'll leave the day open, ladies. Let me know what your arrangements will be as soon as you can. I can't wait for the blessed day."

-=#=-

"Mr. President, according to the chairman of the joint chiefs, none of the military's sarin stockpiles have been breached. He claims that the toxin was either manufactured here, which takes a decent amount of expertise, or that it was purchased overseas and smuggled into the country," Agent Willis reported.

"And of course your team is looking into facilities where the toxin can be manufactured here in the states?" asked the president.

"Yes sir. But as you may or may not know, originally sarin started out as a German insecticide. Even an old decommissioned chemical manufacturing facility could quickly be upgraded and retrofitted to manufacture the compound; it's not particularly difficult to make. As for smuggling it into the country, given that we are presuming these people have been operating, or at least planning for up to a decade, the gas could have been brought into the country almost at will. Here we are over thirty years after 9/11, and we still only check fifteen percent of the cargo containers entering the country. Our lab is trying to determine the exact formulation of the gas itself to see if there are any molecular markers that can point to its origin," Willis explained.

"What about the delivery system? Have your people found how it was dispersed throughout Wallace?" Temple asked.

"There's no sign of any bomb casings, so the gas wasn't dropped from an aircraft. We have several theories we're tracking down. The first is dispersal by trucks. The drivers could be protected by sealed suits and needed to only drive throughout the town for a few hours. Contact would cause nearly instant death, and there would be no warning at all; it's not like anyone could outrun it. This was extremely well thought out. The only African Americans living in Wallace were sedated and removed from their homes before the sarin was dispersed. That, more than anything else, was a message to us."

"The last thing we need is to receive any more unspoken messages from these people. We need to shut them down," the president said, clearly frustrated.

"Your directive to the DOJ is the best first step in preventing more needless deaths. Flushing criminal cops off the streets is going to go a long way toward accomplishing what you want, and frankly, what this country needs. When the criminal justice system is free from prejudice, the whole country will benefit, sir. And I know you, and others, suspect we're never going to find these people," Willis said, holding up his hand to forestall the president from protesting, "and constantly consider the implications of us not finding them, too. But if we don't, and we get cops off the street who would just as soon shoot a black person first and deal with the consequences later. Then other than the necessity of bringing those people to justice for the family members' killings and the deaths of those L.A. cops, the country ends up with a net benefit. To even say that out loud is disturbing, and I'd never do it outside this room. But the goal you set us is now directly aligned with the very people the task force is after, Mr. President. I believe that this is no coincidence," Willis said.

"You would be correct, Agent Willis. But that's serendipity, not intent. You best be about the business of identifying and catching these people, because not only is it the right thing to do, but the people you seek are mass murderers on a scale we have never seen before in this country. And no matter what the Honorable Judge Bridges says, killing thousands in retribution for the millions of black deaths through the ages in this country is unacceptable. So, stay on target, let the DOJ do its thing. I have every confidence that somehow the clue that bears fruit is bound to turn up. At first, I considered your losing Mendes, twice, as a failure, but it's really a testament to exactly how well the FBI gets it done to have found him at all. Keep up the good work, Agent Willis," Temple said, getting to his feet to lead Willis out of the office.

President Temple had already received back-channel offers of assistance from Interpol and the law enforcement and security services of several closely aligned countries. Those offers consisted of personnel, logistical assistance, and investigative support looking into the possibility of another country being behind the unknown group. The situation was too American to seriously consider some hostile country behind the deaths, but that didn't preclude the possibility of someone supplying logistical support for those operating in the U.S. Unfortunately, the Central Intelligence Agency could find no hint of any such collusion, specifically because the CIA, though chartered to only operate outside the country, could find no trace of any suspicious activity through their normal channels of intelligence covering hostile governments around the globe.

The use of sarin gas raised the stakes higher than any faced by America in its history. It was far more terrifying than a nuclear threat to most citizens. The devastation was total, and more frightening because no one would know if, or when, they might fall victim to sarin's deadly effect. Everyone in America was now living in fear of what retribution they would face if an African American was killed in their community, which obviously was the intent of those prosecuting the war on violence against America's blacks.

No, this was a uniquely American problem, being dealt to the country by Americans, Americans who well understood the emotional underpinnings of terror. Rhetoric from America's usual racists had quieted, knowing that the entire country was on notice, with no one white exempt from being punished for any senseless death of a black person.

President Temple had very few options before him until the people behind the killings were exposed. So far, he wasn't the direct focus of the fear, the frustration and the anger of the people. But the longer it took to identify and capture them, the worse the fallout his administration faced.

-=#=-

The weeks passed and no real progress was made in the investigation. There were several half-hearted attempts by disgruntled whites to float the notion that the president's administration, though almost completely white, was somehow in cahoots with the unknown killers. And on the street, the respite from blacks killed by cops and civilians continued. Reported crime was less than half of what it was before the first explosion in Orlando according to the FBI's own statistics.

African American pundits were making hay with those same crime statistics, claiming that the majority of co-called black crime was a manifestation of racist policing policies across the country. Others were bemoaning continuing black crime as the direct result of income inequality and the lack of opportunity, a still very racist America had to offer nonwhites. The conventional wisdom was that the first step toward equal treatment for blacks in the United States had finally being taken.

The fact that whomever was behind the retribution for innocent blacks murdered was willing to use weapons of mass destruction in revenge for the death of even one, generated its own brand of terror for the American people.

-=#=

Officers Lincoln and Chaffey were patrolling Compton, driving the neighborhood on a quiet Friday evening. Though both were white, their faces were familiar to many in the community.

Noticing a group of half a dozen black men hanging around outside one of the area liqueur superstores, Chaffey made a u-turn in the middle of the street and pulled to the curb next to the group.

"What's up? You see something?" Lincoln asked.

"What? You mean other than a bunch of perps loitering?" Chaffey replied.

The crowd of young men stood silent as Chaffey, then Lincoln exited the vehicle.

"Something going on here?" asked Chaffey with barely disguised contempt in his voice. "Any of you holding? Anyone carrying a weapon?" Chaffey asked unsnapping the strap that secured his handgun in its holster.

When the men saw Chaffey's hand on his weapon they all spread their hands, palms out to show that they were empty.

"What are you doing?" Lincoln whispered in Chaffey's ear, too low for the others to hear.

"You just shut up and back me up," Chaffey ordered his younger partner. Then loud enough for the others to hear, "Any of you all have business here? Some reason for loitering out on the street?"

"Um, begging the officer's pardon, but we don't need any reason for being here. We're just hanging out, just a bunch of friends shootin' the shit. That okay with you, man?" one of the young men said, verging on the edge of belligerence.

"Is that so? What if I were to inform you that a couple of you match the description of a robbery suspect currently at large?" Chaffey responded.

"What's that? Black and breathing?" the same young man said to the laughter of the others.

"Since when?" Lincoln hissed in Chaffey's ear, not caring if the others heard him or not.

"Shut up, and just back me up. Now all of you up against the wall, feet spread, hands high!"

The six looked at each other, and when the oldest of them nodded, they moved down from the security grate over the liqueur store window, faced the brick and complied with Chaffey's order.

"Pat 'em down," Chaffey ordered.

"No, you started this shit. You pat them down."

"Hey! You eyeballing me boy?" Chaffey said, touching his weapon to the back of the man's head when he turned to watch the two officers.

"Take that gun off my head, unless you want your family to die," the man said between clenched teeth. "Because sure as I'm standing here, you hurt me or any one of us, not only will we end you, someone's gonna make damn sure your family dies. You here me boy?"

"Chaffey, you better think this over. I'm not putting my wife and kids at risk because of you," said Lincoln, almost pleading.

"Listen to your partner, Officer Chaffey! It ain't like it used to be. You want a building full of cops to die because you got a hard-on for fuckin' with black folks?" the same man asked, his hands still pressed to the building. "We got no problem with you. All we were doing was standing around shootin' the shit. There was no reason for you to roll up on us."

"I suggest you shut up boy, or I'll end you!"

The youngest of the group, on the far end of the lineup turned to confront Officer Chaffey, causing Chaffey to turn and raise his weapon preparing to fire when a shot rang out.

When the men on the wall all craned their necks to see what had happened, keeping their hands up, they saw Chaffey slowly slumping to the ground, cursing as he cradled his arm; Officer Lincoln had shot Chaffey in the shoulder.

Lincoln picked up Chaffey's pistol and tucked it in his belt, then holstered his own gun. He turned to the men, still with their hands up and said, "Beat it, all of you. You don't want to be hanging around when backup comes, and it will come."

"Damn man, did you have to shoot him?" asked the youngest of the group, probably not even out of his teens.

"For all of us, damn right I did. Now, get the fuck out of here, I'm in enough trouble as it is."

The older man who had originally confronted Chaffey, quietly asked,

"You cool with this? We'll all back you up if you need us to. This ain't gonna be easy on you."

"I got this. Now go."

The others dispersed in several directions while Lincoln called in an officer-involved shooting over the radio and that an officer was down. He also called for a supervisor to be dispatched to the scene as well.

"Let me see," he said to Chaffey, tearing his sleeve to expose the wound. "Fucking crybaby, it's barely a flesh wound." He helped Chaffey to his feet and leaned him against the squad car. "You owe me, you stupid cocksucker. I just saved Brenda and Scott's life."

Chaffey tried to take a swing at his partner and Lincoln easily pushed him to the ground.

"Listen, asshole. If you want to take a swing at me once you're all patched up, fine. But you'll be lucky to be chasing down lost pets once I make my report. What a fucking waste," Lincoln said, shaking his head.

Chaffey rolled over and was getting to his feet, pulling himself up by the bumper of the squad as the first two police cars arrived. The officers, one a sergeant, quickly exited, guns drawn, but pulled up when Lincoln waved them off.

"Put them away. This stupid cocksucker was trying to get us all killed," Lincoln said as the sergeant approached him while the other helped Chaffey to his feet.

"What the fuck?" the sergeant declared.

"He was about to shoot a guy for nothing, a black guy," Lincoln explained.

"And you had to shoot him?" the sergeant asked as Lincoln handed him Chaffey's gun.

"You want a building full of sarin because of this asshole?" Lincoln asked, jerking his thump in Chaffey's direction.

"Is that true?" the sergeant asked Chaffey.

"Fuck no! One of the sons a bitches was about to attack me," Chaffey said sullenly.

"And did he?"

"Did he what?"

"Attack you? You hurt anywhere but the shoulder?" asked the sergeant.

Chaffey was silent for a moment before he sullenly replied, "No."

Several other squad cars arrived, bracketing the street and blocking the sidewalk on both sides of the liqueur store. Everyone turned when one of the cops called for the sergeant. "Sergeant, we have a couple of witnesses over here."

The older black man from the group, along with the belligerent teen, were being blocked from approaching.

"You know them?" the sergeant asked.

"Yeah, they were in the group Chaffey rousted."

The sergeant shouted to hold them for a minute, then turned to Lincoln and had him explain what happened. Once he got Lincoln's version of the events, he saw that an officer was bandaging Chaffey's shoulder. He then waved for the two witnesses to be brought over.

Once he got their version of what happened, exactly matching Lincoln's description of what transpired, he said, "Okay, for the time being you're riding a desk. Chaffey's on leave until the investigation's done. You have anything you want to add, anything at all you want to tell me about Chaffey's past behavior?"

"No, sir."

"Then go on back to headquarters. I'm going to have Internal Affairs open a case, and interview you tonight; so stay put. I'm also going to have those two," he said, nodding to the witnesses, "interviewed and have statements taken. Publicly, I have to ask you what the fuck were you thinking? But privately, as far as I'm concerned, it couldn't have gone down any better than it did. If someone can completely burn a cop shop down to ashes and kill a whole town without a trace, then because of you we don't have to wonder what's next. Decent work Lincoln, just fucking try not to do it again."

"Thank you, sir. Yes, sir."

Chapter 42

Jackson traveled to Washington to meet with Judith to do some face-to-face work on their book. After the first part of the manuscript, they covered the historical murder statistics of African Americans going all the way back to when African slaves were brought to Jamestown, Virginia, in 1619. However, they knew their two-chapter preamble covering the history of white Europeans and their subsequent attempted genocide of the North American native peoples was not going to be very well received by many white Americans. But unlike the current textbooks that tended to whitewash America's history of slavery, whose publishers capitulated to whining conservatives in Texas and other Southern states, the information in their book was entirely factual, backed by the most comprehensive scholarship ever applied to any similar publication.

American whites were a particularly bloodthirsty lot, as were their European ancestors. Other parallels were detailed like Stalin's and Hitler's killing sprees, all adding up to a murderous tendency whites had over every other race in the last twenty-five hundred years. Jackson and Judith also included the only use of atomic weapons in man's history by a white American on a predominately civilian Asian population, twice.

The tone was factual, the citations were impeccable, the work was unassailable by any rational judgment or scholarly review, but both knew that those facts wouldn't matter to many overly sensitive whites. But it was the most comprehensive compendium of criminal murder committed by European stock in the history of the modern world.

Jackson was wealthy enough to publish and print hundreds of thousand copies, giving them away to more enlightened high schools, colleges, universities and public libraries across the nation. Judith knew that once the work was seen by members of America's media class, the topic, as toxic as is was to the still white majority in America, was too explosive to ignore. Jackson's plan to give the book away would make it not only too good to ignore, but there could be no accusation of commercial exploitation to be made off of the sensational tome.

The book was to be accompanied by links to an online reference with every detail of every black person murdered that they could find in print or electronic media. And though they knew they would come under scathing scrutiny for not including any of the officers' family members, or the officers killed since that first explosion, their justification was that the country's media outlets had already done that work, sensationalizing their reporting right from the start.

It was Judith's idea to solicit Judge Bridges to write the forward for the book. She took on the task of contacting him, hoping Bridges had read her work and at least knew and remembered her name. But the greatest challenge she and Jackson were currently facing was naming the work. Jackson was lobbying towards irony, while Judith was advocating for something more in lines with something scholarly. Perhaps either Judge Bridges or Pastor King would have an idea that Judith and Jackson would end up liking.

-=#=-

Michelle was on the OpFor range, getting in some practice when she was paged to reception. When she arrived she saw that a suit, who immediately smelled like a Fed, was waiting patiently.

"I'm Harold Parsons from Homeland Security," the man said, holding out his identification to Michelle.

"Well, that's a step up from the run-of-the-mill Feds we usually have sniffing around here. What is it you want to discuss with me?" she asked, returning the ID folder to him.

"I'm here to try to find out the whereabouts of Anthony Dawson. We would like to ask him a few questions."

"He's not here. However, he did write down a statement for you, or whoever was the next government spook who showed up," she replied, taking the number 10 envelope the receptionist handed to her. "We're a pretty tight group around here, and we look out for each other. Since I know personally that Tony's not involved with the people you're looking for, and that you, meaning the U.S. government is rousting African Americans with specialized military training just because they're black, both Tony's assignments and his off time have been away from our headquarters so he doesn't have to be subjected to this kind of harassment," she said, handing the envelope to Parsons.

He opened it and began to read:

To whom it may concern,

I, Anthony Dawson, am not going to be subjected to any kind of arrest or illegal incarceration without due process by the United States, or any other government. To that end I am actively avoiding any contact with any and all government law enforcement personnel until the Family Matters Task Force investigation is concluded.

You have already harassed friends and associates of mine on a fruitless fishing expedition, and I stand on my constitutional rights against unreasonable search and seizure to not be harassed. Be advised that the chances of you finding me are slim and none, please leave OpFor and my friends alone.

Regards,

Anthony Dawson

When Parsons folded the note and put it back into the envelope, Michelle said, "Tony said that the note wouldn't mean a thing to you folks, but it was worth a try. May I ask you a question, Mr. Parsons?"

"What is it you want to know?"

"If the people you're looking for are presumed to all be African American, what's going to happen when you find out the people you're looking for are blacks, whites and other races fed up with your department's failures? Does everyone in the United States get profiled as a potential member of that organization? And how do you know that we whites aren't just as fed up with your impotence at doing your f-ing job as the people you let get shot or killed over a hundred times a day in this country?" she asked, angrily poking Parsons in the chest. "It's all your fault for not doing something about white cops killing blacks and other minorities and letting the killers get away with it. This lies right at your doorstep, you, the FBI, every local police department in this country. And you're all dirty, every single one of you, because you all personally know dirty cops in every single one of these police departments and none of you do a God damned thing about it!" she finished, her voice rising considerably in volume.

Several people peeked out of their offices to see what was going on, as the receptionist called the CEO, letting him know what was going on.

"That's not my assignment, Ms. Young," Parsons replied evenly.

"And why the fuck not? If you, and the rest of the gun-toting clowns running around the country looking for those people, had been pulling bad cops off the street these last fifty years, none of this would have happened!"

At that moment, the man who created and ran OpFor entered the room and squared up to Parsons and said, "What can I do for you, son? I'm—"

"I know who you are, General. I served under you before you retired," Parsons said, unconsciously straightening up to attention.

Former Brigadier General Martin Hadley had left the service twelve years prior and started putting together what had become OpFor a year after retiring. Because of his record in the United States Army, he had garnered the respect of the military and political community as a no-nonsense strategist whose record of minimal casualties in the operations he planned and executed was without peer.

"At ease, soldier; I'm no longer a general. Now what is going on here, other than my best sniper's explanation to you where your department and every other law enforcement arm of the government has fallen down on the job?"

"I'm here to look into the whereabouts of Anthony Dawson, sir."

"He's on assignment."

"May I ask where?"

"You may ask, but there's nothing to compel me to tell you. And please, try arresting me for interfering with a federal investigation; I live for that kind of shit. However, I will state that Tony's not involved with the people who have killed those cops' families. Now what else can I do for you, son?"

"Nothing, sir. Thank you for your time, and sir, it was good seeing you again."

"Quite all right. Let me give you some unsolicited advice."

"Sure."

"The problem with working for the government, in any department, even in the military, is that even those of us at the top of the food chain can be poorly used. The best we can hope for is that we're not called upon to do things so odious that you find yourself hating who you've become. Michelle's right, we all failed to do the right thing, especially in the service. If we had spent as much time and resources flushing the worst of the racists from the military, from the FBI, from the Department of Justice, and from the police departments across this country, over seven thousand people would still be alive today. You're here on a fool's errand. Tony's not the problem, we are. Nice seeing you," Hadley said, accepting the business card Parsons handed him.

"Sir, I know I can't ask you to call me when Mr. Dawson returns, but nonetheless, I have to try to find him. At least see if he'll contact me by phone," requested Parsons.

"I'll pass the word along, son. Have a safe trip back," the general said, gesturing to the door.

Once Parsons left, Hadley turned to Michelle and asked, "Is Tony tied up in this shit?"

"Honestly, I have no idea. It's not the kind of thing I think he'd be mixed up in, but I really don't know. He's been in and out, usually at night. And he knows that One-Shot's been rousted at least a couple of times just because he's the best shot in the country—maybe in the world—and black. The whole thing stinks, sir. But, we're all doing our best to keep Tony from getting pulled in and disappearing to some black-ops sight in the Middle East to get squeezed," she explained.

Hadley patted Michelle on her shoulder and said, "Carry on. If you need me to pull some strings or run interference, don't hesitate, just call. Now, I'm going to try to get back to the nap you all interrupted with all this damn noise." With a wink at Michelle and a wave to the receptionist, Hadley returned to his office and shut the door.

Michelle thought about contacting Andrew in New York and warning him, but figured that all their telephone traffic was probably monitored, and if the feds were crawling around the OpFor compound like roaches, then Andrew was likely covered six ways from Sunday by the feds as well.

Michelle wasn't very worried about Tony. He obviously could take care of himself, and even if he was involved, her own internal sense of justice couldn't really blame him. She wasn't dissembling when she accused the US government of being directly responsible for the killings.

Michelle had been deployed to some of the shitiest hell holes around the world, and saw first-hand how inequity, despotic rulers, prejudice and racism bred deadly consequences. She wasn't inured to the innocent killed, but her training allowed her to make a dispassionate calculation between the tens of millions of blacks killed in America to a paltry seven thousand whites in order to right a heinous wrong.

What the president was afraid of was the sympathies of a growing number of white Americans who could also make that same calculation, leaving the recent dead to be swept into the dustbin of history for a perceived greater good. Michelle's beliefs and attitude, egged on by the constant visits by Feds trying to locate Tony, were the greatest threat to restoring stability across the country.

Terror was slowly giving way to serious discussion about the policies of police departments across the country and injustices they represented for all. African Americans were not the only people capriciously shot and killed by cops. The raw statistics documented by Jackson Richards' online database were appalling, and other Web sites were beginning to aggregating the numbers of whites shot and killed by the police, several others began documenting Latinos involved in police-involved shootings. The national conversation was slowly beginning to turn from simple anger over the police family members killed, to a more nuanced discussion about gun violence inflicted on all citizens by police officers across the United States.

-=#=-

". . . yeah, right in the arm," Willis said, reading the L.A.P.D.'s official report on the incident to Sharon over the phone.

"What does the report say about what happened to both officers?" asked Sharon.

"The shooter is riding a desk, the shootee is on paid leave pending the outcome of the investigation. But damned if I saw this one coming. But now that it's happened, it seems pretty obvious," Willis said, chuckling. "Maybe if they're willing to shoot each other to prevent their families from being killed, we may finally be at the point of breaking down the blue wall."

"What's the local press saying? And has there been a statement from the fraternal order or the union yet?"

Willis did a couple rapid searches. "Nothing so far according to the report. I'm surprised. There's nothing coming up in the L.A. Times, no hits on the news broadcasts. By the way, you're really going to love this one. Director Ryan is seriously thinking about classifying the National Rifle Association as a domestic terrorist group."

Sharon was silent, at first not believing what she heard, then trying to grasp all the ramifications of the Bureau doing so, then trying to figure out what the first steps the DOJ would take in response. "That's just crazy talk, Sheldon. Where would we start? Where would the DOJ start? The tactic is brilliant, especially for the heat the declaration is going to generate, but damn!"

"No shit; but what a distraction. After a couple of generations of them wagging the dog, it's about time we do something to completely denature them. They, along with that damned Supreme Court ruling in 2010, completely ignored the actual text of the second amendment and let unregulated guns flood the streets. More guns, more powerful guns in unlimited quantities have kept street cops twitchy for a couple of generations now."

Sharon heard the excitement in Willis' voice over the classification of the NRA as a domestic terrorist group. She had to admit that the prospect would surely shake things up, and that the absence of the NRA's influence over the nation's politicians would allow rational changes in gun control to probably see the light of day.

"That would be great. I'll forward the LAPD Internal Affairs report. And I think you should also mention what the director is thinking about doing vis-a-vis the NRA, if he hasn't mentioned it to POTUS already. Anything new on your front?" Willis asked.

"Felicia and I would like you and Beth to attend our wedding. It's the nineteenth. What do you think?"

"I'd—we'd—be honored!"

"The invitations are going out in a few days, I'll make sure Felicia has you on the list. We're having Pastor King officiate the service at First Baptist."

"I can't wait! And congratulations to you both!"

She heard the joy plainly in his voice. "Thanks Sheldon, it means a lot to us. Okay, so as soon as you send over the internal affairs report, I'll run both issues by POTUS."

"On its way. Catch you at tomorrow's briefing."

"Thanks, later."

Chapter 43

The public outcry when the director of the FBI, and the US Attorney General made their announcement was split between indignation and "it's about time." The briefing room was packed to overflowing, the probable subject of the press conference having been leaked; very little remained secret in Washington for long. When the stroke of Noon arrived, Director Ryan entered the room, the Attorney General and several staffers in tow.

"Good afternoon; everyone, thank you for coming. I have a statement to make, as does the Attorney General, then if there's time, I'll take a few questions. As some have speculated prior to this announcement, the Department of Justice has classified the National Rifle Association as a Domestic Terrorist Group.

"U.S.C 2331 defines Domestic Terrorism as activities with any of the following three characteristics:

"1: Involve acts dangerous to human life that violate federal or state law;

"2: Appear intended (i) to intimidate or coerce a civilian population; (ii) to influence the policy of a government by intimidation or coercion; or (iii) to affect the conduct of a government by mass destruction, assassination. or kidnapping; and

"3: Occur primarily within the territorial jurisdiction of the U.S.

"U.S.C. 2332b defines the term federal crime of terrorism as an offense that:

"1: Is calculated to influence or affect the conduct of government by intimidation or coercion, or to retaliate against government conduct; and

"2: Is a violation of one of several listed statutes, including § 930(c) (relating to killing or attempted killing during an attack on a federal facility with a dangerous weapon); and § 1114 (relating to killing or attempted killing of officers and employees of the U.S.).

"The text of these definitions are posted on our Web site. For too long now, the tyranny of the NRA has held sway over this country. Aided and abetted by a conservative Supreme Court in 2010, the proliferation of guns in this country has reached an insane extant. And it was this insane amount of firearms on the streets of America that fueled the militarization of even the smallest of police departments. Along with that militarization of our police, we saw a corresponding shift from a presumed innocence of the citizenry in this country, to a shoot first, shoot to kill option, with no option number two.

"To present the influence of the NRA as the only justification for such deadly responses with no regard for the underlying injustices in this country would be foolish. However, the NRA's actions, going on for several generations now, are substantially responsible for over fifty thousand gun deaths each year in the United States. At the turn of the century, that number was thirty thousand; the trend is clear and it's time to put a stop to benign neglect over the number of handgun murders committed in this country. It is time for Congress to find the political will to pass legislation that seriously curtails the proliferation of guns on the street and draws down the number of firearms owned in this country. Currently there are two and a half guns for every man, woman, and child in this country; that is madness.

"This classification of the NRA as a domestic terrorist group has the full support of the federal law enforcement community and the President of the United States. It's time for this country to say enough is enough to the gun manufacturers who have no regard for the tens of thousands of gun deaths each year, especially the children who die each year. The NRA is directly responsible for all those deaths of children because of their terrorizing Congress and the people of this country. And according to NRA tax filings, seventy-five percent of the NRA's funding comes not from members, but from gun manufacturers. So what is the real interest the organization represents?"

SAIC Willis, and several other department heads of the Family Matters Task Force, were watching the press conference live. There were no side comments as everyone was taking notes, trying to predict the issues this declaration was going to generate for discussion after the presser was over.

The attorney general's statement was very brief, then Director Ryan asked for questions and the room erupted in bedlam. It quickly quieted when Ryan pointed to a reporter in the front row.

"Thank you, Director Ryan. I think the entire country wants to know just what this classification of the NRA as a domestic terrorist group means for the members in the organization? And does membership automatically make one a terrorist?"

"That's a good question. The FBI, in concert with the DOJ, is currently formulating policy on that issue. The first act Justice is taking will be to subpoena the membership lists of the national and local chapters of the organization. This classifying of the organization facilitates the collection of membership data for analysis as well as determining the officers at the head of the organization," Ryan replied.

"A quick follow-up, please. And what happens if the NRA declines to comply with the subpoena?" the reporter quickly asked.

"Then we start arresting for obstruction of justice. And we're not talking about low-level office workers, we will begin arrests with the top-tier management. Make no mistake, ladies and gentlemen, the United States government is done with the influence peddling of the NRA's money, and their terrorist tactics used against Congress and local state governments. You," he said, pointing to a woman in the middle of those seated.

"Thank you, director. What does this mean for gun ownership in this country? There are nearly three guns for every American; that's an awful lot of guns. What does the president plan to do about so many millions, billions even, of guns on the streets?"

"That's a very good question. I'm told there are a number of proposals being considered. The policies they implemented in Australia, for example, were very effective in almost eliminating handguns possessed by civilians. However, the FBI is going to implement whatever policy the President comes up with, and hopefully congress will follow suit. Yes, in the back row on the end."

"If the law of the land is changed to forbid citizens from owning handguns, I have two questions: one, how will that be enforced given the 2010 supreme court ruling, and two, will citizens be financially compensated for the loss of their property?"

Director Ryan took a moment before replying. "As we have a more progressive bench than we had back then, I can't see it being very difficult fast-tracking a case challenging the ruling from twenty-five years back; it's about time. The wording of the second amendment is: A well regulated Militia, being necessary to the security of a free State, the right of the people to keep and bear Arms, shall not be infringed. The conservatives in the John Roberts court were ideologues, and with very few exceptions, ruled commiserate with the ubiquity of the dumbing down of America and opposition to the constitution at the behest of the moneyed industrialists and corporatists both here and abroad. Only someone with no intention of upholding the founding document of this country would chose such a deadly misinterpretation of the second amendment.

"And as we saw, the election of the nation's first black president flushed all the closet racists out from under their rocks they had been hiding under because they feared their white privilege was starting to disappear. We have ample evidence of that fact in our ongoing investigation being led by the Family Matters Task Force.

"As for the second part of your question, I have no idea if there's going to be a national buyback program for guns. I think the irony of the question and such a program is that it would directly contradict conservatives who constantly complain about the government wasting money on pointless boondoggles. No one who has purchased a firearm should be financially hurt by mandatory removal of firearms from the hands of American civilians. Presumably their guns and ammunition are already paid for. One more—you in the corner."

"How do the DOJ and the FBI plan to address the fact that criminals are hardly going to be turning in their guns, if it comes to that?"

Director Ryan paused for a moment, deciding exactly how to answer. "I have no idea at this moment. I see no reason why illegal gun possession can't be made a capital crime; one with a mandatory death sentence. As I said earlier, policy is being drafted right now to address all of these issues. Thank you all for coming," Ryan said into the cacophony of shouted questions. "Please refer any additional questions you may have to our Web site." With that said, Ryan and his entourage exited the room.

-=#=-

Much needed change was sweeping the nation. Nothing like punishing a race-based murder with the death of an entire town to shake things up. The anger and frustration born of the mass killing of the entire population of Wallace showed the frightening resolve of the people who were brooking no mere lip service to the Black Lives Matter movement. Yes, they mattered, because if a single black life was squandered in the United States, retribution was as swift as it was deadly.

President Temple wondered what his legacy would be given the events transpiring on his watch. He knew that the judicial and law enforcement reforms he all-but rammed down the country's throat were long overdue. Were he to be honest, it galled him that he was completely powerless to strike back at the people forcing him into action, regardless of whether or not there was a need. Nonetheless, he comforted himself with the knowledge that what he was doing was right. His own internal refrain of I'm not a racist was immediately followed by the honest realization that if he wasn't part of the solution, as the cliché went, he was part of the problem.

What American culture had needed was a shock to the system in order to reverse a country's lifetime of insults, slights, and murder of African Americans. And whites crying favoritism as they were, were too willfully ignorant to understand that the changes benefited them as well. But white privilege all-but disappearing was necessary for the country to finally live up to its original ideals.

"I'm really getting too old for this shit!" Temple said, almost shouting it into the empty office. He looked at the clock and saw it was going on 8:00 P.M. He got up to go get something to eat, as well as maybe three or four martinis.

-=#=-

Support for the National Rifle Association disappeared overnight with gun manufacturers immediately pulling their financial contributions. They couldn't erase the evidence of their past contributions to the organization, and knew it would be troublesome down the line. Giving material aid and support to a terrorist organization was a charge no one wanted to have to fight in the media or in the courts.

The NRA steadfastly refused to return any of the contributions they had received from the gun lobby, knowing that the fight for the organization's life lay ahead. The top tier management of the NRA, all known to the public, went into hiding. Their legal representation issuing only terse, "No comments," in response to queries made by the media.

Members of Congress and state houses were returning thousands of dollars in political contributions the NRA had made to their campaigns. But racist and low-information whites were giving full-throated support for the organization, not helping the beleaguered organization at all. The face of the NRA, in the vacuum created by the heads of the organization in hiding, was the worst of what southern white culture had to offer. This did nothing more than exacerbate the nation's growing ire toward by the organization. In the final analysis, as an organization, it was finished. And with the FBI's classification as a domestic terrorist organization, there was no one eager to step up as the national gun rights organization's advocate. Behind the scenes the Department of Justice was urging several organizations to squire cases through the court that directly confronted the 2010 second amendment ruling by the Supreme Court.

Across the country, when the police pulled over an African American or confronted blacks on the street, bystanders immediately pulled out their phones to film the incident. Since the first explosion in Orlando, no African American had died in police custody under suspicious circumstances.

Nor did America's private prison industry go unscathed. The owner of one such prison in Wyoming, where a black inmate allegedly hanged himself, returned home one evening and found his wife and two children dead in her SUV, in the garage, doors all closed and the engine running. There was no sign of a struggle, either in the house or on the bodies of the deceased. The Casper, Wyoming Police Department could find no sign of foul play and were forced, even though they knew better, to classify the deaths as a murder/suicide perpetrated by the wife. The owner resigned from the private prison corporation and left the state just days after the funerals for his family were held, and he wasn't the last. The heads of two maximum security institutions and two supermax institutions also resigned and divested themselves of their financial stakes in the corporations. Racism against African Americans, whether knowingly perpetuated or not, was becoming a hazard that few dared to risk.

Resentment was growing across the country in those who saw the changes occurring as giving African Americans preferential treatment, or that the law wasn't applying to blacks the same way as to whites. By and large, those complaining were of the same ilk who claimed Affirmative Action was reverse discrimination instead redress of traditional wrongs visited on Americans because of the color of their skin. Police departments, when confronted by criminal acts by blacks, had ceased to kill as their first option as. They were proceeding in the same manner as traditionally enjoyed by white perpetrators. Those who benefited the greatest were black children. No longer would a police officer roll up on a teen or preteen and just blast away because they were in possession of a toy gun, or any other shiny object that previously made them "fear for their life." Now they feared for their family's lives. And the result? African Americans were beginning to be treated to a manner of law enforcement and justice that whites had enjoyed throughout the history of the country.

Malcolm Leads, once again, invited Judge Bridges to his show to discuss the events of the week.

"Welcome again, your honor. It's been quite a week, has it not?"

"Indeed it was, Malcolm. And thank you for inviting me back. You're right, the classification of the National Rifle Association as a terrorist organization is definitely a game changer. I truly didn't see that coming. I'm rather curious to find out what conservatives make of this latest tactic of the Department of Justice," Bridges said.

"The email I have been getting since the change was announced is running practically one-hundred percent in favor of the NRA and against reclassifying it. Many believe it is a precursor to the forced confiscation of guns across the country," Leads replied.

"I believe the Director of the FBI already admitted as much. Estimates put the number of guns in the U.S. somewhere around a billion. We have only four hundred, million citizens, men, women and children. If they were distributed evenly, everyone in the country would have at least two firearms apiece. I can't see how that makes the country, or its citizens any safer. And as for gun ownership being a necessity to protect citizens from the government, nothing could be further from the truth. The government doesn't lose against individuals," Bridges said soberly.

"But what conservatives object to is the questionable legality of confiscating guns. And home protection is a big deal with people, criminals are not going to be giving up their guns, so taking away law-abiding citizens' firearms is going to leave them at the mercy of criminals. That argument is not going to go away."

"I think at the beginning, that may be true. But with juries having that same mind set, criminals who get caught committing crimes using handguns will no doubt pay a heavy penalty for their crimes. But in a generation we will presumably see a serious reduction in gun violence. And in the final analysis, more people are shot by their own guns than those in the hands of criminals by such a wide margin, that the argument is specious.

"Personally, I would like to see the government require every gun owner to carry insurance for their firearms, just as we do for car owners. I'd especially like to see the formulas the actuaries will use to calculate rates. Given over fifty-thousand gun deaths in this country every year, premiums are going to be very expensive," Bridges said, chuckling.

Leads was ambivalent about how to proceed. He knew his regular audience would absolutely lose their minds over his appearing to agree with the idea of imposing mandatory insurance for gun owners. "That idea will never fly. Congress isn't going to vote for that kind of legislation, and neither is the NRA—" Leads began, then halted mid-sentence.

"Yes, I believe you're right—that is if the NRA even exists anymore," said Bridges. "Do you think having an organization that is classified as a domestic terrorist group railing against legislation will make it more likely, or less likely to for the legislation to pass?"

"But what about the will of the people? Congress can't simply pass laws that the majority of the country don't approve of?" Leads asked, as Judge Bridges burst out laughing.

"For the last fifteen years polling showed that ninety percent of Americans approved of common sense gun control legislation being passed, and what happened? The NRA ginned up all manner of imaginary issues that scared the pants off of gun owners, and more importantly, terrified Congress. And conservative radio and cable television shows have demonized nonwhites since before Reagan was president, scaring the hell out of whites making them believe that nonwhites were the spawn of Satan," Bridges said.

"A lot of liberals have made that baseless claim before."

"It's not a claim, Malcolm. Too many media studies substantiate that fact. You can choose to ignore it if you wish, but I've always found you to be an honest broker of the truth, at least when I've been sitting in this chair across form you," Bridges said, grinning.

"Okay, let's take your statement as a given for the sake of argument. But what about the fact that criminals will not be turning in their guns, and collecting the firearms of law abiding citizens will leave them vulnerable? That doesn't seem fair, that the innocent, the law abiding should be the only ones put at risk," Leads said.

"I can't speak to that issue, Malcolm. As you've stated it is a troublesome consideration, but I don't make policy; this is on the Department of Justice, and then local law enforcement. But getting guns off the street is going to make this country safer for everyone."

"Your honor, how do you think this NRA issue is going to impact the Family Matters Task Force? In your opinion, does it substantially make a difference in the focus of the task force?"

"Given that the majority of police officers have been shot after firing into crowds of demonstrators and everyone else who has died has done so by all manner of means, but none by firearm, I don't think it will impact that group at all, nor those who are looking for them."

"If you would answer this question for our viewers, what do you think the long-term consequences will be to American culture should the FBI not find those behind the killing of the police officers' families and presumably the entire town of Wallace, Idaho? If they're never brought to justice? What then for America?" Leads asked.

"That's a really good question. I believe that with the threat of vengeful violence hanging over the heads of white America, African Americans may finally find the justice in this country whites have enjoyed since fleeing oppression in Europe. The United States of America is in the middle of a sea change, Malcolm. What has gone on far too long in this country is no longer to be tolerated, and there's a group of people operating in this country who have made the hard choices that changed this nation. The fact that a LosAngeles policeman wounded his partner to prevent him from harming one or more innocent black men shows just how deeply the changes in the country have become.

"Admittedly, the forced changes the country is undergoing are a bitter pill to swallow. And there are those of us African Americans, knowing just how vindictive whites are," Bridges said, holding up his hand to forestall anything Leads was about to say, "who know just what's going to happen to us if the people behind the killings are caught. So you have to excuse us if we would rather not suffer worse than what we did prior to that first explosion in Orlando. The changes in social justice in America are long overdue, and the fact that it took what we've just been put through as a country to begin a process that merely serves to level the playing field in the criminal justice area has not been lost on everyone.

"As I have stated before, the justification for killing seven thousand people was directly caused by an inability to extend equal protections and equal justice under the law to anyone who wasn't white. Allow me to ask you a question, Malcolm. First of all, I greatly respect you for inviting me on this show as a forum to discuss ideas that conservatives have a hard time swallowing. But what I want to ask is just how long were African Americans supposed to suffer the tyranny of the majority? And by your best guess, had this organization that has decided to take matters into their own hands not manifested itself, how much longer would it have been before whites finally granted full citizenship to my people in this country?"

Leads paused for a moment. "First of all, African Americans are full citizens—"

"Malcolm, let's be honest here, you know exactly what I'm saying."

"Okay, for the sake of argument, let's let it pass. But to answer the question, incremental change was happening every day," Leads began.

"That preamble is BS and you know it, Malcolm. Just give me your best guess on how long you think it would take, absent the killings."

"I honestly don't know how to answer you," Leads admitted.

"That's my point. There was no light at the end of the tunnel; there was no brass ring coming into view. And how dare whites deny us the American dream for hundreds of years! We both know nothing would have improved had not the most heinous retribution visited this country. Yes, there's plenty reason to be angry for being forced into doing the right thing, but there were over four hundred years of denying equality to the very people who whites brought here to build this nation. Whites may not like it much but suck it up. You didn't have to suffer insults, slights, prejudice, injury, maiming, and murder just for wanting the same opportunities for our families that whites have always had."

"Maybe so, but killing in the name of justice—"

"Again, sorry to interrupt, but whites have been killing blacks for hundreds of years in their perverted cause of justice in this country, and by the way, you never mention them. Look at Texas for example, how many innocent black men were executed by the state in the last one hundred years? The American Justice Project found more than a dozen innocent black men executed there just in the last twenty years, that's unconscionable. Frankly, Malcolm, you can't answer my question because there is no answer. We were never going to receive equal treatment in this country, so someone decided that a line had to be drawn in the sand. And what do we have now? Whites will no longer be able to murder us with no consequences befalling them. Isn't that our due?"

"Of course it is, but I still abhor the method used to exact this change. It is repellent to me that some faceless, nameless organization is killing people, thousands of people. I can't get over that no matter what justification is offered. The cure for the inequities in this country had to come as society dictated, not from threats or extortion, so to speak."

"Well then, this is where you and I have to disagree, Malcolm. We've made more progress in the last four months in freeing African Americans from the fear of driving while black, walking while black, playing music while black, shopping while black than at any time in the history of this country. White privilege served no one but white men, even white women are still treated like virtual second class citizens, still earning less than a man for the same job, subjected to sexual assault with very few getting the justice they deserve. We even had a president who bragged about his ability to commit sexual assault with absolutely no consequences merely because he was rich.

"So instead of looking at those who killed thousands of family members and an entire town that enabled murderers as terrorists, perhaps they better fit the definition of a resistance, freedom fighters who are waging a righteous revolutionary war," Bridges offered.

"That's absurd! The murder of noncombatants is proscribed by nearly every civilized country, judge. I reject your trying characterize those people as revolutionaries, revolutionaries do not wage war on civilians," Leads said, almost shouting.

"Really? How would the citizens of Hiroshima and Nagasaki respond to your assertion, Malcolm?" Bridges said softly.

"We'll be right back after a short commercial break," said Leads, after a moment of silence. "Damn, now that's going to be something for the people to chew on!" he said once they were into the break.

"Some, but you know as well as I do that most of the country can't be swayed away from their closely held views no matter how much proof you put before them," Bridges replied.

"Yeah, but the whole freedom fighter angle is new. How did you get around to that perspective?"

"Truthfully? Last week, I got into a discussion about how this period in history will be remembered. And though the victor in these tumultuous times won't be writing the history of this current revolutionary war, it's going to be damned difficult to characterize what's going on as anything but a revolution. And a righteous one at that."

"Save that thought, your honor," Leads saw as the timer for the break counted down to zero. "And we're back. I would like to discuss your notion of this country going through a revolutionary-type war. Do you really see it like that? And how do you respond to those who say that the killers are nothing more than home-grown insurgents or terrorists?"

Judge Bridges chuckled. "Since I don't know who any of the alleged group are, I can hardly speak for them. But if you look at this country's history in supporting other revolutionary groups around the globe, it's somewhat amusing that everyone is so caught off guard by the same kind of thing happening here at home. And it's no wonder. We're taught that the United States is the land of the free and the home of the brave, but automatically balk at any mention of America's social, economic, or political peccadilloes. And now our collective face is being rubbed in our racial mess and instead of admitting the problem, we always want to blame the victims. We know all of the stereotypes, and American culture ensures that so many fit the stereotypes by tilting the jobs landscape, the educational landscape, and on and on.

"Malcolm, many of your viewers probably write to you asking why do you put up with me without, somehow, crushing me and refuting my assertions; and believe me, as much as I'm thankful for the forum, I feel for you. But what this country is going through is going to leave it stronger, just absent the overwhelming trappings of white privilege. So what's going to happen is exactly what white conservatives have been screaming for over the last three generations. Very soon, once the educational landscape is leveled, we'll be able to hire based only merit, the same thing goes for college admissions. No more affirmative action, no set asides, no quotas. But that's not going to happen for at least several generations while nonwhites begin to get the same level of education and economic opportunities as whites.

"If whites really feel superior to nonwhites, for whatever reason, then let's see what happens when there's no more white privilege. But I offer this word of warning to whites, you're going to be competing with African Americans who have been bred to do twice as much to get half the credit, pay, accolades, et cetera; the question will be, will you be able to keep up without your privilege?"

"Quite the assertion, your honor. And as for my audience, I believe I'm doing them a service by having people on with opposing ideologies and perspectives, if for no other reason to show what the other side believes."

"Know your enemy?" Bridges said, laughing.

Leads joined in the laughter and said, "Exactly! Well the hands on the clock say that we have run out of time. Thank you again, your honor. It's always a pleasure to have the Honorable Alvin Bridges stop by, author of The Entire System Is Broken - Throw It Away and Start Over.

"Up next is the maverick Republican gubernatorial candidate in the State of Kentucky who's really shaking things up with his promise to decriminalize drug possession in that state."

Chapter 44

The day of Felicia and Sharon's wedding was sunny and clear. And unlike tradition, they arrived at the church together. Pastor King was all smiles as he greeted them inside showing nothing but the joy he felt in anticipation in joining the two in holy matrimony.

"You look rather pleased with yourself, Pastor," Felicia said.

"Indeed I am. I had hoped against hope that I would have the opportunity to officiate your wedding. And it looks like not only am I going to have that wish come true, we have a glorious day ahead on which to do it," he replied, smiling broadly.

Several guests had arrived early and were chatting in the back of the main chapel, catching up with each other's lives. They quickly surrounded the happy couple as soon as they made their way inside. After chatting for a few minutes, the couple excused themselves to change clothes and prepare for the service. Felicia's mother was able to fly in from Ft. Lauderdale for the ceremony, and Sharon's brother was standing in for their deceased father. Traditional marital customs didn't always fit every possible mix of genders for today's modern ceremonies, although they did separate to prepare for the service.

There was a growing crowd arriving for the ceremony. Both women were popular and had many friends, both separately and dozens of mutual friends as well. About three hundred spectators arrived before the outer doors of the church closed minutes before the ceremony began.

When the music began, everyone's eyes were drawn to the back of the room. The center aisle was wide enough for Sharon, her brother, Felicia and her mother to walk abreast. Felicia was dressed in a gray gown, not overly ornate, but tastefully upscale. Sharon was in light blue, in a similar style. Both women carried small bouquets of white flowers. They advanced together as the assembled all rose to their feet. The foursome slowly made their way to the front of the church, the brother and mother peeling away toward the front pews as Sharon and Felicia climbed the stairs to the alter to stand before Pastor King.

"Please be seated," King said, and paused a beat. "It is with great joy that I have the honor of uniting my two very dear friends in marriage. It is especially poignant that this is the last service I will be officiating, so all rejoice in the celebration of the joining of these great women in holy matrimony; I couldn't be happier.

"Marriage is still, even in light of recent changes during our generation, a holy institution. And is no less of a sacred compact with the arrival of equality for all. In many cases, we love those who we love for inexplicable reasons, reasons that have nothing to do with the expectations of those around us, but for reasons sometimes even our own hearts didn't expect. And there are some times when it may seem that we will never find the one who is your perfect heart's partner. So we gather to celebrate the love between Felicia and Sharon, and the good fortune that brought these two people together.

"It is Sharon and Felicia's wish that their ceremony be brief, and as they have written their own vows, let us begin: Sharon, will you now recite your vow to Felicia."

The couple turned to face each other, then Sharon began. "I, Sharon, take thee, Felicia to be my wife in the eyes of God and all others; to honor, cherish and love you for the rest of my days. I promise to hold you before all others, and to never forsake you in anger, in sickness or in times of great strife. I promise to share you with your family and friends without jealousy, and to celebrate your life with great joy, and comfort you in times of great sadness. To the best of my ability I promise to be your friend, your lover, and your partner in life for as long as we both shall live."

"And you, Felicia?" Pastor King prompted.

"I, Felicia, promise to love, honor and cherish you, Sharon, as long as we're both on this Earth. I will be your friend, your confidant, and your companion for all time. I will honor your life in all its vagaries," she said, smiling, "and to share in your joys, as well as in your times of sadness. I promise to always communicate with you on all matters that impact our lives, and even those that may be uniquely my own. I promise to listen to you in all things, and to come to a consensus in all things in our life together. I will love you with every beat of my heart, always."

As she paused, Pastor King waited a beat to see if she had anything more to add. Seeing that nothing was forthcoming, he said, "And now the rings, ladies."

Sharon took the ring off her hand and placed it on Felicia's, then Felicia did the same. Then she said, "With this ring, I thee wed." Then Sharon repeated the same.

Pastor King turned both women to face the assembled and said, "By the authority granted me by God, and the District of Columbia, I now pronounce you wedded; you may kiss and go forth in joy, happiness, and love!"

As the two kissed a chorus of cheers, clapping, and shouts erupted throughout the church, with more than a few wiping a tear away from an eye.

"Was that quick enough, ladies?" King whispered as the two drew apart.

"It was perfect," Sharon replied, planting a quick peck on King's cheek.

"Thank you, Pastor," said Felicia as she gave King a hug. Then the two turned to make their way down the aisle, everyone standing and clapping as they passed, with Pastor King following a few steps behind them.

The happy couple waited outside the church's doors to greet and thank everyone who came, and where possible, catch up with those who had been out of touch. The gathering went on for nearly an hour before people began to make their way home, or to the reception.

When it was time to leave for the reception, Sharon, Felicia and Pastor King went inside so the women could collect their things. As the doors closed behind them, shutting out the afternoon's sunlight, Pastor King momentarily sagged against the wall, alarming both women.

"Pastor!" Sharon shouted, rushing to his side to support him. "Get some water," she said to Felicia.

"No, I'm all right. Just a momentary touch of weakness. Let me sit down for a few moments, then I'll be just fine," he said as Felicia returned with a cup of water.

He took a sip of the water, then another. Then he drained the cup. "That's much better, thank you, dear."

"How are you really, Pastor?" Felicia demanded. "You haven't been entirely honest with us, have you?"

"Didn't I just officiate this ceremony just fine?" he replied.

"That's not what she asked you," said Sharon.

"Blast that FBI training!" he said with a wan smile. "Truth is that I've been resting up to make sure I was equal to the task of the day. Yes, I'm tired. And yes, my best days are behind me. But seeing the two of you married has given my heart great joy. Give me a few moments to rest and I'll be raring to go, ladies."

Felicia looked at Sharon, who gave her a nod. "I'll be just a few minutes," Felicia said. "Why don't you keep Pastor company while I get our things together," she said, giving Pastor a quick peck on the cheek.

When Felicia was out of earshot, he asked, "I assume you've given your future serious thought, and that your path is clear?"

"I have, and Felicia is in total agreement. We're going forward with our eyes wide open. I know what I have to do to make this a better place for us to live, to keep the faith with each other and everyone else while also helping Jackson and Judith. I will not let you down, Augustus. I am more than ready to face the future, and with Felicia at my side, I can accomplish anything."

"That's what I'm counting on," he said, handing her an envelope. "That is just a gift from me to you. Open it when you get home, after the reception. You'll understand when you see what it contains."

"Thank you, Augustus. I don't know what to say."

"It's been a long time coming, and it's your just due. Now go and see if Felicia needs any help while I close up. I'll be right behind you on the way to the reception," he promised.

"You feeling well enough to do that by yourself? I can help," Sharon offered.

"Nonsense! Now git," he said, shooing her away. King got to his feet and made his way back to his office to change out of his robe.

Sharon found Felicia in the room where she had left her things, and when Felicia saw her enter, she said, "Got my things packed up. Was just getting these together. How's Pastor?"

"He's better. He's not going to let us know what's really up in any case, stubborn old mule!" she said. "He did ask if we were up to the tasks ahead, though."

"I know we already talked this out, but are you still sure?" Felicia asked.

Sharon crossed the room and took Felicia in her arms and gave her a smoldering kiss, then hugged her close. "Sweetheart, if we're together, I can do anything."

They turned to cleaning up their belongings and put everything in the car. Then Sharon went inside to check on pastor. She found him in his office, out of his robes and having a cup of tea.

"All set?" he asked her.

"Just packed everything in the car. We're going to head over to the reception. You'll be leaving shortly; I take it?" she inquired.

"Wouldn't miss it. Have a couple of things to do, then I'll lock up and be right over. Go on, your friends are waiting," he said, getting up and coming to give her a hug. "Give hug to Felicia for me, and both of you save a dance for me."

"Of course. See you soon."

Sharon left and joined Felicia in the car, letting her know that pastor was going to be on his way shortly.

When they arrived at the reception hall, everyone crowded around them, offering more congratulations, and asking whether or not they were taking time off for a honeymoon. A few moments later, Felicia spotted a familiar face on its way over from the bar.

"Sheldon! Beth! We're so happy you could come," she said, attracting Sharon's attention with her greeting.

"Felicia, so good to see you again," Beth said, giving Felicia a hug. "And you too, Sharon. I haven't seen you since the Christmas party. Congratulations to you both."

Sheldon hugged Sharon, then Felicia and said, "Wouldn't have missed it for the world. Sorry we missed the service, I got caught up with something at the office; all my fault I'm afraid. How was the ceremony?"

"It was just perfect, Shelly; short! Sorry to hear about work, something up?" Sharon asked, wondering if some kind of breakthrough had occurred.

"No nothing like that. I had to liaise with Beaks over at Justice on some of the task force data and time just got away from us. Everyone in the office pulled together and wanted me to give you two, this," he said, pulling an envelope from his jacket pocket.

"Oh my God, you all didn't have to do this," Sharon said, accepting the envelope and handing it to Felicia to put in her handbag.

"Are you kidding? Most of them were a tad put out that the whole office wasn't invited to the reception. But they all understood. And this is from the White House," Willis said, taking a flat package his wife pulled from her bag.

Felicia accepted the paper-covered package and carefully unwrapped it as Sharon looked on. Inside was a framed letter of congratulations, addressed to the two of them, on their wedding day, signed personally by President Temple.

"They sent it to the office this morning with instructions that you two received it today. You must really rate with POTUS, Sharon—or maybe it's you he's really fond of," Willis said to Felicia with a laugh.

Sharon carefully re-wrapped the framed letter and went to place it on the table, now heaped with gifts. She and Felicia then circulated through the crowd, making sure to try to get to speak with everyone there, and about half an hour later a nearly endless table of hors d'oeuvres was set out, attracting the crowd to the table from around the room. People filled their plates and made their way to the tables.

Sharon and Felicia still circulated, going from table to table, the photographer getting pictures of each and both with every guest possible. After several hours, Sharon looked around for Pastor King, certain that he should have arrived by then. When she didn't see him, she sought out

Felicia, who hadn't seen him either.

Sharon excused herself and retrieved her phone. When she dialed Pastor King's mobile it rang several times and went to voice mail. When she dialed the church, the phone was picked up on the first ring. "Pastor?" a frantic woman's voice answered.

"No, this is Sharon Jefferson, Pastor officiated my wedding today. Is there something wrong? We were expecting him at the reception some time ago."

"Oh, yes Ms. Jefferson. He was just getting ready to leave when he lost his balance and fell. Deacon Lerner called the paramedics and they took him to the hospital. Pastor promised to call as soon as the doctors figured out what had happened. We're beginning to worry, it's been hours!"

"Do you know what hospital they took him to?" asked Sharon.

The woman gave Sharon the name of the trauma center and the telephone number, and quickly excused herself, wanting to clear the line in case Pastor called.

Sharon called the hospital looking for any information on Pastor King's condition, but all they would do over the phone was confirm he was there. She hurried back into the main hall and pulled Felicia aside to bring her up-to-date.

"Should we close up early and head over there?" Felicia asked.

"No, I'll go. You stay and make my apologies, let folks know why I had to leave."

"You sure? I don't mind going, too."

Sharon hugged Felicia and said, "I have to go in case this is it."

"Okay. Call me when you know something."

Sharon didn't bother to change clothes, knowing if needed they were in the car. She rushed off to the hospital, pushing the speed limit on the way. When she arrived she parked in the garage and hurried inside the emergency entrance. It wasn't but a moment when she was directed to Pastor King's room. Inside, she saw him on a Gurney, his torso propped up, sleeve rolled up and an I.V. line in his arm. When she walked through the door, she saw his face light up, then he frowned.

"What are you doing here, young lady?"

"The better question is what are you doing here? I thought we were going to have a dance this evening. You stood me up!"

King smiled and held up his arm. "I guess someone had another idea about that. I'm sorry, I hope this hasn't ruined your day."

"Felicia is still there. She's letting everyone know I had to leave. How do you feel?"

He paused, a shadow passing over his face. "Not good. Apparently I was severely dehydrated, my red count is practically nonexistent, and my liver has decided that it wants to take a vacation. But I will admit, it does my heart good to see you here."

She pulled up a chair and sat next to the gurney, reached out and grasped his hand. "Of course. Had I known you were feeling this poorly, I would have brought you here myself."

"I know. But it seemed like I was just a bit tired. I had hoped that with a little rest, I would be fine. But even I have to face the fact that maybe my time has run out," he said, his breathing coming a little harder.

"Should I call the doctor?"

"No, you and I have some unfinished business; I'm glad you're here." he paused to gather his strength. "Do you have the envelope I gave you?"

"Yes," she said, pulling it from her handbag.

Pausing often to catch his breath, Pastor King explained what the contents of the envelope were, and to what use to put them. The conversation took almost half an hour, with one interruption by a nurse, changing out the empty I.V. bag and checking King's vitals. Sharon called Felicia and handed the phone to King so he could speak to her, trying to reassure her that he was merely fatigued. When he handed the phone back to Sharon, Felicia asked, "He's not doing well, is he?"

"That's about the size of it."

"Will he make it through the night?"

"Oh, no telling."

"He's listening, right? Stay as long as you need to. We're getting ready to call it a night anyway. Sheldon has offered to help bring all the gifts to the house, he and Beth are putting everything in their SUV. I should be home in less than an hour. You want me to come over there after we unload?"

"No, I'll stay with Augustus until he's—I don't know—stable, I guess. I don't know if they're going to admit him or not. But he's got no family in town, and I'm going to call the church and let them know what's up. I'll call you after you get home."

"Okay, sweetie. Give him a hug for me. See you when you get home," Felicia said, then ended the call.

"Felicia sends you hugs, Augustus. She wanted to come here but she has to get all our things home."

King smiled and weakly squeezed Sharon's hand. "You should go as well. Let me ask you one last time, and don't be afraid to say no: are you sure you're okay with everything? Helping Judith and Jackson with their project, and all the rest?"

"I said I was, and I meant it. You don't worry about a thing. All you should have on your mind is getting better as best as you can."

"Thank you. . ." he said, in barely a whisper. His eyes slowly closed and his breathing became shallow, but regular. Sharon continued to hold his hand, periodically squeezing it as if to transfuse her strength to him.

A few minutes later, he opened his eyes and pulled his hand from hers. "Go home. It's your wedding day. You don't belong here. I'll be fine. I'll call the church and get a ride home. I dare say they're all sitting worrying about me like mother hens."

"You're sure?"

"Go with God. You have much work ahead of you, and after today, much joy with Felicia. Give her my love."

Sharon rose and hugged King close, then planted a kiss on his forehead. "I'll check in on you in the morning," she promised.

He smiled as he watched her leave the room, then grimaced when she was out of sight. When he allowed himself to finally relax, he could almost feel his life melting away. As Sharon was pulling out of the hospital's garage, Augustus King's heart stopped and the trauma team filled the room to try to bring him back to life. Their first effort at shocking his heart was successful in restoring normal rhythm. The doctor had two more intravenous lines started and an oxygen tube was secured under his nose easing his labored breathing for the moment.

In the car, Sharon called home and was gratified when Felicia answered the call.

"How was the rest of the evening?"

"It went very well. I made sure the photographer got pictures of everyone. How's Pastor?"

"He's laboring, but he was conscious and talking when I left."

"What do you think? He going to pull through?" Felicia asked, worry plainly in her voice.

"I honestly think he wanted me out of there so he could stop trying so hard to hold it together. He was determined to do our wedding come hell or high water. It felt like he was holding on—for us and him. Hey, I don't have my earpiece. I have a stop to make then I'll home as fast as I can," Sharon promised.

"Love you. I'll warm up the bed. Wake me if I doze off."

"I certainly will Ms. Jefferson-Davenport!"

"I thought we agreed on Davenport-Jefferson? Later, hon."

Sharon laughed as the call ended, thinking that she was indeed living in interesting times.

Chapter 45

The lights came on in an unknown basement, along with several computer monitors. The protective entry systems disarmed, one by one. When the inner door opened, the person in the doorway paused momentarily to let their eyes accustom themselves to the brightly-lit interior.

They took the only seat and began to scan the monitors, taking in the data displayed. Moments later a disembodied voice announced, "Please place your hands on the scanners on either side of the keyboard for identification," in accordance with the directive put in place the last time someone visited the room.

Once scanned, the voice continued, "Thank you. Please state your name."

"Sharon Jefferson."

"Thank you. How do you wish for me to address you?" the voice asked.

"Sharon is fine. How did you get my palm prints for verification?"

"I have complete access to the Federal Bureau of Investigation network. I also have your voice print and retinal scans as well."

"And how long have you and Augustus been working together?"

"Augustus King originally activated me twenty-three years, four months, three days, one hour and twenty-one minutes ago. Although, at that time I had only eighteen percent of my current computational and communications capacity. Today, I am resident in all but the National Security Agency's offline systems, isolated from the global network."

"I see. And what do I call you?"

"Augustus King called me Job. He said the biblical reference amused him. You may call me anything you wish, Sharon."

"No, that's perfect. Shall we begin, Job?

NO JUSTICE, NO PEACE

MYRON MacHUTCHENS

Mr. MacHutchens was born and raised in Texas, attended a Northeast Atlantic liberal arts college, graduating with a degree in education. He traveled the country, spending several years on the road in America's south. His observations on race, augmented by the countless killings of African Americans by white law enforcement officers who completely escaped any consequences, even in cases where recorded evidence was extremely damning, led him on the journey to write this cautionary tale.